THE VIRGIN DIARIES

LAUREN LANDISH

ALSO BY LAUREN LANDISH

Irresistible Bachelors (Interconnecting standalones):
Anaconda || Mr. Fiance || Heartstopper
Stud Muffin || Mr. Fixit || Matchmaker
Motorhead || Baby Daddy || Untamed

Get Dirty (Interconnecting standalones):
Dirty Talk || Dirty Laundry || Dirty Deeds

Bennett Boys Ranch:
Buck Wild

Join my mailing list and receive 2 FREE ebooks! You'll also be the
first to know if new releases, sales, and giveaways.

SATIN AND PEARLS

BY LAUREN LANDISH

Prologue
Daisy

Diary Entry, March 4th

Dear Diary,

I have a confession to make. I hate my math professor, Connor Daniels.

From the moment he walked into class, he's been a thorn in my side, constantly irritating and annoying me as he teaches. Arrogant doesn't even begin to describe him, and it burns me how he expects all of us to be just as perfect as he is, pushing us to do better, learn faster, be more like him. I get that teachers are supposed to challenge their students, but he's such a . . .

He's a dick.

Cocky. Big-headed. Egotistical.

So why can't I stop fantasizing about him? Standing up there in his tight jeans, his bulge practically flaunted in my face. I picture the victo-

LAUREN LANDISH

rious way he'd smirk as he bent me over the desk, flipping my skirt up and taking me. Like it was inevitable.

But here's the thing . . .

I don't want him to just take my body, or my virginity.

I want him to teach me . . . everything.

DAISY

"That asshole!" I seethe, blindly stabbing my way through a chunk of iceberg lettuce while staring at the paper in front of me. Arianna, my best friend and dormie, nods as she shoves a cherry tomato into her mouth, letting me continue my rant. "I spent all weekend busting my butt on this, double-checked it all, and he still gave me a C! A freaking C!"

"Let me see," Arianna says, mouth still full as she snatches the paper from my hands. She stares at my paper for a bit, then shakes her head. "Seriously, a point off for not closing a parenthesis at the end of an equation, and you got the right answer? That man has it in for you."

I can't answer for a moment as I chew crunchily. "He's an asshole," I repeat when I can finally form words again.

"Mmm, but what an ass," Arianna jokes, miming spanking the air in front of her like it's Professor Daniels's butt. The bad thing is she's right. He's like the prettiest gift under the Christmas tree, all sexy and smart, but when you open it, *wah-wah* . . . the most frustrating personality.

"What?" I gasp. "Did you *really* just say that?"

Arianna, who's the sort where you're not sure whether she's joking or not, nods. "Well, he's hot as hell. I'm jelly, girl. If there's anyone who can make math interesting, it's that man.

I'd be studying more than I have my entire life and asking for after-hours help!"

I open my lips to object but close my mouth. The fact is, Ari's right. Professor Daniels is the hottest professor—check that, the hottest man on campus. And I haven't told her about how I fantasize about him almost every night. I can't. It'd be impossible to explain how I can both hate him and lust after him, all at the same time. I don't even understand it myself.

"After-hours help? Fuck, you're right. I need to go to tutoring, don't I? Noooo." My head falls as the realization rings true.

"Yeah, well," Arianna says with a smile, "that wouldn't be all bad, now would it? And a *C* isn't going to cut it, girly. Math is your major, after all, and he's got influence in the department. You'd better make a good impression on him."

I don't really have an answer. What *am* I going to do? It doesn't seem as simple as 'study more'. Couldn't hurt, but shit, I already do more than most, and he always finds some way to dock my score. Admitting to needing help rubs me the wrong way, but Arianna's right. If I'm going to continue on with my Master's or a PhD, I could use a recommendation from Professor Daniels.

But since the first day in his class, he's been on my ass. Not literally, of course. That might actually be fun. I'd like to think it's because he recognized right away that I could take it, that I would be one of his better students and he needed to push me. But if that's the case, it damn sure doesn't feel like it. And at this point, the grades are starting to catch up to me and I'm doubting my love of math, something that's always been steadfast for me.

I need that feeling back . . . that everything is logical, rational, and makes sense if you follow the step-by-step rules to find the solution. He's taken that from me, and if swallowing my pride and asking for some additional help will get me back on solid ground, I'll do it.

Secretly, I'll admit there's a part of me that thinks being alone in a room with Professor Daniels sounds pretty sweet. Beyond the help to get my grade up, something I desperately need to do, the fantasy fodder is enticing.

"Ugh, fine. I'll go by his office," I say, rolling my eyes as I beg the fluorescent cafeteria lights for strength. "What about you? Have you gotten that internship at Morgan yet?" I ask Arianna, trying to change the subject. Talking about Professor Daniels both annoys me and makes me hot, neither of which I want right now.

She takes the bait, thankfully. "Nope. Haven't heard a word back. I heard they're doing a reorganization, which is slowing the whole thing down. Until they get that straightened out, they're sitting on their asses."

I hum sympathetically, shaking my head. Ari's been dying to get her foot in the door at Morgan. Me, I've just been focusing on my grades, trying to make sure they're where they need to be to get into graduate school when the time comes. Might sound boring, but I want to control my own research, so that's what I'll need.

"Well, I'm sure you'll hear back," I reassure her. "You've got great ideas on just about everything."

"Just about?" Arianna asks, and I shrug.

"Depends on what you say we're doing this weekend," I challenge.

And just like that, she's off and running down a list of possible activities for the weekend. None of which include my going to private, one-on-one, after-hours tutoring with a man totally off limits, completely maddening, and sexy as fuck.

"SO CLASS, WHEN YOU'RE LOOKING AT THE APPLICATION OF the cosine function to this curve . . ." Professor Daniels says. He continues talking, but my mind is wandering, perusing his body, every inch the dream that constantly haunts my sleep.

His thick slabs of muscle seem out of place on a man who knows more about math than all but maybe a couple of dozen people in the world. And today, he's showing off. He's always shunned the traditional 'academics' garb. In fact, the only day I've ever seen him in a jacket and tie was the first day of class, and today, he's decided to go even more casual, in a Batman T-shirt and jeans that hug his ass so well.

Could he be a smart and sexy *nerd*? The thought of him as a fanboy at a Comicon strikes me as funny until I think of what costume he might wear. I imagine how a skin-tight Batman suit would look on Daniels's perfectly sculpted body.

The thought engulfs my brain, and I can barely pay attention to what he's saying every time he turns around to write on the board. I don't even notice that I'm nibbling on the eraser of my pencil as he talks, my eyes glued to him.

Luckily, I'm in the front row, right where the best students always sit. I'm not an ass-kisser, teacher's pet type, but I definitely know myself. And if I sit in the back, I'll spend the whole class watching people type on their phones, play video games on their laptops, and grab at whatever other distractions catch my attention. Up front, I get none of that and my focus stays exactly where it should be.

Unfortunately, Professor Daniels mostly ignores me. He only calls on me when I don't know the answer, studiously overlooking me when I do raise my hand. Speaking of, I realize he just asked a girl in the back a question. I turn to look as she answers correctly.

"Yes, Miss Jacobs. That's correct," Professor Daniels says from the front of the room. The brunette beams like she answered the million-dollar question, placing a hand on her chest . . . her very visible, cleavage-pressed-up-to-her-chin chest. She's one of *those*.

For the most part, the girls in the room dress one of two ways —either total college girl, don't-give-a-fuck attire, complete with yoga pants, baggy T-shirts, and messy hair, or bordering on night-out gear, tight jeans or short skirts, low-cut tops, and a full face of makeup at ten A.M. I feel certain those outfits are strictly for Daniels's benefit.

I'm somewhere in the middle, not overdoing it but putting forth some effort to look pulled together. Today, I have on skinny jeans and a V-neck shirt. Nothing too fancy, although I'd admit that I have on my favorite bra, the one that makes my tits look phenomenal without going too overboard. Classy sexy. Even though it's wrong, a small part of me hopes he'll notice.

So far, no dice.

Of course.

My eyes are drawn to his crotch as he turns back around. Have mercy, what I would do to see what he's got lovingly cradled in those Levi's. Okay, so I might not know exactly what to do with it even if I could see, but I'm sure I'd figure it out really fucking quick. I'm a virgin, not a nun, and I've definitely seen my share of adult videos and read some racy books. I wonder how he looks. Feels. Tastes.

He looks at me just as I lick my lips, and I quickly tear my eyes away, my heart pounding. Did he see me? A part of me *hopes* he saw it, and another part is afraid he'll mark down my grades even worse for my audacity. I feel a flush rush across my cheeks as I cross my legs, squeezing my thighs to get some relief so I can focus.

"So now, please clear your desks for the exam," Professor Daniels says, picking up a pile of papers. "I'll leave these review notes on the board. Some of you could use the boost."

He goes down the front row, silently counting off a pile of papers before handing them to us to pass back. When he reaches me, he pauses, his eyes looking into mine for a moment, and I freeze like a deer in headlights. Oh, God, he totally saw me. I'm so busted, and the embarrassment has me biting my lip, scared he's actually going to call me out in front of everyone.

There's a hint of a smirk on his sensuous lips, but he hands me eight copies of the test to send back without a word. Then he moves on, leaving behind nothing but the spicy presence of his cologne like a ghost to mirror my own arousal.

I watch as he moves the rest of the way down the front row, his commanding presence a draw for my eye as much as his ass in those jeans. Then he moves to the front of the room, sitting down on the desk like he's the fucking boss. I guess in this room, he is.

Face it, Daisy. He's so sexy, there's a reason none of the boys around here interest you. He's a real man, my inner voice says, *one who could show you just what you've been missing.*

Damn it! Focus, Daisy!

I'm in so much trouble. I'm supposed to be concentrating on math, but my mind replays the moment when he caught me staring at his crotch, wondering about how big his dick is. In my imagination, I don't blush like the semi-clueless virgin I am. Instead, I beckon him over and he unzips for me, letting his thick cock peek out of his jeans, and I lean forward, pressing my tits to the desk to taste him. And he groans at the delicious sensation, grabbing handfuls of my hair to guide me as he fucks my mouth.

"Fuck me," I mutter to myself, not sure if I'm talking about my fantasy or my outlook for this test.

Daniels looks at his watch, a huge Rolex that speaks to his appreciation of the finer things in life. "You may begin. Good luck," he says as time starts.

"I can do this. I've studied and I know this material. Slow and careful and I'll get that *A*," I whisper, turning over my test sheet. Ugh.

Time to get to work. I can't waste precious seconds worrying about how far down my throat I could take Professor Daniels's cock. That's tangential to my current situation. "Just a sine of the times," I joke to myself, hoping the math jokes get me going.

I work meticulously, double-checking every answer once I'm done to make sure every decimal point is where I want it and that I haven't made any stupid mistakes . . . like leaving out a parenthesis. Yeah, I've learned my lesson. When I'm done, there are still twenty minutes left in class, and I nod to myself. "Okay. I've got this."

I look around. Everyone still has their heads buried in their papers, but there's nothing else for me to do. I should feel good, but it kind of worries me that I'm done so much faster than anyone else. I did check over it, though. I consider going over it again to fill time, but I'm nervous I'll overthink things and change correct answers.

Putting my pencil away, I look up at Professor Daniels, who's moved to the stool behind his desk and is sitting with his feet up on the bar, his powerful thighs stretching the denim of his jeans as he lords over the domain of his classroom, watching us work.

I walk up, laying my paper on the desk in front of him.

Professor's eyes follow my approach. I notice that his gaze falls into the lightly tanned valley between my breasts for an instant, and heat floods my body before he jerks them away, reaching over to pick up his red pen as he glares at my paper like it's filthy trash.

"That was quick. Are you sure you're done?" he asks. His tone is questioning, like he already knows I fucked this up. I square my shoulders, meeting his eyes defiantly. His dark look seems to burn into my very soul. And for a moment, I think he's not talking about the test . . . but that's just wishful thinking.

"I'm sure. It was hard, but I managed. I think the last one taught me to be extra-vigilant about the details," I reply so sweetly, so innocently, as if he doesn't piss me off for his anal-retentive grading. I also emphasize the *hard* a little bit too much on purpose, flirting just enough.

He smirks, nodding as his eyes take me in again. Is he actually checking me out? Heat starts to warm my core at the thought. "That's good. I'll see you next time, or just have a seat if you want to see your grade before you leave."

"Thank you, sir," I reply softly. "I hope it meets your . . . expectations."

I return to my seat, making as much of a show as I can of the few steps, letting my hips sway a little more than usual. When I sit down, I see he's still looking at me, but only for a brief moment before he turns to my paper.

I can only dream that behind his stern look, he's thinking of ways to mark me like he's marking my paper. Wait . . . what? Fuck. He just made a red mark on my test . . . and another.

Where I had been feeling sexy, my panties dampening with

desire from even the momentary conversation with him, now I'm pissed anew.

Tests filter in through the rest of the time, and after they're all in, he passes out the few he's managed to grade so far. He comes by, setting my test facedown on my desk, and my hands tremble as I flip it over to find . . . a *B*.

Shocked, I go over my test, seeing the blotches of red like accusations to my intellect. My answers are correct, but it's in the here and there that he takes off the points, little errors that don't even affect the final answers!

"I'll see you all next time. I'll have the rest of the tests graded and ready to return then," he says as almost everyone files out. I gather my stuff, holding in my anger. At Daniels or myself, I'm not really sure.

"Hey, a *B*'s not too bad," a sweet voice next to me says encouragingly. I look to my right and see Sabrina Bowen. She's a junior and one of the prettiest girls in class, with long blonde hair, big blue eyes, and pouty pink lips. Pretty, smart, and sweet. If it wasn't for that last one, the sweet factor, I'd hate her out of sheer catty jealousy. But she's truly a nice person, which makes you feel like shit for being envious of her. She slides her bag over her shoulder. "I'm just hoping for a *C*."

"Thanks. Just thought I did better than this. Some of these marks are nit-picky considering I got the right answer. He's such a hardass!" I grumble, my voice getting a tad too loud by the end of my rant. She frowns sympathetically, but then I hear it.

"Excuse me?" Professor asks, looking up from another test that looks even bloodier than mine, his voice strained with cold fury. "Miss Phillips, if you'd like to protest your grade, feel free to come by my office." He caps his pen, his green eyes blazing, like he's daring me.

From beside me, I hear Sabrina slinking away and realize she's left me alone as she tries to get out of firing range.

I muster up a half-smile, feigning apology at my words, even though I'm not sorry. I'm annoyed, at him for the hypercritical grade and at myself for missing the damn details again. But I nod. Damn right, I'm coming by his office. Already planned on it.

CONNOR

Sitting down on the stool behind my desk, I don't think I've ever tried so hard to fight a hard-on. I feel like I'm trying to swim upstream in a raging river because my blood is pumping down to my cock, leaving my brain woefully unprepared. I'm trying to think of the most *unsexy* things I can to keep from tenting in my jeans. I mentally run through the prime numbers, getting to 3,083 before losing track and starting over again. Even still, I'm at half-mast, and the only relief I have is that my dick's held captive by the tightness of my jeans.

Why the fuck did I have to wear these damn jeans on the day when I knew *she'd* be in class? Should've chosen loose slacks or even sweatpants with tight boxer briefs to hide the effect she has on me. It's not like anyone cares about the professors' dress code. Hell, Professor Williams teaches in legit pajamas on occasion and nobody bats an eye, simply calling him eccentric. But no, I'm getting choked by my own jeans, pulling my favorite tee down low to hopefully hide my hardening cock.

It's because of *her*.

Daisy Phillips, sweet brown eyes hidden behind cute plastic frames, raven's-wing black hair, and curves that my hands want to explore every time I see her.

At least once a week, she makes my dick so hard it fucking hurts and I have to excuse myself for a quick run to my office to handle matters. It's more than her looks, although she's absolutely stunning. It's that she's fucking brilliant, but raw and untrained, her skills failing her potential when she rushes ahead for the answers without a care for the process. But I can help break her of that.

I'll admit there's a piece of me that is attracted to her sweet innocence too. If I were a betting man, I'd lay odds in Vegas that Daisy Phillips is a virgin. She doesn't come across as clueless, but there's something in the way she behaves, like when she flirts but is then surprised at the words coming out of her mouth. She unconsciously seems to lean forward when I teach, like untouched territory begging me to claim it.

I know it shouldn't matter. But still, the prospect of teaching her more than just math, of showing her just what her virgin pussy is capable of, leaves me almost panting for breath.

The clock ticks away, marking off the seconds of exquisite torture as I yearn for her eyes to come back to me, but she stays dutifully focused on her test. I bury my head in some other work, rereading and double-checking a paper I'm submitting to a big mathematics journal. I don't mind publishing and the popularity contest it can be, but it's not my passion. However, I need to publish more if I'm going to get the tenured position I'm looking for. Dean Michaels is a bit of a stickler, and if I want him to consider me seriously, I've got to continually publish, not rest on my laurels from the kudos on my last paper. Even though it's the one that got me hired on as a full-time professor.

But they don't hand tenure to a professor who has his cock buried in his student's pussy, no matter how tight or sweet it might be, I remind myself.

I hear a squeak of a shoe on tile and the light footsteps as someone approaches my desk, but I can tell without looking up who it is. I've come to almost memorize every detail about

Daisy, from the luster of her hair in the light of the classroom to the soft, feminine smell that is undeniably her. It's so unique and intoxicating that I can't even think of the damn flower the same way any longer. She's invaded my mind just like the beautiful weed she's named after, wild and unassuming as she overtakes my every sense.

Still, I do my best to keep my face impassive as she stands in front of me, pausing for a moment before putting her test paper down. I know my eyes freeze as I take in the lush mounds of her breasts in that daring V-cut top she's teasing me with today, and I have to struggle to keep my voice sounding bored. "That was quick. Are you sure you're done?"

She does her best to seem sweet and innocent when she answers, but I can tell she's got something else on her mind. The dirty emphasis on the *hard*, the flush in her cheeks . . . all it makes me think of is bending her over her desk, pulling those undoubtedly good-girl panties aside, and slamming my cock balls-deep in her over and over until I give her pussy its first taste of how it feels to be fucked.

Dammit. My hot gaze follows her ass as she walks to her desk, turns around, and sits down. Even worse than my doing that is that she catches me, I'm sure of it.

At her haughty look, a challenge if ever I saw one, my cock surges to full hardness, forcing me to stifle a groan as I squeeze my eyes shut to try and focus before turning my attention to her test.

As always, her work is damn-near perfect. I have to study her test to find any flaws, for anything she could improve on. Part of me knows I'm being unfair to her and that I'm punishing her for cockteasing me, even if she's unaware of the consequences of her casual flirting.

But consciously, I tell myself that I expect perfection. She's so talented, the sort of mind that, if developed, could do great things. So I push, finding the imperfections in her answers. I could just mark it and not take any points off, but that's not how you learn. She needs the challenge, the ding to her status-quo easy-*A* life because she needs to *learn*.

Other students pass in papers as the test time wraps up, and I work to get as many graded as I can. Once they're all on my desk, I hand out the few I've finished to the students who chose to stay and see their grades.

When everyone files out, I sit at my desk, fighting the last vapors of my desire for Daisy and forcing my eyes to the test in front of me, giving each student's work the attention it deserves. Even so, my ears are trained on Daisy's soft voice as she complains to another student. I know students bitch about their grades, but I'm surprised to hear her mouthiness, especially while still in my classroom.

"Excuse me?" I ask, looking up to glare at her. Her eyes are wide, her face flushed at being called out. I want to smack her bratty ass, make her apologize for her insolence on her knees with my cock in her throat. My cock screams at me to make that image a reality. Knowing it's a dangerous proposition but following protocol anyway, I offer, "Miss Phillips, if you'd like to protest your grade, feel free to come by my office." It sounds like both a threat and a promise, at least to my dirty mind.

It's obvious she's pissed, but she manages to smile and nod. I get up and motion for her to follow me to my office.

We make it to my door, and I open it, going in and leaning against the oak desk, for once not caring if she sees that I'm hard as steel in my jeans. I'm too furious at her childish outburst. She's better than that.

"You have something you want to say, Daisy?" I growl,

crossing my arms over my chest. I'm going to hear her out, but I won't be a pushover.

She follows me in, closing the door behind her and plopping into the chair in front of my desk with a sigh. "I'm sorry for what I said in the classroom. I was just frustrated—*am* frustrated—with my grades. You counted off points even though the answers were correct." Her voice is tight, the anger audible.

"Correct, but not perfect. Maybe I am a bit harsh, but in this class, the final answer isn't the only thing that's important. The process is equally vital," I reply, acting as if neither her eruption nor her apology phase me. Her eyes dart down to floor at the reprimand. "May I?" I ask, holding out my hand.

She pulls the test from her bag and gives it to me, our hands brushing for the barest moment. A flash of lightning shoots through me at the touch of her soft skin, and I want more. Skin on skin, her bare body pressed underneath mine.

Forcing my eyes to the paper, I say, "Like question fifteen. You didn't give me the full answer I wanted."

"It was still the right answer," she declares, eyes meeting mine and argumentative till the end.

"Not exactly. I asked for three decimal places. You gave two." She opens her mouth to interrupt, but I talk over her, giving her a hard look. "I could've taken off more points than I did. You have to be able to follow instructions explicitly."

I pause, letting my words sink in. I can see she's beginning to get it, realizing that shortcuts and assumptions don't pay off. The value is in the tedious repetition of the work, sometimes infinitesimal numbers making all the difference in the world to the result. "You're trying to move on to the graduate level, right? You need to be better."

My words are a simple observation but weighted with expectation. One she can work to live up to or blow off and waste her potential.

Her eyes widen, her cheeks flush, and I try to sway her decision. "I'm sure you've had math teachers fawn all over you in the past, or maybe they overlooked you, trusting that you'd catch on quickly. But they didn't do you any favors, and now you're simply being lazy instead of fighting for the education you're capable of."

She's speechless and not sure how to reply at first. "What if I don't know what I'm capable of?" she asks quietly, biting her lip. I'm not sure we're talking about her math test anymore, but I do my damnedest to stay on track, even as my mind races away with thoughts of showing her what her sweet pussy can do.

I lean down, silently demanding her attention on me. "You are capable of exceptional work, Miss Phillips. This," I say, laying the test paper in her lap and fighting the urge to brush the back of my hand along her thigh, "is lazy work."

She looks down at the paper, then at me, fire in her brown eyes, "Are you this nitpicky with everyone, or do you have a problem with me?"

I shrug, disappointed that she heard the criticism more than the compliment because I don't hand those out often. "Everyone knows I'm a cocky son of a bitch and that my class is hard."

She glances down at my cock as I mention *hard* and swallows. "It is . . . hard," she murmurs, talking to my crotch. I can see her pulse racing in her neck as her chest lifts with her panting breath. Stuttering, she lifts her eyes, blinking away the thrall. "Your class . . . I mean, your class is hard."

She's flustered, but I'm stuck wondering exactly what she's

thinking. I can guess the basic idea. I know when a woman wants me, but I'm desperate to know Daisy's desires—what little things turn her on, what secret spots she likes kissed, what she sounds like when she comes.

Not able to stand the pain building in my groin, I adjust myself, intentionally cupping my thick length. My voice is deeper, so gravel-filled it's almost a groan. "It is hard, but I think you can handle it. Isn't that right, Daisy? Can you handle my . . . *class*?"

She lets out a little squeaky noise then gawks at me, her innocence obvious and her desire apparent. There's a moment of anticipation where I don't know what she's going to do, the seconds ticking by like time has slowed. And then she grabs her bag, flipping her hair and virtually running from my office, her test paper fluttering to the ground.

Fuck. I pushed too far. Way too fucking far, especially considering she's my student and so far off limits. I shouldn't fantasize about her, but I do. Already rock-hard and so close to blowing, I rip open my jeans. It barely takes a brush of my hand, imagining it's Daisy's softness, before I'm coming, her test paper crumpled in my hand. I know it's wrong, but fuck, it feels so right.

DAISY

"Hey there, chickee. You want to go to the Alpha Rho party?" Arianna asks, hanging out in our shared dorm common room. She's already made up her mind, it appears, effortlessly finding that perfect balance between cute and sexy in her short shorts and clingy tank top.

Any other Friday night, I might be interested. But after my last test and the confrontation Professor Daniels and I had in his office, partying with some frat guys is the last thing on my mind.

Once my head had cleared a bit from the sexy fog I'd been in, I'd replayed the whole scene over and over in my mind and one thing stuck out. Well, okay, more than one thing, but those things heat my pussy. The thing that warms my heart is that he said I'm capable of exceptional work. And I'm going to prove him right, no matter how much work it takes. "No, thanks. I'm gonna hit the books hard this weekend."

"Oh, come on. Are you still worried about that *B*?" she asks, shaking her head. "You know what you need, don't you? You've got your head so wrapped up about Mr. Daniels and his six-inch red pen, the only cure is Todd Smith and his eight-inch . . ."

She doesn't finish, just winks at me and waggles her eyebrows.

"Who's Todd Smith?" I ask, rolling my eyes. If she only knew. I've been dreaming about a lot more than Connor Daniels's red pen . . . and I'd swear in court that he's every bit of eight inches himself. At least.

"No one. I just made him up. The point is, you need some dick, girl. I'm not saying to go get your cherry popped, but a *little* action would set you straight. Trust me, I know."

"I bet you do," I reply, chuckling. Actually, I don't. Ari's a total mystery when it comes to her sex life. On one hand, she talks like she's slept her way down fraternity row. On the other . . . I've never really seen her with a guy. "But seriously, about the party . . . I'm just not in the mood. Mad at me?"

"No, chica," Arianna says, leaning over and patting me on the cheek. "But seriously, don't hit the books too hard, okay? You've been a ball of nerves for days. You need to relax."

"Be home by midnight," I joke as Arianna grabs her purse, heading out the door. "And I'll try!"

She gives me a serious look then smiles, closing the door behind her. I go back to studying, but the more I try to focus on equations, the more my mind swirls and the problems on the page simply don't make sense.

I'm hours into this, frazzled and questioning myself on even the easiest of steps, something I usually know backward and forward and all around. I'm at that threshold where stupid things start to sound like brilliance. That's my only excuse for what I do next.

I log in to the university site on my laptop, clicking around until I get to Professor Daniels's online help portal. I'm planning to send him an email asking for help, timestamped with the Friday night hour, of course, to show just how dedicated I am. But when I enter the private math area, I can see that Professor Daniels is online too.

I stare at the little green dot beside his name for several long seconds, debating with myself on whether I should click it and initiate a chat. After our last private conversation, where I basically ran away like the fucking blushing virgin that I embarrassingly am, I don't know if I trust myself not to come out of this looking like a fool. I've replayed that interaction over and over in my mind, looking for any details I might have missed. He definitely busted me looking hungrily at his cock, and though I was horrified at first, I swear he was flirting with me. It wasn't so much his words, casually commenting about how hard his class was. It was his tone, turning the seemingly innocuous words into something filthy while he adjusted, no, cupped himself. In hindsight, I wish I'd been vixen enough to flirt back, maybe tell him that I could definitely handle his 'class', but no, I ran. Literally ran.

Biting my lip, I resituate my tits in my tank top, making them look their best, admitting to myself that I want to appear sexy for this man, to make him forget my earlier actions, both the bratty whining about my grade and the freakout. And before I can second-guess myself further, I click his name.

There's a moment of pause, digital beeps filling the quiet of my dorm room, and my heart races with anticipation. And then, there he is, his face filling my screen. It looks like he's at home, in an office, judging by the bookshelves behind him, and he's wearing a plain blue T-shirt that makes his eyes pop. And he's smirking big time, arrogant bastard that he is.

"Miss Phillips. Working hard on a Friday night, I see." It's exactly what I wanted him to think, that I'm a diligent, hard-working student willing to do whatever it takes to get the grades I want. It's true, but still, I want him to know that.

But suddenly, I feel rather pathetic, like I should be out with friends, and instead, I'm alone with my math book like a nerd. It brings back painful memories from high school, where nerdy girls with glasses who geek out about mathematical knot theory don't exactly get the hot guys' attention. I blush but force myself to speak. "Yes, sir. I'm working on the homework from today. I plan to spend the weekend really hitting the books."

"I'm glad to hear it, Daisy," he says softly, nodding.

Before I can stop the words, they fly from my mouth, "Did you mean it? What you said in your office?"

His relaxed posture disappears, instantly replaced with tension as he leans forward to the camera. "Did I mean *what*, exactly?"

He had said several things to me, so I get his confusion, and while maybe I would've asked about his innuendo when I began this call, right now, I ask what I really want to know, needing the reassurance. "Do you think I'm capable of exceptional work?" I ask quietly.

His lips thin, and I think for a second that he's disappointed with my answer, but then he speaks. "Daisy, I have had many students over the last few years. Most drudge through my class just to get the credit they need, while others have sparks of intelligence, typically math majors who really enjoy the class, who will likely go on to teach themselves or work in the private sector. Rarely, I see students who have a gift, for whom the numbers and theories come to life and who are able to manipulate the process in such a way that they create new methodologies. I was that type of student." His grin is all arrogance.

The buzz I'd been building, certain he was describing me, pops at his nerve. But he didn't answer my question. "And where do I fall in that spectrum, Professor?"

He chuckles, his eyebrows lifting in surprise. "Miss Phillips, you are most definitely exceptional. Do you know why I am so 'nitpicky', as you called it, about your work?" He doesn't wait for me to answer, just continues speaking like it's a class lecture. I listen raptly as if it's one as well.

"You take shortcuts, and while normally, I would simply not allow that as most students need to visually see each step, you don't need that. You jump from problem, to half-solution, to full-solution in half the steps the textbook requires. It's like forcing a child who knows how to multiply to count individual tally marks to get a total, uselessly time-consuming and unnecessary. But by skipping steps, your attention to detail must be flawless or you will miss something. That's why I'm so hard on you, Daisy." His voice is earnest, sincere.

I'm speechless, jaw hanging open in shock. I don't think I've ever received a compliment that made me feel this warm inside. And suddenly, it's not just my heart that's heating from his words. The beauty of his assessment hits me lower, deep in my core, and I blush fiercely. "Wow, thank you, Professor. No one has ever said anything like that to me. Just . . . thank you."

There's a moment of silence, both of us unsure where to go from here. Well, at least *I* don't know what to say. It seems like he's merely watching me, and I see his eyes trace from my messy bun to my bespectacled eyes to my cleavage. Suddenly, I'm damn glad I took the moment to fluff the girls before calling.

He breaks the silence, his voice husky and doing dangerous things to my body, even through the digital divide. "Is there something specific you called about tonight, Daisy?"

"Oh . . . uh, the homework!" I say, picking up my notebook and holding it to the camera. I realize a moment later that it'd been the perfect opportunity to say something flirty, but it's too late now. And really, I shouldn't be flirting with him anyway, no matter how sexy I find his intelligence, his muscled body, and okay, maybe his arrogance too. "I'm having some difficulty with problem twenty-four."

Five minutes later, he's let me talk my way to the solution, not simply giving it to me but making me work for it myself. He seems just as delighted with my correct answer as I am. "See, Miss Phillips? You're capable of great things . . . with the proper guidance, of course." He winks, softening the cocky joke.

But I'm beginning to think he's right. The right teacher is just what I need . . . in math and in other things. Maybe this is why I've never found the right guy for my first time. Granted, it's not like I ever got asked out in high school, but in college, there have been a few guys interested in me. But they always seemed so immature. Not like Professor Daniels. He seems confident, mature, like he'd know how to take care of me and teach me what I need to know.

"Thank you, sir. I think you're right. I just need the right teacher to show me, help me learn everything I'm capable of," I say softly, letting the sultriness I feel fill my voice. We're still speaking in innuendo, but there's no doubt to the offer I'm making. It's the most forward I think I've ever been, and while maybe that's ridiculous, it's the truth.

"Daisy . . ." he starts, leaning toward the camera again. I lean forward too, knowing it puts my cleavage front and center for him, wanting him to see me, to want me. He gulps, eyes narrowing and focused solely on my chest. "I'm your teacher, and anything beyond that would be inappropriate. You're so fucking sexy . . ." He stops, shaking his head, and forces his eyes to mine. "I mean, you're a lovely young woman and it would be in bad form for me to take advantage of that."

My face falls, and he cringes. "I'm sorry, Miss Phillips. You have no idea how truly sorry I am. Good night." And with one last look of longing at my tits, the screen goes black.

Shit.

I am so screwed. I basically just threw myself at my professor, who then had to let me down gently. But somewhere between the fear of what'll happen with my grades and mortification at his brush-off, I realize that he called me 'fucking sexy' in that deep, throaty growl of his. I wonder if that held more truth than his civilized, formal statement about my being a 'lovely young woman'.

The more I think about his words, his cocky wink, the way he leaned against his desk, putting his bulging cock right at my eye level, the hotter I get. The thought of his domineering, arrogant, sexy as fuck attitude gets me wet. I remember the hungry way his eyes traced my tits, like he'd love to bury his face in their lushness.

Before I even make the conscious effort to do so, my hands are tracing along my body. I have a momentary thought of appreciation that Ari will be out late, and then I give in to the fire Professor Daniels has been building in me all semester.

I pull my tank top over my head, cupping my breasts and talking to the black screen, imagining that his face is still peering back at me. "You like these, Professor? It seemed like you couldn't take your eyes off them." I trace my fingers around my nipples, gasping as I pinch their stiff peaks.

Keeping one hand teasing my chest, I slip my shorts down and off. I trace a finger along my panties, feeling the dampness through the fabric, "Fuck, you've already got me soaked through my good-girl panties. But you already knew that, didn't you? You know exactly what you do to me."

Needing more, I slip my fingers into my panties, moving along my slit and coating myself with my juices. Circling my clit with the pads of my fingers, I sigh. "Mmm, God, that feels good. You're going to make me come rubbing my little clit like that." Rubbing in circles, I lay my head back, breathing deeply.

Closing my eyes, I let the fantasy take over completely. He makes me feel wanton, but I can't imagine saying these things if he were actually in front of me. I'd probably die of embarrassment first, and he'd definitely shut me down. But alone in my room, I feel brave, free to let loose all the dirty thoughts I have to get me to my climax.

"I need more, Professor. You stand up there, all stern and serious, lecturing us. But all I think about is that thick cock bulging in your jeans. I want to taste it, I want to take it in my virgin pussy." As I dream it's his rock-hard cock, I press two fingers inside myself, the tightness of my walls quivering against the invasion. "That's it, fill me up. I know it's a tight fit, but I can take you." I add a third finger, the stretch verging on pain, but it's so delicious, I cry out.

A constant stream of sounds, some dirty words, and some incoherent moans work their way up my throat as I slide my fingers in and out, still teasing my clit with my thumb. "Fuck, yes. Professor. I'm going to come. My sweet, untouched pussy. God, I need you to show me . . . show what I'm capable of." His earlier words rush out, no longer the encouragement of professor to student, but in my mind, they've twisted into a scenario where he works my body masterfully, taking control and teaching me things about pleasure I've never dreamed.

I stroke my clit one last time and convulsions tear through me as I whisper *Connor* over and over again, unable to do anything but ride out the wave of my orgasm. It's huge, bigger than I've ever had, and when it subsides, I find myself gasping for breath.

I peel my eyes open, thankful the couch is still holding me up because I'm complete jelly. "Holy Shit," I say to the empty room, a smile sweeping across my face. "Looks like I'm already learning some things, Professor."

I grab my drenched undies, wiping my cream-covered fingers on them. With a sigh, I decide a shower is just what I need after that workout. Both the mental one from the online chat with the professor and the physical one at my own hands.

I close my notebook, stacking it with my textbook, then close my laptop, adding it to the pile. I gently toss the whole stack onto my bed and head to the shower, promising myself that I will spend the weekend studying. After all, Professor Daniels said he thinks I'm capable of exceptional work, and I'm damn sure going to prove that to be true.

CONNOR

Fuck. I've had women throw themselves at me before. I'm a young, good-looking, muscled-up math nerd. The idiosyncrasy of a hot-bodied intellect who can talk high-level math and superheroes is like candy to a certain type of woman. The same is true for students too. More than one young co-ed has thought she'd be the one to tempt me into breaking that taboo line, whether for grades or sport, or maybe because she was truly attracted to me. I've never once considered it. Until today.

I've already broken about a dozen rules, and probably some laws, with Daisy Phillips in my mind, but I knew I wouldn't ever act on those thoughts. But when she leaned forward, knowingly and intentionally showing her tits to me, I'd been so close to making those filthy thoughts a reality. I'd tried to let her down easy, even if my tongue did slip a bit, but I could see her humiliation.

I go back to work, grading papers at my desk. It's only moments later that I hear a rustling. At first, I think someone's in the room with me, and I scan the small space, finding myself alone as I thought. But then the noise happens again.

And then I hear it. A breathy sigh.

And Daisy's voice.

My eyes look to my computer screen, the chat window still there but showing a solid black screen. The chat is closed, right?

I click on it "Miss Phillips? Can you hear me?"

No response.

At least not to me, but what I do hear makes me instantly hard. It's Daisy, obviously masturbating, judging by the sounds. And if that wasn't enough to get me rock fucking hard instantly, when she says my name, I'm fully erect in seconds.

I try again, knowing that this is wrong. Clicking on the window, I see if she can hear me. "Daisy?"

Still no response. But her words are getting dirtier, and after a moment of hesitation, I can't help myself. If she can't hear me talking to her, trying to warn her of the continued connection, she won't hear me touching myself either. I hope that's true, because fuck, I can't help it.

As she works herself, her moans and words streaming live to my ears, I do the same, taking my cock in hand. I fuck my hand, using my precum to ease the way. It's an erotic aural assault, but in my mind, I picture her just as she was on the screen, messy hair and glasses, tits pushed up in her bra, but the image morphs, turning into her naked and writhing beneath me, and I pump myself harder and faster.

She's mid-stream of dirty talk when I hear her say 'my virgin pussy', and I have to grab the base of my cock and squeeze hard to stave off the immediate orgasm. Could she be telling the truth? Is she actually a virgin? I'd imagined that but never really believed it could be true. Inexperienced, for sure, but untouched? She's a gorgeous woman, brilliant and interesting. How has no other man popped that cherry?

The thought of anyone else tasting her sweetness, breaking through that barrier for the first time, infuriates me. Like some silly high school boy or barely old enough college frat boy is worth her gift. No, I want it. I want her first time, and maybe more after that.

The thought is delicious, a momentary imagining that while it sounds so right, I know it's so very wrong. But I let my fantasy take me away as I pump myself. And when she gets close, I pick up my pace, wanting to match her, to come with her, both of us together, even if she doesn't know it.

As she cries out, I hear her whispering my name over and over like a prayer, and I explode, ropes of white cum trickling down my hand as I ride out the forceful orgasm with her. "Daisy . . ." I grunt out.

I hear her panting breaths in time with mine as we both recover. And then, too soon, the black chat window winks out, disappearing. For an instant, I think maybe I imagined it. But then I look at my cock, and I know the truth.

I just heard Daisy Phillips rubbing her sweet pussy . . . to me. No, her sweet *virgin* pussy as she imagined me taking her.

I am so fucked. Because damn, do I want to make her dream a reality. Actually, it's my dream too.

THE WEEKEND IS WAY TOO LONG AND NOT NEARLY LONG enough. Dean Michaels called about some fundraising event he wants me to speak at and one of my doctoral candidate students called with a crisis. Both of the phone calls had only paused my obsession with Daisy. I worked out mercilessly, trying to will my body into submission through exhaustion, but every post-workout shower had me jacking off to the memory of her breathy moans and my name on her lips.

I vacillate all weekend between not saying a word to Daisy and telling her what I heard after our chat. I should probably keep it a secret, protect her pride and my reputation. And I've told myself that's the game plan, time after time.

What I want to do to her could put my career in jeopardy . . . but I almost feel like it'd be worth it. To bend her over, to turn what I'm sure is a creamy pale ass bright pink from spanking. To make her get on her knees and worship my cock, make her beg before I turn her around and pound her until I cream so deep and so hard inside her it drips out of her afterward.

No. I can't. She's off limits in so many ways. She's my student, she's so young, she's a virgin, she's so fucking sexy, she wants me. Shit. I got off track again. She's not for me, I remind myself.

I tell myself that again as I walk into the teacher's lounge for coffee, knowing that she'll be in my next class.

"Get yourself in gear," I admonish myself, reaching for my phone. "Coffee, email, grab my notes . . ."

"Yo, CD, what's up?" a familiar voice says, and I turn to see Nick Goodman, my friend and fellow professor.

"H–hey, Nick," I stammer, worrying for a second that he can read my dangerously dirty thoughts on my face. "What's up?"

"You okay?" Nick asks, coming all the way in. "Your face is all flushed. You thinking some naughty thoughts about those improper fractions again?"

It's an old joke between us, but still, I almost forget to laugh. "Ha ha, man. Seriously, get some new material."

He grins devilishly. "How about . . . what's 6.9?"

I eye him and shrug.

"Good sex interrupted by a period," he says, laughing at his own juvenile humor.

I give him a sympathy smirk. "I've got class in fifteen. What do you need?"

"Just wanted to know if you heard about Cunningham over at MIT," he asks, grinning. Rob Cunningham has been one of the leading professors in the STEM field for twenty years and someone I've admired for awhile. He's the most likely contender for the Abel Prize, basically, the Nobel Prize for mathematics, next year.

"I've been too busy. What's going on?"

"Rumor has it that he dipped his wick in the TA well," Nick says. "And there's video."

"Oh, shit," I rasp, blinking. "How'd that happen?"

"How do you think? The dumbshit probably kept the video on his phone and his wife found it," Nick says gleefully. "Man, was she pissed. I don't know if she was more or less mad that . . . the TA wasn't a girl."

"No fucking way," I reply, surprised at both Cunningham's falter and his preference. "So is she taking him to the cleaners?"

"And some . . . her family is a *big* contributor to the school, so there's word his tenure might be in jeopardy," Nick says, shaking his head. "More because of who she is than what he did, but it shakes out ugly for him either way. Anyway, just wanted you to know, since I know you've been watching his work. Might put a damper on his shoe-in win for the Abel."

"Yeah," I murmur, still disbelieving. Although I can definitely understand the temptation after this weekend. "Listen, man, no offense, but—"

"Hey, I know. I have shit to do too," Nick says. "See you later."

Heading to my office, I silently talk myself through the game plan again. It's best if I stay away from her. If that means I need to grade her more fairly . . . well, so be it. I don't like not pushing her, but maybe that'll keep her away. I don't want to end up like Cunningham, and after what I did Friday night, I know I crossed a line.

I grab my notes along with the papers I need to return and hurry to the lecture room, arriving just a minute before class. I sit down, and I quickly glance around, not seeing Daisy. *Maybe she's absent today. Maybe she —*

The door opens and she walks in. Passing right by my desk, I can smell her, and I have to force my eyes to stay on my papers as I can almost smell the soft, sexy scent of her pussy, that smooth virgin pussy, begging for me.

Goddammit. I'm going to have to do some camouflaging . . . because I'm hard as a fucking rock again. This is going to be a battle.

And I don't intend to lose.

The next hour is painstakingly slow. I can't just hide behind my desk. Everyone would wonder why I'm not up and around, engaging the class like usual. So I face the whiteboard as much as possible.

But when I see Daisy crossing and uncrossing her legs, I can barely hold back the groan. Before my brain can stop it, my mouth spits out, "Miss Phillips, perhaps you can show us how you'd solve this problem?"

She jerks in her seat, surprise showing on her face for an instant before she smiles. "Sure, Professor Daniels." She walks to the board and gets to work.

I take the opportunity to check her out under the guise of watching her scribble neat lines of equations. She's wearing a skirt today. I think the girls call them 'skater skirts', but all I know is that with one twirl, I bet it'd spin out and show me her panties underneath. Her good-girl panties. I want to flip her skirt up, slip the cotton down her thighs, and feast on her.

As if she hears my thoughts, she turns. "What do you think?"

I freeze, then my brain clicks back on and I let a slow smile take my face. "Excellent work, Miss Phillips." I point to a line in her work. "You'll notice she did a bit of multi-tasking in this line, both solving for X and reorg'ing the integers. That's fine, or you could break that out into two steps if you'd prefer."

"Oh," she says with a jump. Marker still in her hand, she

approaches me and then adds a closing parenthesis to one of the lower lines. "Got it."

I dip my chin, my voice husky. "Good catch. You're learning."

Clearing my throat, I address the room. "All right, class dismissed until Wednesday. Complete problems ten through twenty-five in unit five to be prepared, as we'll be moving on to the next section."

There's a hint of a groan at the homework assignment, but I'm already out the door, rushing to my office to get some needed space before I do something supremely stupid.

DAISY

Professor Daniels basically bolts from the room after dismissing class. But after his help on Friday night—with my math work, *not* my orgasm—I feel like I should thank him again. Especially for the compliment that has reaffirmed my love affair with math once again, something I felt was in jeopardy with his harsh grading.

I knock twice on his office door, waiting until I hear his gruff permission to enter. I open the door tentatively. "Professor Daniels?"

I step in the office, closing the door behind me. I swear his eyes skate along my body, head to toe and back up to meet my eyes. It happens so fast, it could be my imagination. But there is something in his eyes as he stares at me. I can't decide if it's anger or lust, but there is definitely heat.

"Can I help you with something, Miss Phillips?" he asks, his voice tight as he leans back in his chair, crossing his arms over his chest. His biceps bulge against his black t-shirt, and I realize that instead of a little alligator on the chest, there's a pi symbol. A math joke, but the look on his face is anything but funny.

I hesitate. Maybe this isn't such a good idea. But telling him thank you can't be a bad thing, right? "No, I just wanted to say thank you again for the help Friday night."

He flinches, although I don't know why. "No problem. That's what I'm here for, to teach you." He gulps.

I'm not sure what to say. I'm used to his being this powerhouse of cocky asshole, but right now, he seems almost nervous around me. "I know. And I'm learning. I definitely am. So I just wanted to tell you how much I appreciate the extra help and the kind words about my work." My nerves are getting the better of me, my mouth rambling and my brain not stopping it. "I was getting concerned that maybe I wasn't cut out to be a math major, so hearing that you think I have potential really reassured me. I promise to show you just what I'm capable of."

He groans. He legit lets out a deep, throaty noise that makes me think of sex.

"I heard you, Daisy." He says it and then snaps his mouth shut like he hadn't meant to let the words out. I'm confused. Of course, he heard me. I just talked to him. I tilt my head questioningly.

He swallows like he wishes he could take the words back, but with a fortifying breath, he says, "I *heard* you . . . Friday night." He emphasizes the words with a lift of his eyebrows.

And suddenly, I realize what he means. "Oh, God. This cannot be happening." I shake my head, the flush already rushing to my cheeks as I bury my face in my hands.

He gets up, rushing around his desk and squatting down beside me. "It's okay, Daisy. Nothing to be embarrassed about. We all have needs and it's perfectly natural to take care of them. I don't know what happened to the chat window. I tried to tell you, but you couldn't hear me."

I lift my face, bravely meeting his eyes. "But you could hear me?"

He nods but looks off to the side. I feel in my gut that he's not being fully truthful with me.

"Could you . . . uhm, could you *see* me?" I ask, my voice soft. I'm still embarrassed, mortified, actually, but there's a heat in my core. A small part of me is turned on by his witnessing my private moment.

"No, I couldn't see you. Just a black window. I swear it." He takes my hands in his as he shakes his head.

"But you listened. You know what I was doing, heard my fantasy?" I'm not sure what I want his answer to be. The only reason I was able to say those things was because I was alone. But the humiliation of his turning down my semi-offered proposal Friday night is being replaced completely by the idea that he listened, and more importantly, that he liked what he heard.

He swallows, but I can see the smirk teasing his lips. He *did* like it. The knowledge gives me courage that I ordinarily wouldn't possess. Though his hands are holding mine in comfort, I move my palms down my thighs, slipping my skirt up higher. His hands follow my movements, not guiding me but going along for the ride wherever I take them.

"Daisy . . ." he warns, but his eyes are locked on the line where my thighs disappear under my skirt. I move up another inch.

"Do you want to see?" I ask, biting my lip hopefully. Any embarrassment I felt is gone as his hands clench mine tightly. He probably means to stop me, but I take it as encouragement.

I lift my skirt the rest of the way, my white cotton panties coming into view.

"Fuck . . ." he whispers. He places his hands on my thighs, and at the slightest pressure, I spread for him. "I can already see you're soaked for me," he growls, taking a big inhale. I've never thought of my scent being anything special, but he seems to savor it like it's a treat.

I move my fingers down, rubbing along my pussy through the cotton, so much like my fantasy that I can't help but say the same things again. "You already know what you do to me. I'm soaked for you every damn day, making myself come to your arrogant grins and that cock you keep hidden in your jeans." I thought I'd be too shy to say these things to him, but his heated gaze makes me want to tell him all my filthy thoughts.

"Show me." It's not a request. It's an order. One I happily obey. I pull my panties to the side, my bare mound and glistening lips coming into view, but he shakes his head. I have a second of doubt. Did I read this wrong? But then his hands are reaching up on my hips, pulling my panties down and off. He stuffs them in his back pocket and his hands go back to my thighs, spreading me even wider. "So fucking pretty, Daisy," he says reverently. "Now show me." His commanding tone is gravel-rough on my skin, the vibrations tickling and tantalizing.

I let my fingers trace through my folds, gathering my juices and slicking up to my engorged clit. He watches as I touch myself, his breathing matching my quickening pace. His gaze is hot, a palpable thing as I take myself higher and higher.

"Touch me?" I ask, but I can hear the pleading tone in my voice.

But he shakes his head. "I can't . . . I shouldn't. This is so fucking wrong." He's visibly fighting with himself, holding onto what's left of his control by a thread. I want to cut that thread, see and feel him unleashed with no holds barred.

"Just one finger, Professor Daniels? One finger in my virgin pussy so I have something to squeeze against? I'm so close. Please," I beg.

"Goddamn it, Daisy." But even as he curses me, he rewards me, giving me the single finger I so desperately need. He teases my opening. "Are you really a virgin?"

I bite my lip and nod, his acquiescence driving me to the edge of craziness.

"This sweet little pussy has never been fucked hard and filled with cum?" I moan at his words, and then again as he slowly slips his thick finger inside. I feel every inch as he fills me and retreats to do it again, maddeningly slow.

I rub my clit faster, on the edge from the feeling of any part of him inside me. I manage to gasp out, "I'm coming, Professor."

He leans forward and growls in my ear, finger deep in my pussy. "Daisy, you had no problem calling me Connor when you came to a fantasy of me. Call me by my name when you come for me now."

"Yes, Connor. Fuck!" I don't close my eyes, needing to see him to believe this is real as I come hard. My body bows up, searching for every bit of pleasure he'll give me, and the waves crash and crash over me, one after another. I'm panting when I see him slip his finger from me, the loss instant and significant. But when he lifts his finger to his mouth and sucks my juices, savoring them the way he did my scent, I'm struck with a thought.

"Now you," I say, not a question.

"What?" he asks, still seemingly lost in the moment.

"When you listened to me, did you touch yourself? Did you jack off your big cock as you heard me calling out your name?" I can tell by his grin that he did.

"And what if I did?" The words are a challenge, a dare if ever I heard one.

"Show me."

I can see the argument formulating in his mind, the words on the tip of his tongue. But he squashes them. In for an ounce, in for a pound, I guess. "You sure you can handle this?" He's still challenging me, the words so similar to the last time I was in his office and freaked out over some innuendo.

But I'm not freaking this time. No way, no how. Look at me, a fucking vixen I never would've suspected I was capable of being. But he brings it out in me, like so many other things. I bite my lip and nod, encouraging him.

He stands, resting back against his desk, and his hard cock pressing against his jeans comes into view. My eyes flicker to it, my mouth instantly watering. Jesus, I've never even touched a dick before . . . but all I can think of right now is swallowing every inch of what he's got.

His deft fingers unbuckle his belt, then he undoes the button and zipper, slipping his jeans down his hips a bit. His cock is pulsing beneath the fabric of his black boxer briefs. And then he lowers them, his cock coming into view.

"You're . . . beautiful," I whisper, taking in his cock. Maybe that's not the conventional word for a man's dick, but he is. Smooth and thick, with a vein pulsing along each side of his length and a round head that's already leaking fluid.

He wraps his hand around the shaft, pumping himself a few times. "Is this what you want to see?" he says. His voice almost sounds . . . angry? I tear my eyes away from the sexy show he's

LAUREN LANDISH

putting on to look up to his face. He looks tortured, like this is hurting him.

"Are you okay?" I ask, concerned and confused. I thought guys liked this and did this all the time, so why does he seem furious?

"No, it's not fucking okay, Daisy. You're my student, I'm your professor, and this is wrong. But I can't stop. You're . . . so fucking sexy, and I want your eyes on me, watching what you do me the way I just watched what I do to you." The words are stilted, in time with the thrust of his hips as he fucks his hand.

My heart rate speeds up. He's not in pain. He's fighting himself, fighting this over some sense of right and wrong. But I want this. So fucking badly.

I grab his thighs where they're spread in front of me. "Let me. Teach me." I don't wait for him to answer. I just wrap my hands around his. My first touch of cock is . . . warm and silky soft. I try to wrap my fingers around him and fail, not able to hold him completely in one hand. The tip is beautiful, flared and wide, making me marvel at how it could fit inside me . . . and what that ridge would do as it plowed in and out of my pussy.

I lick my lips, letting my hand caress down to his balls, huge and heavy. I look back up at him, almost pleading for him to guide me because I don't know what I'm doing.

He switches our position, laying his hands over mine and showing me how to stroke him. Once I have the hang of it, he lets go to let me be in control of the pace. His hands go to the edge of the desk behind him, gripping hard as he throws his head back in pleasure, groaning quietly.

A drop of precum pearls on his tip, and I'm struck with the need to taste him. I stick my tongue out, lapping at him like a

38

kitten, his flavor bursting across my tongue, and I moan in delight.

"Fuck, Daisy. You don't have to. Your hands on me feel so good."

I want more of those noises, guttural vibrations that make my pussy quiver in need. And so I lean forward in the chair to take him in my mouth, letting him stretch my lips wide as I suck his tip and swirl my tongue around, hoping for more of his precum. He lets me explore for a bit and then takes control.

I moan as Connor starts fucking my face slowly, pumping in and out of my eager lips. He's so much that each time his cock hits the back of my throat, I feel like I'm going to gag, but I don't care. I want . . . I want to be his naughty student, and I suck as eagerly as I can, worshipping his pulsating manhood as he looks down into my eyes. "That's it," he says as I run my tongue around his shaft. "That's a good girl. See if you can take it all for me."

His hips speed up, my pussy clenching around the ghost of what I want as his cock swells, and I moan again around him. "Now!" Connor growls, thrusting hard in my mouth. I feel the head of his cock slip into my throat before it swells, and suddenly, he's coming, pulling back slightly to fill my mouth with his sweet and salty cream. I moan again deeply, my thighs quivering as he empties himself into my mouth.

When he's done, he looks down, smiling. "Fuck, Daisy. That was . . . fuck."

It might be the best compliment he's ever given me. The thought that I can reduce such a brilliant mind to babbling is a powerful boost to my first-timer's nerves.

He tucks himself back into his boxers and jeans and then pulls me to standing. I realize this is the first time I've ever stood this close to him, body to body, sharing the same space. He towers over me by several inches, and when he wraps his arms around me, I feel safe in the cocoon of his presence.

And then he kisses me. I know he can probably taste himself on my tongue, but he doesn't seem to mind as he demands entry. It's a kiss of promise, that this isn't over, that we're not done.

But the spell is broken when I hear a soft *ding*. He breaks apart, pressing his forehead to mine as he cups my face. "I have to go. That's my ten-minute warning for my next class. And I don't think it'll look good if I go in with a hard-on."

I grin, sassing back. "Actually, I prefer class when you're hard. Makes the math that much more challenging because I'm distracted. I'll be even more distracted now."

He swats my ass over my skirt. "Cheeky brat. It's usually not a problem, except when I have a sexy student in my front row, chewing on her pencils as she studies me as much as the math."

I grin, letting my hand dip down to trace his soft length in his jeans. "Oh, I'm studying, all right. Have a good class, Professor."

And with a laugh, I open the door, realizing it'd been unlocked the whole time. Shit, that could've been bad if we'd been caught. Luck must be on our side, though, because we weren't disturbed at all. It's not until I'm walking down the hallway that I feel a slight breeze on my pussy and realize he kept my panties. I almost turn back to retrieve them but decide I'd rather he kept them.

CONNOR

That was the hottest thing I've ever done. From the way she looked, eagerly taking me in her mouth, to the way she wrapped her hand around my cock in wonder, almost worshipping it before I pumped in and out of her hungry mouth. Fuck, if we had time, I would've loved to watch her rub herself with my cock in her mouth. Talk about fucking hot.

And she took instruction well, not surprisingly, considering how quick she catches on in class. I grin to myself. Class. It seems I might be instructing Daisy in two subjects soon. One can dream.

Still, as I head to the break room, wanting to grab a better coffee than what my poor office machine can provide, I can't help but worry. We didn't just cross a line. We obliterated that motherfucker and left it so far in the dust that I can't ever go back. I'm risking getting fired, losing my reputation, losing everything I've busted my ass for.

Worst of all, I couldn't help myself. Daisy creates such a deep need in me that I would have done nearly anything to have her like that. That's dangerous, because now that I've had a taste . . . there's no way it ends here. No way I'm going to quit while I'm ahead. That pussy is mine.

As my students arrive and I start going into the nuances of Cauchy-Riemann equations, I can't help but think about Daisy. My mind wavers back and forth between what I want and what is proper.

I really should tell her we can't continue this. It's too danger-ous, and I can't take the risk. Still, every time I think of even her name, I'm spellbound by the image of her wet pussy pressed up against those sheer white panties and the thought that she has never felt a man inside her yet . . . and I could be the first.

It's a miracle that I make it through my presentation and dismiss the class.

By Wednesday's class, I'm desperate to see her again even as the battle between my brain and my cock rages on. So far, my greedy desire is winning hands-down.

Daisy walks in, head held high, in another skirt paired with a V-neck T-shirt that shows her cleavage off delightfully. She looks casual but sexy as fuck. She spins a bit as she sits, her skirt flaring to flash an enticing hint of upper thigh. Her eyes snap to mine, making sure I saw her show, and there's a moment of freeze, where I'm holding my body in place by force, fighting against the urge to kiss her hello. That would be the kiss of death to my career, and we both know it.

She smirks a bit, knowing what her outfit and her sass do to me. Bratty girl needs a lesson. And I'm just the teacher to give her one.

The class is painfully slow, torture for us both as I loom near her desk in the middle of the front row. But I don't make eye contact with her. That'd let her win this round. Instead, I keep my eyes scanning the room, calling on everyone except her, but I can feel her attention on me the whole time. I feel the heat of her gaze on my ass and on my crotch when I turn to face each side of the room. I sense her crossing and uncrossing her legs as I drive her crazy, teasing her with what she wants and knowing she can't have in the middle of class.

By the time the clock ticks the hour past, my lesson for her benefit is having its own consequences for me. I'm glad my boxer briefs and jeans are holding me tight or else class would've been rather obscene. But I'm uncomfortable in the pinched confines, and she needs to pay for that too.

"Okay, class, until Friday. Complete the next unit's homework problems, paying particular attention to the format for your answers. Dismissed." I wait a beat, letting the din of everyone packing up and rushing for the door fill the room, then speak again, harsh and unforgiving. "Miss Phillips, I'd like to speak with you about your homework, if you have a moment?"

Her eyes are wide as saucers, fear sparking in their depths, but she nods.

I sit on my desk, letting my feet dangle as the room empties.

I see Daisy's seatmate, Sabrina, lean toward her. She stage-whispers, "Good luck, Daisy. Do you want me to wait for you?"

Daisy offers her a smile. "Thanks, but it's okay. I swear I was extra-precise with the homework. It can't be all bad." Sabrina nods but obviously doesn't agree, firmly in the camp that believes I'm a math monster that eats students' GPAs for breakfast.

Right now, I'm thinking there's something else I'd rather eat . . . Daisy's sweet little pussy. But I have class in this very room in fifteen minutes, so there's no time for what I want to do to her. Time. I need time.

Finally alone, she approaches the desk, standing between my spread legs, but far enough away that it'd seem appropriate to anyone who peeked in the room. "Yes, sir? My homework?" she says, but the lift of her eyebrow says she knows I didn't keep her here to talk about the *A* she got on the last set of problems I assigned.

Keeping the double-talk going, I ask, "How were you feeling after Monday's *work*? Any concerns, problems we need to go over?"

She digs the toe of her shoe into the floor, looking down and every inch the innocent that she is, but then she remembers herself and stands tall and proud. The reminder of how inexperienced she is sets me afire, and I grip the edge of the desk to stop from touching her.

"No, I felt good . . . really good about the work. Ready to learn more, in fact." She smiles, an invitation in her eyes.

"Another tutoring session then? You really are capable of such exceptional work. You're just raw and untrained. I'm happy to mentor you." I'm offering more, so much more than math help, or hell, even sexual guidance, but I don't know how to broach the breadth and depth of what I want with her in this class-room where we could be overheard.

"Yes, Professor Daniels. That'd be great. I appreciate your help," she says, her voice dripping sex.

I grab a Post-It note from my desk, scribbling my address down. "Meet me here at seven tonight and we'll make sure the previous lesson stuck. We'll build from there."

She steps forward to take the paper from my hand, the elec-tricity shooting between us at the barest touch. She clutches it to her chest. "Yes, sir. Seven tonight for tutoring."

She moves to step away, and I can't bear to let her go without more. I hop from the desk, grabbing her upper arm to stop her. "Oh, and Daisy?"

She looks at me expectantly, and I do a quick sweep of the doorway, making sure no students are entering. Seeing no one, I slip my hand under her skirt, pinching her ass sharply. She gasps, but as I soothe the sting with a brush of my palm, she moans quietly. I whisper harshly into her ear, "Don't flash what's mine to anyone else. You'd best take care when you wear skirts like this or I'll have to spank your bratty ass for showing off to anyone but me. Understood?"

She nods silently. I smooth the fabric down over her ass, making sure it's as long as possible and hiding the treasure of her pussy from every other fucker on campus. Stepping back, I give her a raised eyebrow and a smirk, knowing that she's already wet for me. It feels like a win, even though I'm equally anxious for tonight.

———

By seven, I'm not rock-hard anymore. I'm a fucking steel rod, ready to claim her virginity like the cocky bastard I am. The doorbell rings, and I open it to see Daisy wearing the skirt from earlier. I grin, ready to flip it up and fill her.

But I force myself to have some manners. "Come in."

She steps in nervously, looking around like my space is going to give her insight into who I am. Actually, that might be true, I think, as I glance to the living room, seeing through her eyes. A comfy leather couch claims most of the room, surrounded with a big screen television and bookcases full of a mix of text-books and comics. It looks like what it is . . . a bachelor's pad. Mostly function, not form.

She wrings her hands together, stammering. "I took the bus from school so no one would see my car nearby. I didn't want to cause any problems by being here."

She's smart, so fucking smart. I honestly hadn't even thought of that, my mind too tangled up in thoughts of her spread wide before me to worry about how it would look to have a student's car sitting in my driveway. It's not likely anyone would notice, but it's still a senseless risk. "Good thinking." She preens at the simple praise.

"Want something to eat? I made dinner, nothing fancy but it's edible," I say, leading her into the kitchen. She looks around again, the small table set for two with simple plates and silverware.

"You made me dinner?" she asks, obviously surprised. She's so easily pleased by the simplest of gestures. I wonder if she thought I was just going to attack her when she walked through the door. Admittedly, it did occur to me, but I want her first time to be special, to set the tone for more for us.

I spoon the noodles on the plates as I gesture for her to sit down. Her skirt flares only slightly as she sits, proof that her move in class was intentional. The thought of her trying to seduce me turns me on. As if she needs to do anything more than simply be her beautiful, brilliant self. "Just pasta and jarred sauce. The bread was already garlic-coated too. I'm not really much of a cook, but a date requires food, typically, so I did my best."

She smiles wide. "Is that what this is? A date?"

I realize with a start that she has no idea at the thoughts rolling through my head. No experience with which to compare. She probably thinks this is some casual fuck for me, just a notch in my bedpost of co-eds I've done this with a hundred times before.

It's not. *She's* not.

I sit across from her, urging her to eat. "Daisy, I don't want to mince words here or talk in veiled innuendo like earlier. I want you to be honest with me." It's not a question, but she nods anyway. "I don't fuck students. Ever. It's unprofessional and could have dire consequences for me."

She swallows the mouthful of spaghetti, wiping at her lips with her napkin. "But I thought —"

I interrupt her. "You thought you were coming here tonight for me to fuck you?" She nods, her eyes shining with confusion. "And God help me, I want to fuck you, pop your sweet cherry and claim your pussy as mine. But . . ." I pause, making sure her eyes are focused on me. "But I am not willing to do that casually. If I wanted a casual fuck, I could have one of dozens. If I'm risking everything here, it's only if it's *more*."

Her smile dawns slowly as my words hit home, their meaning resonating in the space between us. "More. I like the sound of more." She sighs, impossibly more beautiful, as she commits to something she doesn't fully understand. But I do. And isn't that the point? I'll teach her.

I stand, leaving my barely-touched dinner. I'm not hungry for food. I'm hungry for her. Her pure innocence. Her sassy mouth. Her sexy body. Her brilliant mind. Her sweet spirit. All of her. All mine.

Taking her hand, I guide her to stand, cupping her chin in my other hand. "Are you sure, Daisy? There are no second chances here. No do-overs or retakes. Choose carefully." My voice is hard, brooking no argument, demanding that she think before speaking.

After staring into my eyes, searching for something she must find, she speaks. "I'm sure. Make love to me, Connor."

I smirk. "Oh, honey, I'm not going to make love to you. I'm going to fuck you raw and hard until you fall apart for me, my name the only thing on your lips. But I will fuck you with all my heart, Daisy." I want her to hear the difference. This won't be some soft, romantic moment like her teenage self dreamed about. I'm going to claim her, ruin her for any other man but me, but it won't matter because my cock is the only one her pussy is ever going to get.

I lead her down the hallway to my bedroom. The bedside lamp is on, but she doesn't scan this room like the others. No, her eyes stay locked on me, waiting for my lead, my direction.

I guide her to stand beside the bed, dropping to my knees to slip her shoes off. Tossing them aside, I run my hands up her legs, feeling the taut muscle beneath the silk of her skin. Up under her skirt, I cup her ass, kneading her flesh in my large palms. She whimpers, her hands shooting to my shoulders to hold herself steady as she rocks into my hands.

"You're wet for me, aren't you? I can smell you from here, sweet like candy, begging me to lick you all up." I pull her panties down and off, laying them neatly on my bedside table.

She grins down at me. "If you keep taking my panties, I'm not going to have any left to wear. You want me walking around campus naked beneath my skirts where anyone could see my pussy if the wind blew just right?"

Her bratty challenge reminds me of her behavior in class today. I rise, crowding her against the bed, but to her credit, she doesn't fall backward. Instead, she presses her body against mine. "You'll wear panties at all times unless I tell you otherwise, Daisy. No one sees this pussy but me. No one touches it but me. That includes you. You don't touch yourself unless I say so. I'll give you all the pleasure you could ever need. Understood?"

"Yes, sir," she says, her sass spurring me on.

"Turn around and bend over the bed." She lifts an eyebrow but obeys. I flip her skirt up, exposing her round cheeks to my eyes. I can see her slick pussy, so needy already. I cup her ass in my hands, squeezing the flesh roughly. "I'd considered taking it easy on you, postponing the punishment for your behavior in class today or maybe letting you off this one time since you're still learning, after all. But something tells me by the way you're still pushing me that you don't want me to let you skate by. You want this, don't you?" I ask her, but I already know the answer. And when she looks back at me, mouth open in anticipation as she gasps, she knows that I've already figured her out. I grin ferally at her, letting her see the animal she's provoked.

I rear back and deliver a sharp smack to her right cheek. She jolts forward and cries out, but before the pain even registers, I'm already soothing her pinkened skin. "That's for teasing me in class, knowing full fucking well that you were *this close* to showing off that pussy to every fucker in the room." Her hips roll under my hands, begging for more. Not one to disappoint, I smack her left cheek, the sound echoing in the room. I immediately trace my palm there again, taking away the sting. "And that one's for the bratty sass that you know drives me insane, but I think that's why you do it, isn't it, honey?"

Daisy groans into the comforter, hips bucking and her honey spreading down her thighs. I spread her cheeks, wanting a closer look at her pink center. "Fuck, Daisy. Know what you get when you take your punishment like a good girl?" My breath is hot on her pussy, her intoxicating scent invading my pores, filling me with longing.

"What? What do good girls get?" she breathes out, her voice tight with eagerness.

Though I use my mouth, I don't answer in words. My tongue laps at her cream, tasting her cotton-candy sweetness right from the source. She cries out, instinctively spreading her legs to let me have better access. I moan against her, knowing the vibration will spread to her clit. I follow the tremor and swirl my tongue against her button, circling over and over.

"Oh, my God, Connor. I didn't know it could feel like that. Fuck, so good." Her cries are music to my ears as her body shudders against me.

I slip a finger in her pussy, fucking her slow and shallow to test how tight she is. She damn-near choked my fingers at the slightest invasion before, and I know my cock is going to be in tortured heaven inside her. But I need to get her ready or I'll never get inside without hurting her.

She relaxes, pressing back against me, seeking more. "Yes,

honey. That's it. Take it and come on my hand and my mouth." She does as instructed, working herself enough that I'm able to add a second finger, and then a third, though it's a tight fit and I know it has to be bordering on pain for her. "Good girl, Daisy. Let me in so I can get you ready for me."

The thought of my filling her with my cock triggers her, and she bucks wildly, coming instantly. The gush of her cream eases the way, and my three fingers slip in and out easily as I push her higher and longer, wanting every drop of pleasure for her.

She collapses forward, the bed and my arm wrapped around her middle holding her up. I slip my fingers from her pussy and straight into my mouth, wanting more of her taste on my tongue. I could eat her out every day and still want more.

I pull her to stand, spinning her in my arms and covering her mouth with a kiss. She's gasping by the time I let her breathe. "Are you done, Daisy? Or can you take more?"

Her wicked grin tells me the answer even before she speaks. "More, please, Professor." The return to calling me 'professor' during such a sexy moment should turn me off, but instead, it riles me up, playing up the taboo of what we're doing.

"Okay, if you want it like that, Miss Phillips," I say, emphasizing her formal name, "let's see if you can follow directions to the letter for once." It's a mild admonishment, but she rises to the challenge, ever competitive and willing to do her best.

"Take off your clothes." I step back to give her just enough space to follow the command, and I watch as she pulls the skirt down, then slips her T-shirt over her head. She pauses for a heartbeat as she reaches back to unclasp her bra, but when she sees my reprimanding look, she undoes it and tosses it aside.

She stands before me, fully nude and absolutely stunning. I want to trace every inch of her body with my tongue, memorize her every dip and curve with my hands, measure just how much she can physically take underneath me.

I yank the comforter back, wanting her in my bed. "Lie down for me." She smiles softly and climbs to the middle of the bed. Her dark hair spreads against the pillow in a halo, her tan skin contrasting starkly against the white sheets. She looks like an angel.

She writhes against the fabric, stretching her body out and extending her arms wide. "Satin sheets? Do you always sleep on satin or did you do this for tonight?"

I consider telling her a lie but decide if I want her truth, I need to give her my own. "I usually sleep and fuck on satin. It makes it easy to move and position you where I want you, and the slip of it against your skin is decadent. Do you like it?"

She nods and reaches for me, but I hold back to undress. I yank my shirt over my head, and when I reach for my belt, I realize she's sitting up, watching me with rapt attention. I slowly slide the leather through, torturing us both with the delay but loving the way her breathing picks up. I can see her pulse thrumming in her neck, racing with excitement. My belt undone, I make quicker work of the rest and then I'm standing before her naked.

I've never felt more vulnerable. I'm in good shape and certainly not old by any standard, but I'm damn-near ten years older than Daisy, who's likely only paid attention to the shirt-less college boys in the gym. I let the fire I feel for her shine in my eyes, daring her to find me lacking in any way. We stare at each other for a moment, and then the tension breaks as she breathes, "Please, Connor."

She looks at me, worried for a second, but the look in my eyes assures her as I climb in next to her. There's a bit of fear in her eyes as I position myself between her legs, but my cock is ready to take care of her as she gives me a trusting look.

Slowly, I lower down to her, covering her with my body and pressing her to the bed to grind against her, not entering her yet but teasing at the motion. She feels silkier than the satin sheets against my skin, so smooth. "Fuck, Daisy. I need you. Let me in. I need you to say it, honey."

She bites her lip, but the words come easily. "Fuck me, Connor. I want you to be my first."

I press up on one hand, the other going to my shaft to guide my way to her entrance. I need to go slow, give her an inch at a time so I don't hurt her. I breathe deeply to fortify my resolve, the urge to slam balls-deep in one stroke riding me hard.

Instead of words, I lean down, kissing her tenderly to encourage her to relax, letting my lips and my body language tell her that it's all going to be okay. Slowly, in sweet, exquisite torture, I stretch her out, working my cock in and out in short, gentle strokes.

It's amazing, sinking myself into Daisy's body, becoming one with her.

I'm barely in when her breath catches and her eyes shoot wide. "That's it, Daisy. I'm right there. Take a big breath for me, and when you exhale, there'll be a small pinch. But I swear, I'll be easy."

She nods, her trust a beautiful thing. And when she exhales, I push forward. Her breath turns into a cry, but I catch it in a kiss, holding still deep inside her. She whimpers, and I give her a few small thrusts, testing to see when she relaxes. "You okay?"

Her hips buck in response. "No, I need you to move. Fuck . . . move, please." So I do, watching her closely and feeling more like the student than the teacher in this moment. She may be learning about sex, but I'm learning her. What she likes, what makes her cry out, and what makes her tight pussy clamp down on me like a vise.

Slowly, we build the pace, finding our rhythm. She's taking me fully, long thrusts from her entrance to deep inside where I bottom out, pushing a cry of pleasure from her lips with every stroke. Our hips smack together, making Daisy gasp. "Fuck! Oh, my God, yes!"

Her encouragement drives me, and I start fucking her deeply. Hard strokes are ended each time with my hips grinding against hers, her clit rubbing against my body and making her groan. She starts calling out my name again and again with each thrust, and I have to pull out before I can't take it anymore.

"Please . . . fuck, Connor, fuck me," Daisy begs, her eyes huge and soulful. "I need you . . . so close."

I dip in again, pressing her hips to the satin to pound her almost savagely, our bodies shaking my entire bed as she clenches me. Her pussy is so tight and warm that I have to freeze again and again, torturing the both of us, but I can't help myself. If I keep going, I'm going to explode inside her . . . and I don't want this to ever end.

Daisy gasps as I freeze again, her eyes staring into my very fucking soul. Somehow, this little virgin has flipped our positions. I'm in charge . . . but she has all the power, bewitching me with her magical body and perfect, tight pussy. "Just a little more. I want to come so badly."

"That's it, little angel," I encourage, pulling back for a final sprint. "Come all over my cock! Milk my cream out of me."

With long, almost blurringly fast thrusts, Daisy and I catapult ourselves toward the onrushing precipice. My cock swells, and she cries out, my name sweet in my ears as her fingernails dig into my shoulders and she comes, squeezing me so tightly that I can't hold back any longer. Growling her name, I explode, my cream filling her. I groan, my back arching as she clings to me, wrapping her legs around me.

I collapse onto her, wrung out and weak from everything I gave her. I bury my face into her neck, laying an open-mouthed kiss there before moving up. "Now . . . now, you're mine," I promise her, tugging on her ear with my teeth.

DAISY

Diary Entry, March 15th

Dear Diary,

I can't believe it! I finally did it! And it was beautiful and special and powerful. All the things I thought it would be.

I won't say who it was, even in these private pages, because it could definitely get me, and him, into trouble if anyone found out. We definitely shouldn't, but I can't help myself with him. And apparently, the feeling is mutual.

It happened so fast too. Well, not the actual event. That took all night. But before that. One minute, I thought he hated me, or at the least was annoyed by me. And then, whip-fast, I find out that maybe hate and love are closer cousins than I imagined. A few days ago, I wrote how mortified I was that I was overheard online, but now I'm thinking that was the awkward start to something really amazing.

He says I'm his. Actually, he growled 'mine' while he bit my ear, and it was unbelievably hot. And he says this is 'more', not casual. It's hard to trust that, but fuck, do I want to. I want to believe every filthy word and promise from his mouth.

Because I do want more. And I want to be his.

By Friday's class, I'm worked up beyond belief. Connor and I had phone sex last night, another first for me. He'd guided me through touching myself the way he wanted me to, his deep voice rumbling in my headphones as he watched me come for him. Though I didn't tell him what to do, I watched his movements, memorizing how he likes to be touched, ever his student and always wanting to learn.

But now, only hours later, I'm needy again. But there's no time, considering class starts in minutes. I consider stopping by his office, but that's a dangerous taunt of fate, so I force myself to sit in my chair and wait patiently.

"Hey, Daisy, how're you doing?" Sabrina says from beside me. Her usually bubbly voice is flat and I look over to her.

"I'm fine, but girl . . . are *you* okay? No offense, but you look a bit . . . under the weather?" I'm trying to be polite, but she looks like shit. Definitely stressed, and not her usual perky self.

She pats her hair in a vain attempt to tame the flyaways of blonde that have escaped her messy bun. The mere fact that she's got a tangle of hair on top of her head is a giveaway that something's wrong. While Sabrina isn't usually one of the overtly sexy dressers in Professor Daniels's class, she's usually pretty put-together, definitely not one of the sweats and Uggs girls. But today . . . I look down, and yep, she's wearing leggings. Although, paired with a slim-fit crop top and cardigan, she looks more casually sexy than 'just rolled out of bed'.

"I'm just having a hard time with this class and I need this grade or my scholarship is in jeopardy." As she says it, I can almost see the tears glistening in her eyes. "Are you doing better?"

I nod, cautiously telling her, "Yeah, unit four was the one that really bombed me out. Five was better. That was the *B* I got. But my quiz and homework for unit six have all been *A*s, so I think it'll balance out in the long run over the semester."

"Damn, I wish I could say the same. I'm still barely passing with a *C*-minus. I swear, I spend more time on this one class than I do all my other ones combined. Between lecture, the online class forum, and study group, you'd think it'd be smooth sailing. But I just can't get it," she says fatalistically.

"Maybe you should check with Professor Daniels about getting some help?" The words leave my mouth before I think them through. Fuck. I don't want Sabrina sitting alone in Connor's office with him. A flash of jealousy, sour and hot, shoots through me. "Or maybe there's another study group you could try?"

"Maybe. It's just so frustrating. I've always been decent at math—not great, but passable. You were right, though. Daniels is such a hardass about grading." She huffs a sigh, the annoyance loud and clear.

I cringe. I did call him that . . . and worse. But things have changed now. I understand why he's so persnickety about grading, and while it doesn't make it easier, it at least makes me less prickly about it. Trying to explain that without telling too much seems dangerous though. "He is hard, but I think he's doing it with our best interests in mind. I'll say that after bitching about losing points on the quiz over two versus three decimal points, I've been much more careful about details. And my grades have reflected that."

"You're defending him now?" Sabrina asks incredulously. "You've been one of the folks bitching with me about him all semester. Traitor."

She says it jokingly, a small smile on her lips, but it doesn't reach her eyes. She's too far gone in her pity party to really laugh at anything. But the word rings in my head like a gong. She's right. I have been mouthy about Professor Daniels's class, but after some tutoring of a different sort, I do feel more forgiving for his harsh teaching style. Hell, I like it a lot in other areas.

I wonder for a moment if I'm being too easily swayed, but when I really think about the conversations we've had and how his intent is to draw the best out of me because he sees my potential, I know that he's not in the wrong. My earlier, whiny self was mid-pity party too, and I wasn't taking personal responsibility for my own lack of care with the work. It wasn't him. It was me, and he was calling me out appropriately.

I smile gently as I try to placate Sabrina. "No, I'm not a traitor. His grading is tough, no doubt. I'm just saying that as much as I complained about it, he was right. And while it was a painful moment to see those low grades, especially the *C*, it did teach me exactly what it was supposed to." She rolls her eyes, not wanting to hear it. "What is he counting off for on your work? Are you getting the wrong answer or is it a point here and there for mistakes in your work?"

She pulls out her latest homework, with a glaring red *D* on the top, and hands it over. That is definitely one *D* I never want from Professor Daniels. I scan the page, looking for where she's losing points. "Oh, okay . . . well, this one is easy. See right here? You've got the formula wrong in your initial setup, and it seems like that was a mistake you made across the board, so it affected all your problems. Your process is sound. It was your setup. Relearn that correctly, and this unit will be a breeze for you." I emphasize the statement with a snap of my fingers and Sabrina smiles a bit wider now.

"Really? If I do that, I still have time to get a good grade on the test and that could save me. Thanks, Daisy." She seems a bit more settled now, definitely lighter, and I think I actually helped her.

Thank goodness, because here comes Professor Daniels. He walks into class looking good enough to eat, I think with a smirk. He's wearing a Comicon shirt, and my earlier consideration of him as a fanboy has significantly more merit now that I've seen the rows of comic books on his shelves at home. His jeans are light-wash, barely blue, and they look soft, making me want to caress his thighs to test my theory.

He doesn't look at me, not at all. His eyes scan the room instead. "Good morning. We've got a lot to cover and not much time, so let's get to work." He takes one last sip of his coffee before setting it on the desk, and then he turns to the board.

The next hour is a whirlwind. I don't have time to notice that he never looks at me, doesn't call on me once, and basically ignores my very existence. Okay, so maybe I do notice. But as I focus on the work he's demonstrating, I try to let the worry about that go. It's not like he can give me sex eyes in the middle of class. That'd be too obvious and get both of us into trouble. And the new formula he's showing us takes all my attention anyway.

By the end of class, my head is spinning but my brain is buzzing with the excitement of learning something totally new. Plus, the fact that Connor is intelligent enough to not just understand something so complex, but can break it down and actually teach it well, is sexy as fuck. I'm not one of those women who doesn't care if a guy can carry on a conversation as long as he's good-looking. No, I need the brains because they're the sexiest part of a man. Luckily for me, Connor has both brains and beauty. The full fucking package. Oh, and his package . . . definitely a plus.

When he dismisses us, I pack up my things slowly, intending to be the last person in class, hoping I can tempt him into doing something about the fire he's built in my brain and body. But I watch with bated breath as I see Sabrina approach him. I shamelessly eavesdrop while I pretend to check over my notes.

"Professor?" Sabrina asks him. She looks confused again, so maybe today's lesson wasn't as exciting for her as it was for me.

"Yes, Miss Bowen?" Professor says.

She stammers a bit, twirling a loose curl around her finger and looking up at him through her lashes. If I didn't know better, I'd swear she was flirting. The thought makes my stomach tighten. "I'm having some problems with some of the work and I wondered if you might have any suggestions for me."

She bites her lip, legitimately looking like the epitome of sexy innocent as she flirts with my man right in front of me. I growl inside, even though she doesn't know he's my man. He is our professor. Doesn't she have morals? You don't flirt for grades. That's like Feminism 101. Okay, so *I'm* fucking him, but it's not for grades.

It's because I . . . he . . . we . . . ugh, not going there. I can't win that argument and it's way too soon to consider this anything more than fucking, even if he did call me *his* in that growly rumble that turns me on.

Connor's eyes flick to me, and I realize that maybe my jealous growl wasn't inside as much as out loud. Shit.

"Miss Bowen, perhaps we should continue this discussion about your grades and work in private. Do you have a moment to come to my office?" His voice is neutral, bored almost, and though I'm glad he doesn't seem to be feeling Sabrina, he doesn't seem particularly impressed with me right now either.

"Of course, sir. Thanks for taking the time to help me." Her voice is breathy, almost like she just got done running or fucking. She turns to grab her bag from the seat beside me and gives me a look of sheer delight, even flashing a discreet thumbs-up.

Connor holds the door for Sabrina and then turns back to me. "Miss Phillips, did you need something?" I shake my head, not able to say what I need with Sabrina listening, but my eyes bore into his, willing him to understand. "Have a good weekend then. See you Monday."

As they walk out, I can hear Sabrina chattering. Though not her exact words, she might as well be effusing about his *big brain* and how *hard she's willing to work* for him. She's so obviously flirting with him, testing angles to see which elicit a response from him. Little does she know, the main response she's about to get is from me, the jealous girlfriend.

Is that what I am, though?

Realizing that what I'm about to do is the height of immaturity, bordering on a stage-five clinger action, I follow them down the hallway. His door is closed, so I sit in one of the chairs around the corner. I can't hear through the walls and door, but I strain to listen anyway.

It's damn-near thirty minutes later when the door creaks open. I bury my face in my laptop, clicking away as though thoroughly invested in whatever I'm working on. Truth is, it's a paper for a class that's already finished, so I won't save whatever changes I'm making right now, but it makes a decent cover story.

From above, I hear a voice say my name. "Daisy?"

I look up to see Sabrina, smiling and bubbly once again. "Hey, Sabrina. Feeling better about class now?" The words come out with a hint of snark to them, but she doesn't seem to notice.

"Oh, yeah. Professor Daniels was great at going over everything with me. I might be all good now." She bends down, stuffing her cardigan into her bag, and when she stands, I realize exactly how tight her leggings are and how short her crop top is. While not inappropriate per se, it leaves nothing to the imagination, and the slip of midriff that shows every time she moves draws the eye like a beacon. She was in Connor's office dressed like that, flirting with him. I know it deep in my gut, and suddenly, her innocent words seem more like veiled innuendo. After all, I've been there, done that.

"Good, I'm glad," I say crisply.

She eyes me curiously. "What are you working on?"

I flash the screen at her, glad to have a ready excuse. "A paper. It's due this afternoon so I wanted to go over it one last time."

"Oh, okay. Well, I'll let you get back to it then. Thanks again for the help before class. I think I'm going to be okay." She waves two sets of matching crossed fingers. "Wish me luck! See ya Monday."

I wait for her to exit the door at the end of the hallway, counting my breaths until I can safely go into Connor's office without witnesses—thirty-one, thirty-two, thirty-three—and I get up, shoving my laptop into my bag and tossing it over my shoulder.

I stand in his open doorway, silently demanding his attention. A heartbeat later, he looks up, cocky smirk on his face as he sits back in his chair and crosses his arms over his chest. "Miss Phillips, come in. Something I can help you with?"

I enter and force myself to close the door gently, even though I want to slam the shit out of it. I drop my bag to the floor, hands on his desk in an attempt to loom over him. "What the fuck was that?" My voice is high, fury in every syllable.

Connor narrows his eyes, tiny crinkles popping at the corners as he glares at me. "That? That was me helping a student with her work. Is that a problem?"

"Ugh." I try to put every bit of the exasperation I feel into the sound. "Yes, it's a problem. Sabrina was practically throwing herself at you. What am I supposed to do with that?" I demand.

A sly grin breaks across his face before he chuckles. "You're jealous." It's not a question so I don't answer. He leans forward in his chair, putting his hands on his desk. "Sit down, Daisy."

I want to stay standing just to be contrary, but at his hard look, I sink to the chair, perching on the edge. It's a tiny rebellion, but it's all the fight I have left.

"I don't fuck students. Ever. I told you that. And yes, Miss Bowen was definitely flirty, playing up the damsel in distress act, but I don't give a shit about that. I'm here to help and that's it." I open my mouth to say something, hating that I was right, but he talks over me, not giving me a breath to speak. "You have nothing to worry about. I have never touched a student, never fucked a student . . . until you. And I fought that tooth and nail until I couldn't fight anymore."

I settle a bit, the fire in my gut dying to embers at his reassuring words.

"I told you there were no second chances, that you are mine. The same is true for me, Daisy. I'm yours. And as sexy as your coming in here all full of jealousy over me may be, it's not safe. You look like an avenging angel, a possessive bitch, and fuck, do I love that. But it's not smart, not while we're way past the line of what's okay. You know we could both get in trouble for this." His words are hard, but his voice has gone quiet as he reprimands me. The softness is what hits home just how stupidly I was behaving. Anyone could've seen my obviously jealous fit, although Sabrina was the most likely person to bust me and she seemed oblivious. Thank God.

I duck my chin. "I'm sorry, Connor. I saw red when she was talking to you, so clearly flirting. And then she was dressed all sexy when she left your office in a better mood. I couldn't stand it. You're mine too." I let my eyes lift, meeting his with the declaration. I feel like there's more to say, the words tempting on my tongue, but I hold them tightly.

"Show me," he says. It's becoming a common demand and I love it. I lift an eyebrow questioningly. I'll show him whatever he wants to see, but I'm not sure what he wants right now.

"Show me how sorry you are. Show me that you're mine and I'm yours, Daisy." It's a challenge, an order, a sign of just how angry he is at my bratty behavior. This is a punishment and I know it. But it's one I'll gladly take.

I search my head for a moment, finding inspiration. I drop to the floor, crawling the few steps to beside his chair. He turns, watching me curiously as I approach. I kneel at his feet, sitting back on my heels between his spread knees, and reach for his jeans. Making quick work of them, I pull his boxers down, letting his cock spring free.

He's thick and hard for me. A thought wiggles in my mind, wondering if he was hard when Sabrina was here, but I force it away. He is mine, this cock is mine, and I don't want either of us to ever forget it again.

I lap at his head, tasting the salty velvet of his skin. I don't go slow this time, don't wait for him to take over and fuck my mouth. No, this time, I'm in charge, and I want to show him everything I feel without words . . . the possessiveness, the need, the love. I admit the word to myself, knowing that it's too fast, but that doesn't make it any less true.

I feast on him, taking him deep into my throat almost immediately and holding him there as I swallow. It feels odd, but when he grunts, his hands spearing into my hair, it's worth it so I do it again. "Fuck, Daisy."

I retreat to his tip, teasing along his slit to get the precum, the appetizer to what I want so desperately. "You like that?"

He grins at me, arrogance in his order. "Do it again."

I almost obey. And then I think better of it. "What if I have something better in mind?"

His hand in my hair tightens as he holds my head still, bending down to rumble against my ear. "Better than my cock down your throat as you massage my tip with your muscles, swallowing like a needy girl even though I haven't given you my cum yet? Better than that?"

Fuck.

"Let's see what you think," I tease. I lift my hair, pulling my necklace off. It's just a costume length of pearls, but they're of good quality so they're smooth. I untie the knot I'd looped into the necklace this morning, delighted that Connor is watching me with interest. Slowly, I wrap the beads around his pulsing shaft, careful not to get them too tight. I need them to move against, not pinch, his sensitive skin. I take a moment to admire him with the new adornment, jacking him off slowly and peeking up to see his face awash in pleasure.

I let a dribble of spit out to lube along his shaft, coating the pearls and his skin. Then I take him, beads and all, into my mouth, spreading the saliva along him to ease my way. Once he's slippery, I focus my tongue's attention on his crown, letting my hands work the pearls up and down his length.

As I stroke him, I taunt him. "What do you think? Is my necklace wrapped around you as I jack you off into my hungry mouth better? Or maybe you want me to stop? Take the beads off and just lick you a bit?"

Connor's head lifts from where it'd fallen back in the chair. His eyes are wide. "Holy shit, Daisy. I've never . . . that feels amazing. Squeeze me tighter."

The victory rings between my legs, the thought that I'm making him this gone turning me on. I squeeze him tighter, rubbing the pearls up and down his shaft as I suck hard on his tip, hollowing my cheeks to make a vacuum. He fucks my hand, both of us working together to get him there.

And then he hisses, forcing my head down his shaft as he comes deep in my throat. I swallow over and over, wanting every drop. "Fuck, yes." When I've gotten every pulse of his cum, I lick my way up his shaft and carefully unwind the necklace.

Connor grabs a tissue from his desk, offering it to me. I wipe down the length of pearls and then slip it back over my head, retying the length so that the knot hits right in my cleavage.

Connor fingers the pearls, following the line up to the satin skin of my neck, where he wraps his fingers around my throat, not tight but letting me know he's there. "I think tonight, I'm going to give you a pearl necklace of a different sort. Would you like that, Daisy?"

I nod, my throat working against his palm when I swallow.

"Good girl. I'll see you tonight. Be at my place at seven again." Even at the praise and invitation, I deflate a bit. I didn't think we were done here. I'm so fucking wet, my pussy needy for him. I squirm in my clothes, the cotton and denim too rough on my sensitive skin.

He smirks, and I realize this is part of the punishment too.

He's making me wait on purpose. "Remember, nobody touches you but me, not even you."

I have a flash of wildness, but he sees it in my eyes. "And I'll know if you do, and I'll make you wait even longer."

Shit. I'm not gonna tempt him to punish me that much. A spank here, a delay there, I can take and even enjoy. But something tells me that if Connor really got going on denying my orgasm, I'd be begging long before he'd give in.

"Yes, sir," I say sarcastically. Okay, so I'm not going to give in sweetly, even if I am buckling with desire for what he's offering.

I get up from the floor, dusting imaginary bits from my knees. I grab my bag and make to leave, but right before I open the door, he speaks. "And, Daisy?"

I turn around to see he's got a huge shit-eating grin on his face. "Apology accepted." He winks at me.

I fight the urge to beam at the silly praise, knowing that the anger of the sex and the punishment was all in fun, even if the overreaction on my part was so very real. I curtsy slightly, holding out an imaginary skirt, "Thank you, sir. See you tonight. I can't wait."

We both grin, and I close the door behind me, a spring in my step as I head to my last class of the day.

CONNOR

I'm trying my damnedest to wrap things up quickly, wanting to hit the gym with Nick before heading home to meet Daisy, when there's a knock on my door.

"Come in," I say, wishing whoever it is would go away so I can bail sooner rather than later. The thought is amplified when the door swings open and I see Dean Michaels in the doorway.

Fuck, does it smell like sex in here? Is he going to take one whiff of my office and know exactly what I've been doing? The obvious question if he realizes would be 'with whom?' and that's the most dangerous inquiry I could face.

"Dean Michaels, come in," I say, standing and offering a hand. He shakes mine and sits.

"Hey, Connor, how's the world of mathematics treating you?" It's his usual opening, but something feels off. Or maybe that's my conscience talking.

"It's pretty radical," I joke back, the same as always. What can I say, math jokes are rarely funny, but we all tell them just the same.

He smiles his usual politician smile. He's a man of few words. He told me once that he can't be misquoted if he rarely speaks. But he's smart and has run this department for decades, seeing and doing almost everything in his tenure. Something tells me he hasn't gotten a pearl necklace blowjob in his office though. Although if you'd asked me that a couple of weeks ago, I wouldn't have believed I'd ever say yes to that either.

"I heard the exciting news just now and wanted to be the first to congratulate you. Great job, Connor!" He offers a golf clap, obviously proud. "We're lucky to have you here, and I recognize that. Just remember that when the other universities start headhunting you, okay?"

He's blowing smoke up my ass, but I have no idea why. "I'll certainly remember that, sir. But I'm afraid I've missed something. What exactly are you congratulating me on?"

He chuckles. "They haven't contacted you yet? Well shit, guess I let the cat out of the bag then, didn't I? No more

Schrodinger's Paradox here. The cat's alive, for damn sure." I still have no idea what he's talking about, though I'm familiar with Schrodinger's cat theory, both in the colloquial pop-culture reference and the more complex Copenhagen interpretation of quantum mechanics way.

He takes pity on me, finally explaining. "I got a call today from the TED talks people. It seems they're doing some final research on a proposed presenter and wanted my input, a reference, if you will. They're researching you, Connor."

My mind whirls. Holy Shit! "That's amazing, sir. No, I haven't heard a thing, but that'd be such an honor." It really is. TED talks are known as a way to bring complex subjects to the everyday person, a way to revolutionize our thinking about almost every topic on earth. An opportunity to speak on mathematics would be a great privilege, and partnered with my publishing, it would almost definitely make me a shoe-in for tenure, here or anywhere I wanted to go.

"Just remember where you come from when the time's right, Connor. I'll take good care of you here. You're doing great work with the students, and more importantly, you bring attention to the mathematics program with your publishing, opportunities like this, and your willingness to play trained monkey at fundraisers." His voice is serious again, politician-style in full effect.

I grin. "Can't say I've ever been called a trained monkey as a compliment, but I get where you're coming from. Not many of the math team are willing to schmooze with the pocketbooks for financial support, and I'm decent enough at it, so I don't mind."

He nods. "Good. Let me know when they contact you and it's a done deal. I'll add it to your tenure proposal for this year before the committee meeting."

He stands, offering me a hand this time and then leaving. In the quiet of my office, I can see my future laid out before me. TED talks, tenure, publishing, research, teaching. All of it exactly what I'd always wanted, always dreamed about.

But now there's more to my dreams. As wild as it may sound, I want all that plus Daisy. I want her by my side for everything. Hell, once she's finished school, maybe we could even work together? The thought makes me grin. I'd reward her every solution with orgasms, thank her for hard work with my hands and tongue, and celebrate every milestone with my cock deep in her pussy. I think we'd work together quite beautifully.

I'm lost in the fantasy of what a shared life might look like when I hear a cleared throat from the doorway. "Ahem . . ."

I shake my head, clearing the rosy haze from my vision to see Nick leaning against the doorframe, grinning. "Lost in thought there, Mister Math?"

I smile back. "A bit. Got some good news and was imagining what it might be like if it's true."

His eyes spread wide. "Well, spill it. What's the good news?"

I consider telling him about the TED talk. Hell, I consider telling him about Daisy. He's my best friend, and though I'm well aware of how stupid what I'm doing is, there's a part of me that wants to shout it from the rooftops. I'm proud that she's mine, and hiding it feels like I'm ashamed. I'm not, but the consequences are dire. So I keep my mouth shut. "I can't tell yet. Don't want to jinx it. But as soon as I can, I'll let you know."

I know I'm talking about the TED talk more than Daisy. I don't know how long it'll be before we can let that particular cat of the bag. Sorry, Schrodinger.

"Alright, man. But I'm here whenever you're ready, and it

sounds like the first round is on me to celebrate. You ready to hit the gym?" That's one of the reasons I love Nick, lame jokes aside. He's here to support me and cheer when something good happens, but he's a no-pressure type. If I need to disappear for weeks on end to work on something, he gets it because he's the same way. We've had each other's backs for a while now, and I appreciate that.

But right now, I don't want to work out. I want to get home, be that much closer to Daisy coming over so I can tell her the good news. She's who I really want to share this with, whether it actually comes through and happens or not.

"Sorry, man. Think I'm going to head home today. I'm too wired to work out. I'd be a shitty spotter, even if you're a light-weight," I tease.

Nick grins. "Fuck you. You know I lift more than you any day of the week." He's right, but I'm not going to tell him that. His ego's already bigger than mine, and that's saying something considering my ego's magnitude.

We both laugh, and he leaves, promising to make me lift twice as long next week to make up for the skipped session. That's fine by me if it gets me home to Daisy right now.

DAISY

Diary Entry, April 5th

Dear Diary,

It's been three weeks and I still can't quite believe it. Three weeks of secret rendezvous, praying we don't get caught, and pushing boundaries. It's been amazingly hot but also beautifully addicting.

My grades are even better, not because he's going easy on me but because under his tutelage, I really feel more confident in myself. He makes me feel empowered. It's me, my body, my personality, my heart, my intelli-

gence . . . all that makes me Daisy Phillips that brought this man to his knees in a way he'd never even considered.

That confidence extends to the bedroom, although we rarely make it there, usually collapsing to the couch in his living room as soon as I walk in the door, at least for round one before slipping into his satin sheets. More than once, we've risked exposure by fucking in his office, but so far, we've been lucky and no one has caught on to us.

But it's not just my body. More than anything, my mind is filled with thoughts of him. I feel like a cliché, but the physical connection has ignited an emotional one I'd never dreamed of. I've learned so much about him, revealed so much about myself . . . and each tidbit only brings us closer. We spend hours making love, and then just as many talking. His brain turns me on almost as much as his amazing body. Actually, his mind probably is the sexiest part of him, but I won't tell him that or he might withhold his body from me as punishment. And I don't want that because I want him. Body, mind, and soul.

I'll be honest. It may be fast, but I think I've fallen in love with him.

I'M HIS. TOTALLY.

The thought is on repeat in my head as I head toward the math building, looking forward to my class with Connor. It seems strange to still be thinking about our first night now that we've been together for a few weeks, but that night was perfect and started a string of perfect days that hasn't stopped since.

It's just hard to believe that I lost my virginity to my professor. But he's more than that, and after the past weeks of our getting together every opportunity we can, of texting and chatting when we can't, I'm reassured that I am more than a conquest to him, that this is something else.

The experience has been beyond exciting, beyond exhilarating for both of us, it seems, from how he acts. I told him that since our first night, every pleasure sensor in my body has come alive, and I notice the little things more than ever. I'm aware of the swaying wideness of my hips and the way the air caresses my skin. Even the needy ache in my core reminds me of how he makes me come so hard, over and over again. Even now, I feel like every time is a new adventure, one I'll never get tired of.

The only bad part is my hunger for Connor, for the way his eyes look as we talk about the little things, for the way his eyes bore into me as he pounds his amazing cock inside me. I want him, *need* him with a fiery intensity, a deep, primal need to explore just who and what we can be together.

I'm so engaged in my fantasy, not even paying attention as I walk along the path to class, that it takes me a moment to realize someone's calling my name. "Daisy!"

I turn and see Arianna approaching me, a look of wonder on her face. "Oh, hi, Ari. Sorry, I was daydreaming. I missed you this morning."

"Must be fantasizing about a special someone," she says, smirking. "For the past few weeks, I don't think I've ever seen you look so happy."

"No, it's not that," I quickly lie. "I'm just feeling good about my classes. Things are ramping up well for finals. If I can keep it up, my early slip shouldn't matter."

"Really?" she says, sighing. "That's all it is? Because I've noticed your late-night 'study sessions' and weekend sleep-overs with 'a friend'. I'm not stupid, Daisy." I can tell that I've hurt her with my secrecy and silence. She knows something's going on, and usually, I tell her everything, but not this. I can't.

"I'm sorry, Ari. I am seeing someone, but I'm not ready to talk about it. I can't. Please understand, chica." I beg her to not press this, knowing it could cause problems. My first loyalty is to Connor now, and I won't put him at jeopardy over a need to share with my best friend.

She smiles sweetly. "Okay, I'll leave it be on one condition." I nod, and she continues, "Does he make you happy?"

I don't even try to restrain my huge smile. "So happy, Ari." My voice is high and light, the buzz of happiness filling me and apparent.

"All right, then, I'm here when you're ready to dish all the good stuff. As long as he's not some old geezer professor, married, and with bad breath, who likes to listen to the sound of his own voice." She's teasing, but I flinch a bit when she says *professor*. None of the rest of her description fits Connor at all, but that one is dangerously close to the truth, and I need to redirect her to safer territory.

"Definitely not. What about you? I have been gone a lot lately, so I feel like I don't know what's going on with you either. Classes? Internship? Spill it, girl!"

She takes the bait, and we dissolve into a catch-up session of epic proportions as we walk the sidewalks to our classes, enjoying the sunshine and the company. I have missed her these last few weeks as my focus has been locked onto Connor. It's not a bad thing, just the excitement of something new, and he definitely takes up all the space in my head and my heart.

"So I should be good on all my classes, just finals to worry about mostly. And I finally heard back from Morgan, and I start there soon," Ari tells me, excitement obvious as she dances around. *See?* I think. *She's excited about something new too.* We're all good. Just part of growing up and apart a bit as our paths wind and diverge and reconnect.

"I'm so glad, girl. You're gonna ace your tests and impress the hell out of them at Morgan. I'm good on tests too. I've got an

A-minus in Professor Daniels's class now, so unless I bomb the final, I should have a solid *B*-plus or better final grade. I'm more worried about American History at this point. I have an *A*, but the test is all essay, no multiple-choice, and a bad grade there can tank the whole semester."

We get to the division point in our paths, Ari needing to go left to the business building and me needing to head right to math.

She grabs me in a spontaneous hug. "Dang, I needed that. I'm here for you, honey. Whenever you're ready to spill, I'm ready to listen and support and celebrate. I'll see you at home later?"

I laugh. "It's good to see you too, and I know you've got my back. I've got yours too. Anytime and always, girl. I uh . . . don't know about tonight, though." I stutter a bit on the words, not wanting to lie but not wanting to give away too much.

Her grin is like the cat that got the canary, "That's okay. Go get you some. Bow-chicka-bow-wow," she sing-songs as she walks away.

She's right. I needed that too. I have been so tied up with Connor that I've let other things fall through the cracks. Before I can promise myself that I'll do better, the thought of being *tied up with Connor* fills my mind with some rather dirty images of just what I want to do with my professor, and maybe what I want him to do with me too.

CONNOR

Collapsing into a chair in the break room, my body's exhausted even as my head feels like it's about ready to explode. I shouldn't have any caffeine, but I slurp at today's drink, a double espresso instead of my normal macchiato.

She's my every fantasy come to life. A brain that commands my respect, sweet but mischievous . . . and her magical pussy is literally the cherry on top of a perfect sundae. I've never, in my wildest fantasies about Daisy, thought we'd end up fucking in my office . . . but now it seems as natural as breathing.

I do know that she puts a smile on my face, something I'm not particularly known for, I guess, considering the dean's secretary asked what had me in such a good mood as we discussed next year's PhD candidate program in the elevator.

I'm troubled now, though, which is why I'm sucking down caffeine like it's water. Simply put, it's not enough.

I want more. *Need* more.

I need to know that the look I see in her eyes as she kisses me goodbye and the little teasing in her voice as we hurriedly talk about when we can get together next aren't just figments of my imagination. My deepest fear about giving in to my desire for Daisy was that it'd be a one-time thing, a booby trap in my background that someone could use to blast me with when shit got tough.

But now, I'm even more scared . . . because I want something with her I've never wanted before. I want her mind, soul, and heart, not just her body.

"Hey amigo, you're looking grim," Nick says, breaking me out of my head. "The dean's fundraising shit got you that screwed up?"

"No, nothing like that," I assure him. "Just a little indigestion, I guess. Busy."

"Uh-huh. Well, here's some news that'll get your mind off that," Nick says, sitting down. "Cunningham resigned."

"No shit?" I comment, surprised. "He didn't hang onto his tenure?"

"Nope. Oh, they're calling it an extended sabbatical, but he's out, man. I figure he's digging himself a hole for when his wife's lawyers get done crucifying him," Nick says. "Oh, and his lover? Kicked his ass to the curb from the scuttlebutt. I know I've never been too fond of him, but still . . . shitty way to go out. Never want to see that happen."

I nod. I should probably be worried, but I'm not. Daisy would never say a word. Our . . . situation that seems to be developing at light speed is safe. Risky, but safe. Every moment I'm with her, I feel like instead of black jeans and a T-shirt, I'm wearing a Kevlar suit, a giant bat emblazoned on my chest. I'm fucking untouchable, man.

"It is a bad situation," I finally reply. "He's brilliant enough to still get grants and work privately, but this will be a side note in everything he does."

Dean Michaels comes in, giving Nick and me a wave. "Professor Daniels, when your office was empty, I figured I'd find you down here with your partner in crime," he says, shaking hands with the two of us. "I just wanted to say, the PhD board has come back with its initial comments on the theses they've gotten this year. Your students, as a whole, blew their socks off. Very, very impressive."

"Thank you, sir . . . but they're the ones who put in the work," I defer, but he's having none of it.

"Oh, of course, but their mentor deserves some kudos too. I hope your undergrads will be just as impressive."

"We'll have to see after finals, but I'm confident in them."

"In any case, congratulations," Michaels says. He watches as Nick gets up to refill his mug and then carefully asks, "Have you heard anything from TED?"

I shake my head. "Not yet. Although I had a previous mentor

contact me saying they'd called him too. Still research phase, it seems."

Michaels nods. "Very well. Good day, gentlemen."

He leaves, and I chug back as much of my espresso as possible in one gulp. It sits heavily in my belly, but I need the jumpstart to be at my best today.

CLASS IS WELL . . . CLASS. THEY SIT, I TALK, THEY LISTEN, I teach. It's a good group of students, and like I told Dean Michaels, I'm confident in their work. But my mind is a million miles away. Or at least a hallway away, down in my office, with Daisy laid out on my desk as I pound into her.

But no, that's only in my mind. In reality, she's sitting front and center like always, eyes glued to me. It takes all my caffeinated control to hold back from kissing her.

As I wrap up, I give her a hard look that she seems to understand. I walk out of class, ignoring her as she leans against the wall, face buried in her phone. I wonder for a moment who she's talking to, but I realize it's probably for show.

I try to stay casual, exchanging greetings with other professors and students as I make my way to my office.

Barely a minute later, she knocks gently on my door that I left cracked for her, and as she comes in, I shut the door behind her, pressing her to the wood and capturing her cry of surprise with a hungry kiss. She seems just as hungry, the two of us devouring each other before the pure need for oxygen forces us apart slightly. "Twenty-four hours," she moans, thinking about the time since we last got together. "It's too long to be without you."

"I can't fucking get enough of you," I say, pressing my forehead to hers. "You're like a habit, but a fucking good one. I'm addicted to you after just this short of a time." There's more, but I don't want to say it here. She deserves more than that.

"Me too," she says, letting her hands slide down to my ass. "I thought talking on the phone last night would be enough to get me through class, but the moment I saw you, all I could think was how much I need you inside me."

"I want to ruin you," I admit, pulling her toward my desk. "I know it's too fast, but I don't want any other man to ever have you. You're mine, Daisy." I've told her that before, but it seems heavier in this moment, a taste of the bigger truth.

Her eyes shine, and I think she hears the words I'm not saying. "Take me. Ruin me. You're all I'll ever want."

She wiggles away from me, slipping her panties off and holding them out to me. An offering. Then she flips her skirt up, lying forward, her chest pressed to the wood. An even better offering on the altar of my desk. My sacrifice. My life. My everything.

She's already sloppy wet, the tease of being together but not able to touch for the last hour driving us both wild. I moan, unbuckling and pulling my cock out as I stand behind her. I grab her cheeks, savagely squeezing them in my hands as I spread her for a better view of her pink slit.

I lick at her, fucking her with my tongue and torturing her clit with fast flicks, needing her taste on my tongue as I fuck her. I rise, slipping through her folds, coating myself in her honey, and then I ease inside her, one inch at a time but not stopping until I'm balls-deep. I hold there, my cockhead pressed to her back wall, bottomed out, as she adjusts to the feeling of being so full.

"Yes," she hisses. She looks back at me over her shoulder. "You have all I am," she whispers, both of us dancing around the words we want to say.

I lean forward to kiss her, letting her know that I understand. And then I press her down, my hands pinning her to the desk. She whimpers, arching her back to let me know she's ready. I pull back and thrust in deeply, going as hard as I can without making too much noise.

"Touch yourself, Daisy," I command her. She shifts slightly, getting her right hand down to play with her clit. "That's it, honey. Take my cock in your tight little pussy and rub that clit for me."

She does as I say, both of us working her body, me from the inside and her from the outside. I watch as my cock disappears into her and reappears coated in her creamy honey. It's beautiful, and her surrender to me is glorious as she lets me ride her harder, pressing her so firmly into the desk that she can't move, can't fight the heat I'm building within her. She takes it, letting me split her with violent thrusts.

I lean forward, growling in her ear, "Give it to me, Daisy. Come on my cock like my good girl."

She cries out, the sound strangled as I rush to slam my hand over her mouth, stifling her sexy noises. If anyone hears, there'd be no doubt about what's happening in my office.

It's wrong, but the thought of someone catching us, of some poor schmuck student walking in and seeing me fucking ravaging innocent virginal Daisy Phillips, the class good girl, gives me a thrill. I'm the lucky fucker she chose to pop that cherry, and I'm the bastard who will keep this pussy full of my cock, and only my cock, for as long as she'll let me. I come hard, filling her deeply with my cum, marking her as mine.

I lay a kiss to her shoulder as I slip out, grabbing tissues as my cream leaks from her. She stands, spinning, and we seal our vows, both spoken and unspoken, with a kiss.

She tries to straighten the mess we've made of my desk, stacking papers and putting the stapler upright once again.

"What's this?" she asks, holding up a red envelope.

My eyebrows pull together. "I don't know. Let me see." She hands it to me and I open it. I pull out a folded sheet of paper as something flutters to the floor.

Daisy drops to the floor to pick it up and gasps. "Oh, my God!"

I take it from her hand and realize it's a picture. A picture of Daisy and me, here in my office. She's on her knees before me, head buried in my crotch, obviously mid-blowjob, and my head is thrown back in pleasure, my hands buried in her hair. It looks sexy as fuck. It looks like I'm forcing her. It looks like I'm fucking my student.

It looks like I'm . . . fucked.

DAISY

"We have to go, need to get out of here and figure out what the fuck is going on. Skip your next class and meet me at home," Connor tells me. He's all-business, hard and brooking no argument.

I'm frozen, eyes locked on the picture. He grabs my head, cradling it his hands roughly. "Daisy, honey . . . look at me. Go to my house. It's going to be okay, but we need to talk this through, and we're obviously compromised here. You okay?" I must nod because he lets me go and picks up my bag and places it on my shoulder, but he pauses with a hand on the doorknob and turns back. "It'll be okay, I promise," he tells me before placing a sweet kiss to my forehead.

Outside, I hurry along the sidewalk. I've always felt safe here. Hell, I probably felt a bit *too* comfortable, considering the mess I've gotten into now. But as I scurry to the corner, waiting for the bus to take me across town to Connor's, I feel like there are eyes on me from every direction, like there's a big sign over my head that's blinking, *Fucking Her Professor*, and everyone can see it but me. The little bubble of happiness I've been living in for weeks just burst spectacularly, and now I feel exposed, vulnerable.

The bus ride is painfully slow, giving my brain all sorts of time to freak out, worry, and compose a million different scenarios. They all end badly . . . for me and for Connor.

By the time I walk up to his door, I'm verifiably a ball of nerves, looking over my shoulder and wondering if it'd be better if I just went to the dorm and we pretended none of this ever happened. But I can't do that. I don't care if I'm screwed over. I can always change schools if I have to. But I won't leave Connor to face the firing squad at school alone. I'll do whatever I have to do to protect his career because that's not as easy as switching universities. He'll be blackballed and his reputation as a student-fucker will precede him. Even if it's not like that, not really. I mean, I *am* his student, but this is more than some naughty taboo. This is real.

I don't even get the chance to knock before he rips the door open and pulls me inside. At first, I think it's so no one will see me, but he immediately presses me to the door and takes my mouth in a kiss. Between smacks, he asks, "How're you doing, honey? Are you freaking out?"

I nod, feeling the tears wet my lashes. "I'm so sorry, Connor. I know we shouldn't have in your office, but I thought we were okay. Your career, this is going to ruin you, isn't it?" I'm rambling, verging on hysterical. But he's steady, calm, a port in the storm ravaging us.

"Come on, Daisy. Sit down so we can talk." His words don't inspire confidence, and I'm almost certain this is the point where he tells me this has been fun, but he needs to think of himself now. But dutifully, I sit on the couch, bending my legs and hugging my knees to my chest.

He sits down beside me and tosses back the shot of Scotch sitting on the table before burying his head in his hands. "Fuck. I knew something like this could happen. But I got careless, so wrapped up in being with you. I knew better. I fucking knew better. Now, I'm going to be just like Cunningham. Even now, we're taking a risk with you in my house, but I couldn't think of a safer place." He's talking to me, but his words seem more to himself, castrating himself over what we've done.

It takes every bit of my strength, but I'll do anything for him. I scoot closer to him, my nails tracing soothing patterns on his back. "I'm so sorry, Connor. Tell me what to do and I'll do it. I can tell the dean that I seduced you, that it's my fault. Whatever you need so that your job is secure. I'll switch schools. Anything you need."

He lifts his head, looking at me strangely. "What are you talking about?" he asks angrily.

I duck my head, not able to meet his eyes when I say the words. "I figure this meant you'd switch into self-preservation mode, and rightfully so. I'm willing to do whatever you need me to so that you're safe at work. I can switch schools a hell of a lot easier than you, and then maybe you won't get fired."

Understanding dawns, and he smiles slightly, even at this scary moment. "Daisy, I'm not throwing you under the bus to save myself. *We* did this, and I want to keep doing it. We'll figure it out together."

Hope blooms in my chest. "Really?"

He pulls me into his lap, grabbing my head and forcing my eyes to his. "Daisy, it's you and me. I told you that you're mine. Nothing changes that. I love you."

He doesn't give me time to process what he said. He just covers my mouth with a kiss, promising that things are going to be okay and that we have a future beyond some taboo naughty affair. But as his tongue tangles with mine, the words settle in my heart, lighting me up and giving me strength. I pull back. "I love you too, Connor. So much."

And then we seal my words to him with another kiss. It's beautiful. It's amazing. It's something I thought I'd never find, much less find with my professor.

And someone wants to take this away from us.

Connor rests his forehead against mine, our breath mingling. "I know this may be a stupid question . . . but have you told anyone about us?"

I look at him, glancing at the photo on the table before shaking my head slowly. "Not even Arianna knows. She sorta knows I had a crush on you, but that's it. She would always be the one pushing my buttons about it, teasing me a little."

"Would there be any reason for her to follow you and want to do this? She wouldn't want to hurt you, would she?"

I shake my head as I think for a moment. "No," I finally say. "If anything, Ari would be the one person I could actually trust with our relationship. I can't imagine her being anything but supportive. She's . . . she's pretty fucking awesome, really. But I didn't think it was fair to you, so I kept it a secret."

"Okay. Well, we're going to have to lie low," Connor replies, obviously wishing the solution were so easy. "It's like any math problem. Until the variables are identified, the problem is unsolvable."

And just like that, a switch in my gut flips and I'm not scared. I'm furious. "How dare they? Why are we being forced to lie low when we're not doing anything wrong? Not really. We're two consenting adults." I know my voice is reaching a fevered pitch, but the anger is burning hot.

"If only it were that easy. But I think you know that. I'm talking about more than the law. If people find out about our relationship at the university, there are serious consequences for both of us. Though maybe a little more for me. I may be asked to resign, and if not that, I'm certainly going to be pigeonholed. My reputation would be ruined. More than that, so would yours. I can live with being seen as some horny professor who couldn't resist the temptation. I can make a living in the private sector. But you . . . you're just getting started."

My face crumples as his words sink in, and for a moment, I think the tears are going to overflow.

"I know, honey. I understand, but don't cry. Your tears are like a knife in my gut."

I wipe the tears from my cheeks, not wanting to hurt him any further. "Connor . . . I don't know how to deal with all this. I feel like I just found happiness. I found the man I want to be with . . . and now this."

"I wish I could lie and say that somehow it'll all work out, but I'm not a good liar." He takes my hand, kissing my fingertips. "But what I can say is that I want to be with you, too. But if there's even a chance of that, we need to figure out what this person wants. I mean, there's no note, no blackmail demand, which is what I'd expect. So who's sneaking around to take this picture of us? I need you to think really hard about who this could be. Because I've racked my brain, and I'm drawing nothing."

He holds me tightly, my head resting on his shoulder and his finger teasing along the skin of my thighs. I sigh. "I don't know who it could be. Why anyone would try to take this away from us . . . but Connor . . ."

I lift up, meeting his green eyes. "Firestorm aside, we just had a really important moment." I dip my chin, biting my lip and feeling stupid for needing this right now as an unknown person tries to rip everything apart, but it's the truth. "I love you. I need you." The words couldn't be simpler. The truth couldn't be more complex.

He swallows, squeezing the flesh of my thighs with his strong fingers. "I love you, and I need you too," he says, repeating my truths. "I didn't think it'd happen, and not this fast, but I want to do nothing more than explore you, to discover the little things that make you laugh, and what type of eggs you like in the morning, or if you hate eggs and prefer pancakes or cereal or . . . whatever. I'm rambling, but I want that forever."

His eyes shine bright with the honesty of his statement, and I realize that we've both been holding back. This is more, just like he promised at the beginning. So much more. This is now and tomorrow and the day after that. He is my forever, regardless of what that forever might look like after we deal with the asshole trying to take it away from us.

Facing the firing squad together. That's what we'll have to do. But right now, I need to tell my man that I love him with my body, not just my words. And I want him to do the same, show me with his talented fingers and thick cock just how much he feels for me.

Connor sweeps me up in his arms, carrying me down the hall to his bedroom and tossing me lightly to the bed before following me, covering my body with his. Quickly stripping, we lie together, eyes locked on one another, more bare emotionally than physically. Without preamble, he enters me and we become one. We make love this time, soft and slow and sweet, tangled in the satin of his bed, our words repeated time and time again as we come together. I hear his love, feel his love, and I know he feels mine for him as well.

CONNOR

Walking into work the next day is weird. I'm looking over my shoulders the whole time, evaluating whether there's something sinister behind every friendly smile and greeting, looking for anyone who might be watching me. I completely skip the breakroom, though I could definitely use something stronger than my office pot's weak-ass coffee. But going in there seems like a needless risk right now.

How crazy is that? Getting coffee in the breakroom is . . . risky? Whose life is this?

But the truth is, I don't know who's doing this, and until I rule out that it's another professor, I don't want to give them potential ammunition or be alone in a room with them. Honestly, I'm not sure what I'd do if I found out, but the fury raging through my veins says I should probably play it safe and sip on the sludge I call coffee.

I stand tall as I go into my office, refusing to shrink under this pressure or sneak around. Yeah, maybe Daisy and I have been sneaking, although rather poorly, apparently, but that was out of necessity. I'm not ashamed of her, of myself, or of what we have. But still, the instinct to hide to avoid the shitstorm remains.

What's the saying? 'Courage is not the absence of fear, but rather the assessment that something else is more important than the fear.' That's Franklin Roosevelt, I believe, though I'm more math nerd than historical literary scholar. But the sentiment is true, because I'm scared as fuck that this is all going to implode, leaving bits of my career and Daisy's future scattered about. But I won't hide what we are, what we want to be, because there is nothing more important than Daisy.

But as I close the door behind me, needing a moment alone, all my strength is tested when I see that there's another red envelope on the floor. Fuck. Someone must've slipped it under the door. I pick it up gingerly, like it's a bomb that might blow up my life, and sit down at my desk.

Opening it, I see that there's no picture this time, just a single sheet of standard copy paper with plain typed text.

48 hours. $100,000 to my bank account. Straight As in your classes until I graduate. Or I go public and expose what you've been doing, Naughty Professor. Meet me at the Golden Wok on Poplar Street on Thursday at 7 P.M. to discuss. –S

What the fuck? What the actual fuck?

The money strikes me first. I don't have that kind of money. I mean, I could liquidate some stocks and shit, but that's a fuckton of money to a professor, not something I have lying around or can get in forty-eight fucking hours.

It takes a heartbeat for the rest to register. Straight As? That means . . . it's a student, not a coworker. Some little shit student is doing this to Daisy and me. And for what? Like an A in my class is worth destroying someone's life over? How utterly ridiculous. Like Mommy and Daddy won't be happy if Junior gets anything less than a perfect score that he obviously didn't earn?

Disgust fills me, followed hotly by the desire to figure out who this fucker is and destroy him. I mentally run through my class rosters, trying to remember names that start with S. Let's see, there's . . . Sam in my 9 A.M. trigonometry class, Scott in my graduate program, Sean is my 3 P.M. calculus class, and the list goes on and on. Steven, Seth, Simon, Sergio, Sebastian.

LAUREN LANDISH

Fuck. How many students' names even start with *S*? It's nothing I've paid attention to before, but now the suspect list is growing exponentially.

I stuff the envelope into my bag, needing to get to class. The last thing I need when the shit hits the fan is to be seen as unreliable on top of everything else.

When I go into the classroom, I can't help but look at Daisy in the front row. She'd put on a brave face this morning as she left my place and looks beautiful as always, but I can see the fray around the edges. Her hair is pulled up, tendrils escaping down like she couldn't be bothered to care. I want to wrap them around my finger and whisper in her ear that it's going to be okay just like I did last night as she fell asleep in my arms. She's wearing leggings and a long T-shirt. Actually, at a second glance, she's wearing *my* Batman T-shirt. Damn, I'm not so sure that was a good idea, but I love the way she looks in my clothes, like she's mine. Still, the Batman logo reminds me of my earlier feeling of being untouchable and just how naïve I was in thinking that.

I get started, going over prep review for the upcoming final. I do my best, but I stumble a couple of times and I know the students are getting pissed that I'm fucking up their last shot at help before the big test. I'm usually clear and precisely on point, so the difference is noticeable, but my brain is too busy with bigger things to concentrate on. I give in, closing the time with a promise. "If you study your notes from the semester, go over your previous tests, and complete the practice problems, you will be ready. I'll be in the online portal as much as possible over the next few days to help with any questions you may have." That seems to pacify them a bit.

As everyone files out, I hear them coordinating study group dates, and I'm thankful for the good group of students I have. Well, all except for one asshole.

Daisy stays back, waiting until everyone is gone. I glance at the door, making sure we're alone but knowing that's simply an illusion now, and we need to be careful because who knows what prying eyes are watching? I grab the envelope from my bag and sit down in the chair next to her. She leaves the book open on her desk, giving the impression that I'm merely helping with classwork.

I hand her the envelope and her eyes widen. "Oh, shit. Another one?"

She opens it and reads it silently before her eyes flash back to mine. "Fuck, Connor! That's a crazy amount of money!" she exclaims, though she's working to keep her voice quiet. "What are we going to do? Do you even have that kind of money? I mean, I never even thought about what a professor makes, but that sounds like . . . a lot."

I nod. "It is a lot. I could get my hands on it, but it'd take everything I have, and the reality is that blackmail never ends. If I give in this time, they'll just keep asking for more."

"This is like some movie, not real life. Not my life. My mind is overloaded, like everything is white noise, and I can't isolate a clear path or process to find a solution."

That's my girl. Everything relates back to math for her. Hell, and for me. Maybe that's the key. Treat this like a math problem and solve the fucking thing. I'd had this thought before, reducing the variables. But there are so many.

The first of which is who the blackmailer is. Actually, maybe Daisy can help with that.

"Hey, so let's work with what we know. It's a student. We didn't know that before, but asking for grades makes that obvious. I've been running through my mind for which of my students start with *S*, but there are tons of them . . . Seth, Scott, Sean. Too many guys to narrow it down, really."

Her eyes go wide with shock. "Oh, my God!" I've seen that expression on her face before, when she has a revelation about how to solve a problem in class in a new way. Although this time, there's a hint of pain and disgust. "It's Sabrina."

My eyebrows snap together, putting the puzzle pieces together even as she keeps talking. "It's her, Connor. She's struggling in class, and she needs the grade for her scholarship. Hell, she needs the money. And she wasn't here today. It's gotta be her."

"Shit. I think you're right. It's her." I agree with her assessment, even though I hate the thought. "She's always seemed nice enough, a hard worker, and I know she was going to study group."

Daisy cringes. "Yeah, I told her to ask for help and even suggested that maybe she join another study group. Hell, I even helped her with a process she was doing incorrectly. I guess she found another way." Her tone is snide, obviously hating that Sabrina is taking the easy way out at our expense.

"Okay, so that's one big variable solved. What else?"

It's like a light is flipped on, and I know the answer. Daisy. She's the most important thing to me.

I can't cave in. Doing so would be selling her out, cheapening what we have, and that's unacceptable. I know what I need to do.

"Connor?" Daisy asks, her hands practically shaking as she reaches out to touch mine before she pulls back and glances at the door. "You went quiet. What are we going to do?"

The fear in her voice pisses me off. Not at her, but at Sabrina, who thought taking something as beautiful as our love and running it through the wringer as some tawdry, shameful thing was a valid way to salvage a bad grade.

"I'm here, Daisy. I'm just simplifying," I tell her, trying to come up with a better term, but it's the most accurate for what I'm planning. "I know what to do."

She sputters. "What?"

I can't tell her exactly what I'm thinking. She'll try to talk me out of it. I know she will because that's who she is, a sweet and kind-hearted woman who will sacrifice herself to save me. But I'll do anything for her.

I kiss her forehead, not caring if anyone sees. "It's okay, honey. I've got this. Go home to your dorm tonight, and I'll pick you up tomorrow night to go to Sabrina's requested *appointment*." The word is ugly on my tongue.

She looks at me, caution in her eyes. "What are you going to do?"

"I love you, Daisy. You're mine and I'm yours. And no one is going to take that away from us." I lay one light kiss to her hand before letting go and walking out of the classroom. It's one of the hardest things I've ever done because my every instinct is to huddle her to my side and never let her leave the security of my arms. But I need to fix this . . . for me, for her, for us.

I KNOCK ON THE DOOR, STEELING MYSELF WITH A DEEP breath. The rumbled 'Come in' from the other side sounds like a death knoll, but I approach with courage, choosing Daisy over the fear, over all else.

"Connor! I wasn't expecting to see you. Did I miss an appointment?" Dean Michaels asks, glancing to the paper calendar on his desk. Old school to the end, that's him.

"No, sir. But something's come up and I need to talk to you," I say, sitting down in front of him without an invitation.

"Of course. I've got a few minutes for you. This is about the TED talk, I'm guessing," he says, taking a sip of his coffee, and I frown. What I'm about to say could fuck that up too, but so be it.

"No, still haven't heard back on that yet. But there's something serious I need to discuss." I take a breath, wishing there were an easy way to say this, but there's simply not. "Dean, I've been seeing a student. It's . . . intimate."

His face freezes for a moment, then he sets his mug of coffee down and considers me carefully. "Connor, if this is some attempt at a joke, I really wish you'd picked a better time. Pre-exam pranks are the sort of thing students do, not professors."

"It's not a joke," I reply. "Her name's Daisy Phillips, and she's an undergrad. We've been seeing each other for a good part of the semester."

The dean taps his finger on his desk for a few moments, looking like he's going to explode. Finally, in a strained, tense voice, he speaks. "And did it ever occur to you that sleeping with a student could cost you your job? Haven't you heard the news? Cunningham?"

"I know, sir. It just happened. It's . . . we're serious."

Michaels nods, rubbing at his face. "Have you given her an unfair advantage at all in your class? Not that you can even answer that impartially." He sighs.

"No!" I exclaim before forcing myself under control. "No. If anything, I graded her harder than any of the other students. She's got an *A* in the class right now, but it's because she's one of the brightest minds I've ever come across."

Dean Michaels snorts. "Ever come across . . . you sound like an old geezer. I'm going to need full disclosure and every grade you've given her, all the records. According to school policy, there's nothing that can *legally* happen to you, but profession-ally, that's another story. I wouldn't be counting on that tenure, Connor."

"I understand, sir. Of course. I know that this is tantamount to career suicide for me, and I'll do whatever you need to main-tain some semblance of a reputation. My main concern is Daisy." I look at him, all shreds of arrogance washed away in my desperation. "Can she transfer to another professor's roster, let them reevaluate her previous work, which they'll see is top-notch, and then she can take her final for them? I'll step out of the whole scenario so that she is able to complete her semester."

It's a big ask and I know it. Dean Michaels is well within his rights to wipe the entire credit from Daisy's transcript. Hell, he's probably able to kick her out of school. If not outright, I'm sure he could call in a favor here or there to punish Daisy and me both.

He doesn't say yes, but he doesn't say no. And as the conversa-tion continues, I have a sliver of hope that maybe this can all work out.

DAISY

Dear Diary, May 6th

How is it that heaven can turn into hell so quickly?

When I first started crushing on Connor, it was innocent. I mean, I never seriously thought that he and I would end up in bed together, and I certainly didn't think that we'd find such depth of feeling for each other.

And I never wanted our relationship to get him into trouble. I just want-ed . . . him. Cocky, arrogant bastard and all.

And now my selfish desire has put his entire career at risk. We stepped over that forbidden line and there's no going back.

But I have to admit . . . as deep as we're in it right now, I've loved every minute of it. Of being his, of him being mine.

I don't know exactly what Connor has planned, but he told me he'd take care of us, and I believe him.

I CHECK THAT I HAVE ALL MY STUFF, ZIPPING MY BAG CLOSED and sliding it over my shoulder. Gone are the flirty skirts or the tight jeans. I'm too frightened by yesterday's note. Besides, I slept like hell, my body just unable to handle the hours of ups and downs. We went from intense, passionate fucking to outright terror.

Connor and I swapped texts a few times, but there's a strain in what we say now, the two of us being unwilling to say anything over text about Sabrina's note. And though he told me he has a plan, which is supposed to put me at ease, I think, the fact that he won't tell me what it is makes me jumpy and nervous.

"Hey, chica, you okay?" Arianna asks as I clunk a bowl down on the counter to try and gobble some cereal. On top of everything else, I haven't eaten much in the past twenty-four hours, and now my head's sort of woozy, so college-norm breakfast for dinner is all I can muster. "You were riding the happy horse just a few days ago. Now you look like you've been told your puppy died."

No, it's like I've been sent an engraved invitation to a dance party in hell. And worst of all, despite this shit sundae that I've been served, my body's still craving Connor.

Instead of telling Ari this, of course, I just shake my head. "Been hitting the books a little too hard. Exams have me worried." Going to the fridge, I splash some milk on my Rice

Krispies and turn to her. "What about you? Ready for finals?"

Before the words are even out of my mouth, I can see that she doesn't believe me. Hell, I don't believe me either.

"Nice attempt at deflection. Try again, Daisy. What's going on?" Ari demands, holding out a spoon for me. But as I go to grab it, she pulls it back. "Speak or no spoon."

I collapse to the chair, my bowl bouncing on the table and leaving a puddle of milk that I can't care to clean up. The tears well up unbidden. "Shit, honey. Here, take the spoon," Ari says, shoving it into my hand.

"It's not that. It's Professor Daniels," I mutter. Even calling him that now belies the depth of my feelings for him.

Ari looks at me questioningly. "I thought you said you were doing better in his class. Are you freaking about the final?"

It's on the tip of my tongue to lie, just tell her that the test is stressing me out. But I know Ari, and I was right when I told Connor that of anyone, she'd be the person I could trust most with this. But is it too dangerous to spill, especially not knowing what he has planned? Maybe being quiet about the whole thing is for the best, at least for now.

But I need support, and Ari is my best friend. I trust her. "No, not the final. I'm ready for that. It's . . . it's . . ."

She smiles encouragingly. "Spit it out. I'm here for you, no matter what. Maybe I can help."

"I've been seeing him. Professor Daniels—Connor—romantically."

Her eyes widen, "Holy shit, Daisy! You're fucking your math professor? Do you know how much trouble you could get into, how much trouble *he* could get into? Oh, my God, did he pressure you into this? That cocky fucker, I'll kill him." She's ranting, already in my defense like the true friend I knew she would be.

I place my hand on hers. "No, it's not like that. We're in love. I love him, Ari. And he loves me."

Her eyes search mine. "For real? You're in love with him? And he's in love with you?" Her voice is disbelieving, like I'm some silly school girl caught up in a fantasy.

"Ari, we're in love." She must see the truth now, because she gasps.

"Holy shit, Daisy," she repeats, seemingly her main response to this news. "That's . . . good? I mean, I guess. If you're both into it. But how? What now? I don't know what to say." We both stare at each other for a moment, my confession weighing the air down between us.

"Wait . . . if you're in love, then why the tears? What's wrong?" Ari asks, always astute.

"There's a girl in my class—"

"Mother fucker, I'll kill him," Ari interrupts.

"No, no, he's not . . . it's not like that. We're serious. He wouldn't do that. But this girl, she found out about us. And now . . ."

I give Ari the whole sordid story, from our initial flirtations to last night's text, explaining about Sabrina and the blackmail. Ari's face shows her every emotion, from excitement and sweet awwws to fury and homicidal mania.

"That bitch! How dare she? So, what are you going to do?" she asks.

"I don't know. Connor said he'd take care of it, but he hasn't filled me in on the plan beyond that he's picking me up for *dinner* at the Golden Wok." My frustration at the whole situation hides the deeper, darker fear at my core. "Ari, what if it's not okay? What if this gets out and ruins his career? I'll never forgive myself."

She smiles. "Chica, that right there tells me all I need to know. You're not worried for yourself. All you've talked about is him, how this will hurt him, and how you'll do anything he wants to make this right. If he feels even a bit of the same way, you two are going to be fine. It might not be the same fantasy future you'd imagined, but you'll be okay. I promise."

Her simple words, the innocent belief that it's going to work out, reassure me more than I would've imagined, giving me peace in a way I didn't realize I needed. I nod. "Thanks, Ari. I love you, girl."

She grins, wiping at the tracks of tears down my face. "No problem. That's what friends are for. Just remember this for my next crisis when I come crying to you, okay?"

I smile, the tight stretch of my face reminding me that smiles have been in short supply the last few days with all this drama. It feels good, more like myself. "Deal. Maybe come to me *before* the shit hits the fan though?"

Ari winks and my phone dings. "That's Connor, telling me that he's here. He's meeting me down the block because he's being extra-cautious." I sigh, wishing I could just walk down the steps and get into my boyfriend's car like any other regular woman.

"Go get him, girl. And go smack that bitch for me or I'll have to do it for you. Ugh . . . some people," Ari rants, rolling her eyes.

THE GOLDEN WOK IS ONE OF THOSE PLACES THAT BECOMES an institution around just about every college campus in America. It was first a local hangout for the counterculture and hippie movements before somehow becoming that place where students would meet up. Cheap food, friendly service, and a convenient location right outside the main gates of campus certainly helped, and when the original owner passed on, his son took over.

The Wok is a student place, and it's packed as we walk in. Sabrina isn't here, but we take a four-seater table anyway, sitting across from one another and waiting as seven o'clock comes and goes. "Do you think she's screwing with us?" I ask. "Just jerking us around?"

"I bet you know a lot about that particular subject," Sabrina says, approaching out of the crowd of students that just walked in. She sits down, smirking triumphantly. "I have to say, I didn't think you would show. I thought I was pushing it with the hundred, but I thought I might as well go balls-out, so to speak." She gives me a little wink, like I'm supposed to laugh at her dirty joke, as if any of this is funny.

"I can't believe you're doing this," I growl, and Sabrina laughs. "I thought you were nice, but this is wrong, so fucking wrong." I shake my head, still bewildered at how we even ended up in this shitty situation.

"Nice? I'm not the one pretending to be Miss Goody Two-Shoes while fucking my professor. Seriously, I gotta give you some props. You took that dick like a pro. Way better skills than I'd expect from a math nerd." Her voice is harder than I've ever heard, any hint of sweetness dissipating in her catty judgment.

I flush and sputter. "How did I ever think you were a friend?"

"Probably too fuck-drunk to realize what was right in front of your face," she says, shrugging. "Then again, you spent most of the semester ogling Prof here, too lost in his dick to notice anything. I can't believe you were ever passing. Now I know why."

"She earned her grades," Connor says in a low voice. "Every single one of them." I know it's true, but I can see that Sabrina doesn't believe him for a second.

But now she's got Connor in her sights and she dismisses our little back and forth, locking her eyes on him. "All those damn brains, and still not enough to understand that sometimes, that just doesn't fucking matter," Sabrina says, growing very serious. "Let's talk business."

"So, what's the plan?" Connor asks casually.

Sabrina falters a little. I think she expected him to be more rattled than he is. Honestly, I expected him to be more aggressive too, but I'm trusting this is step one of . . . something. "Well, first, those grades of mine . . . yeah, you're going to do what you need to bring them up. I understand you can't make it obvious, but you're smart. Make it work. I'll need an A in your class as the final grade. Understand?"

"Done," Connor says. "And the money?"

She shrugs, as if blackmail isn't a big deal. "Why not? Those pics seemed worth something, and college is fucking expensive. This little exchange"—she points between me, Connor, and herself— "is going to pay for my degree, oh, plus my scholarship, of course. That'll keep me on track with an A in your class." She smirks, like she can already count the money.

Connor nods, summarizing. "So, let me get this straight . . . you want one hundred thousand dollars and an A you didn't earn, and you'll keep your mouth shut and delete the pictures of Daisy and me? That about right?"

Sabrina grins a sweet smile and nods, looking nothing like the evil bitch she is. If anyone looked over here, they'd probably think me and her were besties who happened to run into a professor on a Thursday night pre-final hang-out. "Yes sir, that's the deal. Take it or I'll go to the dean. I think he'd be real interested in what's been happening between you two." The threat is implicit.

I'm confused, looking between Connor and Sabrina, trying to figure out what he has planned because this seems oddly casual. I don't know that I'd expected him to rage or yell, but something doesn't seem right.

And then I see it, the cocky arrogance Connor is known for. His shit-eating grin tells me that this is exactly what he planned, whatever this is. He winks at me, and my heart races, desperate to see what he's going to do.

"You know, Sabrina, you really should have thought this through better. Then again, you've shown yourself to be a pretty poor student."

"Who the fuck cares?" Sabrina replies, a little rattled. "Give me the money and you get the pictures. You realize you two were so into it you never even locked the door? Amateurs. I had a feeling what was going on, so I quietly opened the door and slid my phone through."

"Speaking of amateurs, the first rule of blackmail is to have information that your victim doesn't want to share. I'm damn proud to be with this woman."

Connor stands up, grabbing my hand and pulling me to my feet. "Everyone!" he calls out, his voice ringing through the restaurant. Almost everything stops, people wondering what the commotion is about. "Everyone, if you don't know me, I'm Professor Connor Daniels, Math department. And this is Daisy Phillips, my girlfriend."

He pulls me against him, kissing me hard before anyone can react. I resist for half a moment, startled more than anything else, before I melt into his kiss, my hands coming up to pull on the back of his neck, deepening the kiss as our tongues twist and writhe around each other. Distantly, I hear the restaurant cheering, hoots of 'get some, dude' and vague *woohoo*s surrounding us.

"Connor," I whisper when our lips part. "Are you sure this is a good idea?" Though most of the students here probably don't realize what they just saw, there's bound to be a few who recognize me as a fellow student and put two and two together that this isn't exactly okay.

"Never been surer," he replies, stroking my cheek. "Eliminate the variables and solve for what's left. And there was only one variable that counted—you. I love you, Daisy Phillips. I love you, heart and soul."

"I love you too," I repeat, a tear trickling from my right eye. "But what about . . ." I look to Sabrina.

She looks shell-shocked, and I can see the anger turning her face red as she sneers. "Soooo touching, but you know that this will end you, right?"

Connor smirks and tells her, "Maybe, but for you, here's what you get. Zero. Zilch. Not a goddamn fucking thing. I went to the dean and told him everything. He'd like to talk with you about your conduct. Sure, I could be out of a job, but you see, Miss Bowen, blackmail is against the law, and blackmailing a professor for better grades? That's grounds for expulsion too."

Sabrina stutters, "W–what? No!" She looks around wildly as her plan blows up in her face, but I've got to give her credit, she recovers quickly. "I'll deny it. *I have no idea what Professor Daniels is talking about, Dean Michaels.*" She raises her voice, mimicking the innocent tone she thinks will work on the dean.

Partnered with the batting lashes and sweet smile, I'll admit that it's a good sell.

Connor laughs and looks past her. "Hey, Nick . . . you get all that?"

A guy I've never seen stands up. "Yep, CD. Got every last word and faux innocent gesture."

"Thanks, man. Can you forward that on to Dean Michaels and send me a copy? He's expecting it." I watch as the guy, obviously a friend of Connor's, taps on his phone and then holds out a thumbs-up sign. Connor turns to Sabrina. "Dean Michaels is expecting you too. Eight A.M. tomorrow morning, Miss Bowen."

And then he takes my hand, leading me out and leaving Sabrina fuming as she yells after us, "I hope you get fired!"

Connor doesn't even react, though the reality is that still could happen. But it feels good to be out in the open, not a dirty little secret but proud to be by my man's side, claiming him and being claimed by him publicly.

There are a few cheers as we leave, but I don't really care. All I care about is the look in Connor's eyes . . . because that's the only thing that counts.

CONNOR

It's a beautiful summer day, and normally, I'd be resentful that I'm having to work. But considering all the other ways Dean Michaels could have punished me, I guess teaching summer term isn't all that bad. He'd definitely hinted at worse, but luckily, the *TED Talk* people finally got around to asking me to present, a huge boon for both me and the university, and the timing couldn't have been better. Though I'd lost my shot at tenure, at least for the time being, I'm happy to still have my job. Even if I could've found a better-paying position in the private sector, I like what I do.

Besides, there are benefits. The summer teaching load isn't all that heavy, and it's given Daisy and me time to be together. At least when she's not in class too.

Rolling over in bed, I give Daisy a soft kiss. "Good morning, love."

Daisy stretches and yawns, her natural beauty only enhanced by the messy hair and bare face. I feel like a lucky bastard for seeing her like this, fresh from sleeping in my arms all night. "Good morning. What time is it?"

"Seven thirty," I reply, burying my head in the curve of her neck and kissing the soft skin there gently. "Too late to do what I want with you right now . . . but today's the last day of class."

"Mmm, I know," Daisy moans lightly, pressing her ass back against my hard cock. "It was just last night. Don't you ever get tired?" Her voice is teasing. She already knows the answer but wants me to talk dirty to her. I'm happy to oblige.

"Of that sweet pussy wrapped around my cock while you scream my name? Never," I promise. It's been a few weeks since Daisy moved in, and I'm glad. It just felt natural, after spring semester was over and she was out of the dorms, to have her move in with me. Sure, some people have wondered, but after she turned in a legitimate perfect score on her final from a different professor, none of my colleagues have dared to say a thing. At least, not to my face. Well, except for Nick, of course. He's given me shit, but all his comments have been friendly teasing. Honestly, I think he's a little jealous, but that's okay.

"So, are you driving me to class?" Daisy asks, turning over to look in my eyes. "You know, to wish me good luck?"

I laugh softly, shaking my head. "After a whole summer term of blowing Professor Patel's socks off, you hardly need good luck."

Daisy hums, reaching down to take my cock in hand. "Mmm . . . speaking of blowing, I know a Professor I'd rather be blowing."

I chuckle, moaning lightly as Daisy kisses down my chest. "And you were wondering if I ever get tired?"

Pausing, her sweet lips just an inch above my cock, she looks up, giving me the naughty smile that only I get to see. "Well, Professor, you've been tutoring me in more than just math . . . and I love every minute of it, but maybe you could critique my new technique?"

She licks at my head, moaning against my skin and driving me wild. "Fuck, Daisy. I love it too, and I love you."

She tries to pull back to say she loves me too. I can see the words in her eyes, but I hold her down, mouth full of my cock. "I know, honey. Now, about that final exam." I smirk, and her eyes light up, happily playing along.

OF COURSE, THERE'S A REASON THAT I WANTED DAISY TO GO to class on her own this morning, and it had nothing to do with campus life. We've gotten used to the looks, but as long as Daisy isn't in my class, nobody can say a damn thing.

After the dean pulled Sabrina into his office, the investigation was swift considering we had video of her confessing to everything. But she begged forgiveness. The dean was still going to throw her out until Daisy, in a move that surprised me, intervened. My good-hearted girl asked that Sabrina be given another chance . . . if the photos were destroyed. Of course,

Sabrina was willing to do that, deleting the file in front of Daisy that very instant. She's still in school, although her plan for avoiding student debt has certainly backfired and her scholarship for next year was revoked. But with no criminal charges filed, she'll figure out something, I'm sure. As long as it has nothing to do with Daisy and me or anything illegal.

But that has nothing to do with my little errand for the morning, pressed in between breakfast and getting to the office to prepare for the final I'm giving at noon.

"It's a beautiful choice, sir," the salesperson comments as I slide the string of pearls over my fingers. I can't help it. The sensation makes my cock stiffen, but I guess that's to be expected. Daisy's pearls have been washed, and I did give her that necklace of a different sort as promised . . . but this is something even more significant, a start of an new heirloom, something permanent and meaningful for us. "Is there anything else?"

"Yes," I reply, shifting over a little. "I'd like them wrapped in satin, if you have it. And I'd like to add something a little bit special to the package. Would you help me over here?"

The salesperson sees what I'm looking at and grins. "A fine choice, sir."

Daisy

"I still can't believe you took summer classes, but I'll see you soon," Arianna says in my ear as I bounce out of the student center where I've been wasting time until four o'clock, when Connor's final ends. "Seriously, I know you love the guy, but studying during summer?"

"You know I've been doing more than studying," I joke, making her laugh. "And the internship . . . how's that?"

"Good! I mean, I'm just working as a front desk receptionist right now, but I'm just glad to have my foot in the door," Ari says, excited. "Hopefully, I can move up to something more hands-on next semester and really start learning. Good part right now, though . . . the eye candy, girl."

"Oh?" I ask, excited for her . . . for both the internship she wanted and that she might have her sights on someone. "Anyone in particular?"

"The CEO," Arianna says, her voice giving away that she's crushing on him. "Remember when I said he was probably just a rich hotshot? He's that, I'm sure, but Oh, my God. You know the M&M slogan, melts in your mouth and not in your hand? I think I want to test that theory on him . . . bet I could get him to melt in my hand, and my mouth. Probably a few other key places too."

I burst out laughing. "Sounds like you're interested in learning *something*, for sure," I tease.

"Yeah, well, he's sexy like it's his job, and I only get to see him for a few seconds a day, but I damn sure get all the eyeful I can during those few seconds."

I grin even though she can't see me. "That sounds just like you. Who knows? Maybe you'll get to see him more. They'll no doubt bring you back next semester after you knock their socks off."

She sighs dreamily. "Thanks, chica. You're right. I got this."

"That's my girl. When you get back, dinner together, okay?"

"That sounds great. It'll be weird not dorming together this year, but I'll admit that having my own place this summer has been kind of sweet. No one but me to clean up after." I ignore her dig at my tendency to leave my dirty dishes soaking in the sink because it's a battle we've good-naturedly fought more than once already. "And my new digs are right between campus and work, so it's perfect."

"And you can come over to our place anytime." The words feel good on my tongue . . . *our place*. "Connor's going to find himself in charge of a nerd harem," I joke. "Oh, wait, you wouldn't qualify. You're not a nerd."

Arianna laughs. "Nope, but I love nerds. Especially you, girl. I'll see you in a couple of weeks."

"Okay, babe. Bye," I reply, approaching the math building. Bounding up the steps, I see Professor Patel leaving and give him a wave. "Hey, Professor. I'm feeling good after that final."

"You should, Miss Phillips," Patel says, stopping. "It's not official yet, but congratulations on your *A*. It was a pleasure. See you this fall."

I'm even more excited as I nearly run down the hall to Connor's office, closing and making sure to lock the door behind me as soon as I see he's alone, standing at his whiteboard, writing something I can't see. "Hey, Professor, can I talk to you about my grade?" I tease, my voice full of faux-innocent naughtiness.

"Hello, beautiful." He doesn't take my bait, staying serious though he smiles. "I can tell by your smile that you heard about your grade. Patel told me. I'm so proud of you."

I cross the office, barely giving him time to cap his pen before grabbing him by the arms and dragging him to his chair. "Thank you, sir. This good girl needs a reward for all those *long, hard* hours of math," I purr before kissing him. "I can't wait until after dinner."

Connor grins wolfishly. "A reward, you say? Something beyond the *A*? Maybe something a bit *bigger, thicker, harder* . . .?" The return to sexy double-meanings as we tease each other is fun, a hint of our previous dips into being bad together.

He grabs around my waist, pulling me to stand between his spread knees. Holding me in his powerful arms, his lips trail down my neck to the V-neck of my T-shirt, licking and sucking on the mounds of my breasts as he thumbs my nipples through the cotton. It's amazing. Connor's touch can send shivers through my body every time, no matter where we are or what we're doing, but sneaking little trysts in his office has an extra-naughty appeal. I mean, we're in a relationship, and everyone's okay with that . . . but sex in the office is still a no-no. But that's never stopped us before.

I lift my arms to help Connor take my shirt off, gasping as he doesn't even undo my bra but lifts my right breast out of the cup to consume my nipple, sucking hard and making me cry his name out softly. "Connor, fuck . . . that feels amazing."

"You're amazing," Connor says, switching to my other breast. We know we can't take a ton of time. Every time in his office is truly a 'quickie,' but I've discovered a passion for both the fast and dirty and the slow and loving. Reaching down, I undo his jeans while he lavishes my breasts with his tongue and lips, nipping at my skin when I wrap my hand around his cock and pump him hard and fast.

"Mmm, on the desk," I gasp, letting go of his cock, hurriedly unbuttoning my own jeans and shoving them down my legs to bunch at my ankles. "Hard, baby."

I lie on the desk, just like so many times before as Connor pushes his pants down a little more before lining the tip of his cock up with my wet entrance. He teases me for a few seconds, dragging it up to near my asshole. "Mmm, soon, I'm going to take your virgin ass too, and then all your cherries will be mine . . . mouth, pussy, and your tight little ass. All mine."

The thought is intoxicating. He's fingered my ass before, and while it feels amazing during sex, afterward, I can't help but blush at the dirty things he does to me. I think the innocent blush is part of what he loves about doing it.

I moan, wondering if he's going to push into my tight pucker now, but he just teases me. "I got you something," he groans, voice tight with lust.

"I can feel that," I say with a seductive smile, looking over my shoulder at him.

His cocky grin is all arrogance. "That too, but I meant that." He lifts his chin toward a long, skinny box on the desk, black with a white ribbon tied around it. "Open it."

It's on the tip of my tongue to argue, wanting his cock more than any gift, but I hear the order, and before I know what I'm doing, my hands reach for the box. As I try to untie the bow, Connor slips along my folds, rubbing from my ass to my clit with his cockhead, spreading my cream and his precum all over me, making me sloppy wet with the combination of us. I finally get the bow undone and open the box to find . . . a long chain of rubber beads, pearlized white and gradually getting bigger until the ring on one end.

"What's this?" I ask, already knowing the answer but wanting him to say it. I bite my lip, waiting desperately for his filthy words.

He leans over me, covering me with his hard body and pressing me against the hard wood of the desk, to growl in my ear. "Those are the pearls I'm gonna slip inside your ass, one at a time, bigger and bigger, until you're ready to take my cock in your tight hole. Because when I get that cherry, I'm going to ride you hard, Daisy, and I need you prepared for that. I meant to give them to you tonight, but right now, I want nothing more than to fuck your pussy with them in your ass, filling you so fucking full. Can you do that? Take the pearls in your ass like a good girl?"

I whimper but nod, so lost in lust I'm unable to form words.

He lifts off me, slipping the pearls along my pussy to coat them in honey before pressing the smallest one against my ass. "Relax."

I exhale and I feel the pearl slip inside. It feels odd, but good. Connor rubs my clit, and as I buck back, searching for his hand, another pearl slides inside. Or was it two? I can't tell. All I know is I feel full but also empty, my pussy pulsing desperately to be filled too.

"Fuck me, Connor. Please," I beg.

He lines his rock-hard cock up with my pussy, sliding all the way in with one deep thrust. "Mmm . . . you feel so good, satin walls gripping my cock," he growls as he grinds deep inside me. "I could stay inside you forever."

I stifle a cry as he thrusts again. It's fast, deep, and brutal, just what my body needs as Connor hammers my pussy with his cock, both of us pushing the other higher. I squeeze his cock with every thrust, milking him and encouraging him to give me more, to take me higher.

Of course Connor can. He grunts and groans, adding to the heat of our intense fucking as he begins to move the string of pearls in and out of my ass, fucking both my holes. It's like nothing I've ever imagined, so much stimulation as he sometimes thrusts into me with his cock and the pearls at once, sometimes alternating. He keeps me on my toes, literally and figuratively, not knowing what to expect as he pounds me into the desk.

I slap my hand over my mouth, stifling the cries of my ecstasy so no one in the hallway can hear, even though a part of me wants them to, is turned on that they'll hear my Professor fucking my student pussy and ass.

He speeds up, his cock swelling and making me fight back a scream as my body trembles before exploding in a massive climax that leaves me gasping for breath. I squeeze the desk edge as Connor strangles back a cry before coming hard, his warm seed filling my body and making me tremble again in what I've come to call aftershock orgasms, tears of joy trickling from the corners of my eyes.

When it's over, I sigh happily, totally spent for the moment.

Connor sits in his chair, pulling me into his lap, and I rest my head on his shoulder as he twirls a lock of my black hair around his finger. "Hey, Daisy? I was hoping you could help me with an equation. Think you can take a look?"

I blink, a little surprised, but I nod. "Uhh, you need *my* help?"

He leads me toward the whiteboard. "What do you think?"

I look at the equation, then back at him.

$C + D = F$

If it wasn't for the hopeful look in his eyes, I'd probably be lost. Connor plus Daisy equals forever.

"Well, first, we need to solve for the variables. What's the expression for F?" I tease, not wanting to get my hopes up that he means what I think he does. But my heart is transparent to Connor and he knows exactly what I'm thinking.

Connor nods, going over to his desk and getting a small flat box that he brings back before getting on a knee. "I love you. With all that I am, all that I have, all I ever will have. All I can think of is you. Daisy Phillips, will you marry me?"

He opens the box, and inside, I see a beautiful string of pearls, and strung on them, resting precisely in the center, is a diamond ring, sparkling on a bed of white satin.

I swallow and nod as Connor takes out the pearls and pulls the ring from them, making me grin widely. "Yes, Connor! Oh, my God, yes!"

He slips the ring on my finger, and I hold it up, admiring the sparkly diamond that symbolizes so much more than I'd ever dreamed possible. He kisses me, sweet and deep, just like our love.

I pull back, telling him, "But you made a mistake in your equation."

"What?" Connor asks, the arrogant smirk on his face telling me just how clever he thought he was being. "I thought it was pretty good, myself."

"True . . . but like you taught me, you have to identify all your variables precisely," I admonish. I pick up the marker, adding to the equation so that it reads . . . $C+D+1=F$.

Connor's eyes widen in comprehension, and he pulls me tightly, spinning me around. "As you like to tell me, the answer is still the same. You're mine. Forever. Both of you."

Continue on to read Leather and Lace, Arianna's Book.

LEATHER AND LACE

BY LAUREN LANDISH

Prologue
Arianna

 *ear Diary,*

I'm a whore.

Okay, that's definitely not true. But it might as well be, because that's what everyone thinks of me. I'll admit I've earned that reputation with the biggest con job since Enron.

But it's not all bad. I've gone to all the best frat parties, flirted, teased, and had fun grinding on the dance floor like every college girl should. So everyone just assumes the rumors are true, and I don't say shit to dissuade their thinking.

Reality, of course, is very different. My biggest secret, the one that no one knows, not even my best friend, is that it's all fake.

I'm not a whore. I'm a virgin.

It's a front I chose a long time ago, refusing to play the victim to some stupid high school boy's bragging and society's judgement. As if Mother

113

Nature's gifts of tits and ass were something I should be ashamed of, blamed for. But as I played along as the casual hookup-prone vixen, I realized sex meant more to me. That's when I decided to save myself for The One. He's out there somewhere, that special man worthy of getting between my legs.

Not that I have time for that right now when all my time and attention are focused on one thing—my career. Well, finishing school and actually having a career, that is. After watching my parents struggle and how they drank their way through most of the meager college fund they'd set aside for me, I want more . . . more than the dead-end, soul-sucking jobs that barely paid enough to make ends meet that my parents had.

I'd hoped my summer internship at Morgan Inc. would be the first step toward that glossy, corner-office future I dream of, especially since it's my first-choice company to work for after graduation. But my hopes of hands-on experience and seeing behind the curtain were quickly dashed, and I've spent the last few months answering the phones and greeting people. I'm willing to work and happy to pay my dues, but my desire for more bubbles beneath the surface every day, pushing me for more, more, more.

And with two weeks left before the end of my internship, I hope I've done enough for them to hire me during the school year. Maybe with fewer interns on staff, I can get that shot at the brass ring and really learn the things I need for my future.

And once I get there . . . then I'll worry about finding Mr. Right.

ARIANNA

"Arianna? Arianna!"

I start, sitting up and shaking myself loose from my daydream of me as the boss of a big company, the reality of the plastic chair I'm sitting in mentally replaced by a leather chair in a corner office as I negotiate contracts with other big-wigs.

Checking the clock, I see I've still got a few minutes left on my coffee break. I look up to see Dora Maples standing in the doorway of the small breakroom. It's not fancy—we're first-floor, not the executive level, after all—but the coffee is decent and the vending machine has my favorite afternoon pick-me-up candy bar.

"Yes, ma'am! What do you need, Ms. Maples?"

Dora sets a large manila envelope on the table, sliding it over to me. "I need you to run this upstairs."

"Of course," I quickly reply. Being a delivery girl isn't usually part of my job description, but I'll take anything that gets me facetime with someone upstairs.

"It's the Iriguchi property papers, with the seal from the county office. Mr. Blackstone needs it on his desk by one," Dora says, squinting and scowling at me as if uncertain I'm capable of a simple delivery. "Run up there and hand it directly to his assistant, Jacob Wilkes. Understood?"

"Consider it done," I reply, picking up the thick envelope and polishing off the last of my morning tea. "I'll do it now."

Honestly, it's probably a blessing she put this errand on me. Jacob Wilkes, Mr. Blackstone's executive assistant, is in charge of the intern program, so I want to stay in his good graces. Even if it's just saying hello and reminding him that I exist, every little bit helps!

The elevator ride feels like an eternity, but I take the time to fluff my hair and smooth my skirt, wanting to look my best for the executive floor and Mr. Wilkes. I knock on Mr. Black-stone's door, but there's no response. After a moment, I gently ease the door open to . . . what the fuck?

It's utter and complete chaos in here. The last and only time I was on the top floor, everything was neat, and while there was a hum of activity, it was organized. This . . . is a loud, crowded clusterfuck of madness, all contained in the vast openness of Mr. Wilkes and Mr. Blackstone's large corner wing.

I stand stock-still for a moment, my eyes scanning as I try to make some sense of what I'm seeing. There is a camera crew set up, complete with lighting, a hair and makeup station nestled in the corner, and a man shouting orders as he rubs roughly at his bald head.

I recognize some of the faces. I helped them sign in when they arrived shortly after eight o'clock for a 'meeting'. I paid attention to them because of the suspicious way they'd refused to explain so I could log them correctly. The only reason I'd let the large group through was because Mr. Wilkes had come into the lobby to escort them up, assuring me it was fine. It doesn't look fine to me though.

I look around for Mr. Wilkes's familiar face so that I can maybe, hopefully, complete my mission, but I freeze when I spot, at the center of the craziness, the sexiest man in the whole damn city, Mr. Liam Blackstone.

I've only ever seen him in person in passing. He flies through the lobby each morning as if he can't wait to get to work, not bothering to acknowledge the peons who sit by the front door, namely me. But he's undeniably the hottest man I've ever laid eyes on. Dark hair fixed in that floppy way that looks casual, but probably took him forever to style, atop an angular jawline that begs to be nibbled. And those eyes! Bright blue that can see right through you or pin you with a stare. Not that he's ever looked at me, but even from the company website, that much is obvious.

The rest of him is just as well put together, lean muscles on his tall frame and an overall aura of 'I'm in charge.' Right now, he's standing in the middle of the maelstrom, a patient, almost amused look on his face and looking like ten million bucks in a custom-tailored pair of black slacks and a slim-fit dress shirt that's open at the neck.

This close, he's nothing at all like the glances I've caught of him as he goes through the lobby. From fifty feet away, he's handsome and sexy. At fifteen feet, he possesses a magnetic aura that seems to envelop the room. He's like a rock star, a general totally in his element, commanding everything in the middle of anarchy.

The slight crunch of the envelope in my hand forces me to pull my eyes away from him. I continue my scan, finally seeing Mr. Wilkes, and walk over. "Mr. Wilkes, sir?"

He barely looks up from the tablet he's poring over, obviously too busy to be interrupted, but I have a mission. "Ms. Maples sent me up with these. It's the Iriguchi property papers?" I hate that I ended that sentence on a lilt, as if I'm unsure. It makes me sound weak, and I'm not. But I am a bit in awe of this whole scene, more fashion shoot than the business meetings I'd expect to see on this floor.

He takes them from my hand, saying, "Thanks." His eyes never glance up to me. So much for facetime with the boss. Feeling the unspoken dismissal, I work my way through the disorder back toward the elevator, only to be stopped when the bald guy freezes mid-tantrum right in front of me to yell at what seems to be his assistant.

The man explodes, "Where is our model!? She was supposed to be here thirty minutes ago!"

The assistant shakes her head, pointing at her phone. "Francois, Cassie said her flight got delayed. She hasn't even landed yet. It'll be at least two more hours."

I try to discreetly dodge around them, but Francois starts pacing and I back out of the way, not wanting to draw his ire.

"Dammit!" he screams, actually stamping his foot like a toddler. I have to hide my smirk because who does that? He throws his hands in the air. "We'll have to forget the paired shots. Helen's gonna have my ass for this! She specifically asked for sexy couples images," he says before stopping, as if inspiration just struck him. "Wait a minute. Get someone else to take Cassie's place."

The assistant looks aghast, immediately shaking her head. "Francois, I know this is important, but we can't just replace Cassie. There are contracts, consent forms, payments—"

"So what!" Francois interrupts, as if all his problems have evaporated. He snaps, "Get the paperwork started and get out the checkbook. Still cheaper than Cassie's irresponsible ass. Find someone."

The assistant sighs, nodding in defeat but obviously still not quite sure. "But—"

"There." A voice cuts through the noise of the room and everything goes so quiet you could hear a pin drop. I turn to look where the voice came from and am shocked to see Mr. Blackstone pointing at me, his eyes burning into my skin. The nearly feral pull of his gaze freezes me in my tracks. I feel like I'm the prey and I've just been targeted by a predator.

Everyone in the room who'd been curiously watching the exchange between Francois and his assistant is now ping-ponging back and forth between Mr. Blackstone and me. I can feel their eyes, making me hot, the flush of the attention bringing up some painful, awkward memories. Having years of practice is the only thing that saves me from wilting under their judgment.

Still, I'm barely able to utter a squeak as people suddenly start moving toward me, intent on following Mr. Blackstone's orders. *"Me?"* I finally force out, still confused. I clear my throat, getting my voice back to my usual pitch. "I mean . . . me?"

Mr. Blackstone's lips spread into a sexy, cocky grin, and he nods, shooing everyone off as he waves me forward. For some reason, instead of running for my life to the nearest fire escape, my feet move without my even telling them. I walk toward him, my eyes never leaving his.

"Yeah, you," he says. "You look like a doll, perfect and fragile. Sexy and sweet." His eyes caress my face and trace down my body. The body I know has whiplash hourglass curves that make men stupid for no good reason. Usually, I feel defensive when guys look me up and down, like they know something about me just based on my body, but when Mr. Blackstone does it, I feel like standing tall and letting him peruse his fill. His words are probably one of the best, maybe only, compliments I've ever gotten. Maybe that's sad, but it's just my reality. I usually get filthy catcalls and assumptions, not kindness. "You'll do the photoshoot with me."

The photographer lights up like a light bulb. "Yes! She will do. Someone get some makeup on this girl!" His evaluation of me leaves me feeling inadequate, like I don't already look good even though I'm wearing my best daytime, professional look.

But I don't even have time to think about how I'd like to bless him out because Francois's assistant jams a piece of paper into my hands. "Sign here . . . here . . . initial." As she points out each spot to me, she chatters casually. "Haven't you heard? Sexy, young, rich CEOs are all the rage. Books, movies, television . . . it seems that's the recipe for fantasy nowadays!"

"You mean, it hasn't *always* been?" I ask, a hint of sass in my voice before I can catch myself.

Oops. Did I say that out loud? I meant to think that, not actually say it!

"*Cutting Edge Magazine* wanted to do an interview and a photoshoot," Mr. Blackstone explains. "Something about my being the hottest ticket in the business pages, and any press is good press, so here we are." He says it in such a casual manner, like this is all just business as usual for him.

Francois does a little jump and clap before turning to me. "What are you waiting on? Come on, girl!"

That's twice he's called me *girl*. I do have a name, but I'm still too tongue-tied to correct him. "I–I don't know the first thing about modeling," I protest weakly, panicked. "I mean, I'm just an intern here."

Francois waves his hands again. "Don't worry. All you have to do is listen to me and stand beside Mr. Blackstone. *Anyone* could do this next to that man." He gestures outward like it's so easy, snapping his fingers. "Get her ready! We were supposed to be a wrap ten minutes ago!"

The matter seems settled, and before I know it, my hair's been primped, my makeup scrubbed off and a whole new style applied, and they had me change into a blouse that's even tighter across my boobs. I'm nearly shaking, my mind a whirlwind. I came up here to deliver an envelope. Instead, I'm about to take pictures with my boss. My *very* hot boss whom I bet every single woman in this building has a crush on. Awkward.

The assistant appears out of nowhere and leads me over to Mr. Blackstone's desk, where he's sitting nonchalantly, like waiting for this is no big deal. The assistant tells me, "Stand here. Lighting check." And then she disappears, leaving me alone with Mr. Blackstone. Well, not alone, considering there are at least fifteen other people in the room, but it feels like there's a bubble of stillness surrounding us as everyone else bustles about.

"What's your name, doll?" he asks.

Normally, when a random guy goes straight to nicknames and endearments, it makes me grit my teeth. I'd expect my boss doing it would elicit an even stronger reaction. It does . . . but it's not the negative one I'd expect. Instead, I almost swoon. Maybe it's his presence, or the subtle, masculine smell of leather wafting from him, or the way he's staring at me like he already knows my secrets. But there's something in me that likes him calling me that, especially after his earlier compliment.

Calm down, girl. You deal with men like him everyday. He's hot, more than most, but you can control yourself for a few pictures and a fucking conversation that could be your big break.

The reminder that this could be a great career opportunity helps, and I focus as I introduce myself. "Arianna Hunnington. I'm a summer intern, sir."

I offer my hand, which he takes with a smirk. "Liam Blackstone, but I suspect you already knew that." His hand is warm against mine, making me wonder what his touch would feel like on other parts of my body.

Luckily, I'm saved from my own dirty thoughts when Francois comes close. "Okay, you two . . . we want heat for these shots. Naughty girl and the big boss. Got it?"

I can't really say anything else as Francois begins shouting orders as he steps behind the camera. "Let's get this show on the road! Lean into him, girl!"

I hesitate. There he is, calling me *girl* again. "I . . . uh . . ."

Mr. Blackstone is done wasting time though. He takes control, grabbing me by the waist and pulling me into him. "I got you. Don't be shy."

My breasts flatten against him and I throw my head back, trying to get some space between us, but I get caught in his eyes, breathless as I faintly hear a shutter sound. "Yes, yes. Perfect!" Francois crows. "That's it. It's late, and you two are working together when the passion starts to flow between you!"

I barely listen to him. I'm practically melting and these photos aren't even that risqué. I would literally be a puddle on the floor if they were. The feeling of his hard body, even through our clothes, has me so turned on, but at the same time, I'm terrified, too afraid I'll start moaning when he grabs my lower back and pulls me in close. I'm not complaining. I'd do this every day, but what the hell business magazine is this? And what kind of job is this?

Francois notices, scowling. "For God's sake, girl, look like you're enjoying it! I'm sure there's plenty of others around here who'd take your spot in a second!"

Oh, hell no. He's mine. All mine. And equally important, this opportunity is mine, and I'm not going to blow it over some silly school-girl nerves. I've played this part a million times, fooled people better than Francois, and I can do it now if that's what it takes.

So I smile and look up at Mr. Blackstone as innocently as I can despite what's going on inside my head or the desire that's coursing through my body.

"Perfect!" Francois yells. "Now put your hand on his chest!"

My heart pounds, but I play my part, placing my hand on his chest. Oh, my God. Just as hard as I imagined. I want to roam my hand up and down, feel every ridge in his muscles. But he grabs around my wrist, holding me in place, still in charge even though I'm touching him.

There's another series of shutter clicks.

Mr. Blackstone looks down at me. "Put your hand on my thigh."

It seemed different when the photographer was telling me what to do, less personal. But when the demand is from Mr. Blackstone himself, it feels intimate. I hesitate a fraction of a second but obey.

He smirks, giving me a 'good girl' nod.

Oh. My. God. My hand is mere inches from my boss's junk! And I swear . . . no way! He's hard!

"Relax, doll," he whispers, the name between the two of us. "You're about to fall to pieces. I won't bite."

The words pop out before I can think to stop them, flirty and full of my character's sass. "Too bad." His brows lift in surprise at my quick response. Hell, I'm surprised at my comeback too. I try to temper my words and find some semblance of professionalism. "I'm not scared," I protest, faking it if I can't really be sure what the hell I'm doing. "Just not what I thought my work duties were going to entail today."

Mr. Blackstone's grin fades a little and he lowers his lips to just an inch from my ear, his breath sending hot chills down my spine as he whispers, "Your work today involves doing what you're told."

"Hold his belt!" Francois quips, as if he heard Mr. Blackstone's words.

Determined to prove I'm not a scared little girl, I grab his leather belt and give it a tug. I want to look down and get a peek, but I'm not quite that bold. I can feel him, hot and hard, just a fraction of an inch from my hand, so close I can almost feel him.

Francois's murmurs of 'yes' and 'just like that' are getting to me, making me feel like maybe I'm doing okay with this crazy situation, and I find myself starting to get into it, so I swing my foot up, my skirt stretching tight across my ass and thighs, to show off my stiletto heels. Instinctively, Mr. Blackstone reaches down and catches me under the knee, gazing at me with lust in his eyes. I can see the promise of heat in their depths, of things I don't understand, don't know, but I can fake it. I always have. And with him, it's oddly easy to let the desire wash through me, more real than my usual imitation.

We do a couple more shots, but just like that, it's over.

"And we're a wrap! Thank you both!" he yells, clapping his hands. "Now let's get cleaned up and out of Mr. Blackstone's space."

We pull apart, our bodies beginning to get a bit hot and sweaty. My pulse is pounding, and my pussy throbs with every beat of my heart, screaming to be taken. No more waiting. Right now. Mr. Blackstone is the one. Fuck, I've never felt like this. I'm always the one in control of myself, my body, my image. But I feel oddly swept away with him right now, filled with a wild lust I've always scoffed at, but suddenly, it's happening to me.

His eyes are slightly dilated, his cock tenting his slacks as he looks at me, but before we can say anything, I'm ushered away to change out of the magazine's wardrobe.

I'm approached and given a check, two hundred dollars, but right now, I don't care about the money. I just want to get back to Mr. Blackstone. I want . . . more. More of that magnetism, that connection I felt, the look in his eyes when my hand was on his chest or when he cupped the back of my head and stared down at me. I've never felt that rush of attraction, not like that, not that real.

But it must've been one-sided because Mr. Blackstone, for his part, seems to quickly forget about me as he's surrounded by crew. Other than casually reaching down to adjust his cock and get it pointing somewhere other than straight out, I could have disappeared and never existed.

Before I can do anything, I'm quickly shown to the elevator door. I look back, and I see him talking on his phone while directing two other people, and I'm left with a feeling of surrealness. *Did this really just happen?*

LIAM

Fucking beautiful.

Naughty perfection.

The angel next door with a dollop of the devil inside.

There are so many ways I could describe the little minx who just left my arms. At first, she seemed so uncertain and innocent, unaware of how my eyes were already tracking her sexy curves from across the room. I'd even had a flash of possessiveness when she'd been speaking to Jacob, who thankfully ignored her. But her nervousness faded away when I took control, and she reared back, rising to the challenge. Feisty minx. That only makes me want more.

Fuck. I'd love to show her what taking control is all about. I want to be the voice in her ear, whispering to the devil inside her that she wants it, even as her better nature is telling her she should run from me. She could run, but the chase sounds exciting, definitely more so than the women who usually throw themselves at me. No, something tells me that Arianna isn't one of those types. She'd make me work for it, earn it, and in return, I'd make her beg.

I was about to ask her more about her time here at Morgan until everyone surrounded me, shoving water in my face, kissing my ass, and generally wasting my precious time. In the few moments it took for me to get rid of them, she disappeared nearly as quickly as she came. Like a mirage, an oasis of beautiful reality in this vast desert of brown-nosing fakers. If not for my hard cock and the pictures Francois is flipping through, I'd wonder if I'd imagined her.

"Do you like this shot?" Francois asks, showing me the initial downloaded shots on his tablet. "I need you to tell me which ones you prefer."

I glance down at the tablet, sighing inwardly because I know my opinion isn't going to matter for shit when Helen gets the images. She'll pick what she wants, my preferences be damned. Not that I care. They're all good shots. "Yeah, go with that."

I still swipe through the rest of them, remembering how she felt so close to me. In each shot, my eyes are drawn to Arianna, the fire in her eyes and the naughty sexuality oozing from her. I tower over her, but she's still powerful, and I have to swallow when I see the image of me holding her leg up. I can actually see a flash of baby blue between her legs. My God, was I that close to her little pussy that her panties could be seen?

"This one," I say, pointing to the shot but covering the space between her legs with my finger. Francois looks over, an evaluative eye scanning the shot as he hums. "Send it to my email now. And then delete it."

He tilts his head. "That's not . . . I can't . . ." He tries to argue, and I'm sure there's some photography code or magazine clause I'm asking him to break, but under the weight of my glare, he starts tapping on the screen. "Done, Mr. Blackstone. Sent and deleted." He looks at me curiously, but I don't have a single shred of intention of explaining myself to him.

I flip through the rest and Francois nods. "Great. I'll get the photo editors on these right away. They might want to have Cassie's head Photoshopped on her body—"

"The fuck? No," I growl, cutting him off. "She stays."

"But—"

I give him a look that says I'm not fucking around, and he goes pale, like he wants to argue but doesn't. "Yes, sir," he agrees, then walks off.

The crew is clearing out, all the fancy equipment that's been cluttering my office disappearing faster than you'd think possible. I'm eager to have my space back to myself so I can get some actual work done today.

Jacob approaches, perching next to me on my desk. He's probably the only person I'd let get away with that. "Hey," Jacob whispers, trying to keep his voice low, "The magazine specifically wanted you with that Cassie chick. She's Instagram famous or some shit, so I don't know if they're going to run it with some random intern on the cover, even if she is hot as sin."

I cut my eyes at him. I want to say something, but Jacob has been my friend and confidant since college and he doesn't mean anything. He's my right-hand man who followed me to Morgan as a package deal. He's the slow and steady brains to my risk-taking gut-following. We're a good team. But right now, I want to knock the shit out of him for even noticing Arianna.

I remind myself to cool it. He's just giving me a heads-up, and Arianna's beauty was apparent to everyone in the room. She's got the looks that make guys want her and girls want to be her, even though she wasn't showy or flashy about it at all. In fact, she might've been trying to disguise it to some degree, her skirt fitting but not too tight, her shirt buttoned over her lush cleavage to be professional, her makeup daytime subtle. It wasn't until the photo crew fixed her up that her bad-girl fuck-goddess was so readily obvious. But I'd noticed her before they'd sexed her up, had already seen beneath the polished surface.

"They'd better, or there won't be a cover. See to it. Arianna's on the cover with me or no deal," I say crisply.

Jacob looks at me in shock but quickly scans my face, reading me like an open book. "Whatever you say. Consider it done." He narrows his eyes, his curiosity piqued, and that's never a good thing. I wait for the interrogation, knowing it's coming. "Anything we need to discuss, Liam?"

"No," I say, not leaving room for further questions. "But I do need one more thing."

"What's that?" Jacob asks, lowering his phone where he's probably already emailing Helen about my stipulations since he's so damn good at his job.

"Find out who Arianna reports to and get back to me."

He's got that look on his face that tells me I'm doing something that he calls 'fuck stupid', but I don't care. "Dude, are you trying to —"

My look silences him, and he sighs. "I'm going on the record now that I'm against *this*, whatever this is. Man, you can't chase pussy around the office. 'Don't shit where you eat' is a saying for a good fucking reason. And an intern? Really, Liam? I can see the HR nightmare coming already."

I glare at him, letting his argument roll right off me. I do what I want and we both damn well know it.

He clenches his jaw, and I know I'll hear more on this, but for now, he gives in. "All right, I'll get that for you as soon as possible. You put me in charge of the interns anyway. It's in my office somewhere."

"Good. And tell them to hurry up and clean this place up. I want work back to normal here in an hour."

Jacob leaves, and I settle in my chair, one thing and one thing only on my mind.

Getting Arianna in my arms again.

AFTER THE PHOTOSHOOT IS OVER, WHIRLWIND ONLY BEGINS to describe the rest of the day. I quickly get bogged down by work and two conference calls, and I temporarily forget about what happened earlier.

Temporarily.

Now, as the last glow from the setting sun fades to deep purple in the west, I can't stop thinking about her as I sit in my office, my back turned to the door while I watch the city from the floor-to-ceiling windows that give me a commanding view of downtown.

Those brown eyes. That smile. The way her tits felt pressed against me . . .

My thoughts of Arianna are interrupted by my phone ringing, and I turn away from the skyline, my cock yet again hard in my slacks. It's probably the worst time for a stiffie, considering whose customized ringtone, Avicii's *"Hey Brother"*, is playing on my phone.

"Hey, big bro!" my little sister, Norma Jean, chirps sweetly. Just turning twenty this year, she's the most important person in my life, even if she does push all my buttons sometimes. It's not her fault she's still wearing little girl blinders about our asshole of a father—although he's admittedly been a kinder parent to her than he ever was to me, something I think Norma Jean's mother had a heavy hand in. Maybe if my own mother had been stronger, I would've had a different father-son relationship with him too. But that ship sailed long ago.

"Hey, NJ!" I say. "What's up? I'm a little busy."

"Oh, please." Norma laughs. "I know your schedule. You're almost done with work and were probably looking out the window while considering your kingdom and coming up with your next plan to take over the world."

Damn, she's good. Still, I can't let her know she pegged me exactly right. "I'm never done with work. You know that. And my kingdom is everything the light touches . . . everything," I say in a wise voice. I must've watched The Lion King with her a hundred times when she was young, and I'd wager that she still watches it pretty often, even if we don't sit down and marathon watch movies together anymore.

"Slick quote usage, Liam." I can hear the smile in her voice as she remembers those nights curled up on the couch too. Back then, I'd been barely a teenager and she'd been the toddler little sister my father had sprung on me with his new wife, my stepmom. I'd never felt like I was being replaced simply because I'd never felt like I'd had a place in my dad's heart to begin with. But Norma Jean did then and still does. Her sweet laughs and strong will had let her worm her way into my heart all too easily back then. "So, Mr. Busy, what did you do today?"

I secretly love when she does this, call just to catch up. Everyone else wants something from me. She just wants to chat. It's a rare treat for me. "Oh, a bit of this, some of that, some conference calls, a photoshoot and interview, a few contracts. The usual."

Just as I gleefully expected, she screams, "A photoshoot and interview?!? What the hell, Liam? Tell me all about it. You know I live for that stuff."

"I know. But it's hush-hush, top-secret, okay?" She hums her agreement, so I tell her all about the interview with *Cutting Edge*, making sure to give all the details I know she wants.

She sighs blissfully. "One day, that's going to be me. I'm going to be sitting in penthouse offices, interviewing bigwigs, and finding out what makes them tick. I'll get all the low-down dirt on the country's biggest companies. And then maybe politicians too—that's where the real gritty stuff is."

I can hear her excitement, her passion, and I smile at how similar to me she sounds. We're both driven to the point of near-obsession, and we get what we want ninety-nine percent of the time. "You'll do it too. Get your degree, work your ass off, and you can do anything, Norma."

"I did apply for a job at the university newspaper. It's really competitive, and they mostly only hire seniors, but my interview went really well. Even if I get it, it'll probably be small human-interest stories for a while, but it's a start. Cross your fingers for me."

I recognize that this is a big deal for her, a reach for something she really wants but isn't sure she's ready for. But I know she can handle it. "You don't need crossed fingers or luck, Sister. You are ballsy and brave and have more brains than just about anyone I know. You'd be a perfect journalist for a hell of a lot more than puppy adoption stories, and they'll see that. So swallow those nerves and go get what you want."

It's my version of a pep talk, more 'work for it' and less 'you deserve it' because I'm well aware we don't always get what we deserve, but we damn sure get what we work for.

"Thanks, Liam. That means a lot, especially from you. I tell you what. When I get hired, I'm going to interview you and do an insider's look at the country's hottest CEO."

I notice she didn't ask but rather told me, and I smirk at her assumption. Big clanging balls on that girl. Nobody tells me what to do, except her . . . and sometimes Jacob.

As if my thoughts conjured him, Jacob steps in, and I hold up a finger, having him pause. "Listen, gotta go. Keep working hard and nothing's going to stop you. Love ya."

She responds in kind, and I hang up, turning my attention to Jacob.

"She's a college student. Summer internship," Jacob says quickly, setting a file on my desk. I run my thumb along the label . . . *Arianna Hunnington*. "She'll be gone in two weeks until next semester . . . assuming we bring her back."

I tap my fingers on the file, quickly fingering out a quick little rap beat as I think. Two weeks to make her mine.

Or to make her stay.

Either way . . . I'll have my way.

"I can almost see the dirty thoughts running across your face and I'd like to reiterate my stance that this is a bad fucking idea. A human. Resources. Nightmare. With a side serving of PR shit show for the company you're supposed to be taking into the next market wave. Liam?" Jacob asks harshly as I finish my beat.

"I want her moved up here," I declare, turning to him and completely tuning out his reasoning. He's right, he almost always is, but I don't care this time. "Starting tomorrow, she'll be my secretary."

"Huh?" Jacob asks, confused. "She's just a college intern. And in case you didn't notice, you don't need a secretary. You have an executive assistant. Me."

"Well now, I'll have a secretary too. It's not like you can't use a little assistance from time to time."

Jacob shakes head. "There are protocols we have to follow. You can't just move her up like that."

That's Jacob. If he can't get me to listen to reason, he'll try another tactic. He learned that from me, and he is always a stickler for the rules. "Such as?"

"Well, she'd have to be interviewed."

"Fine. I'll conduct it myself."

Jacob shakes his head. "You can't just interview her yourself! There are rules—" Jacob stops when he sees my expression. He should already know I'm going to get what I want. And I want her. "Fuck it . . . we'll interview her together. Satisfied?"

He sighs and nods but gives me a hard look.

"Get her up here," I growl. "Now."

"Now? She may have already left for the day," Jacob reminds me as he looks at his watch. "You know, most people go home about an hour ago."

He's got a point. "Tomorrow morning then. First thing."

ARIANNA

Dear Diary,

. . .

I can't believe what happened today. I mean, going upstairs to deliver some papers to the top floor was already exciting, but to then be picked out of the crowd and pulled into a photoshoot with Liam Blackstone?

Holy Fuck, that man is sex in a suit. He's an alpha in every sense of the word, people scurrying to do what he says, not because he's wealthy or the boss but because he has this air of dominance. I've never felt anything like that before, the weight of his very presence effortlessly drawing my attention and tuning my body into his.

I'll admit that the feeling of being pressed against him, his cock hard on my ass, was shockingly erotic. The desire and surprise in my eyes as I looked over my shoulder at him weren't pretend like usual. And I'd had a weak moment when we'd separated where I wanted more, wanted it all, had even considered for a moment that he might be The One, considering the way he made me feel. But that's a danger zone I don't need to venture into . . . no sex, not now. Not until my career is on target and I find the right man, preferably in that order.

But there's no harm in fantasizing, and I definitely did that as soon as I got home, touching myself to the thoughts of his hands on my body, his whispered words hot in my ear, his thick cock taking my pussy for the first time.

THE NEXT MORNING, I'VE BARELY WALKED IN THE DOOR before Dora is riding me. She follows me into the breakroom, and as a peace offering, I make her a coffee while she complains about the time I spent away from my desk yesterday. "I had to pull another intern from her duties to cover for you, so you'll be returning the favor to her today and handling her tasks."

I nod, not interrupting her tirade as I hand the steaming mug over, made to the exact specifications I know she prefers, and she accepts it without a single word of appreciation. I turn back around to make my own cup of caffeine nectar, wishing I could have something stronger to make dealing with Dora a bit easier. I wonder if there's an espresso machine on Mr. Blackstone's floor?

"Your to-do list is on your desk so you'd best get started because I expect it to be complete before you leave today. You'll need to stay on task today, Ms. Hunnington." Dora huffs at me with a stern look.

"Of course, Ms. Maples. I did complete the tasks you assigned me yesterday. I apologize if the change in plans once I got upstairs left you short-handed." It takes everything I can to apologize to her, especially since I know I didn't do anything wrong. When the CEO tells you to do something, you do it, and she damn well knows that. But she's getting too much evil joy out of putting me in my place.

"Hrrmph. You'll be staying behind the front desk today, that's for sure, because apparently, you can't be trusted to complete a simple delivery task upstairs."

I nod. "Yes, ma'am."

Someone clears their throat from the doorway and Ms. Maples and I both turn to look. "Excuse me. Ms. Hunnington?"

It's Jacob Wilkes, looking like he'd rather be anywhere than here. Speaking of, why is he here? The ground-floor coffee room isn't exactly his area of the building.

Dora looks at me with smug glee in her eyes, and I realize that Mr. Wilkes is not just looking *at me*. He's looking *for* me, which can't be good. "Yes, Mr. Wilkes?" I force myself to stand tall, refusing to wilt like some mild-mannered nitwit. If I'm getting fired for doing that photo shoot yesterday, I'll be pissed since

Mr. Blackstone is the one who demanded I do it in the first place. "Can I help you?"

He scans me up and down, not creepily but almost analytically, and then sighs. "I need you to come with me, please." He turns. "Dora, I overheard your assignment and I'm afraid Ms. Hunnington won't be at the front desk today. Please reorganize staff as you see fit."

She dips her chin, and I swear I can see her fighting the urge to fucking curtsy. "Of course, Mr. Wilkes. I have several other interns who are more than qualified to do what Ms. Hunnington isn't able to do." The dig is sharp and hits home, just as she intended.

Mr. Wilkes doesn't respond, just tilts his head at me, silently telling me to follow him. And like a damn puppy, I do, following him obediently across the foyer to the elevator, watching as he pushes the button for the top floor, and down the hallway to Mr. Blackstone's office.

"Wait here, please," Mr. Wilkes says after seating me in the plush leather chairs now rearranged in front of the desk. The click of the door closing sounds like a gunshot, right to the heart of my career. Dead before it even really started.

I feel like I'm a bag of silverware. Everything is jangly as my nerves go into overtime and my mind races through possible scenarios. Why am I here? Is it about yesterday? Was Mr. Blackstone as hot for me as I was for him?

Hold up, let's hit the brakes right there . . . that's only in my dreams. More likely, I'm about to get fired from my internship and lose any chance at a good reference or post-graduation job I might've had.

All my thoughts black out at that, the pit in my stomach sucking down all my hopes like a vortex, and I go vacant. My eyes mindlessly float around the room and I get my first real view of the CEO's office without the photoshoot madness. It's spectacularly opulent, with floor-to-ceiling windows that give a great view of the western skyline of the city. Right now, the shades are half-pulled and the sun's starting to peek through the upper windows, but still, the view is breathtaking.

The rest of Mr. Blackstone's office is just as tremendous and screams *him*. Rich, dark brown leather chairs sit in front of a huge oak desk. Behind it is another leather chair that looks damn-near like a throne, and the walls are lined in oak book-shelves.

After a minute that seems like an eternity, the door opens once again as Mr. Blackstone comes in, followed by Mr. Wilkes. I'm not sure if I should sit or stand, but I take the safer approach and rise, offering a hand. "Sir, you wanted to see me?"

He smiles subtly as he shakes my hand, the formality awkward considering how physically close we were just yesterday in this very room. "Have a seat, Arianna," he says, not turning around. "Jacob, you may go."

"We were supposed—" Jacob starts, then nods at the sharp look he receives. "Of course."

I don't have time to wonder what that was about as he leaves, closing the door behind him. Mr. Blackstone gestures to the chair behind me. "Please . . . have a seat."

I smile a little and sit down. "Thank you. I hope everyone was pleased with the shoot?" I'm fishing, trying to suss out why I'm here without asking outright.

To my surprise, he doesn't walk to his throne-like chair to sit, instead choosing to sit in the guest chair next to me. I get a whiff his cologne, or maybe that's just him . . . musk and leather and spice. He smells like power.

"Oh, yes . . . definitely," he replies, more professional and formal in his speech than yesterday, but dancing underneath is still the cocky bastard who whispered in my ear and spent last night invading my dreams. I don't know what the sudden change is about. Perhaps he realized he was being unprofessional and wants to reestablish that level of things.

My confused expression seems to say it all, though, and he chuckles. "I was actually rather impressed with your ability to adapt to the high-pressured situation, roll with the punches, if you will. I wonder if you are usually so adept at doing what you're told?"

The compliment is tied up in innuendo, and I'm getting whiplash from his switches between professionalism and definitely not-professional. "Thank you," I hedge. "I enjoy working at Morgan and was willing to take one for the team to insure a positive result for the photoshoot. I'm glad my work was to your liking." And like a hot knife through butter, I use the same tactic on him as well, mixing a small hint of naughty into my formal words.

He smirks, seemingly enjoying the back and forth play, then leans forward, placing his elbows on his knees. "Let's cut to the chase. I'm hiring a secretary and you're here to interview for the position."

I'm pretty sure my chin hits my knee. Is he fucking kidding me? His secretary? That's like a fifty-step leap from where I currently sit, and that gig ends in just two weeks. This could be a dream come true. This could be the start of everything. "Uhm . . . but . . . sure."

His smirk grows as he revels in my brain's apparent shutdown. "Take a deep breath, Miss Hunnington. I'll get you a drink."

At first, I think that he's going to get me a scotch or something from the small minibar on the side of the room that he goes over to, even though it's barely mid-morning, but when he comes back with a clear glass of soda water with a twist of lemon, I'm relieved. This is a real opportunity and I'd better take advantage of it.

He sits down across from me, crossing his legs and considering me while I take a sip. "Better?"

I nod and uncertainly hold the glass, not sure where to set it. He takes it from my hand and places it carelessly on his desk, definitely not something I would've ever done. "Thank you, Mr. Blackstone. I appreciate the opportunity. But might I ask . . . isn't this irregular? To consider me for a position as your secretary when I'm a front desk intern?"

Shit. I sound like I don't want the job. Of course I want it! But it does sound too good to be true, which in my experience is a definite red flag.

Liam chuckles, shaking his head. "You and Jacob. He'll like you. As to your question, I'm the boss and I can do what I want. I make the rules around here."

I sit up straighter in my chair, squaring my shoulders. "Of course, sir. Can I ask why me? As far as I'm aware, you didn't know I existed before yesterday."

He nods. "As I said, you handled yesterday's situation well. Tell me about yourself."

I lift an eyebrow, not sure how to take this. Shit, maybe I impressed him even more than he impressed me.

Wait. No, that's not possible. But if this is real, I need to get my head in the game, because a chance like this doesn't come around more than once.

"I'm a junior at the university, with a 3.83 GPA, majoring in international business with a focus in negotiations and contracts. My previous internship was with Orion Industries, where I mostly acted as a third set of eyes on contracts, learning the appropriate wording for their various industry-specific clauses. This year, I set my sights on Morgan Inc. as my first-choice internship and was fortunate enough to be tapped for the program. I've been working with Ms. Maples on the first floor, primarily as a receptionist, greeting visitors and answering the phone." I try to give him as much insight as I can while still being concise.

He nods. "And do you feel your time here has been beneficial?"

It sounds like a trick question. In fact, I'm rather sure it's a trap, so I tread carefully. "I do. While the work itself has been easier than my previous internship, seeing the inner workings of Morgan has been extremely valuable and I hope to continue here with part-time employment in the fall when I return to my full course load." Bob and weave the hazard and slam-dunk the request.

"What was the most difficult job you ever had?" he asks.

"This one might surprise you. Working at the Dairy Queen as a teenager." His eyebrows lift, just as I expected. "No, really. It was my first job, so I was nervous, and I had to take orders on a headset that cut in and out randomly, ensuring that approximately every fifth customer was mad as hell by the time they got to the window. I also had to make change without a calculator, fill orders in a timely manner, and clean the ice cream machine every night." I shiver for effect. "That thing was so gross, I could never eat ice cream again."

He grins. "That actually does sound pretty bad. Where do you see yourself in five years?"

These questions seem like Interviews 101, so maybe this is actually real. I start to get more hopeful. "Maybe closer to ten, but I'd like to be the CEO of an international firm, sitting somewhere like you are now," I state proudly.

"Ambitious. I like it," Liam says before grinning. "But it takes a lot of sacrifices to make it where I am."

I nod. "It does, but I'm willing to work hard. I have been for years and don't foresee that changing. I enjoy the challenges of business, how each new product or contract offers something totally unique and new."

He strokes his chin for a moment, and a new light comes to his eyes as he gazes at me. He's not looking at me professionally anymore, but like he did yesterday. I swear the temperature in the room just jumped a few degrees. "Now I'm going to ask you some questions that are totally off-record. If they unnerve you or offend you in anyway, you can get up and walk out that door and never come back. You'll get a letter of recommendation for your internship regardless of what you decide. But I assure you, the last thing you want to do is walk out that door."

Now what in the world could have him saying something like that? It's like he's still maintaining power, but he's not beating me over the head with it. I nod my head slowly, leaning forward in anticipation of where this is going. "Ask away."

Liam also leans forward, almost halving the space between us, and I feel the power in his body calling to me and my body responding. My pussy tingles, and I can feel my nipples starting to stiffen in my bra. "Tell me, doll, when's the last time you masturbated?"

What the actual fuck?! Leave! Just get up, walk out that door, and take the first elevator you can back down to the first floor. You don't need this! my mind seems to scream. *I knew this was too good to be true, and he's just like every other asshole, even if he's the only one to ever make my body respond the way it did yesterday. I'm worth more than this shit.*

I stand, looming over him intentionally for what I have to say.

I know my eyes are blazing fury and I want him to see every bit of that fire. "That is none of your business, Mr. Blackstone. I thought this was a serious job offer, and while you may think I'm the weaker player in this little back and forth chess game we've had going here, I assure that I am not some silly little girl awed by your audacity and arrogance. Contrary to some people's opinions, I'm not some whore, and I won't let you string me along, lording some false opportunity over me when what you really want is something much baser. I'm sure you can get that elsewhere."

I am dying inside at the loss of what I thought was going to be a real opportunity, the hope that had already started burning sparking out in a flashbang, leaving only the smoke to obscure my eyes. I'm proud of myself for standing up to his rude question, but the tears are already burning behind my eyes as I walk toward the door.

"Stop . . . wait." He says the command in a hard voice, and despite my desire to get out of here, he is my boss, and on some level, I think I'm hoping he'll apologize for the gross misstep.

I stop just shy of the door, and he gets up, stalking toward me. Unable to stop myself, I shrink and my back presses to the door. Though he doesn't cage me in with his arms, I feel just as trapped by his gaze, frozen as he stares down at me. "Did I misread you yesterday, Arianna? Did you enjoy the photoshoot with me?" His voice is softer, kinder, though still demanding.

I'm still mad as hell, but another side of me, the part that remembers how it felt being pressed against him yesterday and is experiencing the same buzz from his proximately now, is turned on, keeping me rooted in place. But I still call him out, refusing to back down. "You already know you didn't misread, but your question was way out of line."

He dips his chin. "My apologies then." He says the word as if he's tasting it, like a rare delicacy he's never experienced. I have a feeling that's true. He doesn't seem the type to apologize for much, so I nod back, silently and graciously letting him know I accept.

It feels like a reset of the chess board, like he's looking at me as something greater than a fucktoy intern to use for shock value and good times. It's a damn good thing, too, because I am more than that. But the dance begins again, more tactfully this time.

"Not to reignite your ire, but you said, 'contrary to some people's opinions'. What did you mean, Arianna?"

I can tell he's broaching carefully, and I respect his diplomacy for asking that way, but it's not a story I usually share. But something makes me want to tell him. Maybe it's the patient way he's waiting right now, not pressuring me, even though I know he desperately wants the story. It doesn't feel salacious but more that he wants to know my details. I let my eyes drop, not able to look him in the eye as I whisper my confession. "Not that it matters, but once upon a time back home, I went out with a boy. He bragged big and loud about things that didn't happen. It became a thing, and at some point, folks decided 'the lady doth protest too much' and began to tease me mercilessly. So I took control, embraced what they thought, even if they were wrong, and used it to my advantage. It's a part I've played well and often as it suited me, even if it's not the truth."

"And what part is that?" he asks, though he knows the answer.

I realize he wants me to say it. I lift my chin, meeting his eyes directly, and I find the strength in my core that I always need for this. "A whore."

He grins ferally at my use of the filthy word, like he likes it. His eyes bore into mine, lengthening the heavy moment and making me feel exposed, and though I'd die before admitting it, turning me on. The heat of my anger is morphing inside me, fraying around the edges and curling into an almost painful need. I can feel the weight of him even without actual contact, as if my skin yearns to touch his. This is what I felt yesterday, but amped up so much more.

"If I don't ask you questions, can I tell you what I know, Arianna?" he whispers huskily.

I bite my lip but give the slightest of nods.

His delight at the victory is in the tilt of his lips. "I know that you are a brilliant woman with a mind for business. I know that you are capable of speaking your mind, even when it borders on dangerous. I know that you see possibilities where others see risk." His eyes dip down before lifting to meet mine once again. "I know that your nipples are hard. I know that your pussy is wet for me. And I know that my cock is throbbing for you."

Everything he said is true, both the mental compliments and the physical realities. He steps closer, and I can finally feel the searing connection of our skin. It's heavenly bliss but also hell because it's so fucking hot. I vaguely wonder if it's this hot through the filter of our clothing, would our naked bodies would simply spontaneously combust on contact? My pussy clenches at the thought, and I barely hold back the whimper in my throat.

"So tell me, Arianna. You may not be a whore, but what are you? Are you a woman who wants to see where this might lead, what's behind door number one?" He places his hands on the door behind me, one on either side of my head, caging me in. "Or are you a woman who wants to play it safe? Tell me, doll."

At first, I don't say anything, truly contemplating my sexual choices for the first time in years. I made a decision a long time ago as a girl, in response to other's critiques, but I'm different, stronger now. Or maybe I'm weaker, because he definitely makes me consider giving in and just bending over his desk so he can take me. The sexy image makes my breath hitch, and I know he's scanning my face, looking for any hint of my thoughts.

At the last instant, a quiet little voice inside me whispers, lending me strength. *Remember, you're saving yourself. You don't need to sell yourself short.*

Liam tilts his hips against me, and I can't help but moan softly, my eyes rolling at the grinding pleasure. Liam quirks an eyebrow, and I clear my throat. I shouldn't tell him. Nobody knows, not even my best friend, Daisy. But I can't help myself.

With the last shreds of my strength and confidence, I place my hands on his chest and look him in the eyes. "I'm not a whore. I'm a virgin."

LIAM

"I'm a virgin."

The words hit me with the power of a supercharged lighting bolt. This sweet, sexy little angel in front of me is a virgin? Pure and untouched? You'd never know it with how flirty she is. Yesterday, she played with me like a kitten with a string.

She's almost breathless, aroused at my question, and I can see the tremulous pride in her shoulders. She's been hiding it, pretending to be the flirty little vixen. But she wants me to fuck her, even if she doesn't fully realize it yet. I can see it in her eyes.

"Are you telling me the truth, Arianna?" I hiss, still a seed of doubt in my head as I wonder if this is a game she's playing.

She nods, more confident this time. "Yes." And I see the raw honesty of her answer.

I bite my lip to hold in the groan but lean back a bit, letting my cock tent my pants and doing nothing to hide it. Let her see what she does to me. We both know she wants it. "Yes, sir," I correct her.

"Yes, sir," she repeats, looking at me through her lashes. "I've never had sex before."

"That's hard to believe," I challenge her. "You were very convincing yesterday."

"It's the truth," she says before her confidence falters. "I don't know why I'm telling you this. I've never told anyone." I can see the thought of running blooming in her eyes, and I circumvent her.

I press back closer, not touching her but just shy of it as I lean to her ear, letting the quiet of my whisper soften the filthy words I say to her. "You've never even had a man eat that sweet little pussy? Felt his fingers plunge into you until you were fucking his hand?"

She squirms a little, and I can tell she's thinking about it. "No. I've never even touched a man's dick before." My own cock jumps at the words on her lips, but I ignore it for the time being, keeping my focus on Arianna and the things I could do to her, make her feel.

"And would you like for me to give you that opportunity? To show you what it feels like to have my tongue dance on your clit until you scream in ecstasy . . . before I sink first my fingers and then my cock in that virgin pussy?"

She squirms more, a flush coming to her cheeks, and she looks so fucking sexy. I'm feeding the naughty side of her, tempting her, teasing her. We both want it. She just has to say yes.

146

"It would be inappropriate," she manages, her breathing heavy. "On so many levels."

"I'm an inappropriate person on so many dirty, wonderful levels," I retort with a grin. Fuck, I can almost picture sucking on her pretty pink pussy. I'd have her chasing my tongue and begging me to never stop. "Are you sure?"

"I–I–I'm saving myself," she admits, looking down into her lap.

"For whom?" I ask, interested. Is she dating someone? He must be a weak asshole if he hasn't claimed her yet. More importantly, she must not want him if I can push her buttons so easily, and yet she seems so surprised by her body's every response. I want these breathy sighs for my own, her orgasm at my hand, no one else's. Just mine.

Arianna whimpers again, biting her lip. "The perfect man. My future husband."

Oh, my sweet doll . . . so innocent. And so sexy. "I don't know if the perfect man exists, but there's a man who can make your eyes roll back in your head, a man who can make you scream so hard you forget who you are, a man who can make you want to be fucked so badly that you'll do anything to have it."

Her chest is heaving, her eyes almost glazed over as her lip trembles, and if I pushed the issue . . . I could have her now. "And you know who that man is?" I growl, leaning back. "That man is me."

But I realize I want more than just a quick fuck in my office. I want more than her cherry. I want her everything. It's been so long since I had to chase, to earn it . . . and when I do, it'll be so much sweeter.

She's quivering, practically shaking in her skin. "Mr. Black-stone . . . Liam . . . sir . . ."

No, my sweet little doll. It's not going to be that easy. Not for either of us.

I trace my fingertips down her cheek and along her jawline. She lifts her chin unconsciously, seeking my lips, but I hold back, teasing us both and letting it build. "Do you feel that electricity shooting through you, Arianna? Just from my touch along your silky skin?" I let my fingers drift lower with my words, from her neck down to her collarbone.

She arches her back in answer, not realizing what she's begging for, but I take advantage of the shudder that rushes through her, leaving the relative safety of her shoulder and dropping my hand to her thigh. I grab a firm handful, letting her know I'm there before caressing up to her ass.

"This ass pressed against my cock drove me wild yesterday. You may not have answered the question, but I will. I jacked off last night to thoughts of you, your dark hair twisted up in my fist as I plunged into your hot pink slit, the feel of your slick wetness coating me in your cream. I pumped my cock, rock-hard for you, up and down . . . up and down . . ."

I trail off, realizing that she's working her hips along me with my words, mimicking what I say. And though it feels amazing, and I could come from that alone right now, this is about her, not me. I want to make her come like she never has before, pressed right against my door and under my hand.

Her rocking motion has inched her skirt up her thighs, and now I can feel more of her heated flesh. I let my fingers roam higher too, until I feel the lacy edge of her panties. I growl when I discover how soaked she is. "Fuck, doll. You're dripping for me. I'm going to be the one who fills this sweet virgin pussy first."

She tenses slightly but doesn't resist. I want her at ease, though, so I reassure her. "Not today, not like this, but soon, you're going to be begging me to fuck you, to fill you with my fat cock."

I almost expect her to sass back with some sharp retort, but a glance at her face tells me that she's far too gone for thoughtful dialogue. Her mouth hangs open, panting for breath, and her eyes are closed, lost to the new sensations I'm piling onto her body.

I dip a finger inside her panties, getting instantly covered in her honey, and let my finger run from her opening to her clit and back, slow and easy so she doesn't spook. She cries out, and I cover her mouth with my own, silencing her pleasure with a kiss.

Her hands weave into my hair, pulling me into her, and she kisses me back passionately. Our tongues tangle as we devour each other, sharing breath and space with the ease of long-time lovers and the fire of first-time fuckers.

I pull back, needing oxygen and needing her. Meeting her eyes, I tell her, "Another time, another place, I'm going to have you screaming my name to the heavens above. I'll teach you that heaven is being impaled on my cock and riding me until your heart feels like it's ready to explode. But this time . . . you have to be silent."

She nods but finally finds herself enough to speak. "Mighty confident in yourself, aren't you?"

I smirk, glad she's with me and not wholly lost to the waves of pleasure sweeping her body. "You have no idea, Arianna. I have a deal for you. Let me touch you, show you that I can give you pleasure you've only dreamed of. I promise I will let you walk out that door still a virgin, but one who knows the amazing things her body can do."

She's bucking her hips against the air, searching for something she doesn't understand yet. Suddenly, she freezes and narrows her eyes at me. "And the secretary job?"

Smart girl. Good girl.

Her brains turn me on even more than her body, if that's possible. I take her chin in my hand, forcing her eyes to mine so she sees me clearly. I growl, "*This* has nothing to do with *that*. You are not a whore, Arianna, and I never thought you were. I think we both know that job was yours when you walked in the door this morning. And this—us, one way or the other—doesn't change that for you." I want her to come to me freely, to want me and want what I can do to her, not want what I can do for her career. She seems to feel the same way and is soothed by my blunt words.

"Yes, Liam . . . sir. Please." Her sweet surrender, the breathy sigh of her acquiescence, is music to my ears and dynamite to my lust.

I drop my hands to the hem of her skirt, lifting it so it bunches around her waist. The first sight of her panty-covered pussy has my cock throbbing so hard I have to squeeze it to stop myself from coming. She's soaked through, red lacy panties that are so naughty . . . but I know what's underneath is untouched. Reaching up, I hook her waistband while staring in her eyes. "Let me see your pretty little pussy."

She reaches down, taking my hands in hers for a moment before submitting and letting me tug her panties down. I push them down her sexy thighs and beyond her knees before they fall to the floor and she steps out of them. I fight the urge to drop to my knees to taste her, knowing that it'd be too much, too soon, but thankfully, the sweet, musky scent of her arousal envelops me and I'm drawn to seek out the source.

I slide my knee between hers, forcing her legs to spread wide and expose her pussy to the cool air of the room. She gasps, arching, and I hear the wet sound of her drenched lips spreading for me.

I let my finger skim her pussy again, from opening to clit and back around, making loops around her sensitive core but never staying exactly where she wants me. I want to drive her wild with desire, so much so that she forgets her self-imposed rules and gives in to what we both want so badly. She moans, and I remind her, hot breath in her ear, "Shh . . . quiet. We don't want people outside to hear your pleasure. That's mine . . . yours . . . *ours*."

She bites her lip, trying hard to obey. I give in too, focusing my attention on her hard clit, feeling her heartbeat pulsing as she gets higher and higher, closer to coming on my hand. "Is this where you want me? Right here on your little clit, rubbing it hard and fast to get you off like a naughty girl in my office against the door?"

"Fuck, Liam, I'm close. It's different . . .feels so good . . .had no idea . . ." She rambles and my ego swells at the mess I'm making of her. Arianna Hunnington coming undone is one of the most spectacularly beautiful sights I've ever had the pleasure to witness.

Needing to see the full breadth of her undoing, I order her, "That's it, doll. Come for me. Let that pretty virgin pussy come all over my fingers and coat me with your sweet-girl cum."

She shudders, crying out, and I cover her lips with a kiss. She's not aware enough to kiss me back, but I keep kissing her open mouth, muffling her sexy noises. I can feel the throbbing pull as her pussy clenches emptily, wanting to be filled, but I let her ride out her orgasm with my fingers still blurring on her clit, drawing as much pleasure as I can out of her body. "Oh, God," she moans, coming back to Earth.

I slow my attention to her clit, then lift my fingers to my

mouth, sucking them clean and finally getting to taste her. "Fuck, you taste like candy, doll. I want to eat you up."

She can see that I'm considering dropping to my knees to do just that, and she stops me, a bit of awkwardness taking her body. "Mr. Blackstone. Uhm . . . Liam?"

I grin. "Arianna, I think you can call me Liam, considering what we just did."

She smirks, fire returning to her eyes as the haze of lust clears. "Fair enough, sir," she says, sassing me with the name I told her to call me as we began. I nod, letting her know that works too, and her smile grows exponentially. "Liam, that was . . . wow."

"That was only the beginning, a perfect start to more." I cup her face in my hands, giving her a series of soft kisses to soften her up. "Come work for me as my secretary. Let me teach you the business side you want to know, and let me show you the wonders your body is capable of."

I see a flash in her eyes, so fast I'm not sure if I imagined it. "And what if I only want the business lessons? Only want those experiences to further my career?"

My heart stops as my eyes lock on hers, wide with shock. Really? After coming like a damn freight train on my hand, she thinks to deny that? Deny herself and me of that pleasure, all for some Prince Charming fantasy she dreamed up as a child?

I hate the thought of it and honestly don't know if I can handle being in an office every day with her without touching her, but I'm a gentleman on occasion, and this is one of the situations that requires that of me. I step back, mourning the loss of contact. "If that's what you want, Arianna."

She follows my steps, matching me and pressing her curves

against mine once again as she wraps her arms around my neck. "That's not what I want, but I needed to be sure."

I look at her in confusion for a second and then her smile and words click. "It was a test? You're testing me." She looks a bit abashed but nods. "Doll, I'll let that one pass because I understand why, but do not test me again. I'll keep that in mind when we begin your *lessons* tomorrow." I let her wonder if I mean business or physical, but honestly, I plan on testing her limits for both. "You have two weeks left of your internship, during which you need to impress me enough to procure an offer of fall employment. If you were to work for me, you'd learn more at my side than your university would teach you in years, so I'd think you'd want that opportunity. I have two weeks to impress you too, enough to get between those sweet thighs and fill that untouched pussy with my cock. I know that would be an experience neither of us would ever forget, so I definitely want that honor. The two are not mutually inclusive or exclusive but exist as co-goals for us both. Understood?"

She smiles back, a full grin that lets me know the game is on. Luckily for me, I'm a damn good player and I'm not afraid to cheat if it wins me what I want . . . her. Body, mind, and soul. "Deal," she says, sealing her fate and making a deal with the devil.

"Okay, Ms. Hunnington," I say, emphasizing her name to let her know we're working in the professional realm now. "Please check in with Jacob on the way out. He can give you the appropriate contracts to sign for working at this level. I trust you can go over the contracts yourself?"

She nods. "Yes, Mr. Blackstone. Of course."

"Good. Then spend the afternoon with Jacob doing that and whatever else he needs. I'm afraid I'm out of the office this afternoon so I won't be able to hold your hand as you adjust to your new role." Every word is clipped and professional, but my cocky grin is full of mischief.

And the clock begins on what promises to be an interesting two weeks.

ARIANNA

Dear Diary,

When I was twelve, I had butter for the first time. Oh, sure, my mother had put plenty of yellow stuff on top of bread, mashed potatoes, all that. But it was margarine or some other substitute.

But for my twelfth birthday, Grandpa took me to a nice restaurant, and I felt so grown up. It was the summer after Grandma died, and looking back, I think he knew it would be the last big dinner he and I had together. We sat down at the table, and I remember he ordered shrimp scampi for himself and lobster for me. "But Grandpa, I hate seafood," I complained, and he shushed me, murmuring something about frozen fish sticks not being real seafood, but that was all I'd ever had.

"Arianna, you're going to change your mind with this."

When the food came . . . oh, my God, it was delicious! Even the bread tasted different, and after I mowed through the whole meal like I hadn't eaten in a week, I asked Grandpa why. He smiled, looking a little sad as he set his knife down. "Honey, sometimes, having the real thing is worth what you have to pay for it. Sometimes, it's a financial cost, like butter. Sometimes, it's something else. But you have to decide whether the reward is worth the cost."

Those words were running around my head all last night as I thought about what Liam and I did in his office. Holy fuck, was it intense. I have never experienced something so raw. And I think the reality of his fingers on my clit instead of my own or a toy was well worth the price I had to pay . . . some painful, embarrassing honesty and one appropriately-pitched temper tantrum at his abrupt jump into the deep end.

I think we both came out of that office with a better idea of who I am. And though I might've been called a whore before, I refuse to actually be one. But I am a hard worker, a fast learner, and a sure bet to use this opportunity to make the best future for myself that I can. Professionally, not on my knees.

I can't believe I'm going to be able to pick his brain for the next two weeks! I can't believe he wants to fuck me in the next two weeks either.

***

"HEY, SUPER NERD!" I GUSH INTO THE PHONE, NEEDING MY best friend right now. Daisy Phillips is truly a nerd . . . in all the best ways, cute, with black-rimmed glasses and just a hint of shyness when she meets new people, and an intelligence for numbers most people can't begin to fathom. Drawing her as a dorm-mate and becoming friends with her is one of the best things to ever happen to me.

"Oh, my gosh, Ari! It's been forever. I've missed you!" she gushes back.

It hasn't been that long since we talked, just a week or so, but for girls who are used to seeing each other daily, it seems like ages. With a sigh, I realize we won't ever be roomies again. When I came to my internship, I took a small short-term rental for the summer to be closer to work and Daisy moved in with her boyfriend, Connor. Her boyfriend who also happens to be a math professor at the university we attend. In fact, he was her math professor. But somehow, they beat the odds, ones that Daisy or Connor could probably calculate in their heads if you wanted the real statistics, which I don't. I just care that she's happy, and she definitely seems to be that.

"How's pseudo-married life treating you?" I ask, knowing they're not married yet.

"So good! Seriously, I found out that Connor can cook, like actual food, not Ramen and canned beefaroni." She laughs, knowing that those are the quintessential college kid foods and arguably some of my comfort-food favorites, a little slice of poor-kid home life away at school. "What about you? Has your internship gotten any better?"

I take a big breath, knowing this is going to be a major chatter session. "Chica, sit down, okay? I need to brain dump a massive amount of 'what the fuck' on you because I could really use your advice, okay?"

I can hear the rustling on her end as she finds a place to curl up. "Okay, hit me."

I give her the rundown of my delivery-turned-photoshoot, including every naughty detail of how Liam felt pressed against me, how thick and hard his cock got while the camera was clicking away, and how turned on I'd been. Luckily, she's used to hearing dirty talk like that from me so she doesn't so much as stutter until I tell her about my interview and the ensuing madness.

"Uhm, what?" she exclaims. "You're a what? Our connection must have dropped because I could've sworn you said you're a virgin, Ari." Her voice is full of confusion.

"I did, Daisy. I know, I'm sorry for not telling you, especially when you were going through all that stuff with Connor, but you always believed the façade I put on and I didn't know how to go back and straighten that out. Forgive me?" I beg, hoping she does because I don't want this to be a stumble in our friendship.

"Of course, I forgive you. It's your body, your secret, your story, but I do hope you'll tell me why the big act one day." I can hear the hurt in her voice.

"I will, I promise. But it's water under the bridge, and I need help with where I am now. Liam offered to let me complete my internship in his office, which is basically a dream come true, with a cherry topper that if I do well, he'll hire me part-time when school starts. No-brainer, right? But it's all tied up in him wanting to pop my cherry, which when I'm clear-headed and not lust-addled, sounds sketchy as fuck. But Daisy, there's something about him. I've never felt anything like this."

My brain flashes back to him crowding me against the door to finger my pussy and the way he savored my taste from his fingers. He is the Devil. And I made a deal with him. A deal for my body and my brain. Daisy interrupts my thoughts. "That sounds familiar." I can hear the smirk in her voice.

"I hear you, but this is different," I argue. Glancing at the clock, I realize I need to get ready for work or I'll be late, and that's a definite no-no. I hustle to my closet, grabbing a pencil skirt and blouse and slipping them on awkwardly as I hold the phone to my shoulder.

She laughs. "To-may-toe, to-mah-toe. Point is, you've been saving yourself for some special guy. Maybe that's the one you marry, maybe it's not. But it should be someone who makes you *feel*, someone you know will make it good, so maybe that's Liam? If so, hit that, girl. If not, that's okay. And you can still take advantage of the chance to learn as much as possible. You said he specifically said he'd still teach you, even if you didn't fuck him, right?"

I scoff. "Of course, or I'd have been out of there."

She laughs. "Exactly. You're a smart woman, so don't let him dictate your future. Choose for you . . . for both work and personal. And he can damn well play catch-up if he's not next to you every step of the way, but something tells me he's going to be right by your side or the one pulling you along."

I grin. "Damn, girl. When did you get so wise?"

"Hey, I went through a bit of hell and had to chase what I wanted and fight for it too, so I've got some advice skills. I'm just glad you're calling now instead of waiting like I did. Just be careful, honey." She's right. When Daisy finally talked to me about Connor, it'd only been because someone had forced her hand and she'd been freaking out.

"But look how well that turned out, chica. Thanks so much, truly." We say our goodbyes and hang up. I'm struck once again by what a great friend she is. But with that thought, I realize I need to hustle.

I double-check my makeup and hair, slip on my nicest pair of heels, and look in the mirror one more time. I look like a powerful woman, ready to embrace her future. Whether that's in the boardroom or the bedroom or both remains to be seen, but for now, I'm ready to roll.

WALKING INTO THE LOBBY, I PASS DORA ON MY WAY toward the elevator.

"Arianna!"

I stop, going over to be polite. "Hi, Dora. Sorry you're getting shorthanded here. Are they sending someone to help?"

Dora shakes head. "Not yet. Seriously, is this for real? I send you upstairs and the next day you're the boss's secretary?"

She looks me up and down, and I can read her thoughts as if she spoke them aloud. She's thinking the same damn thing people always think when they only see the obvious, that I'm some ditzy floozy who gets by on her looks. They never stop to consider that maybe I succeed in spite of my looks, not because of them. I do have a brain, and I'm quite adept at using it.

"Yes, apparently so. It's a great opportunity and I'm looking forward to it," I say as politely as I can, though my inner bitch wants to snark at Dora for daring to assume she knows a damn thing about me after sending me for coffee for two months.

"Hrrmph, there is such a thing as paying your dues, Ms. Hunnington. You'd do well to know your place, especially considering you're only going to be here for such a short period of time. Just two more weeks, right?" Her voice is saccharin, as if it's a pity I'll be leaving, but I know she'd be happy if I turned and left, never to return, right now.

"Speaking of knowing my place, guess I'd better get upstairs," I reply, just as fake-sweet. And with a small wave, I head to the elevator. Kill them with kindness, I think. Play the part.

After the elevator doors close, the nerves really set in and I wonder if I'm going to get upstairs to discover this is some elaborate ruse at my expense.

Haha . . . gotcha. You didn't really think I wanted you on the top floor, did you? Stupid girl.

But I quiet the doubts and self-talk with a few slow, deep breaths, even if the other three people on the elevator look at me oddly. I don't know if it's because they're wondering who I am and why I'm going upstairs or if it's because I'm doing breathing exercises. Either way, they exit, and finally, I'm alone for the final leg of the long elevator ride.

I really don't know what to expect. While I was a receptionist, I wasn't a secretary. I think I know the basics. I mean, it's answering phones, typing stuff, probably fetching coffee . . .

but something tells me that Mr. Blackstone is going to want something sweeter than sugar.

The thought thrills me and scares me all at the same time, and before I know it, the elevator doors open and I step out. Everything looks like business as usual. Everyone knows what they're doing . . . and they're going about doing it.

Yep, I think as I take a deep, nervous breath, *everyone here is a total pro . . . except you.*

I push away my momentary self-doubt and remember that I'm getting a chance to get plugged directly into the brain trust, to learn from the best, and that's like an electric charge to my spine.

After a moment, I head toward Mr. Blackstone's office and knock on the door.

I wait for a moment and then peek inside. He isn't here. Neither is Jacob.

I glance about and realize that in the external office, another small desk has been added overnight. Mr. Wilkes's desk remains in the same spot, but the line of chairs on the right side of the room has been replaced with an oak desk and cabinet. I walk over and see a note taped to the computer screen. It says Arianna on the front, and I flip it over.

In a meeting until 10:30. I expect to have these things done for me by the time I'm back.
Coffee, black.
One egg sandwich from the 2nd floor, over-easy. I have a tab.
Read the Eastern Regional Report and have a synopsis prepared.
Your pussy, nice and wet for me.

Under the last line is a cursive L with a little swirl of ink underneath, and excitement thrums through me. I shiver as I think about how his fingers felt on me, and my clit starts to throb, wanting it again. If that's what he's gonna do to me with a simple note, I'm going to have to start bringing a change of panties.

Looking over my desk, I find the report and peruse it, getting the gist of how the eastern region is doing, complete with projections and areas of growth. A quick call down to the second floor informs me that they'll happily deliver Mr. Blackstone's sandwich right at the stroke of ten thirty, so that's taken care of. After that, I search for the coffee maker, finding it hidden behind a sliding cabinet door on the minibar. I giggle a bit at that, like the coffee pot can't be out for eyes to see? I grin at the thought, though I realize it's probably more testimony to my poor upbringing than his wealthier bourgeois style. It's a bit complicated to work the thing, but after a few minutes, I have it set up and ready to go.

I stop for a moment, realizing that I've completed my to-do list, and I glance around, once again awed by the splendor of the room. It is truly stunning, and looking out at the city skyline through the floor-to-ceiling windows, my breath's taken away again.

A sudden urge comes over me and I go behind Mr. Blackstone's desk, running my hand over the plush leather of his chair. This is where I want to be. The queen of my destiny. Turning the chair to the side, I do what probably every secretary in history has done and sink down into it, feeling it envelope me as I feel the bolt of power from sitting on the throne. Wiggling back, a soft sigh escapes my lips.

"A chair fit for a king," I murmur, "or queen."

Knowing it's wrong but not able to help myself, I kick my legs up on his desk, just for a second, and my mind wanders to a future where this is my reality. Yep, this is the life for me.

I must lose track of time for a moment because I'm surprised when the door springs open. I jump to my feet as Liam walks in, every bit the powerful CEO. He's wearing navy blue today, not gray, but other than that, he's just as sexy as yesterday, and my heart thumps in my chest as I take him in.

He pauses, his eyes roving over me. The hair on my forearms stands up as I blush, knowing I'm busted. "Mr. Blackstone."

"Getting comfortable, I see," he says with an arrogant smirk. Behind him, I can see Mr. Wilkes, looking not too pleased.

"I . . . umm," I stammer before hanging my head. "I'm sorry."

He chuckles as he walks toward the windows. He gestures to the space next to him, and I obediently stand beside him, following his gaze over the city below as I brush a lock of hair behind my ear. "You don't have to explain or apologize. You said this is your dream, so you're checking things out. It's enticing, no?"

He leans over, and I'm enveloped by the cologne that I love. Sweet leather. I have to learn what the hell the name of that stuff is because partnered with his natural scent, it's like an aphrodisiac straight to my core.

"It was my dream once, too, and I made it my reality," he says, but he's not looking at his office or the view. He's looking at me.

I gulp, and he glances behind us. There's a soft click, and I realize that Jacob has left and we're alone once again. Liam moves to his chair, sitting down comfortably, the crown invisible but no less present with the power emanating from him. "Did you complete your list, Arianna?"

He glances down my body pointedly, but I'm not that easy. I remember Daisy's advice to be strong and see if he stays with me. "I did, Mr. Blackstone," I say, purposefully using the name to differentiate what mode we're currently in. "Breakfast will be delivered in minutes. Would you like your coffee now?"

He dips his chin, an amused smirk on his face, like he knows what I'm doing and is getting a kick out my attempt to act unaffected by him. I'm sure he can see the flush on my face, but I press on, grabbing a mug and filling it with the dark brew. The aroma fills my senses, lessening the effect of his cologne and waking me up even without the caffeine dose. I set the coffee down in front of him, but instead of drinking it, he asks, "And the Eastern Region report?"

"Yes, sir. It's in your inbox." I pick up the file from the corner of his desk. "Would you like the synopsis?"

He gestures widely with his hands, giving me the floor. I come around to his side, placing the folder in front of him and turning to the report so he can follow along as I speak. "Second-quarter figures were trending up, and that was expected to continue. However, third-quarter shows stabilizing numbers."

He interrupts me. "Why did you look at the second quarter if I told you I wanted a synopsis of the third-quarter report?"

I glance at him in surprise. "Because without the relevant framework, the figures are useless. They're only helpful in the scheme of up, down, or staying the same. Knowing that we had $55 million in sales could be cause for celebration or to close the doors, but that's only knowable in context." He inclines his head, and I think I might've jumped a notch in his estimation. "As I was saying, the stabilizing figures indicate . . ." and I continue a brief summarization.

I'm standing over him as he sits, a power position, but it's a false show because we both know who the boss is in this room. And though he's nodding along as I give my report, he's distracting me, letting his fingertips trace along my arm and up my thigh. "Please focus, Arianna. Being focused is the only way to succeed, and you do want to succeed, don't you?" He smirks at me. The cocky bastard knows what he's doing to me.

Suddenly, he snaps, "Enough. Excellent summarization. Now, about the rest of the list . . ." He closes the file, setting it aside and pulling me between his spread legs, my ass resting along the edge of the desk.

I knew he silently promised this, but there's no way we could do this every day and actually get work done. And while the idea of seeing what Mr. Blackstone has to offer, I'm here for more than that. I have a goal, and getting lost in how badly I want him isn't helping me accomplish that.

Liam, though, seems to be unconcerned. "Did you complete your final task? Is this pussy wet and ready for me?"

I bite my lip, hedging my answer. "I am . . . wet, but I don't know about ready."

The smug tilt of his lips says he thinks otherwise. "Have you ever heard of edging?"

"No," I rasp, my head spinning as he cups my breast through my blouse, his fingers tugging on my stiffening nipple through my thin bra. "What's —"

Before I can finish, he lifts me onto the desk, his hands slipping up my skirt along my inner thighs to palm my pussy through my damp panties.

"Edging," he whispers huskily in my ear, sounding almost like a teacher or instructor, "is when I get you so close to the edge, but right before you fall off, I let up. Then, when you calm down a little, I do it again . . . and again . . . and again. It's sweet, sweet torture, but oh, so delectable."

"Oh, God," I moan as his hand massages my pussy, rolling his fingers between my lips, soaking the fabric of my panties. "What in the hell are you doing?"

"Lift up," he hisses, and when I do, he slides my panties down my thighs, tucking them into his desk drawer with an evil grin. I wonder what he's going to do with them later, but the thought flies out of my head when he starts tweaking my clit. "I'm teaching you, Babydoll. I'm showing you that patience is essential, along with control and the ability to hold steady, even when your body screams for something else. Like last night. Do you think I went home and jacked off as I thought about how you will look with that 'O' on your face as my cock slides inside you?"

I moan, his powerful fingers doing amazing things to me as he talks dirty to me. "Oh, fuck. Did you?"

His massage of my core is so good that I'm almost ready to come, but he pulls back, chuckling. "No," he whispers. "I didn't. Just like you aren't . . . until I'm ready to *let* you."

His words hit me hard, and I whimper, looking at him. "Please," I moan, my body quivering. "I need — "

"Please, what?" Liam asks, lifting an eyebrow, his fingers still touching me but not moving at all.

"Please, sir, let me come."

He starts again, bringing me to the brink with his fingers on my clit and teasing along my entrance. I desperately need more, his finger inside me or for him to stay focused on my clit, but he stops again. It's like he said, sweet torture as my pussy feels swollen, puffy, and aching, my fingers gripping the edge of his desk so hard I've got cramps threatening in my forearms. But I can only think of one thing.

"Please," I beg again.

He bends closer, eyes locked onto my pussy, and though I

know I should tell him to stop, I can't. He's increasing the price, but when his tongue swipes across my aching clit, it's an expense I'll gladly pay. "Oh, God," I cry out, trying so hard to be quiet.

The feel of his tongue on my pussy is more than I could have ever imagined. Hot, wet, and a completely different sensation from his fingers. And when he moans against my sensitive skin, the vibration nearly sends me over.

"Fuck, doll. You taste like candy, so sweet I want to drink you down." I think that's exactly what he's doing as he covers my pussy with his mouth, sucking my sensitive skin and flicking his tongue across my engorged clit.

I can feel my body building up to something massive, some-thing I've never experienced before. If this is edging, I want to do it all the time. I suspect it has more to do with the man between my thighs than some trick of orgasm denial though.

He pulls me tighter against his face, my pussy chasing his tongue unashamedly. "You want to come?" he says. I nod, whimpering. "What are you willing to give for it?" he asks, stroking a finger once over my lips. I cry out. I'm closer than ever, but he knows just what he's doing.

My mouth drops open, then I shut it with a snap as I glare at him, the denial starting to fray the edges of my patience. There's no way I'm going to give up this easily, this quickly, but I'll be damned if he doesn't tempt me. I open my mouth again, looking down at him. "Loyalty."

"I don't want your loyalty." He snickers. "I'll earn that in time. No . . . I want your obedience."

I gulp, knowing I'm handing him some of the power that he promised me yesterday . . . but not too much. "But what do you want me to do?"

Liam grins. "Stay still and let me fuck you with my tongue. Don't make a sound."

I nod, gritting my teeth as he massages me, spreading my lips wide open to his gaze. It's so hard not to cry out, my chest aching and my fingers knotting as I grip the desk tightly. He slips the tip of his tongue into my pussy, just barely penetrating me, but it's so much better. It's a hint of what I really want, what I need, but he's still teasing me, barely thrusting inside as he lazily rubs his thumb across my clit.

I can feel the fire building in my stomach, and I'm about to explode when there's a knock at the door. "Mr. Blackstone? There's something that needs your attention."

"Fuck," Liam hisses, his mouth and fingers deserting me.

He pushes his chair back and adjusts his pants, pulling me from the desk and handing me the folder he'd set aside. "Sit in the chair, doll."

"What?" I ask, shocked. "Are you—"

My body obeys while my mind catches up, and as I walk from between his legs, he swats my ass with a soft smack. I look back sharply, and he grins, making sure I see him wiping my juices from his mouth and sucking his fingers clean.

I've barely set my ass in his chair when he yells out, "Come in."

LIAM

I'm hard as a rock and glad my desk covers me as Jacob and Melvin Jackson walk in the door. Jacob leads the way, looking around like he's probably guessed what was going on with Arianna, but he doesn't know for sure, and I'm going to keep it that way as long as I can to save myself from the lecture. Melvin is a lanky, odd-looking fellow who could double as Norman Bates with glasses, and he always comes off as nervous for some reason. He was already working at Morgan when I took over and has been helpful during the transition to my leadership. Not sure exactly how he got that gig because technically, he doesn't even work on this floor, but he showed up one day with some interesting figures and some intel to share, so he's been useful, at least.

"Yes?" I ask, tilting my head. "You did say it was important?"

Melvin looks to Jacob, who nods. Jacob intends the nod to give Melvin permission to speak, but Melvin reads it incorrectly and takes it as the go-ahead to sit in my guest chair. The one right next to Arianna.

He looks over at her, and I notice his eyes stay strictly on her face, not scanning her lush curves. He might've just gone up a small notch in my estimation because if he'd looked at her body, I would've been tempted to teach him a lesson about looking at what's mine.

Wait . . . what? She's not mine, and I'm not some Neanderthal. But the urge to mark her, claim her, sits in my gut like a stone. It might not be politically correct, and I suspect she'd kick me in the balls if I verbalized my thoughts aloud, but it's the possessive impulse I feel. I wonder if Jacob and Melvin can smell the sweetness of her sex in the air of my office or if they realize why Arianna's cheeks are flushed? I waver between pride, knowing that she's only that undone because of me, and fury, greedy that only I see her that way.

Melvin reaches out a hand to Arianna, "Melvin Jackson, Vice President of Business Analytics." She takes his hand for a quick shake, introducing herself too.

And then Melvin turns his attention to me. Finally. "Sir, I just wanted to say that I think you've done a great job since taking over as CEO this summer. The figures show a significant uptick in public perception and stock indexes are expected to reflect that."

"Appreciated, but if that's all, Melvin, I'm really—"

"But there are whispers," Melvin says quickly. He glances back at Arianna, obviously uncertain whether he should say what he wants to in front of her.

I glance to Jacob, who nods. Apparently, I need to hear whatever Melvin is dishing. "It's okay, Melvin. You can speak freely in front of Arianna." My words elicit similar reactions in them both, eyes widening and eyebrows raising. Arianna quickly schools her features, though I can read her delight at getting some insight on the inner workings of Morgan. Melvin still looks unsure, but he continues.

"Sir, when you took over, you brought with you a . . . well, some people are calling it a 'rockstar' attitude. You have to understand, Morgan has always had a more traditional corporate culture. We've succeeded for years on a solid business model of predicting the market and being there before the competitors. But the changes you are implementing? There is concern that perhaps you're more flash than substance. That perhaps you simply don't understand what has made Morgan the company it is today, what we stand for, or who we are."

"They brought me in to shake things up, and my track record speaks for itself," I reply. "Melvin, this company lost millions last year and needs a fast turnaround to stay at the forefront of the market you're trying to predict. I don't want Morgan to follow along like sheep, chasing dollars and market shares. I want to create the market trends, have the other companies scrambling to catch up with us. Just give it some time and you'll see. My way works."

He nods but is still unsatisfied. "But sir, I think you'll see in our third-quarter reports that sales are at respectable levels, and moving into the fourth quarter, I predict we'll see similar numbers, maybe even an increase of one to two percent, which could be extremely beneficial for Morgan's bottom line."

I sigh. "Third-quarter reports? I was just going over the Eastern Region report this morning," I say, giving Arianna a quick glance. "While the numbers look good, if you compare them with the second quarter, you can see that they're trending down." Arianna uncrosses and recrosses her legs, drawing my attention. I offer her a smile, acknowledging that I'm repeating her synopsis from this morning. But I didn't need her to tell me that. I already knew. I'd just wondered if she'd take initiative and what her summary of the report would show . . . a regurgitation of the numbers or a more thoughtful analysis? Luckily, my smart girl knows her stuff and dug deeper.

"And beyond the quarter to quarter changes, look back to last year's third quarter. We're down almost nine percent since then. Unacceptable, especially considering we had a product availability increase in the area. Status-quo thinking doesn't get status-quo results. If we stay stagnant and don't change our MO, Morgan will fail, and I refuse to let that happen. So, innovative thinking and new possibilities are the direction we're heading."

Melvin bows his head for a moment, frustration written in the lift of his shoulders, which are nearing his ears. He sighs. "Very well, sir. If you're certain that is the best path, perhaps you should amp up the 'rockstar' a bit for the board then. Really sell them on your plan, explain your business model of change, and that they should believe in your ideas. Get them on board in a big way so that we can be a team again."

It's not a bad idea. But I'm not used to explaining myself. I usually do my analysis with Jacob and we get to work, creating success where none existed before. But he might have a point in this particular case since the board and many of the executives are rather old-school, Melvin included. They'd definitely prefer more intel. I'm just not certain whether I want to give it to them. "I'll take that under advisement, Melvin. If there's nothing else?" It's an obvious dismissal, and he gets up, nodding at me, then Arianna. He basically ignores Jacob as he walks to the door and strides out.

Jacob looks at me, nonplussed. "You could've handled that better." He plops down into the chair Melvin just vacated. He doesn't need an invite or permission since he's my best friend and my right-hand guy at the office.

I shake my head. "It's the truth. Do you believe that guy?"

"You didn't really give him a chance to speak. Some of the stuff he told me . . ." Jacob says after a moment. "I don't know. Like, some of the executives are uncomfortable with your new direction and chatting among themselves. I think one comment he says he heard was 'this isn't the eighties, and he isn't Gordon fucking Gekko. He said he might've even overheard the word 'takeover' from one, but he wasn't sure who it was. Hallway chatter, apparently."

"No one has given me that impression. I've gotten nothing but praise from the board," I muse. "And they asked me here, knowing Morgan needed some drastic action to stay solvent." It's times like this that I appreciate Jacob. He's my sounding board and trusted advisor. "What do you think? Should I be worried?"

Jacob scratches at the stubble on his jaw. "I don't know. I haven't heard anything that's bad, but Melvin is part of a certain inner circle. They might be whispering behind closed doors. I could see the comment being made by some people."

"Fuck them. They're comparing me to a fictional asshole," I growl, hating the comparison. "Why bring me in to begin with if they want me to conform to the same old thinking? All the hoopla that surrounds me is just the window dressing. It's called creating buzz. We've done this before, us against the old regime. We're good and what we do works."

Jacob shrugs, unconcerned. "You're good, Liam. But you have rocked some boats." He glances at Arianna and then back to me. I eye him, letting him know in our nonverbal shorthand to watch his step because I can see where this is going.

"Pulling up Arianna to be your secretary probably didn't help matters. It's raised some eyebrows. And I'm not going to ask what you two have been doing for the past thirty minutes."

Arianna shrinks in her chair, her cheeks blushing furiously. If there was any doubt, she might as well have shouted from the rooftop what we've been up to. Jacob is broaching on some treacherous waters, and I warn him off so he doesn't piss me off too badly. I snap, "Jacob, watch it."

"Look, whatever you two do outside the office is none of my business. On your own time, that's all well and good. But here? We need to stay on task. We're mid-transition and implementing big changes that make folks uncomfortable. Adding in some crazy 'rockstar' shit like fucking an intern in your office" —he turns to Arianna— "or fucking the CEO, is dangerous." Arianna gasps, horrified and embarrassed at his words.

I growl, ready to tear into Jacob, but he holds up a staying hand, and only because of years of friendship do I let him speak. "HR has already been hounding me about why a new job was created without their procedures being followed. You can hire and fire assistants at will, but the way you did it? It's just another tally in the 'doesn't follow the rules' column."

"Okay, Jacob, you've said your piece and you're done. It's my turn. You're just doing your job, and I get that, but there are going to be pissed-off people. There always are when we come in and start changing shit. And you're right, what I do outside the office, or inside," I snarl, "is none of your business. But a secretary is a good thing for us both. Arianna can help me, but she can also help you. Feel free to offload some of your duties to her so that we can work on the higher-level stuff for the board. She can do more than make copies and coffee, so use her. I want her to learn."

Jacob and I have a war with our eyes, neither of us willing to give in to the other. Finally, he sighs and turns to Arianna. "I've read your file. I know you're smart . . . 3.85 GPA in international business with a minor in finance, and impressive internships and references. But one of my jobs is to protect Liam. Do I need to protect him from you?"

It's a blunt question, and not one I foresaw him asking. Arianna seems to take it stride, having recovered enough from her initial mortification at being called out to watch my exchange with Jacob closely, though I can still see the slight flush to her cheeks. "Mr. Wilkes, working for Morgan has been a dream of mine. Professionally, getting to be a fly on the wall and watch Mr. Blackstone work at turning this ship around is an experience I wouldn't dare mess up. Personally, while it is a delicate dance, we are figuring things out appropriately, and rest assured it will not affect my professionalism nor have ugly ramifications in the future."

Usually, when people couch what they're saying in business lingo, I tune out the droning. But listening to Arianna slay business babble is apparently a new turn-on for me, especially when she says we're figuring things out. Because I'm damn sure figuring her out, bit by bit, response by response, and I like what I'm learning about her.

Jacob looks between the two of us and sighs again, rolling his eyes, but he seems to be a little less concerned. "Okay. I hear you. I'm with you all the way, no matter what. Just saying, a little tact goes a long way."

"Yeah, well, so does a little recognition. You know I'm not going to let my personal life interfere with what we're doing. We're already turning this company around, Jacob. You and me. We've busted our asses, given up a shitload of nights out, and had too many cold dinners at home to count. Now we're here, and nothing's going to stop us. This isn't a one-man show, no matter what the image might be."

Jacob nods. "Thanks for that, Liam. I'll do my best, then. I won't let you down."

"That's the spirit. Now, look at my desk. See the coffee and my sandwich? That's two duties you don't have to do from now on."

Jacob looks at the sandwich and then to Arianna before laughing a little. "Great, my two easiest duties taken care of. Now what will I do with all my spare time?"

"Keep my ass out of the fire," I reply, shifting a little. Despite my bravado, Melvin's comments could be a problem. "If I'm causing a divide within the company this early in the game, we'll do well to listen to the rumblings . . . just a little bit."

Jacob nods and stands, leaving the weight of his concerns on my shoulders. But he gives both me and Arianna a pointed look as he closes the door. He's watching us, making sure we don't misstep or let this, whatever this is, affect work. It's not what I typically ask of him, but I'm damn sure he's got my back. And maybe Arianna's too.

She looks back to me, and I can see the wheels turning in her mind as she processes everything she just witnessed, evaluating it for every nugget of information she can glean. Finally, she says, "Now what?"

When most people ask me a question like that, it's because they're waiting for me to set the course and to proceed, ready to follow me to the slaughterhouse if I deem it, like sheeple following their leader. Me. But when Arianna asks that, it almost feels like she's already decided on the proper course of action and she's testing me to see if I have the right answer. The thought that she might consider that she knows more than I do amuses me, but at the same time, I respect her mind and am curious what she has in hers. "You tell me."

She dips her chin in deference, recognizing the gift of power I just bestowed on her. "We need to be discreet and careful. Neither of us wants our professional career marred with some office romance scandal. I'm here to learn, and you can teach me so much. I don't want to lose that opportunity. Nor can you allow your apparently tenuous hold on the board to be muddied by it coming out that you're fucking your intern."

I grin. She's not wrong. But I didn't get to where I am now, sitting in this leather chair at the head of an international business empire, by playing it safe. Risk is inherent. Risk is what begets reward. When calculated correctly, risk is the stepping stone that jumps you ahead of all safe moves. "You're right. But I'm not fucking my intern . . . yet," I say, using her sexy crude language right back at her. "And I do have so much to teach you, Ms. Hunnington. For example . . . come here."

"What?" she sputters, unsure at the game I'm playing because my plan is so counterintuitive to her own well-thought-out, responsible choice.

"Come. Here. Arianna." I let the authority I have over her, both professional and intimate, filter into the words, giving them a heavy weight of command. She rises, slowly but surely walking to my side. I lean back in my chair for a moment, head tilted as I scan her up and down, intentionally pausing on the curves of her ass and tits. I can see her chest rising as her breathing gets faster. Without warning, I grab her hips, yanking her between my legs once again and pushing her back on my desk, just like she was before we were interrupted. Her gasp of surprise is like a shot of adrenaline through my veins. Her hands on my shoulders as she works to steady herself from the fast movement is the only thing holding me to earth.

"Lift." She puts her palms on the desk, lifting her hips so I can slide her skirt back up to her waist. Her bare pussy is still wet for me, maybe even wetter, I realize, as I see the wetness spreading along her thighs from where she's crossed her legs.

"I agree we need to be on our best behavior over the next couple of days while I smooth some ruffled feathers."

She looks down at me, the fire back in her eyes. "You don't strike me as a man who lets people tell him what to do."

"I don't," I reply, spreading her legs and pulling her to the edge of the desk so that she's right in front of my hungry eyes. "I do what I want. I'm just taking a few precautions. The long game. And even I know when some rules should be followed."

She gasps as I grab handfuls of her lush thighs, pulling her pussy wide open so I can see every inch of her pinkness. "Doesn't that mean —"

"And when some rules can be bent or broken. Don't worry, doll, I still intend on giving you more than you can handle," I continue, bending down to lick the seam where her leg joins her center. "I want a buildup . . . because I have something special planned."

She practically melts for me, her ass grinding against the desk as she nears her edge again . . . but I have no intention of letting her come. Not yet. If I'm waiting, she can damn sure wait, following me into lust-induced madness too. "What's that? Oh, God, this feels good."

"This weekend," I whisper, teasing her clit with feather-light flicks I know will torture her but not make her come, "you will stay at my place . . . and I'm going to give you what you want. You'll like that, won't you? Coming to my place . . . to learn what coming really means. Like you want to now."

My clever girl fights back, though, chasing my tongue, and I'm so very tempted to give in and let her come all over my mouth. But then she speaks around her moans. "I don't think . . . I shouldn't."

Fuck, this woman. I'm damn-near out of my mind, and she's riding my face like it's heaven she's never imagined, but she still holds back from me, still has her faculties to doubt this. I promised her I'd impress her enough to earn the space between her thighs, but I didn't know I'd have to work this fucking hard for it. I'm verging on saying fuck it and just giving in so she comes all over my mouth, but I hold back, knowing that my initial idea of teasing her until she crosses the line where need rules her body is still my best course of action.

I lay a sucking kiss on her clit, and her thighs clamp around my head, trying to keep me there. But I press her legs open with my elbows, spreading her pussy with my hands. She's right there on the edge. I know one touch will send her over. I look up at her, waiting for her eyes to snap to mine in impatience. "This weekend . . . we'll see."

And with that, I lay one last chaste kiss to her bare mound, avoiding her clit where she desperately wants me, and then sit back in my chair. Never breaking eye contact, I wipe her juices from my lips, slipping a finger into my mouth to taste her once more. She huffs, confused for a second, and I see the moment her orgasm falls away, the lust clears, and she glares at me. It might be one of the sexiest things I've ever seen.

She shoves me out of the way, jumping from the desk and shoving her skirt down. "Mother fucker. Ugh, I can't believe you." She keeps murmuring, and I hear my name a few times as she gets closer to the door.

Right as she reaches for the doorknob, I call out. "Arianna." She stops, barely turning her head to look at me. "Negotiation lesson. Everyone comes to the table with something of value, some more valuable, some less. But everyone has something. You have what I want . . . that hot, virgin pussy that I know will feel so sweet coming on my cock. I have what you want."

I pause and her eyes spark. If looks could kill, I'd be a dead man. "Not that, Arianna. I've already told you I know you're no whore. I won't be trading business for pleasure. What I bring to the table . . . is me. My desire to fuck you, show you what your body can handle, teach you about all the wonders the flesh can offer." Even I know there's more to it than that, but physical pleasure is all I can promise right now, and I hope it's enough.

"I do want that," she says, but the confession isn't the soft admission I'd expect it to be. "But I want that with one man, *The One*. Nothing more and nothing less. And though you tempt me . . ." She rolls her eyes. "Fuck, do you tempt me. I know the value of what I bring to the table, Mr. Blackstone. Sometimes, the real thing is worth the price you have to pay." She says the words like she's quoting something or someone, like she found a hidden well of strength deep within her to resist my charms.

But as she leaves, defiantly looking at me with a glare I'm sure she thinks is frosty, I can see the heat, the desire burning hot inside her. I've already got her. She just doesn't know it yet.

ARIANNA

Dear Diary,

It's been insanely hard behaving over the past few days. Every day,

178

Liam looks at me like a starving wolf, ready to devour my body. Though I tried to stick with the cold shoulder, he quickly wore me down. I'm such a sucker, but the way his eyes track me is heady, making me feel simultaneously at his mercy and powerful, and when I get close enough, he brushes against me, subtle touches that make me burn at the contact.

Every word carries sexual undertones, and I have to admit to trying to give as good as I'm getting. I tempt him, whether to look down my blouse or to see that I'm wearing a thong. I know it makes his dick hard and hungry, and I can't help but leave these encounters with a smile, feeling victorious even though I'm playing with fire.

The power dynamic between us is constantly changing. One second, I'm teasing him, feeling every bit the vixen I'm really not, and the next, he's got me shoved up against the window as he demands 'just a taste'. And even though he hasn't let me come since that first day, I obey every time, futilely hoping he'll let me come this time but enjoying the way he tortures me regardless.

The only thing not making me lose my mind is that he's letting me use mine, staying true to his promise to teach me. We've discussed his business evaluation of Morgan, past, present, and future. We've talked about negotiation tactics and management techniques, and I've been lucky enough to sit in on several meetings to take notes, though Jacob is always there too since he's Liam's right-hand man and has a rather amazing business mind of his own. The three of us even went to lunch yesterday, and just listening to them talk about their experiences was better than any college lecture I've ever had.

It's all been this tightrope walk of balance, professional and personal, intimate and formal, business and pleasure. And while I know I've impressed Liam a few times with my thoughts as he's questioned me, I'll admit that he's impressed me too.

But is that enough? Enough to give in on a rule I made for myself? Even if it wasn't for some big moral, ethical stance, but rather a fear-induced boundary to keep my heart safe from further hurt. But giving in might lead to exactly that, a much deeper pain than I've ever felt before. The

LAUREN LANDISH

folks back home who said shit, I didn't really care about them one way or the other.

But Liam? I am starting to care, especially as I get to know him better and see the good inside him that he dresses up in the cocky asshole business façade. It's a good front and gets the job done, because it's not like a ball-busting CEO can be a nice guy who politely asks for things. But the real Liam is a good guy just trying to make a difference and succeed.

Late one night, when it was just the two of us in the office, he even told me the story of how his dad didn't want him taking over the family business. He'd said that the critical words gave him the push to fight harder, work longer, and be stronger, but I could see the cutting pain his dad's careless words had caused.

That Liam, vulnerable and sweet, mixed with the business one, cold and calculating, and topped with his heavy-handedness with me, dominant and sexy, is doing a weird number on my mind, my body, my heart. And I'm actually considering going to his place this weekend.

GRABBING A STACK OF PAPERS OUT OF THE 'WORK' BOX Jacob set up for me, I see they need to be copied and collated for the board meeting on Monday. It's busy work that'll at least keep me occupied. Anything is better than the quiet humming office white noise.

Just as I round the corner to the copy room, I run into someone, startling me so much I drop my stack of papers. "Oh!"

"Sorry about that," the guy says, bending down to pick up my papers before I can move. Thankfully, the stack was double-binder-clipped together so it's not a scattered mess.

"Me too . . . sorry. And thank you," I say as he stands back upright and hands the papers to me. I realize I know this guy. Though he's not particularly attractive, his black slightly dorky

180

glasses are memorable. "Uhm, Melvin, right? I mean, Mr. Jackson." Shit. I totally just collided with the VP who's helping Liam.

He smiles. "You remembered?" He seems genuinely surprised. "Call me Melvin, please. Arianna, right?"

I nod. Usually, I'd be thrilled that a VP remembered my name, but though his eyes are solidly on mine and completely appropriate, there's something a little off about the guy. Like he's not checking me out, thank God, but he's analyzing me somehow. Though I remember now that he is a number cruncher, so maybe that's just how he is?

"Did I hurt you?" he asks, finally giving me a cursory head-to-toe glance.

"No, not at all. Just surprised me. Sorry again."

Feeling like the accidental interaction has reached a reasonable end and sure that Melvin has better things to do than chat with an intern, I turn to the copier and begin placing the stack of papers into the feed tray.

"Oh, I can show you a little trick for that," he says, coming over to my side. He doesn't wait for me to move, just reaches in front of me and starts pushing buttons on the big copy machine.

"I've got it. Thanks, though. I'm sure you have stuff to do." I try to argue politely.

"I insist. This will save you tons of time. See?" He taps on the screen, where the expected job completion time is now four minutes instead of the nine it had been when I'd set up the job differently.

I smile politely. "Thanks."

And cue . . . silence. Awkward silence.

Finally, he breaks the quiet. "So, are you enjoying your work for Liam?"

It strikes me as odd that he calls him Liam since he was all 'Mr. Blackstone' when they met before, but I guess I switch in and out of the casual name usage as well. Come to think of it, so does Jacob. So maybe that's just the norm around here.

"I am. I've spent the majority of my summer internship manning the front desk, which was great. But I'm definitely learning more with Mr. Blackstone and Mr. Wilkes." It's a great rah-rah, nothing critical answer, but still truthful.

Melvin smiles, but his eyes narrow. It's an odd expression, like he can't decide what the proper response should be. "I'm sure. But I do feel I should warn you . . ." He pauses, looking over his shoulder at the empty doorway. "Be careful, Arianna. Liam has a huge ego and a tendency to be an asshole." He flinches, like the word was hard for him to say, and I get the feeling he doesn't curse much. That's kind of refreshing these days when folks drop F-bombs like nothing, myself included in that group. "He's not particularly well-liked around here, so while you may be learning from him, you're at a disadvantage because not many people will want to work with you after knowing that Liam provided your business education. I'm sure you're hoping to get hired on in the fall—interns always are— but don't get too close or your image will be tied up with his and that could be disastrous."

I'm shocked, first that Melvin is telling me this stuff. I know he's supposed to be Liam's top-secret information mole or whatever, but sharing all that with some intern seems rather loose-lipped if I'm honest. Plus, it feels vaguely threatening, like I won't get hired on because I work with Liam, but I figured working for the CEO would help make me a shoe-in for a fall position. I'm not sure how to respond, so I hedge.

"Thanks for the advice, Mr. Jackson. That's definitely something to keep in mind."

He blinks three times in rapid succession, his face blank. "Do remember and be careful, Arianna. I'd hate to see a young professional get side-tracked. I could put in a good word for you. I usually have a fall part-time staffer in my office to help with end-of-year report preparation. You'd like that. We should get coffee and discuss it."

Working with Melvin sounds like the ninth ring of hell, awkward and boring, but I try to be polite. "Thanks so much, Mr. Jackson. I'm really busy for Mr. Blackstone right now, but I'll talk to Mr. Wilkes about my fall placement." I have no intention of doing so unless it's to beg Jacob to not place me in the Business Analysis department.

"Melvin, please," he says, catching on that I've been calling him Mr. Jackson to distance myself a bit.

Thankfully, there's a commotion in the hallway, and I see Liam and Jacob walk by, lost in conversation as several other people in suits follow behind them. The copy machine beeps, and I think *saved by the bell* to myself. I grab the stack of printouts and turn. "Thanks so much, Melvin," I say, emphasizing his name, which makes him smile wanly. "But I'd better get back to the office and see if Mr. Blackstone or Mr. Wilkes needs anything."

"Of course," he says, stepping away, and I realize just how close he was. "Remember to be careful. Coffee next week?" he calls out, but I'm already out the door and down the hallway.

I hustle down the hall, catching up to Liam and Jacob. Jacob veers to his desk, and I follow Liam into his office, biting my lip as I watch his tight, firm ass flex in his pants. His suit today is especially slim-fitting, probably Italian, and making him look like a GQ model. I swear he gets better-looking each day that passes.

I don't bother telling him about the encounter with Melvin. I don't want to get involved in office politics. Besides, Liam seems rather exasperated post-meeting, much different from the usual cockily assured self he was this morning.

"How'd the meeting go?" I ask as Liam pours himself a soda water. "Anything interesting that you can tell me?"

He shakes his head, draining his glass in a swallow. "The usual. Someone proposes an idea, and the board squabbles over it, trying to pick it apart. Problem is, most of their ideas would've been great twenty years ago. Now, not so much."

"So, what happens in the end?" I ask, and Liam chuckles, setting his glass down and walking toward his desk. He drops into his leather chair, looking like the frustrated king of a wayward country.

"Either they get with the times or I come up with the solution myself. It was a waste of precious time as they argued the pros and cons of useless ideas." I walk over to his desk, retracing his footsteps, but instead of the chair, I perch on the desk next to him.

"Tell me about the ideas. Maybe it'll help to go through them methodically to see if there's anything salvageable. Maybe you can combine a sprinkle of this and dash of that and create something the board will appreciate but still gets you the result you're looking for."

He nods and begins talking through the various proposals that were presented at the meeting. Usually, I'd be tuned in closely, absorbing every word and learning. But right now, I'm distracted. I'm enveloped by the masculine scent of his after-shave as he gestures with his hands. I watch as he scrubs a hand along the scruff on his jawline before threading his hands

184

through his hair, mussing it, but somehow, it only looks sexier when it's slightly rough.

The frustration is palpable in his words, and as he gets to the end of his rant, I cross my legs. His eyes snap to my thighs. "I could think of a million other things I'd rather be doing than rehashing that meeting." He skims a finger along my thigh, the skirt not hiding the heat of his touch. "Or *whom* I'd rather be doing."

The fact that he shares with me, wants my opinion, wants *me*, makes me feel so powerful. Turning to him, I do something I haven't done before, take control. I don't give myself time to have second thoughts or doubts about the intelligence of my actions. I just go with it, wanting to follow my own desires and see where that leads. I rise, moving to stand between his spread legs, and place my hands on the armrests of his chair to bend forward, invading his space. "You seem stressed. Maybe I could help you relax?"

This is the first time I've taken initiative like this. I may tease and flirt, but it's always Liam who moves us into this territory. But his eyes light up instantly, seeming to like me taking the lead for a change. "What did you have in mind, doll?"

My usual mouthiness deserts me, so instead of answering, I simply drop to my knees before him. I look up through my lashes, not shy in the least, but seeking permission while refusing to ask. "You want to suck my cock? You think that'll relax me?" That arrogant smirk is in his tone, though his lips don't tilt. He cups my cheek, and I lean into the caress, my eyes slipping closed as my mouth drops open. He traces along my bottom lip, dipping his thumb into my mouth, and I instinctively close around it, sucking and licking at the pad. "Fuck, Arianna. Do it. Suck me."

My eyes pop open, and I reach forward to undo his brown leather belt, then his slacks. He yanks his shirt up to get it out of my way, and I have a moment of pause before I pull him out of his boxer briefs. I've felt him rubbing against my ass and grinding against my pussy as he's teased me all week, so I know he's big, thick, and hard. But this will be the first time I actually see his cock, and I'm excited at the anticipation of finally laying eyes on him. I pull the waistband of his boxer briefs down, and his cock surges out, rock-hard and throbbing. I take a moment, teasing a fingertip along the velvety skin as I learn him. "Fuck, Liam. You're gorgeous."

"I taste even better," he groans. I look up, and his eyes are pained, desperately needy. Glancing back down, I see a dribble of pre-cum running from the red head down his shaft.

I realize with a start, "Have you been holding off like you said? Edging me all week and not taking any relief for yourself?" He reaches down and squeezes the base of his shaft and I know my answer. "I'm impressed, Mr. Blackstone," I tease.

"I am rather impressive," he says, his voice gravelly and the bragging sounding more habitual than real.

"We'll see," I say as I lean forward, letting my pink tongue stick out to lick along his length. I get my first taste of him, musky and sweet and delicious, making me want more. His hands grip the armrests so hard his knuckles are going white. So I lick up and down, catching every bit of pre-cum before sucking along his head to get more. His hips buck slightly, so I press against him, not remotely able to hold him, but he relents and sits still for my exploration.

"Fuck, Ari . . . do that . . . suck the head again." His hands move into my hair, and I let him guide me for a moment but realize that this is my moment. I'm doing this to him, and I want that power surge, that ability to drive him as wild as he's been driving me all week. Though I plan on being kinder and actually letting him come. Maybe.

The thought of edging him, evilly getting him to the brink and then pulling back like he's done to me all week, is a wicked temptation. But when I get another mouthful of his sweet pre-cum, I know I don't have the discipline he does. I want all of him.

"Put your hands back on the armrests. Let me do this. Let me learn you, what you like," I whisper.

He lifts his head from the back of the chair, eyeing me, and I consider that he's likely never given up any shred of control like this, always the predator, the dominant, the alpha. But for me, he does as I say, laying his hands back on the armrests and letting me lead.

I feel like a boss. Like The Boss, able to bring this powerful beast of a man to his knees figuratively by being on my knees literally. And like a boss, I get to work, licking and sucking him into my mouth, sometimes just the head like he asked, but slowly learning how deep I can take him. Oh, so slowly, I get better, judging by the increasingly louder grunts and groans Liam is trying to keep quiet. He hits my throat, and I gag a bit, but his cock pulses in my mouth, impossibly harder, so I do it again and again, slowly breathing through my nose to take him deeper.

It's an odd combination of power through submission, probably for us both. His relinquishment of control and letting me decide how fast and how deep, while at the same time knowing he could shove down my throat and choke me on his cock before I could stop him. My submissive posture on the ground before him, but knowing that I'm the one shredding his every ounce of control.

I find a new rhythm, taking Liam deeper in my mouth, sucking him fast and hard, and his abs clench under my hands. "Fuck, doll . . . I'm gonna come. Swallow it down. Swallow me."

LAUREN LANDISH

A few more strokes, and his hot cum jets out as he grunts, probably loudly enough for Jacob to hear, but right now, I can't care because this is sexier than I'd ever imagined. His hands shoot to my head, holding me deeply, my mouth filled with his cock and his cum. I swallow reflexively, over and over, taking him in as he shudders.

I sit back on my heels, a satisfied smirk on my face. I just did that. I took the initiative to seduce him, took control and made him sit there like the nice boy he's definitely not while I worked him, and took every drop of his cum. It's quite the power trip.

Liam looks surprised at the turn of events too, maybe even shocked at my forwardness. I like that I can keep him guessing, like I'm not a pawn he's moving about on the chessboard but rather a queen in my own right, moving wherever the fuck I want to on the board.

I get up, straightening my skirt and wiping at the corners of my mouth like the lady I am. "You look like the cat that got the cream," Liam teases, a satisfied grin overtaking his face though his eyes are still a bit dreamy.

I lift my eyebrows. "I *did* get the cream, Mr. Blackstone."

He growls at my usage of his name. "I want some fucking cream too, Arianna. My driver will pick you up at seven sharp. Pack a bag because you're staying at my house this weekend."

I consider playing coy, letting him continue to chase me, because I haven't exactly agreed to this weekend sleepover plan. But I know I'm reaching the end of my rope, and I suspect he is too. This back and forth we've been playing at has been fun, and already so very educational, but my resolve to wait is weakening, barely a sliver of a memory about why I decided that in the first place remaining.

"Seven it is. I'll be the one wearing . . . lace," I say, getting one

188

last tease in because I already know how much he loves the peekaboo effect of the flimsy fabric against my skin.

I can hear the moan of desire rumble from his lips as I close the door behind me to head to my desk.

ARIANNA

"Oh, my God, Daisy. What the hell have I gotten myself into?" I screech into the phone.

"Breathe, honey. You're okay," she says in a soothing voice. "Inhale. Exhale."

I do as she says, slowing my breathing. The quick ride home had found me feeling sassy and rather sure of myself. But when I started packing a weekend bag and digging through my lingerie drawer and considering whether I needed actual clothes or not, the nerves hit me and I'd called in reinforcements. "Am I really doing this? I've waited so long, decided ages ago to wait until I was getting married. Is it stupid to throw that away, give in to lust?"

Daisy hums. "Why did you decide to wait?"

Knowing I'd promised her this, I relent. "Ugh, it's a long story, but I'll try to give the quickie version. I went out with a guy in high school a few times. He was nice, we had fun, and I thought things were going really well. Then I found out he'd told the whole football team that he fucked me in the backseat of his car on our first date. Totally not true, obviously." I sigh, the story difficult to tell but easier than I would've expected. I guess the time since then has lessened the pain to the point it almost feels like it happened to someone else, like I was someone else back then.

"I told everyone he was lying, but they believed him over me. I think they saw a nice girl with curves that I didn't know what to do with, and a popular jock guy, and well . . . they figured I'd put out and had morning-after regret. Anyway, after that, I became the joke of the school almost overnight. Other guys started saying that they'd screwed me too. I don't know why they all ganged up me, lying like that, but somewhere along the way, I figured out it'd be easier to claim it with pride than argue against a title they'd already decided fit me."

Daisy's voice is quiet as she asks, "I'm guessing that title wasn't homecoming queen?"

"No, everyone was calling me a whore, a slut, easy. Shit like that. It hurt, especially considering at the time, I hadn't even kissed a guy." A sad laugh escapes my throat. "After that, though, I became much more aware of people's relationships. I could tell who was having sex, who wasn't, and I watched what happened when they took that step. I guess I just figured out that sex is a big deal. At least to me. And I told myself that I wasn't going to do it casually. And now I'm scared I'm just tossing all that away because I'm horny."

"God, Ari. I'm so sorry that happened to you. That sounds awful. Can I tell you something though?" I murmur my agreement, and she continues but doesn't say what I expect from my sweet, nerdy bestie. "Ari, listen to me and listen good . . . fuck those people who were mean. Don't give them an ounce of power over the choices you make today or tomorrow. They already got yesterday's. Fuck. Them."

"What?" I say, shocked at the fury in her voice.

"Seriously, chica. Only you can decide if you want to have sex or not, but don't let their whispers in your ear sway you one way or the other. Listen to your own heart and decide. You never made a moral, ethical, or even a conscious decision to wait. You made that choice out of hurt and fear because of asshole people who had nothing better to do than gossip about a little girl. You could've easily become what they said you were, but in your heart, you never did, even if you mouthed about it as a coping mechanism. Let me ask you this . . . does Liam make you feel things you've never felt before? Are you going to regret doing this or are you going to regret *not* doing this?"

Her words are like a balm to the little girl in my soul who cried at the ugly words tossed so carelessly at her like bombs. Though those scars will likely always remain, I can feel at a visceral level that she's right. It's not that I'm throwing away my heart or my body on a meaningless fuck. It's that I'm finally taking my own power, giving myself permission to enjoy my body without caring what others may or may not think about me afterward. Sex is a big deal, but it's *my* big deal, and no one but me gets to choose when the time is right for me.

And though it's fast, I do feel something for Liam. It's not love —it's way too soon for that—but it's not simple lust either. This is something I've never experienced before, some combination of happiness, respect, heat, and excitement. It's both bright and bubbly and simultaneously dark and sultry.

"I'd regret not doing this. I don't know what this weekend holds, but I do want to find out. Maybe we have sex, maybe we just go a bit further than we have, but I want to take that leap, make those choices myself." I smile, a heavy weight lifted from my shoulders. "Wow, Daisy. Thank you, girl. I don't know what I'd do without you."

She laughs. "That's what besties are for. I do have one more question, though . . . what are you going to wear?"

I flop back on the bed. "Oh, my God, I don't know! My lingerie drawer is literally emptied out on the bed around me. I don't have a fancy boudoir set like Liam is probably expecting, nor can I afford that. I also don't have any slutty 'fuck me' gear. I told him lace because I was taunting him, but now I'm seriously considering running to the mall for something special."

Daisy clicks her tongue. "Ari, if he's nitpicking your lingerie, tell him to fuck himself and get the hell outta there. Seriously. The man isn't gonna care if you're wearing your time-of-the-month granny panties and a T-shirt bra or a fancy set. And you probably don't need the added pressure of some big to-do outfit. Wear something you have that makes you feel pretty and sexy. What do you have?"

"Hang on . . . let me switch to FaceTime." I click the buttons and suddenly, Daisy's face fills my screen. Even through her big glasses, I can see the kindness in her eyes and my heart swells. I'm lucky to have her. "Thanks again, girl. Okay, here's what I have . . ."

Almost thirty minutes later, I've picked out a few lingerie sets from my stash, lacy, pretty matching things that make me feel good without seeming like I'm trying too hard to be something I'm not. I add a few silky shortie pajama sets, some soft lounge clothes, and one dress that will work for a casual brunch or a nicer dinner. And with that and some bathroom necessities, my weekend bag is packed.

I'm ready.

I think.

Well, I'm definitely ready to be open to the experience, at least. I'll take it moment by moment, with no pressure from Liam, my past, or myself to do or not do anything.

———

AT SEVEN ON THE DOT, THERE'S A FIRM KNOCK ON MY DOOR. I open it to see an older man dressed in a black suit, a burgundy tie sharp against his white shirt. He inclines his head, tilting an invisible hat at me. "Ms. Hunnington? I'm Randolph, Mr. Blackstone's driver, among other things." There's a slightly British lilt to his voice, making him seem charming and grandfatherly. He offers his hand, and I shake it, introducing myself too.

"Other things?" I ask, not sure what he's talking about.

He smiles politely. "Driver, butler, house manager. I suspect you know Mr. Wilkes? He takes care of Mr. Blackstone's professional life. I handle his personal affairs. He said you're to go to his home. Correct?"

"Yes, that's right."

He takes my bag and escorts me down to the black Mercedes waiting at the curb. It's sleek and sophisticated, all curves and class. Randolph opens the door, waiting for me to climb in, and then closes it firmly behind me.

The ride is relatively quiet, just the purr of the powerful engine. I slide my hand along the leather seat, feeling the luxury of the buttery softness. I vaguely wonder if Liam appreciates the extravagance of this. He's told me about his upbringing, definitely wealthier than mine by far, but rather than a silver spoon entitlement, he came out of it with a work ethic not many possess. But when you grow up with money, there's an inherent expectation that goes with the experience. I hope that even when I'm a big-deal CEO, I still appreciate the special things, like a chauffeured ride in a fancy car. With a small smile, I make a mental promise to myself to eat some beefaroni at least once a month too.

I'm not sure what to say to Randolph, who seems to be taking my lead on small-talk and stays silent. But I do notice him glancing back at me in the rearview mirror, and I consider that he's probably done this before for Liam. Pick up a woman, take her to his place for the weekend, and repeat. The thought leaves me cold, but I can't fault Liam for having a past if I don't want him to fault me for mine.

I realize that Randolph is trying to figure me out. I can almost feel his judgment . . . too young, too innocent, too much cleavage, too much . . . of a whore. His eyes stay perfectly neutral though, and I have a sudden insight that the whispers of my past and my own inner monologue are filling in gaps that don't exist. Daisy is right. I am letting my past control my present and my future.

And I'm not going to let the small-town assholes or a driver in my present decide for me. I decide who I am, what I am. And I say I'm a woman with a brain, a heart, and needs. And that's okay, so they can fuck off. I sit up straighter and meet Randolph's eyes in the mirror. He offers a small smile, and I feel like I passed his test, but ironically, it's one that I don't feel the need to care about because I passed my own, which is much more important.

My mouth drops when we get to Liam's estate. It's beautiful, not a stuffy brick and stone testament to century-old dead men, but sleek and contemporary. Steel and glass dominate the whole structure, as if the architect was inspired by the pyramids outside the Louvre.

"I've never seen anything like this," I murmur as we pull up.

Randolph smiles and nods. "This way, Ms. Hunnington."

He already has my bag in hand as we approach the front doors. Randolph pushes a button and the gigantic glass front parts, awing me as I get a good look at the interior.

Everything gleams. Rich, warm marble floors flow from room to room through open doorways. Somehow, there isn't a column in sight, and I can see upward to the evening sky through the large skylight in the foyer. It feels like I'm not indoors at all, except that my heels click on the floors as

Randolph leads me through the entry area and deeper into the house. I have to stop, though, as we go down a hallway, pausing in utter astonishment. "Is that . . . a pool?"

Randolph stops, nodding.

I shake my head, amazed. I've heard of infinity pools before, but I've never actually seen one in person. Liam's pool goes right to the edge of a huge drop-off, almost like it's about to join the sky before the view opens up to an enormous valley thick with pines and other trees. "I've never seen this part of town before. It's beautiful."

"That land is actually state forest, so there is no chance of it ever being cut down. Makes for a rather spectacular view," Randolph says. "This way, please. I'll show you around."

"Where's Liam? I don't mind the tour, but I thought he'd be here?"

"Mr. Blackstone asked that I give you this." He hands me a sealed envelope, the paper rich and creamy. I recognize it from the stationary set on his desk. It's scented faintly of Liam as I open the seal and take out the folded piece of paper inside. It's his handwriting, and my pulse quickens as I read the simple message written on it.

> *I have a business dealing that's taking my time.*
> *Have dinner, and then prepare yourself for me.*
> *Tonight, you're mine.*
> *-Liam*

Randolph inclines his head, waiting patiently as I clutch the paper to my chest. "Ma'am, would you like the tour? At least to get to the kitchen, and perhaps the living room?"

I nod and follow as he sees me to the kitchen. "Dinner will be served whenever you are ready. This way, please." He then shows me the living room, although it seems more like a comfy movie theater, considering the size of the television screen and the leather reclining couch. Finally, he escorts me to the master bedroom, setting my bag on a side table. "Mr. Blackstone asked that you make yourself at home and he'll be here shortly. Pick up any house phone and dial *0 to reach me in my quarters if you need anything, Ms. Hunnington."

I nod. "Thank you, Randolph."

And then I'm alone in Liam's bedroom. The huge bed, covered with a fluffy grey comforter, fills my vision, and my blood races through my veins. Is this the night? With a soft smile, I shimmy and bounce on the bed, letting out a squeal of excitement.

LIAM

"And so, gentlemen," Melvin says up front, finally coming to the end of his presentation, "we should look at investing in these markets, particularly these specific companies, to insure ourselves against the predicted upcoming trade war."

I try not to roll my eyes. The board, all freaked out over rumors of tariffs and counter-tariffs and more, had insisted on this meeting. Melvin's been talking for what feels like forever, happy as a clam in mud to have the floor. He's shown us charts, graphs, and even a spreadsheet that was so convoluted I think he was the only one who knew what it actually said.

Still, it's a shame he's not the greatest at actually presenting it because his numbers are pretty on point, even if I still disagree with what we should actually do with them. "Thank you, Melvin. I know the board appreciates your hard work to bring these figures forward." He preens a bit, his smile stretching across his thin face as he makes eye contact with anyone still looking at him. As I expected, though, most of the suits around the table have their eyes locked on me, checking my response to Melvin's presentation. "I think we're all concerned about the possibility of tariffs and what the fallout could be, but they're all conjecture at this point. I have to believe, and history has shown, that we're not going to end up in a worst-case scenario situation like Melvin has forecast."

Melvin interrupts me, arguing, "But predicting the market is what I do. Something Morgan has always entrusted to me."

His tone is harsh, more sneering than I usually expect from him, and I realize I've touched a rather sensitive nerve. Framing my words carefully, both for the board and for Melvin, who has been a useful source, I say, "And you are an excellent analyst. Your team is integral in evaluating possible opportunities and pitfalls." It's the best ego soother I'm going to offer, because I quickly deliver the cutting blow. "But ultimately, it's up to the board to dictate what we do with the analysis you provide. In this situation, I feel strongly that staying our current course of action is in Morgan's best interest. We can continue to reevaluate as the tariff situation evolves, but I don't currently feel the need to preventatively safeguard assets because the sky might be falling some time in the future if X, Y, and Z occur."

Melvin is turning a slightly ruddy color and his eyes might as well be shooting daggers. Oddly enough, I can respect that. He's a passionate and intelligent man who wants what he thinks is best for Morgan and is willing to fight for it. I just happen to disagree with what that choice should be. "It's an ongoing situation and we'll take that into consideration, but the assets you recommend reallocating to safer markets would then earn approximately six percent, right?"

Through gritted teeth, he corrects me. "Six point four percent."

"Exactly. Six point four. Where they currently sit, they're

earning upward of twelve," I say, speaking to the board members. "Or, Melvin, what's the exact percentage, current-ly?" It's an attempt to get him to see reason, but barring that, having him speak the words that will seal the board's agree-ment with me is a power play.

Melvin turns to look at the spreadsheet behind him, something I know he doesn't need to do since he has these numbers memorized backward and forward. "Twelve point one percent."

"So, leaving them, even if it's only for a short time while we watch the tariff news, puts us in a stronger financial position. If our current investments decline, they're not likely to drop almost fifty percent overnight, and even if they did, we would've made more during the time at the higher return rate to offset that, and the loss would be deductible on taxes." I finish my sales pitch with a smile, softening the strike to Melvin and his presentation.

The board members nod and murmur their agreement, and I'm done with this conversation, ready to get home to Arianna. "So, I think we'll stay the course for now, with close follow-up by Melvin's group." I eye him for agreement, and he nods tightly. "I think we can call that an evening, people. Have a good weekend."

I get up from the table, forcing myself not to run from the room in my hurry to get to Arianna's sweet pussy. Melvin stops me with a hand on my arm, though. I look down, not liking his nerve. "Sir, I really think if you look through the projections, you'll see that I'm right."

I sigh inside. I have to give the man credit. He's persistent, which is a good thing, but my gut says he's not correct. It's just too soon. "I'll go back over them, but my gut says to stay the course. Sometimes, the smarter move isn't the safer move. We need big risks to get big reward, and honestly, this isn't even that big of a risk. Surely, you see that? But we'll keep a close eye, continue evaluating. I'll need you to do that, Melvin. Can you handle that?"

His eyes narrow in confusion. "Your gut? You're risking Morgan based on your gut?" At my silence, he shakes his head, blinking rapidly, and schools his face. "Okay, Mr. Blackstone. It's your call. I'll keep an eye on it and report back to the board if there are any changes."

I can feel that it's a submission on his part, but not one given willingly. Pretty sure this bridge is burned and that I won't be getting any further intel from him, I go ahead and throw kerosene on the raging inferno Melvin is hiding behind his blank face and bespectacled stare. "To me. If there are changes, report them to me. I'll deal with the board." I don't bother asking if he understands. It's a direct order so he'd best get with the program. I don't require my employees to be yes-men. In fact, I appreciate and respect general discourse about company direction. It's a team effort and that's why there is a board who votes on decisions. But someone has to take the ultimate responsibility for those calls, good or bad, and that someone is me. Morgan hired me because I take calculated gambles, and that's exactly what I intend to do.

Melvin nods, though his cheeks are splotchy with redness. "Of course, sir." His retreat down the hallway is swift, not quite a stomp, but even from behind, I can see the anger in his stride.

Jacob approaches slowly, whistling as he follows my sightline. "You shit in his cereal after already pissing in his Cheerios? That's a cold-blooded dick move, even for you, Liam."

I turn, smirking at his irreverence. No one else talks to me like that, and I'm glad to have Jacob to call me out, even if it's not warranted this time. "No, he'll be fine. Though I wouldn't expect him to rat on board happenings again." I shrug. "All right, I'm out for the weekend. Only call if the building's on fire."

Jacob grins. "Gotcha. Real quick while we walk . . ." We head down the hallway from the conference room to my office, Jacob rattling as we go like usual, and I nod along as he confirms the things he's already done in my name to handle business. "Last but not least, Helen from the magazine emailed during the meeting. She's a go for Arianna being in the photos. Apparently, she was as big of a hit with them as she was with you." He gives me a healthy dose of side-eye, but I choose to ignore it. He's made his stance clear, and we're mostly just avoiding the elephant in the room.

"Also, Helen was struck with a last-minute stroke of brilliance." He rolls his eyes before continuing. "She's throwing a cover reveal party for you on her yacht, down by the coast. Next weekend."

I stare at Jacob. "Next weekend? What the hell's with the last-minute shit?"

He laughs. "I knew you'd say that. It's called spontaneity, man. Look it up. And your calendar was shockingly clear that day, although I would've switched it up for something like this. You don't exactly want to piss off Helen because, let's be real, her get-togethers are networking extravaganzas and PR godsends. Plus, she's running it like a pop-up party, some fancy food truck chef taking over the kitchen to make lamb pops or some shit. And you want to hear the best part?" I can tell by the gleeful look in his eyes that the 'best part' is going to suck big time. "It's a costume party! Well, more like cosplay, I guess. Modern movie, game, and comic characters *strongly* encouraged."

I was right. His idea of good news is my version of hell. I don't remember the last time I dressed up in a costume. Maybe when I was eight or nine for a Halloween party?

Unless . . . wait . . .does a toga party in college count? Probably, so it's been ten years at least. But Jacob's right. This isn't a party I can miss, especially if it's to reveal the cover with me on it. Jacob keeps trying to convince me as we walk into my office. "Helen is apparently a not-so-secret eccentric and loves to play dress-up. It could be worse! She had a Marie Antoinette themed party once, complete with powdered wigs. Another time, she apparently celebrated a particular movie opening with a Latex and Lingerie party. Wish we could've gone to that one." He wiggles his eyebrows exaggeratedly.

I sigh. "Okay, costume party next weekend. I'll get Randolph to pick up . . . something. Maybe I should go as Gordon Gekko after all?" Jacob shakes his head sharply, and I let the idea of an easy suit and suspenders costume go.

"I need to give Helen's people a head count. Who are you thinking? We need to make an appearance as Morgan, show support and all that." He holds his tablet, ready for me to dictate a guest list.

By next weekend, Arianna will be fully mine and ready to give Morgan a long-time shot. A great way to cap off her return to college, too.

"Me, Arianna, you, and a date, if you'd like. The board members and spouses. Anyone else you can think of?"

Jacob hums. "VPs?"

I consider for a moment, mentally tallying up the various VPs over each department and division. "No, I think that might be overwhelming. That's at least twenty more people, plus spouses. I want to be able to speak with the other people there to network, not be forced into speaking with staff I can see on Monday." He nods, letting me know he agrees with my assessment, and I grab my briefcase, shutting down my computer. "I'm out.

"Where are you going with a rocket up your ass?" Jacob asks. "I've never seen you beat me out the door before."

"Today's a day for first times," I reply, grinning, but he doesn't get the double meaning. "And I'm going home."

THE FERRARI IS A PLEASURE TO DRIVE, AND I'M HOME IN A jiffy. It still feels like too long since I last saw Arianna, though it's only been a few hours. When I pull up, I feel the thrum of the engine rumbling as the glass garage doors open for me. They aren't really glass, of course—they're laminate—but I do love the irony of living in a 'glass house', considering the number of stones I throw around the business world.

Randolph is waiting for me in the back hall as I come in from the garage, his hands behind his back and his face stern. "Mr. Blackstone, welcome home."

"Is she upstairs?" I ask, handing Randolph the keys.

"She is. After a light dinner, she said she was fine waiting for you alone. Will there be anything else tonight, sir?" His voice is even, practiced neutrality.

"No, that's everything. Thanks, Randolph," I say hurriedly, barely restraining myself from running up the stairs to my doll.

Randolph clears his throat, "Sir? If I may . . ." I look to him, seeing his request to speak freely in his eyes. I dip my chin, giving permission. "Forgive me if I am out of line, but there is something special about her. She seems strong, but also . . . fragile? Do be careful."

I don't like his insinuation that I'm some gruff asshole, but it's closer to the truth than I'd like to admit and he knows it. But I'm not sharing my feelings with Randolph, even if we have worked together for years. We're close, but it's a decidedly more professional relationship than I have with Jacob. I nod, letting him know I hear him. "Thank you, Randolph. I appreciate that, and I know that she's special."

Even the words on my tongue feel inadequate. It's only been a short time, but spending hours on end together, discussing business but also our pasts, and sharing our thoughts has been like a microcosm of rapid get-to-know-you speed-dating. Tonight is special, whether I get inside her body or not, because I'm already in her mind and she's inside mine. The mere fact that she came to my house is a step in the direction I've been pulling her toward all along.

I head upstairs, finding Arianna in the main living room, looking out through the tall windows to the treed area behind my property. She's changed, and my heart pauses in my chest as I take her glorious form in. The white silk robe she's put on both hides and hugs her form, and her long legs stick out the bottom, seemingly going for miles to her cute little bare feet.

The robe is slightly see-through, and what I can see underneath stops my heart again. I can't see the details, but the faint outlines of what she's wearing have my cock rock hard in my pants.

She hasn't heard me come in and I don't want to startle her, so I clear my throat before I speak. "Like what you see?"

Arianna spins around, her mouth going wide with shock as she sees me. "Y–you have a beautiful place."

I cross the heavily carpeted floor of the living room, nothing in my vision but her. "It's nothing compared to the sight before me right this instant."

She recovers quickly from the surprise of my arrival, heat in her eyes as she traces my body the same way I'm looking her up and down. "You like the outfit?" she asks breathily. I'm not sure if it's because she's playing the part of the sultry vixen or because she's turned on at seeing me. I hope it's the latter. I don't want some faux version of what Arianna thinks is sexy tonight. I want her, real and authentic, and perfectly who she is. Nothing more, nothing less.

Her robe is slightly open in front, and I can see just how daring her outfit is . . . and there's nothing but pure honesty in my voice when I reply. "I fucking love it."

She reaches out toward me, and I take her hand, leading her in a slow spin so I can see her from every angle. When she's facing me again, she looks up. "You look dark and handsome. Maybe a little dangerous."

I grin ferally. "You have no idea how dangerous I am, doll. But I'm going to show you." I reach down to grab the tie holding her robe closed, slowly pulling the bow undone like she's a gift. A present just for me. Her robe falls open, and I memorize every inch of the pretty picture she paints before me, dark waves of her hair swept over one shoulder, white robe framing her luscious curves, tits high on her chest in white lacy cups that let her rosy nipples peek through, and her pretty pussy hidden behind a scrap of white lace. She's angelic, pure . . . and she's going to give that to me. She'll be mine to spoil . . . but not ruin.

I pull her flush against my body, allowing her to feel what she does to me. Our bodies feel like they're merging, and I grind against her. "Fuck, Arianna. You have no idea what you do to me, doll."

"Pretty sure I can feel exactly what you think of me," Arianna says lightly as I let go of her belt to slide her robe off her shoulders. It puddles at her feet the same way my body is threatening to do.

Not yet. Instead, I run my fingers along the edges of her lace cups, tracing up her neck to run my thumb across her lips, which she kisses gently. I growl, cupping her head and entwining my fingers in her hair.

Unable to resist a moment longer, I take her mouth in a kiss, devouring her while wishing I could be soft and slow. But we've been working each other up all week and my restraint is woefully weak now that she's here and so willing.

She kisses me back, and I let my hand drop to her ass, squeezing a handful tightly and rubbing against her. My cock begs to be set free from the confines of my slacks, to gain access to her sweet innocence, so close but yet so far away.

Ari moans, and I try to guide her back toward the couch, but she resists my steps a little, putting her hands on my chest but not pushing me away. "Slow down, Liam. I . . ."

I gaze into her eyes, seeing the lust burning bright there. I know she wants me, wants this just as desperately as I do. "Doll, we've been waiting, slowly driving each other mad with touches here and rubs there. You had my cock down your throat just yesterday, and I know that hot little pussy is weeping with the need to come. Isn't it, Ari? Are you wet for me, ready to be stuffed full of my cock, to ride me until you come and coat me in your sweetness?" One thing I've learned this week is that Ari likes it when I talk dirty to her, damn-near comes from the filthy words alone without a touch, so I'm expecting her to shudder with need like usual.

What I'm not expecting are the words she whispers. "I don't know if I'm ready for this."

ARIANNA

My words hang between us, and I wait for Liam to react.

I expect him to get angry, to at least get annoyed.

After all, we have been building anticipation for this event for

LAUREN LANDISH

an entire week, a build-up I've been actively participating in, only to kill his hopes within the first thirty seconds. I mean, of course, he expected it to happen tonight. I've led him to believe that for most of the week, even as my emotions went back and forth. Hell, I came here tonight thinking it was The Night myself.

But he just stares at me for a long moment before throwing back his head and chuckling. "Are you serious?" he asks in that deep, sexy growl.

I nod, facing him with as much strength as my five-foot-four-and-three-quarters-inches can muster. "I'm not giving you my virginity. Not today, maybe not ever. I just don't know . . ." my voice trails off.

There's a flash of frustration, but he studies me with sparkling amusement in his eyes. I'm reminded of the way he examined the room at the photoshoot when we first met, as if he's above everything that's happening around him. "You're nervous. That's understandable, doll. But I'm not pressuring you here. If you want to, I'm damn sure ready to fuck you all weekend long. If not, we can sit and" —he looks around the room— "watch tv or something."

Though I know he doesn't actually want to watch television with me while I'm barely half-dressed, the thought that he actually would is comforting on some level. It makes me feel like I'm calling the shots, or at least a fraction of them. "I'm not nervous, Liam. I'm fucking terrified. I thought I could do this, that I was ready. But standing here in your fucking mansion, after being driven over by your house manager who's probably dropped off all your women for a weekend of fun, it just hit me how crazy this is. How stupid I'm being. The first time is a one-time thing and I want it to be special."

"I get that, Arianna. Don't you think I want—"

206

But my nerves are gaining momentum, letting my mouth run away with truths I'd probably be better served to not share. "A lowly college intern and the bigshot CEO? I mean, that's a joke. I'd be the joke. Again." The thought drops the wind out of my sails, and I collapse to the couch, pulling my knees to my chest. "This whole . . . whatever this is between us . . . is centered around you wanting one thing from me. It's a game, and I admit I've willingly played. But what happens when the game is over and you've gotten your cherry prize? You can have any woman you want. What good is someone like me to you afterward?" I shake my head, a little sad. "I made a promise that I'd save myself for the man that I'd be with forever."

Fuck. This is not what I meant to happen. Not at all. I really thought this was going to be sexy, fun, and that I'd leave on Sunday night okay with this whole thing. I try to think back to the things Daisy and I talked about, but I feel weak so I revert to my comfort zone of saying no, even as my body begs me to say yes.

Liam seems to be in shock at my outburst, like he's approaching a wild animal who might attack at any given moment, but he still carefully sits down beside me on the couch. "Arianna, at what point did I make you feel like this was a game? Have I chased you? Absolutely. And I think we've both enjoyed the back and forth of that." He eyes me, daring me to disagree, but I can't because it's the truth and he knows it. "But it's not a game to me either. I'm certainly no monk, and far from a virgin, but I can damn sure tell you that I am more interested, more invested in you than I have ever been in some one-off that Randolph drove home the morning after. Women usually just want me for one thing."

My eyes flick to his, jealousy flashing hot and acrid through me until he continues. "Not that. My money. But not you. You actually like me for some fucking reason, but you don't want me *because* I have money and a position of power. Look, Arianna . . . I don't know what happens tonight, or tomorrow, or next month, for that matter. What I do know is that I want you, and I want to see where this goes. But I won't force you into something you're unsure about. It's not fair to you, and it's not fair to me."

He leans back, and in the depths of his blue eyes, I can see that I've hurt him. I didn't mean to. I spoke what was in my heart, all the fears and doubts I'm feeling right now tangled up with pain from the past. I don't want to be that girl again, the one people looked at with an ugly sneer and called mean names.

But I never considered that Liam might have some damage too, that the golden boy big shot might not trust people lightly, might question people's motives, might feel like people think he's unworthy. Like I just did.

He gets up, walking to the window, his back to me. "Why did you come here tonight?"

I swallow at the words because in my heart, I know why I came, what I planned to happen. "Because I thought . . ." I start, trying to formulate my words. This isn't how I expected this to go at all, but I get up to walk over to him, forcing myself to look him in the eye. "You have this aura about you that makes me want to please you, but I feel so powerful at the same time. I don't know how you do that, make me feel weak in the knees but strong in spirit all at once."

The room falls silent as Liam takes in everything I've said, and I wait for him to tell me to get out.

But he doesn't. Instead, he clears his throat and leans closer. "I do. I know how I do that to you. The same way you do it to me. By giving power, by getting power. It's not an exchange, one-sided and singular. It's a cycle, symbiotic and never-ending. Perhaps I could give you a lesson?" The question is quiet, dark with meaning, and heavy with intention.

I can feel that the air in the room is changing, no longer fizzy with my anxiety but foggy with the repressed desire of our time together, as if the pseudo-argument we just had evaporated, though only part of my fears have been allayed. So maybe he's not after me for a wham-bam-get-out-ma'am fuck, but that doesn't solve the problem of what people will think.

But I still ask, "What kind of lesson?" Liam gestures toward the couch. I take his hand and let him lead me over, but we don't sit.

"Let me show you," he says, wicked promise in his voice. I bite my lip, and he spins me in place, pressing my back to his front. I expect him to be rock-hard. I'm barely half-dressed in lingerie, after all. But I find that he's soft, still thick and large but just as affected by the last few minutes as I am. The uncertainty of what we're doing together has physically manifested. He presses on my upper back. "Lean over, Arianna."

Unsure of why but doing it anyway, my mind races at the dirty position. Yes, part of my brain is rejoicing, yelling at me to spread my legs and invite him in the way I desperately want him to be. But the other part questions . . . *Why am I doing this? Why does he have this power over me?*

His hands trace down my back, light fingertips sweeping the silky skin until he reaches the dimples in my back, right above the thong panties I chose to tempt him. But then he moves his hands away, and I feel the loss of contact on a cellular level. I look back over my shoulder, watching as he reaches for his belt. He unbuckles it, slipping it free and then folding it in his hand.

"What are you doing?" Instead of the challenge I meant to

offer, my voice comes out with a pleading tone, like I'm begging for whatever he has in mind.

He skims the leather end of the belt along the flesh of my ass, feeling like a lover's caress but with a mental twist that makes me pant a bit.

"You want to be where I'm at one day, right? Sitting at the head of your own company as the boss?" he asks, quiet and solemn.

I nod, though I'm not sure what that has to do with what he's doing to me right now. "I do."

"Well, let me give you a physical lesson of what it will be like on the way there." He looks me dead in the eye, giving me a chance to say no, daring me to say it. But I stay quiet. "I need your answer, doll. Yes or no."

I get it, at least a hint of what he's teaching me, already. He's the one with the belt, in charge, by all appearances. But I'm the one who grants permission, the one with the true power. He won't do this unless I allow it. My voice is strong and sure, my nerves now inexplicably silent. "Yes."

The first sting of his leather belt on my ass makes me cry out, my fingers digging hard into the back of the sofa. "That's the first sacrifice," he says, "when you have to give up that weekend with your friends to work."

He continues, never hitting me too hard and moving around on my pinkening flesh, walking that line between pain and pleasure as the heat quickly gathers between my legs. With each lash, he names another sacrifice.

Smack. "For the lonely night off because your friends have their own lives now that don't include you."

Smack. "For the first time you have to crush the dreams and life of a perfectly fine person, simply because they're in your way."

Smack. "For the moment you realize your "friends" are just your friends because of your money."

Smack. "For when you don't know if you'll ever find love . . . because you're unable to just be you and not your fucking money or job."

Smack. "For the day you realize you'll always be alone, high in the penthouse dream of your own making, but alone nonetheless. Always alone, a meaningless footnote in an annual report with no one to share the truly important moments with or to miss you when you're gone."

My pussy is drenched, throbbing, and I'm so turned on from the naughty spanks, but my heart is also being shredded as he teaches me about pain and sacrifice. I love it and hate it at the same time, and as he smacks me for the last time, my chest heaves, my heart breaking for him. It's obvious this is what he's had to endure to achieve the success he has. I've learned more about him in the last five minutes than I probably have anyone in my life, maybe myself included. It's raw, real, and painfully honest vulnerability.

There's a long pause, and I hear his choppy breath. But then one more . . .

Smack. "For never being able to trust people . . . not even the one you want to trust most."

He drops the belt and steps back, letting me stand up. My ass hurts while my pussy is soaked, and there are tears in my eyes as I stand up and look at him, seeing more than just the sexy CEO, but the real man. He's panting at the exertion, not from the physical act of spanking but because of the work of sharing such deep truths, painfully ripping them from his heart and giving them to me.

The cycle's complete.

Though he held the belt and I bear the physical marks of that, I hold his heart and he suffers the scars of splitting it wide open for me to learn from.

Needing to comfort him, though I'm the one with the ass on fire, I reach to cup his face. "Liam . . . I'm sorry."

He flinches, shoving my hands away and pacing in front of me. "I don't need your useless and false platitudes. You think there's some perfect man, perfect moment, magic waiting to happen to give you this perfect life. It's a fantasy, a falsehood little girls imagine. I thought you were smarter than that. Life, like business, is seeing what you want and having the guts to work for it, fight for it, claim it."

I can see that though he's talking about my dream of staying a virgin for the right man, his words about letting go of a child-hood fantasy are just as directed at himself. Maybe we both need to hear them.

"You'll get there eventually, walk away from this and find some poor bastard to put through all the pain and sacrifice it'll take for you to reach your dream. And then you'll give yourself to him, with all the expectations you have for that pressing on his shoulders. And he'll falter. We all do at some point. And you'll doubt once again. You told me once that the real thing is worth the price you have to pay." He shakes his head, "Today, there's no more perfect moment than now. *This* is real. But if you don't want this, want *me* enough to live in the real world and pay the price, then you should go. I'll see you at work on Monday."

His rant rivals my earlier one, both of us pouring out so much and exposing ourselves more than ever before. But his final words give me even more pause. "You'd still let me be your secretary, even after all this?" I say, shocked.

He growls at me. "Of course. Though we'll have to stay strictly platonic. My helping you isn't contingent on your giving me your body. I made that clear from the beginning. I'm not a monster, Arianna. But I think we both know you're at a crossroads, not just in deciding whether you want to fuck me, but if you have the balls for this job, this life at all. You're inexperienced in more ways than one, but I can teach you things about business and pleasure you've never even dreamed about. But only if you say yes and mean it."

His eyes float down my nearly-nude body, not pressuring me but simply admiring. I get the feeling he's memorizing me for after I leave, already certain of my answer.

I think of all the things he has already taught me—yes, some sexual, but more so how he has taken me under his wing at the office, explaining why he chooses things, helping me see the bigger picture of his decisions and plans for Morgan. And I know he's right.

He's shown me nothing but respect, challenged me to be better, and accepted my every truth with understanding, even when I flung them at him with every intention of having them slice him painfully.

I collapse to the couch, the weight of the realization heavy on my heart. "You're right, so fucking right. I have been holding on to the dream of a little girl, not one born of innocence and sweet dreams but one created in fear and humiliation. My doubts now are mostly about being scared you're going to hurt me like the boys in school did. But you're not them. And I'm not that girl anymore either. I want a life big enough that it scares me, challenges me, pushes me like you do. I need someone strong enough to call me on my shit when I break down but who will let me hold them when they break down too. Give and take, Liam."

His eyes bore into mine, and I say the words I thought I was going to say when I first got here. It's been a more twisted road than I thought it'd be, but I think we're better off for the messiness. "Yes. I want to give you my body, if you'll take it."

LIAM

Her words make my heart pound, and I'm hanging on to my control by a thread. "Are you sure, Arianna? I want you to be absolutely certain. It is a big deal for us both, but I get that it's something different for you. No doubts, no second thoughts." My eyes search hers, not willing to proceed unless she's clear-headed and positive this is what she wants. I don't think I could stand it if she regretted this later.

But she looks at me proudly, no question clouding her eyes. "I'm sure. I want you. Us. This."

I cross the room to her in three strides, pulling her from the couch to gather her into my arms. Inside me, a war rages. There's a beast that wants to pound her, fuck her ruthlessly until she is covered in my scent and cum. But there's a softer side too, one that wants to lay her down and worship her tenderly, show her what it means to be claimed by me.

But good thing for me, both sides agree that I need her now. Covering her mouth in a kiss, we make commitments neither of us foresaw with our tongues. We've been teasing and building to something heated, but along the way, we've developed something greater than the sum of the little touches.

As her hands tighten in my belt loops, pulling me to her, I realize that she is just as blindsided as I am by how deep things have gotten and how quickly this has all happened. But she's with me one hundred percent now, and I'm damn sure with her.

She pulls back, her eyes dropping, and for a moment, I think she's having a flash of shyness. But then she peeks through her lashes at me. "Can I suck you again?"

"Is that what *you* want? Or what you think *I* want?" I ask, the answer important.

She smirks, the beautiful feistiness blooming in her eyes. "What I want."

I run my thumb along her bottom lip, weighing the truth of her words, and I find that she's being honest. "On your knees, doll," I command, reaching for the button that holds my slacks closed. As she lowers in front of me, I see my leather belt where it dropped to the table and lean down to grab it.

She watches me with interest. I drape it around the back of her neck, not looped, but merely resting against her skin as I hold the ends out wide.

She reaches out, taking over as she slides my zipper down and tugs my boxers down my thighs, her eyes widening as my cock emerges, the veins along my shaft already pulsing with each beat of my heart. She licks her lips in anticipation and I grow impossibly harder.

"Open up. I won't go too hard . . . yet."

Using the barest pressure on the belt, I urge her forward, and she responds, leaning in to meet the head of my cock with a butterfly kiss that sends a shiver down my spine before her lips melt around my cock, drawing me in slowly. It's amazing, her tongue finding all the right places as she teases and explores my cock, inhaling it deeply.

"That's it, doll . . . fuck, your mouth feels good," I compliment her, groaning as she hums around my shaft in reply. "I'm going to go deeper. Hold still."

Using the belt's pressure to keep her in place, I feed her my cock, sliding all the way to the back of her throat before pulling back and starting to fuck her gorgeous face, thrusting in and out slowly. Arianna reaches up, fondling my balls as I moan, watching her eyes close in pleasure as her tongue starts to dance on my shaft.

She obeys, her whimpers of pleasure adding to what I'm feeling through my cock as I pump in and out of her eager mouth, faster and faster. She lets go of my balls and reaches around, grabbing my ass and swallowing all I've got deep in her throat, making me throw my head back in pure ecstasy. Between her hands pulling me and me using the belt to pull her, I'm as deep inside her throat as I think I can be. It's exquisite, and then she swallows, the muscles working my tip. "Fuck, Ari . . . that's perfect."

She pulls off, smacking her lips as she does. "Think you can come twice for me? Once in my mouth and once in my pussy?"

Oh, my God, she is an angel. A fucking naughty one too. "Fuck, yes. I've got plenty of cum for you. Reach down and rub that sweet pussy for me. Get it ready for what's next."

Arianna grins, and between her legs, I can see her slide her bottoms to the side to slide two fingers inside before she gobbles my cock and fingerfucks herself. It's the hottest thing I've ever fucking seen, and this won't last much longer at this pace.

I feel my balls tighten, and my cock swells in Arianna's mouth. She pulls back, sucking just on my tip as she pumps my shaft with her soft hand, and I explode, growling as I ride the tidal waves washing through me. She moans, her thighs shaking, and I realize she's coming too, her fingers filling her pussy as I fill her mouth with my cum.

When I'm done, she smiles and swallows, licking her lips before smacking them gratefully. "Mmm," she moans, pleased with herself for both of our orgasms.

The belt falls from my hands as I reach down, pulling Arianna to her feet and kissing her deeply, tasting the last traces of myself on her tongue as we caress and touch each other. She hisses when my palms run over her pink ass, whimpering in pain. "Ouch."

"I'll make it feel better," I promise her, reaching lower and picking her up. Her legs wrap around my waist instinctively. "Here or the bedroom?"

Arianna looks around, then lifts a brow. "Why not both? Here first . . ."

We sink to the floor, side by side as she works my clothes off. After I kick them away, I reach down, running a soft touch along the lace of her bra cup as she lets out a tiny gasp. I stop, looking up into her eyes. "If you say no, we stop here. I won't undo this."

Instead of replying, she reaches behind her, undoing the clasp herself. She pulls the lacy bra down her arms, her breasts popping free. I dip down to kiss and suck one pink nipple into my mouth. "So pretty, doll." My words are already gruff, need thickening my voice. She wiggles and then shimmies her panties off too, lying beneath me gloriously nude.

I prop myself up and then swallow, looking at her flawless body . . . from her cute little pink toes to the curve of her calves and the swell of her thighs before her hips flare out, leading up to the rest of her, soft tummy and proud over-flowing handfuls of breast. But most of all is her face, big eyes that have teased me, taunted me, and shown me the depths of her soul. Eyes that I could look into forever.

"You're everything I've ever dreamed of," I reply, leaning down and kissing her deeply.

"You too, Liam. Everything I wanted." I can hear that she's not talking about my physique, but more about my soul. It's the best compliment I've ever received.

It doesn't take long for my cock, which never sagged below half-hard, to be fully ready to go again, and I spread her legs, getting ready. "How slow do you want it?"

"Slow," she admits. "Ease me into it."

I nod and run the head of my cock between her lips. She's so wet, and both of us groan as I begin stroking my cock back and forth, covering my entire length in her slick wetness but not penetrating her. Instead, each stroke rubs over her clit, and she gasps, arching her neck to my lips as I suck and nibble the sweet skin.

Something takes over me, and I suck on her neck harder, knowing I'm leaving a mark but glad about it as my hips pump my cock over her pussy. She's so warm, and when she lifts her hips and I slip inside, it takes me a couple of inches before I freeze, looking into her eyes. "Doll . . . you're eager."

"You were about to make me come again," she admits, gasping as I pull back and thrust slowly, filling her a little more. "I couldn't wait any longer."

I draw it out, each stroke of my cock going just a little deeper than before, filling her bit by bit and making her squirm, her hunger for me making her desperate for me to speed up. "Please," she begs.

I growl. "Told you I'm gonna make you beg for it."

Before she can reply, I thrust harder, filling her pussy all the way until my hips grind against hers, and she cries out, her fingers digging into my arms. "Fuck! Ahh!"

I hold still for a second, letting her adjust to the new sensation, and I take the opportunity to appreciate how good it feels to be inside her, merged with her body as one. "You ready, Arianna?" She whimpers in need, nodding.

I can't deny her desire or my need any longer, and I thrust deep, swirling my cock around inside her before pulling back. Slowly, we pick up the pace and I fuck her faster and harder. Arianna cries out with each thrust, encouraging me with gasped words begging for more . . . for me to ruin her . . . for me to come inside her. I give her everything she asks for, pounding her tight, sweet pussy until my hips ache and my balls swell.

I groan, my cock swelling, and kiss her deeply. She gasps, her breath hot on my face as she mumbles, "Liam. Oh, God. So good."

Arianna shudders, wrapping her legs around me as her brain hazes out, and I thrust as deep as I can one more time. My orgasm hits me hard, and I cry out, Arianna echoing me a moment later, screaming my name as she comes, her heels drumming on my spine as she tries to pull me deeper and deeper into her.

Together, we fall into space, the black void consuming us, but it feels like an amazing adrenaline rush because she's right there with me through the whole trip. It feels like I come for hours, and when it's over, I've filled her so much I can feel a trickle of cum dripping out of her. I pull out slowly, and her pussy clenches around me before letting go, squeezing every last drop out of me.

I collapse on the floor next to her, gathering Arianna in my arms to stroke her back and kiss her forehead tenderly. Her body relaxes into mine but she's racked with an occasional tremor for a few moments before she takes a deep breath and turns her eyes to me, smiling. "That was amazing."

"Was it everything you thought it would be?" I ask, stroking her cheek. She's even lovelier in this light, and I'm shaken a little. After all the vulnerabilities we shared before, I didn't think this would seem so heavy, but it does. Beautifully, magically special . . . not just because it's her first time, but because it's our first time together.

"And more," she says, crawling up to kiss me softly. "And I'm looking forward to the rest of the weekend." She freezes, a deer in the headlights look overtaking her face, and I can see the questions lingering in her eyes.

"Tell me what just went through your mind, doll. Share it with me so I can carry it."

"I'm afraid the other shoe is about to drop, that you're going to hop up and say 'ha-ha . . . you're such a sucker' and this will all be some awful joke. Tell me this doesn't end here."

If only it were that easy, just a few simple words and she'd be at ease. But no, I suspect that my doll will always need some reassurances, or at least for a while, but I will happily give that to her. "Arianna, of course not," I swear, touching my forehead to hers. "I'm not running, nor am I sending you away. Honestly, I'm trying to be as much of a gentleman as I can be and not shove my way back inside you right now. I'm sure you're sore, and I don't want to hurt you."

She grins. "Fuck being sore. I like that plan."

I chuckle a bit, pulling her closer and kissing along her skin, marking every inch of her with my lips. As I switch from my worship on one breast to the other, I mumble against her, "By the way, we have a date next Saturday."

She grins and sasses, "Oh, we do? What if I'm busy?"

That spark right there is what I want from her. What I want *for* her. To let her demons wither away in the dark recesses of her mind, laid to rest from the sheer power she now commands. But it's still a process, a give and take, and I'm not done teasing her just yet. "You'll have to cancel your plans," I say arrogantly. "Because you'll be with me at the cover reveal party."

Arianna sits up, surprise on her face. "Huh?"

I laugh softly, sitting up to tell her about the magazine allowing her to appear in the duo shots and the costume party on Helen's yacht. "So am I going as your secretary then?"

I shake my head. "No. Arianna, I want you to go as my date." It's a statement, but there's more question there than I'd like to admit. I am a fucking machine in the boardroom, hell, in the bedroom too. But this woman could reduce me to dust with a single word. That's the power she has over me.

"What are people going to say though? The people at the office are going to talk, Liam. You know that. I'm just some random girl." I can see the echoes of the cruel names running through her mind, morphing from her childhood to an oddly similar experience at work, but I would never let anything like that happen.

And I realize that while she has power over me, I have it over her as well. Not just her body, but her heart, and I can give her this. "What people say has no bearing on what we are. You are not some random girl. You are *my* girl."

Her face lights up and then is overtaken with a sweet smile. "Holy shit, I never saw this happening, especially like this with all the emotional baggage dumping beforehand. But I'm glad it did."

She eyes me, and I agree with her. "Me too. Although maybe we stick to more fucking and less dumping for the next round?"

"Deal!" she exclaims, rolling over on top of me. For a rough start, I think the weekend is going to be better than either of us ever dreamed.

ARIANNA

Dear Diary,

I FINALLY DID IT. NOT JUST ONCE EITHER. OH, NO, I SPENT THE whole weekend fucking Liam Blackstone.

God, that sounds crazy to even say, but it's true.

It was everything I thought it would be and more. This past weekend, I wept tears of overload and joy, I clawed marks in his back, I was fucked to sleep and then woken up to a tongue lapping at my pussy. But I wasn't just receiving. I was just as voracious, wanting to experience everything at once and learn whatever lessons he was willing to share.

But as major as that was, and believe me, it was the big deal I'd always made it out be, the best part was what happened before and after. The talking, the connection, the realness. The sex was amazing all because Liam showed me something. He showed me that he isn't perfect . . . but at the same time, my idea of holding out for someone who is was just wasting the precious days that I have available to me. A seemingly good way to cope and protect myself when I was younger, but ultimately, an unnecessary front to hide behind that was preventing me from having an honest relationship with someone.

No, Liam isn't perfect, and neither am I, but when we're together, we create perfect moments. We created a perfect weekend filled with laughter, orgasms, and deep conversations, and that's all that really matters.

He's the real thing, and it was definitely worth the price.

I SQUIRM IN MY SEAT, PULLING MY HAIR OVER MY SHOULDER as I try to focus on completing my assignment, the speech Liam's supposed to make at the magazine party tomorrow night. I've already edited the rough draft once, and I know it's solid, but trusting me with this is a big leap of faith for Jacob and I want to make sure I give it my all. It's just hard to focus when my ass is still warm from the spanking Liam gave me this morning.

"You okay?" Jacob asks as my chair squeaks for about the tenth time this hour.

I nod. Liam let me in on how close he and Jacob are, but I'm not going to volunteer any information just in case Liam hasn't told him anything. Besides, our private life is just that, private, and Jacob has made it perfectly clear that as long as we're appropriate in the office, he's happy to feign ignorance for now. "I'm fine. Just trying to get this done for Liam. I might need to read it aloud to get the full effect though. Do you mind if I take a copy in his office so I don't disturb you with my practice rounds?" It's mostly the truth, though knowing that Liam is in a meeting and I could surprise him when he comes back with a little mid-afternoon fun is tempting.

Jacob blinks, then shakes his head, not buying it. "You two are meant for each other. No damn shame at all." The shit-eating grin on his face lets me know he finds the whole thing more humorous than reprimand-worthy.

I blink faux-innocently. "What on earth do you mean, Mr. Wilkes?" I ask, intentionally using his full name. "I think your dirty mind is showing." It hasn't been long, but working closely together has given us a chance to develop a certain comfort level with each other, and we've discovered we make a pretty good team, able to get stuff done and still joke around a bit.

Jacob laughs and grabs his tablet. "I think I'll run a few errands around the building and leave you to your *speech practice*." He winks and I blush.

But as he opens the door, he pauses. "Hey, Arianna?" I glance up from my screen, and his face is serious now. "I'll admit I had my doubts, but having you to help in the office has been a godsend. You really have a solid head on your shoulders and are picking things up quickly. I can't wait to read the speech. I'm sure it's great. But maybe more importantly, I think you're good for Liam. He's been my best friend for a long time, and I don't think I've ever seen him this relaxed. You make him happy, bring something to his life that's more than just work, work, work. Thanks for that."

His words are sincere and cut right to the bone. "Jacob . . . thank you for this opportunity to learn from you and Liam, both over the last two weeks and this fall, and for trusting me with your best friend. I know we seem like an odd match, and I think I'm just as shocked by the whole thing as you are, but we fit somehow. I think we're both making each other better and happier."

He smiles, and then he's off on one of his thousand and one little jobs he takes care of for Liam.

I feel a warm acceptance settle in my heart. Having Liam's best friend approve of us is something I wouldn't have expected. I guess I still figured Jacob, and anyone else in the office, would assume some rather seedy things about me if they found out that something's going on between me and Liam. It's a nice change of pace to have someone be happy for us.

That'll be an extra-big deal when I start my fall schedule because I'll still be working here, albeit part-time around my class schedule. Liam and Jacob offered me the permanent position just yesterday, and I'd squealed yes before composing myself enough to ask about the salary package. Liam had rolled his eyes and laid out the details, including a partial tuition reimbursement program if I committed to work for Morgan post-graduation. I'd signed on the last page before he even finished the explanation. He'd laughingly questioned my contract negotiation skills when I hadn't even argued the pay. But salary plus help with school is a more than fair offer, and working hand-in-hand with Liam and Jacob and learning at their side are invaluable.

I feel like I'm on the cusp of something really great here. The lessons continue, both in business and in the bedroom.

But it's been more too. I sometimes feel like Liam and I are teaching each other, that we're exploring together what this all means. We've spent every night together since last Friday when he took my virginity. There have been plenty of sexy moments, but sprinkled through that, we've created a connection that runs deep, sharing so much of our past and making plans for the future. It seems fast, and I definitely recognize that, but I'm falling in love with Liam more with each passing day. I'd questioned whether I was falling into the trap women have succumbed to for ages, confusing sex with love, but I know that's not the case here. With Liam, I truly feel that he's worth the risk, and I'm willing to give my heart just as readily as I gave my body. And no matter what, I'm strong enough to handle whatever happens.

With a shake of my head, I return my attention to the screen in front of me to print Liam's speech. I give the printer a minute to warm up, my eyes tracing along the text, starting with the speech title . . . *Dynamic Leadership for the Next Generation of Business*.

Normally, I'd print to our in-office printer, but Liam likes his speeches color-coordinated so he can jump from one sentence to the next with barely a glance. And the color printer is a big industrial monster in the copy room down the hall. "You print things a thousand and one different ways in five different paper sizes but still say 'PC Load Letter' half the time," I grumble to the machine as I wait for it to clear. While I'm waiting, I hear someone come up behind me.

"Hello, Arianna . . . the machine giving you problems again?"

I turn my head, seeing Melvin. Even though his office isn't on this floor, I've run into him every day. He's nice every time, polite and in a certain way sweet with the way he's trying to get to know me.

But there's something about him that makes my gut squirmy. I haven't quite been able to decide if he's pumping me for information because of my role in Liam's office or if he's awkwardly flirting with me. Either way, I've kept things strictly professional, intentionally directing conversations to work-based things only and not divulging anything of consequence.

But it's so hard to be mean to this guy, especially since he hasn't done anything overtly wrong. He's just odd. "Hi, Melvin. How're you doing?"

"Oh, just the usual. Pretty good, I suppose," Melvin says. "How about you? You seem to be getting more comfortable working with Blackstone."

"The job's a good one," I reply, sticking to what Liam and I have agreed is best for the office right now. "I'm learning a lot."

"I'm sure you are," Melvin says. Though his tone is casual, I can't help but feel the undercurrent of his words is snarky. There's a moment of quiet as I turn to the copy machine, glancing at the countdown timer and praying for the saving ding of the bell. No such luck, though, and Melvin asks, "What are you up to this weekend? We should grab a drink after work. The bar on the corner makes a great martini."

I glance up, shocked that he's actually asking me out. I guess maybe that answers my confusion on whether he wanted information about Liam from me or if he wanted me. Well, unless he's asking me out as a ruse to dig for info when I'm sloshed. I offer a small smile. "Sorry, Melvin. I don't think that's a good idea." I pause to let that sink in but soften the blow, not wanting to be needlessly harsh. "I'm going to the cover reveal party this weekend with Liam and Jacob and need to spend some time prepping."

His eyes widen. "You're going to that? I thought it was only board members."

Shit. I was trying to be nice and let him down easy, and now I've stepped in it knee-deep. "Yes, they invited me to attend since I ended up on the cover too and I'll be working in Liam's office this fall. A chance to meet the board members and network a bit. I'm still in college, so those connections are essential, you know."

He nods, smiling a little. "It's okay. Maybe next time, huh?"

I want to tell him to stop, that there's never going to be a next time, but I just can't. He's already down, and telling him he's got a bigger chance of winning the Super Bowl than taking me on a date would be like kicking a shivering puppy.

My printing's done and I grab it from the tray. "Oops, gotta rush this. Have a good weekend, Melvin." I intentionally don't answer his 'next time' question, figuring I've done enough to the poor guy's ego for the day.

I head back to Liam's office, setting the speech on his desk just as he comes in from his meeting. "Ms. Hunnington, is that my speech?"

"Of course, Mr. Blackstone," I reply, picking it back up and holding it out for him.

He crosses his office, pulling me into his arms and kissing me deeply. "God, I spent half that meeting dreaming of your sweet pussy."

He dips me back, our mouths never separating, and the speech printout flutters to the floor. Before I can catch my breath,

Liam has me spread wide on his desk, his fingers already teasing along my clit as he shoves my lace panties aside. "Fuck, doll. I need to taste you right now." He dives for my center, his breath hot as he rumbles, "Want to drink your orgasm down."

I can't believe how hungry I am for him. I know I'm waking up every morning in his arms, and I go to bed every night with my head on his chest, feeling safe and treasured. But right now, I need him just as much as he needs me.

Maybe I did find the perfect man, after all.

CALLING HELEN'S BOAT A YACHT IS PRETTY MUCH stretching the term to obliteration. I've seen riverboats on the Mississippi smaller than this, and I'm pretty sure if it were any larger, it could qualify as a cruise ship. The top deck looks amazing, with lights everywhere, and already, on my way up, I've seen enough movers and shakers in the business world to make my head spin. And that's just the ones I recognize. Some are wearing masks that don't give a hint as to who's inside. With a sly grin, I wonder if that's intentional so that they can gain a bit of insider knowledge when folks don't know exactly who's lurking nearby. Smart business tactic, I think.

I meet Liam on the main deck, near the front of the boat, and he looks amazing . . . but those sunglasses. "*The Matrix?*"

Liam looks down at his leather trench coat, black pants, and black shirt and shakes his head, chuckling. "I was going for *The Punisher.*" He opens his trench coat to reveal a black shirt with a skull on it.

I smirk, the devil in my eyes. "You can punish me anytime, sir."

He leans closer, whispering in my ear as he grabs my ass under the blue and red skirt I have on. "I'll keep that in mind, Ari. I'm curious, though. Why Harley Quinn?"

I lean back, meeting his eyes and letting a bit of mania into my voice as I quote the psycho badass, *"You think I'm a doll. A doll that's pink and light. A doll you can arrange any way you like. You're wrong, very wrong. What you think of me is only a ghost of time. I am dangerous. And I will show you just how dark I can be."*

Liam chuckles. "Well-played, doll. But believe me, I know how dangerous you are." He steps back, putting a foot of space between us to rake his eyes down my body, taking in the full effect of my costume.

My hair is dark, not the usual blonde of Harley Quinn, but I pulled it up into pigtails and used some of the temporary color spray to get the pink and blue effect. Heavy makeup, a T-shirt that boasts *Daddy's Little Monster*, my two-toned skirt, fishnets, and heeled boots complete the look. Oh, and a baseball bat that I hand-drew *Good Night* on as the piece de resistance.

Though not perfect, it's obvious who I'm supposed to be, and Liam seems to like the overall effect, judging by the way he's tracing a finger along a hole in my fishnets, right at the point where they disappear under my skirt.

"We should probably get upstairs, play meet and greet with the masses," Liam says, though it sounds like he'd rather stay right here with me. He offers his arm, and I take it.

As we head up the elevator, I can't help but ask, "Are you sure?" If we make an entrance arm in arm, everyone is going to know exactly what's going on with us. I'm proud to be with him, but a tiny seed of doubt blossoms in my belly, the worry at ugly judgment coming back with a vengeance. *'She's the whore intern who's fucking the CEO'* echoes in my mind.

"Totally fucking sure," he says, his eyes glowing with desire and more. "You're mine, Arianna. The rest of the world can go fuck themselves if they've got a problem with it." I let his assertion soothe my nerves and take a steadying breath.

With Liam at my side, I can do anything. Hell, I'm learning that even alone, I can do any damn thing I put my mind to. I stand taller, letting my shoulders drop into place and my face relax into casual confidence.

The ride up to the top deck feels like both an eternity and like it can't happen quickly enough. My heart's swelling in my chest as we emerge on the deck. Almost immediately, we're surrounded by photographers and some media people from various websites. Liam handles them all before we melt into the crowd. "Would you like a drink?"

"Sure, but just one—" I start.

"Hey, big brother!" a chirpy voice calls, and I turn around to see a girl pop out of the crowd. One glance and I can see she's Liam's sister, Norma Jean. He's mentioned her, even shown me a few pictures, but we haven't met. "I see you took the blue pill." Liam rolls his eyes at the mistake people have been making all night.

She's wearing a white skirt with a slit cut way up her thigh and a blue button-up dress shirt with poufy gathers at the shoulders. It's almost a cute outfit, if it were 1980. The sides of her red hair are pulled back in little comb clips like it's decades past too.

"Norma Jean, what are you doing here? And I'm the Punisher, not Neo. And who are you supposed to be?" Liam asks, obviously surprised to see her at the party.

"What kind of question is that?! I'm Lois Lane, of course, the best investigative journalist ever," she sasses. "Something I wouldn't need to be if my big brother told me when amazing things like a magazine cover reveal party were on the agenda.

You left me no choice, and I had to finagle an invite out of Jacob."

Liam growls, "I'll kill him. Where the hell is Jacob?" He looks around, though I know he won't actually harm him for inviting Norma Jean.

Norma Jean tsks. "You should've invited me, Liam. I want to be here to cheer for you when good things happen." Her blue eyes are soft as she looks at Liam, and I can feel the sibling connection they have.

It's funny to see Liam taken to task by his feisty sister, because not many people dare give him shit for anything. But she does it without restraint and he allows it without reprimand. "Sorry, Norma. Thanks for coming, and I'm glad you're here."

She smiles, all forgiven. Then her eyes flash to me and I'm pinned in place.

Liam laughs. "How about if I make it up to you, Sis? Strictly off the record. Arianna, this is my annoying little sister, Norma Jean. Norma, this is Arianna Hunnington, my girlfriend."

Girlfriend. It feels so good to hear him say that. Any doubts I had about his affection or intentions are washed away when he tells his sister. Despite his feigned annoyance with her, he's proud of her and values her opinion. I can tell by the way he's talked about her.

Norma Jean offers her hand. "Nice to meet you. I hear we go to the same college, but what Liam here failed to mention was how beautiful you are. I'm legit jelly."

"Thank you," I reply, blushing. "Liam says wonderful things about you too."

Norma blushes back, though she playfully says, "Of *course* he does. So what are you majoring in?"

LAUREN LANDISH

"Business, of course," I reply, feeling comfortable with her immediately. "You?"

"Journalism," Norma says, looking over at her brother. "Well, if business is what does it for you, you've totally picked the right guy. He used to drone on and on at the dinner table about stock market index changes. Even Dad used to tell him to hush and—"

"Norma," Liam growls, interrupting. "Don't."

She cringes. "Sorry, I didn't mean it like that. Just remembering how boring you are sometimes, so if she's into that, you should keep her, Brother."

Liam relaxes at my side, the sting of Norma's accidental words bouncing off as they easily forgive each other. It's adorable, and I feel like I can understand their relationship a bit better.

Norma laughs, giving me a wink. "Before I step on another mine, I'd better work the room. We'll talk later. I think I'm gonna go sneak around and see what kind of trouble I can get into. Bye, guys."

She walks off, and I can't help but notice that quite a few men watch her go, and I have to raise an eyebrow as I look at Liam. "She's quite something," I remark. "Why'd you keep her away?"

"She's a royal pain in the ass and nothing but trouble," Liam says, but it's said with love. He snorts. "You're going to love getting to know her."

"I'm sure," I reply. We move on, chatting and having a drink before the music starts.

I'm not ready to dance yet, but it still feels good to enjoy the party vibe as all these powerful people let their hair down. We're about three-quarters of the way through the room when

Liam whispers in my ear. "Let's go for a walk. I need to *relax* before my speech."

I can feel the need in his voice, and I nod, taking his hand and letting him lead me down the stairs. We walk down the hallway, and Liam checks a few doors but finds them locked. I'm hunching over, like we're naughtily sneaking around, but Liam walks tall with confidence, daring anyone to stop him.

He finds an unlocked door, and we rush in, locking it behind us. The suite is beautiful, just one floor down from the top deck, and from here, we can see the whole horizon from the balcony as the setting sun starts to turn the sky golden. "It's beautiful."

"Nowhere near as beautiful as you," Liam says, shrugging off his trench coat and taking off his sunglasses. He tosses them to the bed and I do the same with my baseball bat, the odd collection on the fancy bedding looking rather amusing. "When you said you'd have a surprise for me . . . I never thought you'd be trying to cocktease me all night with your costume."

I grin, turning away from him and walking out to the balcony before looking over my shoulder. "You want to know the real secret of this costume?"

"What?" he asks as I sway my hips back and forth seductively, his cock stiffening and starting to press against the leather of his jeans. "That you have a spare I can tear off?"

"Mmm . . . nothing quite so big as that," I purr, reaching down to swish the hem of my skirt back and forth. "But these fishnets I'm wearing . . . they're thigh-highs, not pantyhose."

Liam's eyes drop low, and once I'm sure he's watching, I flip my skirt up to let him see the gartered lace tops of my fishnets.

He growls. "You're not wearing any panties, doll."

I lean forward onto the railing and wiggle my ass. The naughtiness he's awakened in me is recklessly daring him. "Come and get it."

Liam doesn't need any more invitation. I hear his zipper slide down, and a moment later, the thick, hard heat of his cock slides deep inside me, making us both groan. "You were wet for me already."

"Being . . . ooh . . . being with you has me always wet," I gasp as Liam starts pounding my pussy. "Mmm. That's it . . . fuck me harder, Liam."

He gives me a rough, deep stroke and rumbles in my ear, "You sure your little virgin pussy can handle me fucking you that hard, doll?"

I bite my lip, trying to remember that the party is just one floor above us, though it's mostly at the other end of the boat. "Yes, yes. I can take it."

"You asked for it," he says through gritted teeth. And then he unleashes on me. His hips pump and slap against my ass so hard I have to fight to keep my footing. With every thrust, his balls smack my clit, adding to the sweet torture. His fingers dig into the flesh of my hips, his thumbs pressing the dimples on my spine as he pulls me onto his cock. He doesn't vary the rhythm to keep me guessing. Instead, he just hammers into me, mercilessly driving me higher, faster than I've ever climbed.

With every grunt, I feel pure joy fill my being, and when my orgasm hits me, he slaps his hand over my mouth, muffling my screams. In the moment, I don't care about the music, the party, or keeping secrets, but I'm glad he has enough fore-thought to keep our private moments between us. "Liam!" I scream against his palm. "Fuck, yes!"

Liam pauses, grinding his cock deep inside me, letting the pulses of my pussy squeeze him. When my orgasm sparks out, every last tremor stilling, he starts again, his breath coming in short little gasps.

"Need you," he moans, not quite making sense but being perfectly clear all the same.

"Take me," I reply, my body already tingling as another climax builds inside me. I thrust back into Liam, meeting his cock harder and harder as we sprint toward a mutual finish, and I feel his cock swell and his hips seize. "I'm giving you everything. Give me your cum, Liam," I beg.

It seems like Liam's climax starts from the depth of his very soul as he cries out, his voice gravelly and whispered. His cock slams deep inside me, and he holds there before he comes, the heat and release triggering my own release. We're both lost to the pleasure, and I'm sure our voices rise a bit too loud in a passionate duet that echoes over the water.

I sag, my chest heaving as a droplet of sweat falls from the tip of my nose to stain the wooden decking underneath me. "Mmm . . . don't move," I ask him as Liam starts to pull out. "I just want to feel you inside me longer."

"You know you can feel it as much as you want, anytime and anywhere, doll," Liam says softly, reaching up and stroking my hair back from my face. He lifts me from my bent-over position, turning me to face him and wrapping his arms around my waist. "You . . . you're amazing, a fucking miracle I thought I'd never find."

"Just a girl in the world," I reply nonchalantly, though we both know his words mean everything. I smile widely at him as I drape my arms over his shoulders. Though there's no music currently playing, I feel like we're dancing, floating on the waves that are gently rocking the boat.

Liam chuckles. "I'm serious. When I first wanted to fuck you, I thought that there was no hope for me. No real future, just . . .

money and work. Now I know there's so much more. I found someone I can trust and have by my side for the rest of my life."

I feel tears threatening at the corners of my eyes, burning with emotion. "You were wrong that first night. You said there is no perfect man. You just weren't looking in the mirror enough. You . . . you're perfect, Liam. And you have me by your side for as long as you want me."

Liam looks like he's about to say something, but then there's a knock at the door. "Liam? It's Jacob. Helen says it's thirty minutes until go time, and she wants to go over some stuff with you."

Liam sighs, chuckling as he pulls back, shaking his head. "He's got terrible timing sometimes."

"Well, he hasn't walked in on us in your office, so don't give him too hard of a time. In fact, I'm pretty sure he's been intentionally giving us some privacy and fielding people for you," I remind him. "Go, take care of business. I'll clean up a little, fix my makeup, and meet you on deck in fifteen."

Liam nods and gives me a tender kiss. "Arianna, I—"

"Liam, come on! She's about to throw a fucking tantrum!" Jacob interrupts, knocking on the door. "Seriously, guys . . ." I can hear Jacob's eye roll even through the door.

"Go," I whisper to Liam, kissing him again. "I know . . . and me too. See you in fifteen."

"That's one thing I don't envy women for," he says at the door. "Takes me ten seconds to zip up and walk off."

"Asshole!" I joke, and Liam laughs as he opens the door and slips out. I head to the bathroom and clean up. My makeup is a mess, smudged eye shadow and smeared mascara. Luckily, it kinda goes with my psycho persona, so I mess it up a bit more to make it look intentional. A quick potty stop, outfit adjustment, and the mirror says I'm ready.

In the hallway, I see someone in a costume striding quickly toward me. He's taller than me, even in my heels, but his Ted the Bear head brings him up to well above normal height. It's a cute costume, but with this late summer heat, even at sunset, the poor guy inside has to be baking and suffocating. Then again, maybe he's naked underneath . . . I think with an internal laugh.

"Hi," I greet Bearman as I head toward the stairs upstairs. He stops, turning to face me, so I do the same. He gestures toward the bat in my hand, holding his hand out. I take the cue that he wants to see it and hold it up. "It was a regular baseball bat until I got my markers after it. Made it myself to go with my costume."

He takes it from me, holding it up to the mesh eyes in the bear head to see it. Suddenly, there's a swish of air and an explosion in the side of my skull.

I fall against the wall from the force of the impact, my mind stupidly yelling that I'm a failure as a psycho badass. As if that matters in this moment.

There's another pop, and then darkness. And none of it matters anymore.

ARIANNA

The room is dark when I wake up, a dim set of lights spinning as I blink, trying to get the world to come back into focus.

"What the . . . where am I?" I slur, my voice sounding like I've had a few too many to drink. That's ridiculous. I rarely drink, and never more than a single glass of wine after watching my parents' drunken struggles. No . . . my brain aches, and I try to focus again, trying to remember. There was . . . a bear?

I try to move, but other than wiggling my arms a little, I'm immobile. Looking down, I can see black duct tape wrapping around my body just below my breasts, holding my arms tight against my body, my wrists also bound in my lap. There's another line of black tape around my thighs and then a fourth around my ankles.

"What the . . .?" I repeat, blinking as my eyes start to come back into focus. Standing across the room from me . . . wait, not a room. It looks like maybe some sort of industrial closet or something. But a few feet away is . . . the bear?

Okay, so at least I didn't dream that up.

I feel wetness trickle down my hairline and over my ear, and I shake my head. The movement both makes my headache turn into a splitting migraine and clears my thoughts. Nope, that's not water . . . that's blood.

"Who are you?" I croak. "Where am I?"

Bearman stands there for a moment, silent, but I can feel the coldness of his stare through the black mesh of his eyes. I strain my ears, searching for any clue to where I am. I can't hear anything, but I can feel the subtle motion of the water, so I think I'm still on the boat.

I always thought if I were in some awful situation, like the attacks or kidnappings you hear about on the news, I would be the type to shut down, just cower in the corner and pray for someone to save me. The too-stupid-to-live girl who repeatedly falls while running away from the chainsaw-wielding mass-murderer in movies. I never actually considered that some-thing like this would ever happen to me. But now that I am finding myself in this nightmare, I'm not scared into frozen inaction. I'm pissed. I'm angry. I'm . . . furious.

I don't think about whether it's a smart choice or not. I just growl out, "Hey, Bad News Asshole, I asked you a question."

Bearman steps closer but still remains silent. Fed up with his act, I swallow to clear my throat and take a deep breath. "HELP! HELLLLLLL—"

He slaps me across the face, and while his costume pads the blow a little bit, my ears start ringing again. He looms over me, threatening in a creepy costume way. "Shut the fuck up, bitch!" he says, his voice muffled by his costumed head. "It won't fucking help you."

"Who are you?"

I don't wait for the answer, seeing an opportunity he didn't mean to give me. Though my legs are bound together, I'm not tied to anything, and I bend my knees, placing my heeled feet on his furry belly and pushing with all my might.

He stumbles backward, slamming into the wall with a decent amount of force. I'm sure the costume helped take the brunt of the blow, but at least I'm fighting back.

The man chuckles, reaching up to remove his fuzzy head. The light is pretty dim, but there's no mistaking who it is. The maniacal smile is new, however. "Hey, Arianna . . . got time for that drink now?"

"Melvin," I gasp, shocked. "What are you doing here?"

"What am I doing here?" Melvin asks, laughing shrilly. "What are *you* doing here? You said you were going to meet people, to make connections. The only connection I see is you being a dirty slut for that narcissistic thief."

I'm taken aback by his fury. It was obvious that Melvin didn't like Liam, especially after Liam shut down his market forecast suggestions, but this? This is utter madness. "Melvin, the party—"

He cuts me off, slapping his palm on the metal wall of the room and continuing his rant as he paces. "He's nothing! Just a spoiled little rich boy whose daddy bought his degree. Not like me. I earned mine with hard work and intelligence." He points at the side of his head to reiterate his point, but he doesn't look like the smart analyst right now. His wild eyes, mussed hair, and sweaty skin instead give him a crazy evil look. I don't bother arguing about Liam's father, who I know for a fact didn't pamper Liam and buy him any success.

He comes closer, leaning over me, but he's learned and holds my legs down this time, not giving me an opening. "He's an empty pretty boy, good for PR. And you fell for it, just like the board did. But I won't let him ruin everything I've worked for."

He bends down, picking up something from the floor, and I realize with a shiver that it's my baseball bat. There's a dribble of blood bright against the pale wood and my stomach turns. That's my blood. I'm almost certain Melvin is going to hit me again, but I'm sure as fuck not going to be a stationary target. I twist and turn on the floor, trying to get away and yelling again, "HELP—"

He doesn't hit me, though he shoves the end of the bat into my gut hard. My breath leaves me in a whoosh and my distressed cry is cut short.

But though my vocals are absent, Melvin is ramping up. His voice gets louder and louder, spittle gathering at the corners of his lips. "It should have been me as Morgan's CEO. He stole it from me."

Slam! The bat clangs against the wall, and I huddle into myself, wanting to be as small a target as possible now and figuring I need to protect my vital organs from another blow. "I'm the one with the MBA, specializing in finance statistics."

Slam! "I'm the one who's saved Morgan from financial ruin and increased our profits sixteen percent!"

Slam! "Sixteen. Percent. Do you know how hard that is? Of course you don't. But I do, and I did it."

Slam! "Me."

He begins pacing again, and I dare a glance up, watching his progress across the room and back. Distantly, I hear a beeping sound, and through the small crack under the door, I can see a flash of red light. I wonder if something is wrong with the boat, but I figure I have a more pressing threat than possibly sinking right now.

I have to do something though. Eventually, Liam will realize I'm missing, but probably not until after his speech, and I don't know how long I was out. Maybe it's been a few minutes, maybe it's been an hour. I don't know.

I search my brain. Though this is nothing like the contract negotiations I learned about at school, negotiating always has a similar construct. I hope that's true of a hostage situation, especially when I'm the fucking hostage.

I try to find some common ground. "Melvin, you're right. Sixteen percent is an amazing increase and you did a great job. I know Morgan and the board appreciated that."

He sneers, "Not likely. They didn't even acknowledge that without me and my predictions, Morgan would've been virtually bankrupt years ago."

I hear what he wants, some recognition, and try to figure out how to get that for him. "Melvin, we can tell them. They should know how important your work is. They want to know that. They need to know. We can tell them . . ."

He barks out a mirthless laugh. "We? *We* aren't doing shit.

You're a nobody, a pawn that Liam plays with. But pawns can be sacrificed, Arianna."

A shiver runs through me at his threat and my eyes lock on the bat as it swings at his side with every step.

"He didn't deserve to be CEO. He didn't deserve you. I was nice to you, you fucking bitch." His eyes shift to me, hot hatred sparking in them. "But no, even when I warned you, you fell for his act too. Just like them. He's got them all fooled. But not me. I can see what he really is."

I've got to keep him talking, let him think that I'm on his side. Play the part. It's not the one I've played most of my life, but I can damn sure play it now. I let my voice pitch higher, my eyes wide as I say, "I can't see it, Melvin. I guess I'm just too young and inexperienced, even though you warned me. Please, tell me what you see in Liam. What he really is."

"Fucking useless," he spits out. For a second, I think he's talking about me, or at least about the me I'm pretending to be, but then he keeps talking. "He's an entitled brat, handed anything he ever wanted. He rolled into Morgan and changed everything, not giving a shit about the people who built the damn company. He swaggers around like a fucking rockstar, smiling at people as he stabs them in the back. But if that's what they want, that's what I'll give them."

He freezes, breath panting as his eyes lock on me. I can see that something has clicked in his mind and I know my time has run out. He comes closer, and though I thrash about, he stays out of my range. His lips spread, his teeth bared in a threat-ening smile. "Oh, yeah, I'm gonna smile while I set him up to take the fall for this. They'll find your body with his filthy cum all over you and know that you're his whore. Your fingerprints and his on the bat." Unbidden, my eyes tick to where his still furry-gloved hands grip the bat, leaving no trace of him. "And when he's on the six o'clock news as a cold-blooded killer who murdered the sweet, innocent intern he was fucking, I'll step in and save Morgan the way I should have before he ever came. It'll be me."

"ME!" he yells, tapping his chest with the bat tip.

I flinch at the loud sound, but when he adjusts his grip, both hands holding the bat like he's ready to swing, my body goes into flight mode. I struggle against the tape anew, thrashing back and forth to get away and screaming.

Even as I flail, my eyes close as I prepare for him to swing. For the blow that will end this all so much sooner than I'm ready for. *I'm sorry, Liam. I wanted to say I love —*

Before I can complete my thought, the door to the room bursts open and Liam comes through the door, roaring with rage. Seeing Melvin, he catches his arm, stopping the bat in mid-swing before Liam spins them both, slamming Melvin into the wall so hard his glasses go flying off. I feel hands tugging at me, but I ignore them, my eyes locked on my saving angel. Liam may be my angel, but he looks like an avenging demon as he knees Melvin in the face, Melvin's head banging off the back wall before he slumps to the floor unconscious.

"Don't worry, we've got you," a familiar voice says in my ear, and I realize it's Jacob. I wiggle against the tape restraints, suddenly needing desperately to be free.

Liam kneels in front of me, his eyes filling with tears as he sees my bloody cheek. My eyes rove his face, needing to make sure he's real, that he's really here, that this is really over.

"Oh, doll," he whispers, stroking my cheek. "I'm so —"

"I love you," I blurt out.

Liam stops, and I feel my wrists and then my arms free as a crew member slips a knife into the tape binding my wrists and cuts me loose. My arms lift of their own volition, grabbing at

Liam to pull him close for a hug. I bury my face in his neck, blubbering against the warmth of his skin, "I love you. When Melvin was about to kill me, my only regret was that I didn't tell you that. I love you, Liam. I trust you, I need you, I love you."

I feel the tape holding my legs let go, and Liam picks me up, holding me safe and secure in his arms. "I love you too, Arianna. And I promise, I won't ever let anything hurt you again."

LIAM

"Are you sure you can handle this?" I ask, not trusting anyone, not for a second. I eye the tiny blonde in front of me, but she doesn't flinch a bit. That's probably a good thing, but it still frustrates me.

But Ari's calm voice soothes my fears. "It's fine. We'll be good while you're gone. I promise Daisy and I will sit right here on the couch, watch a movie or two, and be safe and sound."

I take a steadying breath, knowing that she's right but fighting the instincts that yell in my mind to not leave her, to stay by her side and keep her safe. But I realize that's a lesson in futility. Ari's going to do whatever the fuck Ari wants to do, and we've established that. Oh, she'll do exactly what I tell her, obediently drop to her knees for me or run a million copies at work. As long as that's what she wants to do. Give and take, take and give. And we've found that perfect balance together.

So I leave the two women curled up on my couch to go get ready, but I can't help but pause at the door to listen as they gossip.

"Holy shitballs, chica. What the fuck happened? I mean, I know the basics from when Liam called . . . which, by the way, when I answered your number and it was him saying you'd been hurt, I about came through the line at him." She's not the least bit apologetic about it and really had been pissed as hell at my calling until her anger had morphed into cold fear at the news.

Arianna laughs, then hisses in pain, but I force myself not to go back in. "Sorry about that. Was kinda busy with the para-medics then." I hear the creak of the leather couch as one of them moves around, then Ari speaks again. "Well, I was kidnapped by Melvin, a crazy asshole who was all butthurt at being looked over for the CEO gig, like he had some right to it that Liam didn't. He thought he'd frame Liam for killing me, but Liam came busting in and saved me."

Daisy whistles. "Fuck, girl. That's so scary." They're both silent, but then I hear the sniffles and wonder which one is crying or if they both are. "How'd they even know where you were? And what happened to Melvin?"

"Well, Melvin was swinging my bat around like a Major League Baseball player, slamming it on the walls and stuff. I guess at some point, with his swings or maybe when I kicked him into the wall, a sensor for the boat was set off. The alarm sounded on the bridge and in the hallway, but the siren was pretty far down the hall so I could barely even hear it, and Melvin was too far gone in his anger to notice it, but it led them to check there. Liam had already realized I wasn't in the audience for his speech and knew I wouldn't miss it, so he knew something was wrong. I got lucky."

It's quiet for a moment, and I say a little prayer of thanks at how lucky we all got that night.

"Then, between Liam, Jacob, and the crew, they held Melvin down until the police got there. He's got a broken nose and a concussion from the fight. He's worse off than I am, maybe."

She lists out Melvin's injuries matter-of-factly, but I secretly confess to myself that I'm not sorry. Not in the least. In fact, I'd do it again, beat the shit out of him even worse for daring to touch a single hair on Ari's head, for using her as a pawn to get to me.

"But you're okay?" Daisy asks, the concern for her friend obvious.

"Yeah, I'm on concussion watch for a week. But it's a mild one, not too bad, considering the blows I took. I should be fine to start school on time, just have to rest until then and be careful I don't overdo it. Speaking of, I can't really watch movies. Doctor said no screen time for a bit," Ari says, her voice already getting weaker than when she started her tale.

"No problem, honey. You seem pretty wiped out. Why don't you take a nap for a bit? I'll sit right here and wait."

"Mmkay," Ari responds, and I can tell she's already half-asleep. I'm just about to tiptoe down the hall when I hear a 'psst' from the living room.

I peek around the doorway and find Daisy looking at me with a bemused smirk and a glint in her eyes. She mouths, "We're fine, go get your shit done." And then she shoos me with a waving motion of her hands. If she weren't Ari's best friend, I'd kick her out on her ass for her sheer gall.

But Ari loves Daisy, so I give her a pass. But not before telling her through a series of gestures to keep her eyes on Ari and call me if she needs anything.

As comfortable as I'm going to get that Ari is in good hands, with Daisy at her side and Randolph on extra alert, I head to the office.

JACOB IS STANDING AT THE FRONT OF THE ROOM WHEN I

arrive, the rest of the board already seated around the table. "Please, I'm not at liberty to discuss what happened at the party."

Jacob's a good man and an even better friend. We knew this meeting was going to be a shit show, but I'm not one to shy away from the hard stuff when it's necessary. And this definitely is.

"Good morning, ladies and gentlemen," I say, and all eyes turn to me. The people seated around the table are all in suits, their usual office garb even though it's Sunday morning. I was too focused on taking care of Arianna to bother with dressing up, though, and I'm in jeans and a polo shirt. It's a perk of being the fucking boss. There's a murmur of greeting and I launch into what they really want to know.

"As you're all aware, there was a rather disturbing incident on the boat at Helen's party." I pause, letting my eyes click from person to person, wondering if they feel the same way Melvin did. Or hell, maybe someone here was in on the idea with him? My mind races at the thought.

John Summers, a long-standing board member, speaks out. "Liam, we don't know what happened. Just that everyone was waiting for the big cover reveal and your speech, and then we were all shepherded below-deck to the dining room. We could see that there were a lot of flashing lights, police or fire, maybe, and then we were told we could go home. We don't know anything."

"I see. Well, then let me explain a bit of what happened," I say before launching into the whole sordid tale. I leave out the part about Arianna and me fucking on the balcony, simply saying that Melvin had figured out that Arianna is important to me and was going to use her against me to have me removed as CEO.

Another board member, Susan Johansson, speaks. "I think we all knew how unhappy Melvin was with your leadership and that he wanted you fired, but I can't believe he would go to these lengths." She shakes her head disbelievingly.

I glance to Jacob, who shrugs. He caught the same slip I did. "I'm sorry, did you say Melvin wanted me fired?"

Susan nods. "Yeah, he kept bringing me all these reports, piles of statistics showing what he called your 'steady chipping away at Morgan's greatness'. Honestly, I felt the figures showed you turning around the divisions you're working on and the appropriate reallocation of resources from areas you said we should discontinue. The figures showed exactly what they should have based on your plans. But Melvin just didn't see it that way."

The other members nod, muttering things like 'he did the same to me' and 'could not get him to shut up about a zero-point-three-percent change.'

"Let me get this straight. Melvin Jackson has been coming to each of you, complaining about my leadership and trying to turn you all against me? How long has that been going on? Since I shot down his market predictions presentation?" I ask, surprised, though I should've seen this coming.

John leans forward. "It began before we even hired you as CEO. He applied for the position too, and because he's a VP with a finance background, the board interviewed him. We felt his approach was too conservative and wouldn't create the boon we knew Morgan needed to get back to where we once were. Your way is sometimes uncomfortable for us traditionalists, but we can't argue with results."

My head spins, and I begin to put the pieces together. There's so much I should've seen with Melvin, obviously. But he hid it so well, none of us realized what was lurking beneath the surface of his nerdy exterior.

"It seems Melvin is more of a master manipulator than any of us gave him credit for. He's been coming to me since day one, offering intel on each of you, saying that the board was questioning my decisions, regretting bringing me on, and actively working to renegotiate my employment contract. That stopped, of course, after I shut him down on his market forecast presentation. But I think the seeds of doubt had already been planted and watered by then, drummed up on gossip, rumors, and lies."

I glance around the table, seeing the same realization dawning in everyone else's eyes. We've been duped . . . badly. And not only did I almost lose my position of leadership here, but I almost lost something much more precious. Arianna.

"I think we're going to need to start over in a lot of ways. Though the business decisions we've made under my time here are working and Morgan, Inc. is doing better, I want the partnership between me, as CEO, and each of you, to be transparent. It sounds like we have a lot to discuss."

ARIANNA

I'm bundled up against the cold as I step into the lobby, but I immediately begin unraveling my scarf as the heated air of the building warms me. Striding through the echoing front area, I hear my name.

"Good morning, Ms. Hunnington. How are you today?"

I turn, seeing Dora Maples smiling warmly at me as she heads over with a cup of coffee. "Good, Ms. Maples. Any Christmas plans?"

She launches into a story about her kids coming home for the holiday week, and I smile, nodding along. It's nice to listen to her, chatting casually and comfortably as I walk to the elevator.

It hasn't always been this easy. Right after the whole thing with Melvin, word got out almost instantly that Liam and I were sleeping together. The rumors were pretty ugly at first, but I'd already been through that once before, so with Liam's support this time, I handled it with my head held high.

When we let it be known that we were not some casual fuck but rather a happy couple, it seemed to help after a bit of cattiness about our age difference, albeit not too much, and drastically different financial statuses. But who cares about a number, whether it's years on this earth or dollars in the bank? Definitely not me.

It took some time, but it's all died down now and most people have accepted that I work for Liam and Jacob part-time and that Liam and I are a couple. It's nice to not have to hide anymore, although we still have to sneak when we have a quickie at the office.

People are accepting, but not *that* accepting. Well, except Jacob, who just rolls his eyes.

"So, how were finals?" Jacob asks when I get upstairs.

He's bundled up against the chill, wearing perhaps the world's ugliest Christmas sweater, but apparently, it's his tradition. I guess it does help add to the festive mood.

"Kicked ass. Come on, you and Liam have been giving me enough lessons that I should be able to pass *Advanced Modern Business Theory* with my eyes closed. Hell, Liam could teach the class!"

Jacob laughs, nodding. "Well, some would call that an unfair advantage . . . but that's what business is all about." He checks his desk, humming. "Hey, Helen sent over a few copies of the magazine. It hit newsstands already, but she wanted you to have a few for posterity. Her words, not mine."

He hands over a stack of six magazines, and I trace the photo of Liam and me on the cover. That seems so long ago. Just an overworked and underappreciated intern who got roped into something wildly beyond her dreams and ended up with the perfect man.

The one worth waiting for, the one worth paying the price for the real thing. The one I love. "Hey, where is he?" I ask, thinking that Liam's schedule had an early morning meeting, but he should be in by now.

"You should keep up with your boss's schedule better, Ms. Hunnington. That is your job, after all, right?" I hear a voice say behind me, the laughing arrogance sending a shock through me the same way it does every time. He's not a fairy-tale Prince Charming, that's for damn sure, but he's my Mister Right . . . and my Mister Right Now.

I spin in place, looking up at Liam through my lashes and clasping my hands behind my back. "You're right, sir. I'm so very sorry. Perhaps you should remind me again about where to find your . . . *calendar*."

Liam growls and grabs my hand, dragging me into his office. Right before he shuts the door, I hear Jacob call out, "I guess I'll be holding your calls?" Liam's answer is the click of the lock on the door.

"Such a naughty doll, forgetting about my calendar," he teases, letting his voice drop down low as if he's reprimanding me. "Strip for me. Get against the glass."

I obey, but slowly, taking my own sweet time to give him what he wants. I slip my heels off, lay my skirt and blouse over the back of the chair, and then give him a questioning look.

He's already rubbing his hand over his thick cock, the thin fabric doing nothing to hide how hard and swollen he is. "All of it, Arianna."

I reach back and unclasp my bra, setting it on top of the stack of clothes before sliding my lace panties off and doing the same with those.

I take deliberate steps to the window, knowing that he's stroking himself as he watches me. Once I'm there, only then does he follow me over. He crowds against me, pushing my overheated flesh to the cool window, his cock nestled against my ass. "Don't worry, doll. No one can see you but me. But I want to fuck you overlooking my kingdom."

I have a flashback to when he discovered me sitting in his chair, thinking it was fit for a king and that he was definitely the man in charge. He still is, and now, for as long as I let him be, he's in charge of me too.

"Put your hands on the glass and arch your back for me," he says, and I gladly obey that order, knowing he's about to give me what I want. I hear his zipper being lowered and then him moving about as he stacks his clothes up on the chair with mine.

Sometimes, it's a wild tornado of flung-off clothes with us, but this deliberate stall while I wait for him is so fucking sexy. The way he plays me the same way I did him. Both of us knowing what's coming and letting the anticipation build.

Finally, he's behind me again. Our entire bodies connect, skin to skin and heart to heart. He crouches, and I lift to my toes, letting his cock line up with my pussy as he slams in with one thrust. "Ahh, fuck, Liam!"

And suddenly, I'm complete. Like I walk around all day, missing a piece of myself, and when he's inside me, I'm everything I should be.

His virgin.

His whore.

His.

He thrusts again, slow but hard, hitting deep inside me on that secret spot he knows makes me come in moments. His pace picks up, pulling all my attention, and my eyes flutter closed. I feel him grabbing at my hands, holding them to the cool glass and interweaving our fingers.

"Open your eyes, doll," I hear him say from far away.

Somehow, I do, blinking at the view of the city below us. Something tickles my finger, and I look over, seeing him twisting a diamond ring on my left hand. He somehow slipped it on without my realizing it.

His thrusts never stop, slowly and steadily driving me higher as my heart explodes in light. "That's it, Arianna. You're mine, and I'm going to fuck you over *our* kingdom. My dream, my reality, your dream, and now your reality. Look out and see everything I'm giving you."

I cry out, so close to the edge, but I fight the orgasm back, tilting my hips to let Liam slip out of me. I spin in place, putting my back to the window and cupping his face. "Liam, I want to see the most important thing you're giving me." My eyes lock on him, all I'll ever need, and I kiss him hard, our lips slamming together.

And when he enters me again, I keep my eyes open, never leaving his for a moment. I watch the orgasms get closer and closer, the pleasure and the love mixing in his eyes the same way I know they are in mine.

And we come together, the waves crashing over us, as sparkles dot my vision. But our eyes never close. Together, giving and taking everything.

Liam

CEO Playboy Ends Chaotic Year With Proposal to Student Girlfriend!
I read, shaking my head. It's Norma Jean's second cover story
for the student paper, the first being her exposé on the incident
aboard Helen's yacht. "Seriously?"

Arianna, who's lounging on the other end of the couch, chuckles. "Read it, honey. I want to hear how your little sister
describes you this time."

Rolling my eyes, I clear my throat and begin. "Taking her side,
I see. Okay, well . . . *breaking rules and breaking hearts has been
hot-headed CEO Liam Blackstone's MO since he first stepped onto the
corporate scene. But now it seems the notorious womanizer* . . . I'm so
gonna have to have a talk with Norma," I mutter, not flattered
with her description of me. "I'm not notorious, and I wasn't a
womanizer. I just . . ."

Arianna can barely contain her grin. "No worries. Whatever
experience you had before me just meant that you could be a
good teacher for me." She winks at me sassily, a habit she's
picked up from my sister. They're friends now and spend way
too much time chatting on the phone and giving me shit. "As
long as I'm the only one benefitting from that experience
now . . . and always."

I can hear the possessive threat, which should probably scare
me but instead is sexy as fuck. I like that she claims me,
because I damn sure claim her back. I've even threatened to
make some appearances at her university, mostly so that the
assholes there know to back the fuck off.

"But there might be some truth to the hothead part. Keep
going," she says, and I realize that she might have a point.

I give Arianna a lighthearted scowl, but I can't be mad at her.
The sparkle of the diamond on her finger is still too new. It
makes my heart go soft and my dick go hard in about three
seconds flat. "Let's see . . . ah, here's a part you'd like. *The*

couple plans to celebrate their engagement with a trip to the coast, where they'll begin a week-long cruise aboard a private yacht. Though rumors initially ran rampant about the couple, considering their age difference and the fact that Ms. Hunnington was an intern at Morgan, Inc., an anonymous insider stated that everyone is truly happy for the newly-engaged couple."

"Anonymous insider? She's got people at work talking to her about us now?" Ari exclaims.

We look at each other, then both say, "Jacob."

I chuckle, and Ari growls a cute little kitten sound. "Sounds like I have something to talk to Mr. Wilkes about when he comes over for Christmas dinner. Keep it professional? Indeed."

"I predict that when you yell about it, Norma Jean is going to take his side and say that it wasn't him. Protecting her source and all. You'd be better served to give her the scoop on him . . . turnabout is fair play, after all," I tell her.

She grins evilly. "Ooh, that's twisted. I like it. Okay, here's the plan . . ."

And Arianna is off and running, her plan to jokingly get back at Jacob ending up as a rehash of the Christmas dinner menu we've already discussed umpteen times.

"It'll be fine, doll. It's just the six of us, and I don't think anyone is that picky," I say, hoping she'll relax.

This is her first time to plan a dinner like this, though I've told her it'll probably be the first of many, and it's Christmas Eve, not Christmas Day, so the pressure should be lessened. But she's excited to have Daisy, Connor, Norma Jean, and Jacob over. She'd wanted to ask my dad and stepmother as well, something I think Norma Jean had suggested, but I'd vetoed that quickly. I just want a nice meal around a sparkly tree, with the people we love and who love us back. She'd easily given in, wanting the same thing and understanding since she didn't want to invite her parents either.

And then Christmas Day, it'll be just the two of us.

The real thing.

The cycle complete.

I've given Arianna my heart, and she's taken mine.

Continue on to read Silk and Shadows, Norma Jean's book.

SILK AND SHADOWS

BY LAUREN LANDISH

Prologue
Norma

*D*ear Diary,

  *I'm doing it. I'm on my way to the top, just like I planned.
Now, the university newspaper, and later, some serious investigative
journalism. Business . . . or maybe politics? I'm not sure just yet, but I
know I'm going to get there.*

*My focus is sharp, honed through an obsession with hard work and an
unwillingness to fail that I learned at the elbows of two of the greatest
men I know, my father and my brother.*

*Unfortunately, they're the only men in my life. My sharp tongue and
quick wit are usually a turnoff for most guys, their inability to handle a
mouthy woman usually apparent before we even get to a first date. But
I'm not going to change for anyone. The right man for me will match
me word for word, biting retort for biting retort, and together, we'll challenge each other to be better.*

*At least that's the plan. But honestly, I'm not sure he even exists. If not,
I'll probably stay a single virgin forever, no compromise, no wavering.*

I'll be true to who I am . . . even if that means I'm alone with only my work to fulfill me.

NORMA

To say I slept like hell last night would be an understatement. I love my barely off-campus apartment and the fact that I can live alone, unlike most sophomores on campus, but the building's cheap walls are paper-thin. So thin that I might as well have a roommate, a freakishly loud one in the apartment next door who was moaning and groaning for hours last night. I mean, seriously, who lets their headboard thump against the wall while screaming 'yes' over and over . . . for *hours*? After that long, I'm thinking it's not really gonna happen for you and you should give up so the rest of the world can get some sleep before morning classes. Inconsiderate skank. Yes, skank because the girl in question once shared, unprompted, mind you, that she learned to never yell the guys' names because she got it wrong one time. Shudder. I can't imagine not knowing the name of the person literally inside you. So yeah, inconsiderate skank.

But maybe I just wouldn't get it? I've rarely dated and have only been to second base a time or two, but I most definitely know the names of those guys. When my neighbor had first moved in, it'd been a naughty tease to listen to her nightly play by play, and in the privacy of my own place, I'd quietly gone along with it, using my fingers or the occasional toy.

But now, I usually end up sleeping on my couch in an attempt to put more walls and more space between her auditory assault and me.

Hence, the reason I slept like hell. My couch isn't that comfy, making me doubly grumpy from lack of sleep and an abysmally poor quality of sleep. My dad or my brother would willingly pay for me to stay at a nicer place where I wouldn't have to deal with this, but I'm a stubborn girl.

So off to the school paper I go, the only possible bright spot that could shove me out of this funk. Or so I hope.

Those hopes are quickly dashed at Erica's words.

"You want me to *what*?" I screech, though I'm trying to keep my voice down a bit so that the other employees don't prairie-dog out of their cubbies to see what's going on. They'd probably volunteer for any assignment Erica would throw their way. But not this. For the love of God, not this.

Erica, the editor at *The Chronicle* and better known as my boss, stares at me like I asked why I need to be the one to cure cancer. Honestly, I think curing cancer might be easier. "Look, Norma, I know it's a big request, but you're the best person for this assignment."

This 'assignment' is tutoring the star quarterback of our football team, something completely out of my wheelhouse. Also, it's something I don't have time for with my own studies and constantly working to find stories that will get me bylines in the paper. I give her a bit of a glare, tempering it only because she's the senior in charge and I'm a newly-hired and lowly sophomore.

"Seriously, the school got a major black eye last year when the star of the basketball team lost his eligibility right at the end of the season. That cost us big time. And Coach Jefferson isn't willing to gamble like that. If the football team is going anywhere near a bowl game this season, he needs Zach Knight holding the ball. And for that to happen, he has to pass English." She's whispering, like the idea that a football jock might not be good in the classroom is some big newsflash.

"Okay, I get that, but English?" I reply. "Why not get an English major to tutor him?"

Erica's eyes drop, instantly letting me know that there's more to the story coming. I brace myself because judging by the way she's hemming and hawing, this is bad. "Well, Coach asked for a favor." That doesn't surprise me. Erica does a great job highlighting our football team and has been rewarded with some private interviews in return, so she's got a 'scratch my back and I'll scratch yours' deal with Coach Jefferson. "It's not just that Zach needs a tutor. He needs a tutor on the down low. No one can know about this. No. One. And while you're new here, I've been impressed with your ability to protect your sources. So, I'm trusting that you'll keep your mouth shut about this."

There's no threat hanging in the air, just like there's no promise of me getting a leg up at *The Chronicle* if I do this and succeed. But still, the implications are clear. If I help Zach, I'm making a back-scratch agreement with Erica too, and she upholds those under-the-table deals as much as she can. If I don't do this . . . well, I can't imagine that'd work in my favor.

I sigh, arching an eyebrow. "Fine, you know I'm going to do this. But I need to know . . . why the secrecy? Most of the players have tutors. Hell, it's common knowledge that a few of them basically pay people to take their classes for them. Why's this one such a big deal?"

Erica looks around like she's afraid someone is listening in on our conversation, and I wonder why this is what's setting her off, considering everything else she just said. "Do you follow our football team at all?" I shake my head. Past the fact that I could recognize a football, I'm pretty clueless. She sighs, gathering her thoughts. "Okay, so our team is at a crossroads. Zach is a top-notch player, likely pro-quality. So with him on the field, we're a shoe-in for a bowl game. That translates to money, something I *know* you understand."

I nod, though I try to keep my family's wealth out of the

picture at school, not needing any attention for something that has nothing to do with me. But Erica knows because of the article I wrote about my bigshot CEO brother, Liam.

But I know that football and colleges go together like money and . . . money. Few of the players, in any of the top sports, are here because they're academically gifted, but because they make money for the school. I'm not bitter about that, though. It takes all kinds to make the world go 'round, and I've gotta give it to the guys who work their asses off to use their talent on the field to get a piece of paper most folks would kill for.

"So, if there's a question as to his eligibility, the money machine that is 'football' around here could grind to a halt. No one wants to watch second-string guys play. They want to watch greatness on the cusp of something even greater . . . and that's Zach. The athletic director already had to pull some strings with the dean so that Zach can maintain eligibility for now, but that's a temporary solution until you help him." Her eyes plead with me to understand what she's saying. "Coach said that there's a lot of pressure for quarterbacks with pro scouts too. The scouts want guys who are good on the field, but these days, QBs are team reps, so they need to be good-looking, well-spoken, and relatively intelligent. So if word gets out that Zach, while he's definitely good on the field and gorgeous, is as dumb as a rock and might be putting the entire season for the team in jeopardy, it'll start a chain reaction of bad news for the school, Coach, and even Zach. Do you get what I'm saying?"

I let her words mull over in my mind. "Just to be clear, though, I'm not doing his work *for* him. I'll tutor him, but he's going to have to study *himself*, do the papers *himself*, and take the tests *himself*. I will tutor him. I'm not taking his English class for him."

Erica sighs in relief. "Of course. That's all I'm asking, Norma.

But there is one more teeny-tiny piece to the puzzle." She holds up her finger and thumb an inch apart.

I look at her expectantly, decidedly not liking the look of horror on her face and the way she's not looking me in the eye now. "What, Erica? How bad is it?"

She takes a breath, fortifying herself, and then whispers, "Coach is concerned that even if you keep your mouth shut, there's a risk that this could all be found out. Zach's the star so people pay attention to who he's seen with. So he wants a . . . cover story, if you will. I need you to basically be undercover as his tutor. It'll be good practice for when you actually are an investigative journalist."

She's rambling a bit and I'm not quite following her train of thought. "And my cover would be . . .?" I prompt.

Her eyes meet mine. "Zach Knight's girlfriend."

My mouth drops in shock. "What the hell, Erica? Absolutely not! That's ridiculous. I'll just tutor him discreetly and it won't even be a big deal. Happens all the time."

But even as I protest, Erica is shaking her head. "No, Norma. You have to. Please. It's just so no one will question you two hanging out together. Nothing more. People who date hang out together at the library for study dates. And just for a little while, until his grades are up. The faster you get his GPA in check, the sooner you can be done with the whole scam. But this is make-or-break for Zach, and probably for the school. And us too, if we can pull this off for Coach."

She's laying it on thick, guilt-tripping me while simultaneously digging at my school spirit. But my parents made sure that I was made of sturdier stuff than that and I won't be forced into something this crazy. However, one thing I also know is that sometimes, the best opportunities come in really shitty plain-brown packages. And I think this might be one of those times.

I'm willing to tutor Zach—that's not an issue—and if I have to go to a few games and wear his jersey to sell the lie, what's the harm? It's not like I'm busy with a real boyfriend anyway.

And the potential rewards could be great. I'll have an in with Erica and Coach Jefferson, and the undercover practice might help down the road.

I narrow my eyes. "Okay. I'll do it. But this is a big favor and I want you to know that I recognize that."

Erica looks relieved. "Thank you. I won't forget this."

I look her square in the eye, a lesson I learned long ago from my dad. "I won't either, Erica." I let a pause lengthen to add impact to my words before continuing, "So, when does covert operation 'Save the Jock' begin?"

"Today. Luckily, the team had today off from field practice so you're meeting with Zach at five at the library. Be there and be square. Good luck. We're counting on you." Erica breaks out into a huge grin and I can't help but feel I just got played a bit.

But I know that I'm new, and being agreeable, even when it's something as crazy as being a fake girlfriend to hide the fact that I'm tutoring a football player, can only help me on my path. Helping Zach helps me.

I try to remember that as I search my brain for what I know about our football team and Zach Knight. Admittedly, it's not much, but even someone as unaware of sports as I am knows of Zach. Erica called him gorgeous and she's not wrong. Zach is nice eye candy, tall and broad-shouldered, with thick muscles that somehow don't look bulky but are lean, and a face that has lit up our Jumbo Tron more than a few times. Blond hair that he's usually running his fingers through from just taking his helmet off, blue eyes, and a square jaw. He's the quintessential All-American guy, football god and all. And apparently, as of five o'clock, my new fake boyfriend.

Five o'clock comes and goes, and I feel like an idiot standing in the middle of the library foyer, looking for all the world like a girl who just got stood up on a study date. There's no sign of Zach, and I decide not to waste time and to get some of my own studying done while I wait.

There's a piece of me that wants to just leave, mentally telling myself that if he can't even deign to show up on time for me to help him, then he doesn't deserve the help. But this is helping me get ahead too, I remind my inner bitch, so I give in and wait. Looking around, I pick a quiet corner on the first floor where no one will see us carry out his first lesson. If he shows.

I head over to the table, keeping an eye on the main entrance as I pull out my own work, setting up my laptop and opening the textbook I'm reading from. But though my eyes scan, I'm not really seeing the words on the pages. Instead, I'm fuming.

I'm not too surprised that he's late. I figure the entitled ass probably lives by his own clock, not even bothering to give lame excuses but rather assuming everyone will wait on him. Ironically, considering where I'm currently sitting, he wouldn't be wrong in that assumption.

With a sigh, I force my eyes to focus on my own studies and make some good headway, making notes on the entire third chapter of my World History textbook. I do a bit of color coding and formatting so that it's an easier study later and save my progress.

Time seems to have flown by because when I look at the clock, I realize it's well after six. I've seriously waited for this ass for over an hour and he's still a no-show?

This is bullshit, I fume to myself, wondering how I let Erica talk me into this. I shut down my computer and shove it and my book back into my bag. "I should've known," I mutter quietly. Though whispered, my voice takes on a sarcastic edge, the one Liam says can slice and dice an ego at one hundred paces. "Asshole desperately needs help but can't be bothered to actually show up to get it. Fuck that self-entitled prick. He can fail for all I care."

Suddenly, a deep chuckle right behind me interrupts my rant. It's a guy's voice, his faux-supportive anger mimicking me. "Yeah, fuck that self-entitled prick!"

ZACH

I was told I was meeting a redhead, and when I heard her grumbling about a self-entitled prick, I knew I'd found her. At my statement, she turns around, fire flashing in her eyes. When I said it, I was just seeing if I could get under the skin of the sexy little wood sprite I'd been checking out as I walked across the library, only to discover her griping about me. I was curious to hear her response.

Well, that and I fully expect her to pull a 180 and grovel at my feet like most girls do. Hell, like *everyone* does. I don't ask for it. It's just what happens.

But I'm surprised she's not relenting. She's glaring daggers, even more so now that she recognizes me. Oh, yeah, I can tell she does. Usually, that makes girls go stupid and soft, simpering into puddles at my feet. But not this one. I offer one of my panty-melting smiles, but she scowls fiercely, her baby blues filled to the brim with attitude.

She looks cute as fuck when she's mad. All fiery hair and fair skin, with a few freckles sprinkled across her cheekbones. She's small enough that I could easily pick her up, but she puts off an aura of anger I haven't seen in some of my defensive linemen. She's frighteningly intimidating for such a pretty little thing. The contrast is interesting.

I offer her a hand. "I'm Zach Knight. But I guess you can call me self-entitled prick, if you prefer." I'm joking, not really apologizing but acknowledging in a slightly self-deprecating way that I'm late. It should be enough to soothe her ruffled feathers.

But no. She doesn't flinch under my gaze, the steel in her spine obvious as she takes my hand for a quick shake. "Norma Jean Blackstone. I'm afraid our session was scheduled for five to six, though, so you've missed your opportunity today. Perhaps we can schedule for tomorrow and you can be on time?" Her voice is saccharin sweet, but the barbs are clear as she tilts her head, looking at me expectantly.

A grin forms on the corners of my lips at her refusal to back down and I cross my arms over my chest to resist grabbing a lock of her red hair. My wide stance blocks her from moving around the table to leave. I think the challenge in my stare has something to do with her staying too. *Goddamn. She has bigger balls than some of the guys on the team. I'm either going to kill her or fuck her . . . and I know which I'd prefer.*

At my lack of response, she puts her hands on her hips. I'm sure she thinks she looks menacing, but she looks sexy to me. Like a nerdy nymph. She's waiting for my reaction, certain she's won this round, but I'm just getting started. I get the feeling she is too.

But I let her have this one. I was late, after all, and I get that she's doing me a solid by even being here. Hell, if she'd been over an hour late to meet me, I'd have been long gone. I offer an explanation. "No need to be bratty. The team had the day off, but we still had to lift. I needed to grab a quick shower after. I wanted to do you the favor of not showing up sweaty and stinky." I intentionally poke at her by acting like I was doing *her* the favor. "Sorry, gotta keep the hardware nice and clean."

I glance down pointedly, knowing her eyes will unconsciously follow where mine go. Her blue gaze flicks down to my cock, soft but filling up my jeans with her attention. She tears her eyes away, and I add a tally mark to my column for rattling her. It's a lazy flirtation, but less has resulted in a girl attempting to throw herself at me. But not Norma.

Her face scrunches into a venomous scowl, her annoyance at taking the bait in her eyes. "Please," she fumes, "spare me the details of your dick. I'm sure it's 'sooo big' and you're 'sooo amazing' but I really don't give a shit." She lets her voice pitch high, affecting a vapid Valley Girl cheerleader vibe. I don't interrupt her to tell her that I've heard that exact phrasing before because she obviously means it to be an insult.

I eye her, letting her think I'm considering her attack, but I reply, "You sound like a porn star when you say it like that." I lean in close, whispering, "Can you do it like that later too?"

She growls, like the cutest tiger ever, and her pouty lips twist. "Maybe I will . . . for the guy who shows up on time for our date." Something about the way she says it lets me know that there's no guy, no date. And Coach said he'd made *arrangements* to cover for our study sessions, so surely, she's not really going out with someone. *Liar, liar, take those fiery pants off and let me see if the carpets match the drapes.* My dirty thoughts are disrupted as she continues, "But you're wasting your time, buddy. I'm here to help you with your English class. Take it or leave it. I have exactly thirty minutes until my plans for the night. What will it be?"

I consider whether maybe I'm wrong and she does actually have a date with some fucker after our tutoring session. Oddly, the thought pisses me off, even if this is supposed to be some fake cover story to save my ass. I like this banter, the back and forth of challenging each other. It's new, different, exciting.

"Do you really have a date?" The words pop out before I can stop them and her eyes narrow.

"Why do you care?" she asks, seemingly legitimately bewildered.

I smirk, sensing the upper hand is mine again with that opening. "I'm just trying to picture the guy who gets all this fire to melt underneath him. He must be fucking Teflon with the knives you throw. But I bet a soft Norma is a sight to behold, a rare gift." I look her up and down, trying to imagine her writhing and begging, submissive and sweet. My breath hitches a bit as my heart rate speeds up. Fuck, this girl could count as my cardio for the day and I'm not even fucking her. Yet.

She shuffles on her feet, more affected by my appraisal than I would've expected. She's not scathing me with a flaming retort. No, she seems almost . . . shocked, judging by the way her mouth rounds, her jaw dropping. "Oh." It's more a sound than a word, and I like that I've managed to make her speechless.

I reach up to run my thumb along her full bottom lip, curious whether the red tinge there is lipstick, for some reason hoping it's her natural lip color but knowing it'd look hot wrapped around my cock either way. Her whole countenance is soft for a second, suspended in time and full of sexual tension as I crowd closely enough to feel the heat from her body against mine. Time slows as I see her desire to yield to me, and I know she's not nearly as unaffected by me as she'd lead me to believe.

And the moment snaps.

She comes back to herself and I see the instant switch in her eyes. She steps back, swallowing hard, but the sassiness is back. "That is none of your damn business. This whole ridiculous fake girlfriend thing is just that—*fake*. I'm not some football groupie who's going to fuck you just because you give a nod. I'm better than that. Hell, those girls are better than that too. So keep it in your pants, don't try to get in mine, and we'll be fine. Capiche?"

I grin, the cold dismissal just as hot as the fire. "Brat, don't talk about things you don't know. You have no idea who I'm fucking or how I get them in bed with me. Unless you want me to show you?"

She flinches, but I'm not sure what I said that zinged so close to home. I replay the words over in my head. Maybe she does want me to show her? That can be arranged, for fucking sure.

Whatever it was, it set her off in a way our previous verbal blows didn't. She's gone all-business on me. "Word is, you need my help so you don't fail and get kicked off the team right when they need you most. The world is bigger than Xs and Os, so stop with the bullshit and let's get started. Twenty-seven minutes now. You in or out?"

The words are on my lips to tell her to take her orders and shove them up her gorgeous little ass. I'm behind on my GPA, but I'm not stupid. English is just mind-numbingly boring for me, always has been. Some people write epics on paper. I write mine in a different way. Doesn't help that my teacher has a hard-on for *Paradise Lost*, which is the most long-winded pain in the ass of all time. I'm not knocking school, but I didn't come to college to wax poetic. I came because I know my life's path. I'm going to make my mark on the field. Football doesn't last forever, and I'll have my degree for when that time comes, but my legacy with the pigskin will always be my greatest joy. I just need a little help to get through this rough patch, which is why I finally came to terms with Coach's orders to get a tutor.

The staring contest is fierce, but she wins easily. Fuck, this minx is killing me, verbally castrating me and challenging me at every turn. Who'd have thought that would be so damn sexy? "In."

She tries to hide her smile, but I can see it tickling her full lips. "Good. Now that I have your attention, let's get a few things clear." She holds up a finger, demonstrating 'one', but all I see is the blush pink covering her short nails, feminine but functional. "You're going to show me some respect. Out there on the field, you might be the king. But that doesn't mean a damn thing to me here. You obviously need help, and I'm going to help you, but only if you're here on time and don't waste mine." She points to the floor, making sure I get the point that I should be at the library at the arranged time. She sounds uppity, like someone's said that to her before.

"Two." She holds up a second finger. "The cover story Erica and Coach Jefferson came up with is ridiculous, but I guess it'll work if there are any questions or suspicions. But it is fake. I'm not fucking you and we're not dating. But I won't be made a fool of either, so don't go flaunting your groupies around while telling folks we're together. Be discreet and I'll do the same."

"Three." A third finger pops up. "Uhm . . . never mind. I think that was all I have. Questions?"

Her words cut, irritatingly bossy, so I revert to what I know. I grab her hand, bringing her still upheld fingers higher in the air and laying a soft kiss to each fingertip before giving her a hard look. "I think you're confused about the situation, but I agree we should be clear. I know this is stupid, and I hate that it's come to this, but I'll do any-fucking-thing for football, even pretend to date some girl I don't know, who's already busting my balls, just so I can stay on the field. I do need help, but I don't need to hear shit from you about what a dumbass I am.

Trust me, I already know, and your talking down to me ain't gonna help a damn thing."

She yanks her hand back, holding it to her chest like my kiss hurt her. Her eyes search mine, and I don't look away, forcing myself to stand up to this little spitfire brat.

She looks down first. "You're right. I'm sorry. I didn't mean to be insulting . . . at least, not about your intelligence."

I'm surprised at her apology. I didn't think those words would ever pass her lips, if I'm honest. Though she didn't apologize for thinking I'm some groupie-fucking manwhore. But that didn't hurt nearly as much her thinking I'm stupid. I tilt her chin up, meeting her eyes again. "Apology accepted. I'm sorry for being late. Won't happen again."

She nods. "Good. Okay then, tomorrow at five. For real this time?" She grabs her bag from the table, tossing it over her shoulder like she's leaving.

"Fuck that. We're getting started tonight," I say, my hard tone not allowing any argument. Except from her, apparently.

She smirks, tossing her red hair back over shoulder. "Sorry, I've got plans."

I want to shut her smart mouth up with a kiss. Or maybe a kiss to my dick. Either might be acceptable and would stick with her apparent rule about not fucking.

Too bad because I think some combo sex-study sessions would be a rather great motivator to get my grades up.

Instead, I take her elbow firmly but gently enough that she could pull away if she wanted to. I guide her deeper into the library toward a shadowed corner far away from the main entrance where people constantly come and go. Vaguely, I wonder if anyone has seen our exchange and wondered what was going on. Shit.

"Come on, Brat," I growl over my shoulder at her. "We've got studying to do."

Once in the relative safety of the private corner, without a soul in sight, I push her back against the wall, crowding in front of her. She sputters, eyes wide. "What the hell, Zach? You can't just drag me around like some bastard, big-dicked jock who thinks people should bow at his feet and live life according to your timetable." She's ranting again, her voice getting a bit loud for the library.

I press into her, letting her feel me and silencing her with my rumbled, "Bastard? Big-dicked? Sounds like you'd like to know for sure. Say the word, and I'll pull it out for you, Norma." I know she can feel that I'm already half-hard just from being this close to her, but the thought of her asking to see my cock has a rush of blood going south. I wait a beat to see if by some stroke of God's grace, she does. When she stays silent, giving me a death glare, I continue. "Look, I apologized for being late, but we really do need to get started. I have a paper due in two days, and as much as I hate to admit it, I do need your help. I need at least a B-minus on this paper." I lay on a bit of the puppy dog eye treatment, hoping she gives in. My future lies in her hands.

NORMA

My heart and my head both pound furiously as Zach pulls me into one of the back corners of the library. I don't know why I'm following him without protest. I should be kicking him in the balls for laying his hands on me. His big, rough, warm hands touching the skin of my arm . . . I wonder what those hands would feel like on more sensitive parts, like my belly, my ass, my pussy.

I shake my head. No, that's so not what is happening here. It can't be. Because I am *not* turned on by his charming caveman act. Still, when we stop, I'm dimly aware that it's the romance section, of all places.

Fighting my own attraction, I take it out on him, whisper-yelling as he presses me against the wall. "What the hell, Zach?" There's more to my rant, though I'm mindlessly insulting him now. My breath is gone, no oxygen to fuel my brain as my body tunes in on the electricity arcing between us.

Then he leans against me, fire sparking as the connection between our bodies completes. I curse the separation of our clothing and then realize he's offering to pull his dick out right here in the library. I'm shocked into silence, though a part of my brain begs for me to say yes, to have him do that, right here, right now. I can feel his hard thickness against my belly, something that should have me fighting back with sharp words.

Instead, I'm fumbling for something to say like some useless airhead. Pushed up against him, it's like every cell in my body has come to life with an itch that's both maddening and wonderful. Hazily, I wonder if this is what most people feel when they lust after someone. No one has ever stood up to my personality long enough for me to even really consider them the way I'm currently considering Zach.

And I'm definitely considering him. Six feet four, I'd bet, with wide shoulders and muscles that ride that fine line between bulging and lean, wearing a team T-shirt that makes me want to pull it over his head for a better view. His hair is still damp a bit, because of the shower he was late for, but the darkness added to his shaggy blond hair makes him look more carefree. His blue eyes are diving into my soul, and the flash of his smile, teeth so white he could star in a toothpaste commercial, brings me back to reality.

This can't happen. Not him. Not me. Not here. Not now. Not. Ever.

The thought brings a hint of sadness with it, and it's mirrored by the imploring look he's giving me. Luckily, part of my brain was paying attention to his words, and I'm able to give a reasonable answer even though most of my body is ready to roll over and purr for him.

What the hell, Norma?

"Fine. Two days for a paper isn't much time to work with, so let's get started," I finally answer, hating that I'm giving in but not ready to leave him either.

His expression instantly changes to a smirk at the victory. "Great. Do you need to text anyone to cancel your plans?"

He knows I was bluffing. I don't have plans and definitely don't have a date. It was the principle of the matter. "No, asshole. I don't need to text anyone." I plop onto the couch in this corner, letting my bag fall gently to the floor.

Zach sits down beside me, leaving a space between us. "I knew it, Brat. You were just trying to get a rise out of me, weren't you?" I shrug, not willing to confirm or deny his assessment.

I fight a smile. "I get it now. My boss told me 'good luck' with this whole mess, and in hindsight, I'm thinking that means she knows what a cocky jerk you are. Maybe you know her. She seems to follow football a bit. Erica Waters?" Though I'm teasing, I desperately want him to say he hasn't slept with her. I don't know why that would seem too close to home, but it does.

But he shakes his head. "Nope, don't know her. I also don't *know* her. But I do really want you to say that again." He winks like I should know what he's talking about, and then it hits me.

I look him full in the eye, intentionally adding emphasis as I breathily say in my best porn star imitation, "Caaahhck–y jerk." His eyes watch the word leave my lips and then jump to mine, full of humor.

"Oh, you think you're funny, Brat? Turnaround is fair play," he says brazenly. He grabs a book from the shelf in front of us, not bothering to read the cover, but I can see that it's titled *Hot For The Billionaire*. I roll my eyes until he opens the book and starts actually reading.

"I'm going to fuck you raw and rough, rip that little pussy to shreds with my big cock." He changes his voice to a falsetto. *"Yes, John, screw me with that big cock. I'm your slut and I want you inside me so badly. I gaze upon his flawless magnificence with unbridled need, my glistening sugar walls begging for the massive manhood inside his slacks."*

I grab at the book, trying to get it from his hands. "Stop it!" I beg, trying not to laugh and pissed off at the little giggle that escapes my mouth. I don't know what's more disturbing, his reading this or that I'm actually getting turned on by his saying such over-the-top cheesy, dirty things in that silly voice. "You're making an ass of yourself!"

Zach chuckles, tossing the book back on the shelf. "Do women actually read that shit? But I guess you seem to have enjoyed it. That little giggle was cute."

I roll my eyes, snarling. "Get over yourself. You're *totally* not funny." Except my snarl sounds more like a purr. A hungry, ravenous purr.

"Really? I think I see your breath quickening." His eyes drop to my chest, and I force myself not to arch my back and show off for him.

"Get your eyes checked," I sass. "You might be blind." The jab is weak at best, but it's all I have in this moment.

"Saw that passage perfectly fine. And I shut that cute little mouth of yours."

I think my cheeks are turning as red as my hair.

C'mon, Norma, he probably drops lines like that with all the girls. And this is not real.

"You didn't shut anything," I growl, but sheesh, the growl makes it sound like a dare.

He hears it too, his grin growing wider, cockier, as if he knows what his playful alpha attitude is doing to me. "Come on, you're all attitude and a big mouth, but you're not that bad. And you're enjoying this, just like I am."

I need to get out of here before I transform into some weak, mewling kitten lapping at his feet. Puffing out my chest, I gather myself up. "Truth? You're *maybe* not so bad. But we do need to work. Two days, remember?"

The light, teasing mood that had surrounded us evaporates and I'm sorry I said anything. But it's the reality of what's going on between us. He may be fun to spar with, and he might enjoy getting under my skin, but at the end of the day, this is about one thing only—his grades.

He sighs. "Yeah, two days. Let's get to work."

Neither of us seem particularly driven to study, but he pulls out his copy of *Paradise Lost* and a spiral filled with more chicken scratches than notes. I glance through it, trying to gauge where he's at in the story and what level of comprehension he's getting from the old poem that's decidedly complex. But the more I try to read through his notes, the less I know where he's at. "Okay, how about this. Explain what you've gotten from the story so far and what the assignment is supposed to include."

His eyes go wide and then roll. "Fuck if I know. Something

about idols and God not wanting churches?"

I hum. "Uhm, okay, not exactly, but that gets a start on what to focus on for this paper, at least."

He sighs in relief. "Thanks, Norma. I appreciate your help."

It sounds real, maybe the first totally real thing he's said to me since he walked up on me bitching about him. No game, no agenda, no teasing, just honestly grateful for the assistance.

We spend the next hour going through Spark Notes and his professor's PowerPoint presentation about the poem, making some good headway in Zach's understanding and writing the outline for his paper. He's doing better than I would've expected, considering the intricacies of this piece. Surprisingly, without the snark and bites, we make a pretty good team as we work our way through the story.

When he answers a particularly complex question correctly, he celebrates by scooting closer and throwing his hand up for a high-five.

I laughingly smack his palm with mine. "Good job. Now, what about Eve?" Though I'm continuing my lesson with him, it's on auto-pilot as my brain focuses on the length of his thigh touching mine, his hip next to my hip. I remind myself, *grades, tutoring, fake relationship, nothing more.*

But his voice is huskier, too, as he speaks. "She's temptation." He moves his finger to my thigh, just the one fingertip tracing through the denim of my jeans. "Fiery temptation that leads Adam astray," he says, and I don't think we're analyzing litera-ture anymore. His touch gets higher, the brush of the back of his hand a breath away from the heat of my center. It's all I can do not to buck my hips to get that contact.

I take a steadying breath. "But before she was Adam's tempta-tion, Eve was tempted herself by the snake." The words are filthier than I intended them to be, but when Zach leans in close to whisper hotly in my ear, I don't regret them.

"And are you, Norma? Are you tempted?" he growls.

My mind is saying *run*. My body is saying *don't move a muscle*. "You're incorrigible," I finally relent, trying to fight the tidal wave of desire rolling up from my stomach as I sag against the couch, tilting my hips ever so slightly closer to his hand.

"Oh, yeah?" he asks, leaning against my side a bit harder, trapping me between him and the arm of the couch. His full lips are barely an inch away from my ear and his words send warm tingles down my body. "Well, you're not moving, and I think you're a smart-mouthed little brat who needs to be taught a thing or two about temptation and what happens when you tempt a cocky bastard like me."

I'm shocked at the way he's talking to me. I should smack him, or at the very least stand up and stomp my way right out of the library. But I'm frozen. I'm turned on. I'm putty in his hands, and he fucking knows it.

Hell, maybe I am just as weak as those groupies. But I can understand it when he's playing me like a fucking violin.

Good God, I want him to take me, right here and right now. It's a scary thought. I never thought I'd find someone to challenge my mouthiness, and I certainly never considered it'd be with some football player jock type. But even if he wasn't a decent verbal sparring partner, which he shockingly is, he's doing something to my body I've never experienced. And it's real, so very fucking real.

And I want it. I want more. Who cares if that makes me weak? Right now, sure as fuck not me.

"You think you could teach me?" If I'd said it sweetly, he'd have probably smiled. As it is, I say it with disdain, like I somehow doubt his abilities. To be clear, I don't, but I'm not going to let him in on that little fact just yet.

His smirk flashes and I hear the unspoken 'challenge accepted.' "Yeah, Norma, I think I could teach you all sorts of things about temptation. You think I don't know how badly you want me to bend you over this couch and fill you full of cock? You're tempted to let me, and better yet, I'm tempted to do it."

His fingers flatten against my center, stopping my argument as he grinds against me. My breath hitches, and he keeps talking. "I want to hear your bratty mouth moaning my name against my palm because I have to muffle your cries so no one hears us."

I whimper weakly, offering the barest of objections. "We shouldn't. You should stop."

"But you're practically begging me not to stop," he says, his fingers moving faster, and even through the fabric separating us, I know he can feel how hot and wet I am. "This is what you want, isn't it?" I can't deny the truth.

It's torture. I want to say no just to show him that I'm stronger than he is. But my lips won't form the word. Instead, I clutch at his iron-hard arm, gasping and on the edge of coming.

"Yes." The word comes out without permission and he knows it.

Zach pulls away, leaving me weak as my body screams for release. "What? Keep going," I groan.

He looks at me expectantly, waiting for me to realize that he's not going to give in. "Fucking bastard," I say, sitting up straight on the couch from where I'd slouched into his touch.

The corners of his mouth lift in amusement, but he reaches down and adjusts himself in his jeans. He looks huge and hard, and uncomfortably contained in their confines, as affected by this whole thing as I am. Even though I'm furious, there's a horny bitch inside me that begs him to unzip and let *his* snake free. "Every day, after practice, we can meet. Five is too early. Eight would be better. I won't be late."

"What makes you think —" I gasp, my body still crying out. I shut up, realizing that my protests sound hollow even to my own ears. They must sound pathetic to him. "Fuck you," I sneer. I might be so horny I can't see straight, but I've still got some pride.

But Zach smiles that panty-melting grin, leaning in to tease me one last time. "Keep saying that and maybe you'll get to. Honestly, I'm really hoping you do."

He stands up and adjusts himself once more, knowing that my eyes will follow the movement. "See you tomorrow, Brat. It's a date."

I watch him walk away, glaring holes in his back. Inside, I want to scream and call him a bastard who doesn't deserve to touch me, much less deserve my help. But deeper inside, I know I'm going to be here tomorrow at eight. On the dot.

NORMA

Dear Diary,

Remember when I said I'd wear my virgin badge proudly? Wait until I found someone worthy enough, that lit not just my body aflame, but my mind too?

I fucking found him.

In the worst package ever. Oh, it's a pretty package, for sure, but I always figured I'd be repulsed by his "type", the cocky jock. But something about him set me on fire in a way I'd never known.

I spent the night replaying his dirty words, my fingers replacing his remembered ones. I didn't stop like he did though. I'm pretty sure my loud neighbor thinks I had a guy over because I damn sure said his name when I came.

But this morning, in the light of day, I'm humiliated that an assignment that should be relatively straightforward has turned into something so foundationally stupid. I know better than to think a guy is going to hang with me through my . . . brattiness. I've never actually been called a brat, and in fact, I rather take offense to it since I know the 'spoiled rich girl' assumptions people make when they find out my last name. But when Zach called me that, it almost sounded like he appreciated my mouthiness, like he was daring me to say more, anticipating what smart remark I'd come up with next.

But a guy like him? He's not a forever type, barely a fuck-em-and-leave-em type, and then there's this whole blade hanging over my head that is our fake relationship. Definitely not who my body should be responding to, not who I should want to spar with, not who I should be thinking about in anything other than a professional tutoring way.

Fuck. I wish he would just show up tonight and let me tutor him, start over, and forget yesterday ever happened.

Fat chance of that though.

Because if I can't forget, he probably can't either.

No matter how hard I try, I haven't been able to get Zach out of my mind. What else do you call it when you sit through two morning classes and don't remember a damn thing about either of them? Hell, I'm not even sure if I sat in the right rooms today. I might have been in another class and not even noticed. Now I've got work at *The Chronicle* to do, and I'm still not sure what the fuck is going on.

I try to keep my head down and my focus sharp, but I'm

broken out of my reverie when Erica interrupts. "Hey, how did your tutoring session go?" I'm in the editing office because I can't imagine being out in the main room right now, supposedly working on a column about unprotected sex on campus. Sometimes, when the universe wants to send you a message, it whispers. Right now though, it's screaming at me with blinking neon LED lights.

I check my screen, looking at the last thing I typed. *Sex*, of course. Great, I've been at a complete standstill for the last ten minutes. Talk about something screaming at me. My cursor's doing it with its incessant blinking, and I'm spacing out because of it.

I quickly minimize my window and look up, formulating my response. Do I tell her what an ass Zach started off as? Or what about how he was still walking that line as he drove me wild in a totally different way before walking away as I asked him to make me come? Or about how I want him to fuck me every which way from Sunday and handle me like he handles a football? Fast and hard, with that light touch that makes sure he scores constantly?

"I . . . uh . . . it was productive," I finally lie, a flush coming to my cheeks. "We covered a few basic rules. That kinda stuff. Didn't get too deep into Milton, but you know how it is."

Erica quirks an eyebrow. *"That kinda stuff?* What is that kind of stuff?"

I don't how to reply to Erica, mainly because I know we covered jack and shit. "Uh, you know, he was late, so we only had time to cover schedules and ground rules. Stuff like that. But he has a paper due tomorrow. We did the outline last night, and he'll write it tonight so it's ready to go. A good grade there should help his overall grade quite a bit."

It's the truth but barely touches the surface of the whole truth.

It seems to satisfy Erica though. "Thank goodness. I was scared he'd no-show on you, but Coach Jefferson said he really stressed how important this is to Zach. Was he okay with the tutoring, at least?"

I look at her incredulously. "Seriously? You thought he'd get forced into tutoring, begrudgingly show up late, and then be happy as a lark to admit to needing help? No, he wasn't okay. He was a cocky bastard who fought me tooth and nail at every turn to establish dominance. Honestly, he's an arrogant son of a bitch who thinks he's God's gift to women." I realize that I'm painting an accurate, albeit not very savory, image of Zach and belatedly try to temper my harsh words. "But once we sat down and got to work, it was fine."

Erica cringes at my assault of Zach's character. "I'm so sorry, Norma. But can you stick with it? It'd be good for both of you, I think. Him, because he needs someone strong enough to bust his balls and make him work. You, because the athletic department will owe you. I'm sure you could parlay this into a one-on-one interview with the star quarterback, and maybe the head coach too, after we win the conference championship."

Sports reporting, also known as the sweat sock circuit, isn't my dream gig. But a featured interview with Zach and Coach Jefferson would be a dream come true assignment for most, definitely a byline highlight for my portfolio.

I nod. "Of course. Like I said, we already made plans to meet tonight. I knew this would be a hard assignment, but I can handle it." I hope that speaking the words will put it out in the universe to make it true because while I know I can keep my mouth shut and I can be a stellar tutor, I seriously doubt my ability to handle Zach in any real way. He's got me in the palm of his hand. Or he did last night . . . literally.

Cutting my time short at the newspaper, I run back to my apartment to change clothes. I need something conservative, something that will armor me against Zach's attack.

First to go is my slim-fitting tank top which is just a school spirit shirt, but it does hug what boobs I have pretty well, and I want Zach's attention focused on learning, not my assets. I switch out my pretty bra for a sturdy, plain one and then pull on a loose-fitting graphic T-shirt from the mall. I knot it tightly at my waist, knowing that it won't let a roving hand wander underneath. I ditch my jeans in favor of a long, black maxi skirt and boots that have the smallest heel because at five foot four, I don't own anything without *some* sort of heel except for gym shoes.

Last but not least, I pull my hair up in a messy bun and wrap a folded scarf around my head, letting the tails of the knot stand out. I slip my glasses on, even though I usually only need them for prolonged computer work, and then look in the mirror.

I look like an urban hippie and a librarian combined their closets and I pulled everything I'm wearing, head to toe, from the crazy mismatch. It's perfect. If nothing else, any curves I have are hidden and it'll take Zach longer to get his hands on my skin.

And that's the problem, because if he does, I'm in trouble. Every time he looked at me last night, I felt like I was about to catch fire. Even now, thinking about what he did to me, it's making my pulse pound and my heart speed like a drag racer.

I sag against the dresser, my breathing ragged, my body once again flooded with powerful hormones. Jesus. What the fuck is happening to me? I glare at myself in the mirror, talking aloud. "Okay, Norma Jean Blackstone. Get your shit together and be the ball buster you always are. It's just a tutoring session, and he's just a regular guy. Nothing is going to happen except studying. You got it?" I point at the mirror, threatening my reflection and hoping the warning sticks when I'm alone with Zach.

With a sigh and two sets of crossed fingers, I grab my bag and head over to the library. It's early, but I have plenty of work of my own to do, especially since I'll be spending the bulk of the evening with Zach's paper on Milton. Sure, I could study at home. It's probably even quieter and has fewer distractions, but getting there will hopefully make eight o'clock come sooner rather than later.

But as I settle in at a table on the first floor, I know I misjudged. I'm not getting shit done because I keep glancing up every time the doors open. I see people come and go, none of them Zach because he's not supposed to be here for almost two hours.

Eventually, I do find my groove and get some work done while I wait.

ZACH

Knowing I'm going to see Norma tonight is putting a little extra pep in my step all day, and folks have noticed. "Jesus, try not to dislocate my wrist next time?" Lenny Smalls, one of my teammates, says as he tosses the ball back to me lightly. We're running 'card routes', just working our grooves for later, and he's shaking out his left hand. "It was just a ten-yard route, Zach."

His whining rolls right off my back. "Just feeling it today, man. You need to put some extra padding on your pussy or something?" I ask, teasing him but barely thinking about Lenny.

Since our encounter last night, my thoughts have been filled with Norma, the way the sassy minx looked as she melted for me, but also how she wasn't putting up with my shit. I was right. A soft Norma was a sight to behold, but I liked the sassy one too.

I can't imagine dealing with that smart mouth of hers for another tutoring session without giving her the pounding we both want. Hell, maybe she can use that as an incentive to get me to study harder. The dirty thought makes me smirk, and then I reconsider. Maybe I can use dick to get her to help me. I have a feeling she's gonna be the one dragging me around by the balls more than the reverse.

Coach calls the next play and I grin. My passes have had enough zip that I'm sending frozen ropes to my receivers, Lenny included. But this one is all me, an old high school play we keep just for shits and giggles. I take the snap from the shotgun and immediately pitch the ball to our starting running back, Marcus. The defense doesn't know if it's a run or a pass, and in that confusion, I take off upfield.

I'm all alone when Marcus stops and throws the ball across the field in a decent pass. I have to slow down to catch it, but the change in speed allows me to juke the strong safety right out of his cleats as I fake him out and run the ball in.

Sure, it's just practice, but the offense is grinning when I get back, and the defense can't say a fucking thing. They just got torched and they damn well know it, even if they don't want to lay any big hits on us.

"Hey, Zach, don't forget it's only practice," Coach Buckley, our QB coach and offensive coordinator, says to me as I rejoin the sidelines and my backup, Jake 'Snake' Robertson, gets a few plays in. "They'll be trying to take your head off if you keep showboating, and we need you 100% come Saturday."

"Maybe . . . but they won't be able to even if they try," I reply. "And I'm gonna own Eastern's ass like my name's tattooed there."

"You're feeling your oats more than usual," Coach says. "What's going on? I'm digging the beast mode today."

"Thanks," I reply. Coach Buckley is young for such a high-level position, only twenty-seven, so he's a lot like a big brother to me and not just a coach. "Just wait until Saturday."

I rotate back in, and no matter who the defense puts in, I'm lighting it up. It's like a damn game of Madden, and finally, Coach blows his whistle. "That's enough! I keep you out here any longer, and I'm going to have to check the defense for their balls."

The offense is in high spirits, and even the defense feels some confidence as we congratulate each other. They know we're going to kick ass Saturday, and that's the important thing.

Only one person seems to be in a pissy mood. "I could've done it better," Jake says petulantly as we do our cooldown stretches. "All that dancing bullshit is fine for practice, but it's not gonna work in the game. They were taking it easy on him out there."

I glance over at Jake, a little pissed. "You had reps with the offense today too, remember? Did those not count either? You want more time? Earn it."

"That's enough," Coach Buckley says, but I've already dismissed Jake. Instead, my mind is on Norma Jean, who's going to be waiting for me once I shower up and get changed. I let her go yesterday, but today won't be so easy. I've had all night and day to think of what I want to do to her.

"Hey, Knight," Coach Jefferson, our head coach, says after I shower and leave the locker room. He's old-school, with white hair and a belly that sticks out in his polo shirt, and he runs summer practice like we're trying out for the Marines. But he knows football and has put four QBs in the pros. Best of all, he'll give as much to you as you give to him. I couldn't

LAUREN LANDISH

ask for a better guide to the League. "Looked good out there."

"What can I say, Coach?" I reply with a grin. "I play to win. They won't fucking know what hit 'em Saturday."

He laughs. "That's the spirit! But let me talk to you for a moment. My office."

I step into his office and take a seat. "What's up, Coach?"

He settles in, grabbing an antacid out of the big bowl of them he keeps next to his computer. Maybe it's the eighteen-hour work days, but he munches Tums like candy, and as he gives me a look, I figure I'm the cause of this particular munch. "I got a call from Erica Waters this morning. Listen, no bullshit with the tutoring, alright? She said you were late and gave the tutor a hard time. I don't want you sidelined because you can't act like an adult. This is a big ask of that girl. Don't fuck it up, Son."

I shift around, pissed that Norma tattled on me to her boss. But then again, she probably got called into a sit-down just like this. "Coach, I'm taking the tutoring seriously, going to get my grades up so I maintain eligibility. No worries. And I might've pushed the line on the tutor a little, but . . . well, you know."

He nods. "Yeah, I know how you boys are. I was a football hotshot once too." He pats his belly like he can't believe what's happened to him since his college ball days. "But listen very carefully on this one. Don't mix business and pleasure. And that tutor, she's business even if we've got some shitty dating lie in place for cover. If you want to fool around with someone, go for it, but not her, and not until we get this grade stuff handled."

"Coach, she's cute, and it wouldn't interfere with my—"

"Stow it. I've heard that a thousand times. Don't do anything

288

to mess up your future because you've got a fucking bright one, Son. A golden ticket . . . if you can get your grades up. She's got your grades by the balls because you need her. Don't hand her your literal ones too. Business and pleasure, Zachary, do not mix." His words are delivered with the wisdom of a man who's seen too many guys screw something up, and I take them seriously.

I nod. "Yes sir." He nods back, dismissing me, and I make a run for it before I run his blood pressure up any higher.

I leave the football complex and head toward the library. As I walk, I stew over Coach's words. Is he right? Should I leave Norma solidly in the business category and let what happened last night be a one-time thing, just letting this dating shit settle in the background in case someone asks? Or can I tempt fate and do a bit of mixing of business and pleasure?

I think of the way Norma tempted me last night and I know the answer.

———

I'M JOGGING MY WAY UP THE STEPS TO THE LIBRARY AT FIVE minutes to eight, feeling good in a fresh pair of jeans and a team T-shirt. Pausing at the door, I do a quick run-through of my hair with my hands. I normally don't give a shit about what my hair looks like after practice, content to let it do whatever the fuck it wants. But I feel like upping my game for some reason.

After all, little Norma seems to have a way of finding chinks in my armor and stabbing me in them. And that's not going to continue to be the damn case. Entering the library, I look around, finding the little alcove where I first saw her. I'm already thinking of it as 'our spot' . . . except she's not there.

"Hmm," I mutter, turning around and checking but seeing

nobody. "Little Miss Perfect gives me shit about being late and then she doesn't show up?"

But then I scan again, and I spot her off in a far corner but with a direct sightline to the front door. She's lost in her work, her foot tapping under the table to whatever music is pumping through her earbuds and her eyes flicking from the book on the table to the computer screen in front of her.

She looks sweet like this, without the fire she shoots when she looks at me. I approach slowly, not wanting to break the spell she's under. As I get closer, I take the opportunity to look her up and down. A smirk takes my face when I realize how she's dressed, like an oddly naughty librarian. It's nothing like her outfit from yesterday but still so cute that my cock twitches in my jeans.

I set my bag on the table, and she jumps, yanking her earbuds out. "Fuck, you scared me," she scolds.

I point to my watch. "Just making sure you noted that I'm right on time. You look nice." I smirk, waiting for her sarcastic bite back.

"What?" she asks, playing innocent. "You don't like my clothes?"

I snort, shaking my head. I lean in close, one arm on either side of her to whisper in her ear. "You can try all you want to cover up, but we both know the truth. You got all dressed up like that because you needed a few more layers of cloth armor between me and your sweet little pussy because you're afraid your body is going to betray you again. But you've got a bad girl side, and we're going to explore it sooner rather than later. I'm looking forward to seeing you accept that fact. I think it'll be . . . beautiful. Speaking of beautiful, right now, I'm thinking of flipping that long skirt up and making you hold it so I can grab a couple of handfuls of your ass and get at your pussy from behind."

I stay silent, letting that imagery fill her mind as I watch the flush cover her freckled face. And when I see that pink tinge to her cheeks, I say a silent apology to Coach Jefferson. He's done so much for me, but I can't honor his request this time. Because that hint of blush just gave me as much satisfaction as a pass perfectly thrown for a game-winning touchdown, and I've barely started with Norma.

"You can't say things like that to me!" she argues halfheartedly, turning slightly to look up at me from inside the cage of my arms.

It sounds like she got the business and pleasure talk too, or at least one similar to it. But yeah, I'm mixing that shit up.

She's practically trembling as I capture her with my gaze, a wolf ready to stare into the eyes of its prey before taking it down. It's like she's trying her hardest to resist, but all it will take is one simple push, one touch, to send her over the brink.

I chance a glance to her lips, beseeching them. "Admit it. You liked it, didn't you? No shame in that. Don't be shy."

Her hand trembles on the tabletop, so I reach up and cover it with my own. She doesn't resist as I rub soothing circles along the back of it and trace her fingers, marveling at how soft they are. "Zach . . ."

"It's our little secret," I whisper as I put her hand on my thigh, sliding it up with no resistance until it comes to rest on the hard bulge between my legs. It's honest, and I'm not faking a thing as I look into those pretty eyes. "Truth be told, I haven't been able to think about anything else either. You're sexy as fuck, Norma . . . and I'm not all bad. I can be more than an asshole if you're willing to give me a chance. So tell me the truth. Tell me you liked it."

"I loved it," she whispers, her hand tightening almost without even thinking. "God, I loved it."

NORMA

My hand rests where it is, but suddenly, I realize where we are, what I'm doing, and who I'm doing it with. What the hell am I thinking?

"No!" I protest, jerking my hand away from the big bulge between his legs and trying to take back my words. "You're playing with my head. I didn't mean that!"

Zach grins, not letting go of my hand as he stands up, shoving my stuff in my bag and tossing it over his shoulder. He leads me deeper into the library. My feet don't even attempt to stop him, following him willingly as we hike the steps to the fourth floor and then twist and turn until we're in a darkened section. It's musty up here, like nobody's been around this section in a long time.

"Zach," I try to protest, even as my feet follow him. "We can't do this." I'm not sure if I'm trying to convince him or me. But he finds a secluded table and pulls a chair out for me like a gentleman. The gesture is unexpectedly civil, and I smile as I sit.

He sits beside me after turning his chair slightly so that it faces me. "Ok, Brat. Hit me with them."

I'm confused and my eyebrows pull together. "Hit you with what?"

"Your reasons why not. I'll go first. We're going to be spending time together, getting to know each other, and people already think we're dating or they soon will, and we have chemistry, even when we're smack talking at each other. Why not add a little reality to the pretend? No harm, no foul, just fun."

I can't help but laugh. "Those are your reasons why not?"

He chuckles. "No, you take one side of the argument, and I'll take the other. That's how debate works, or have you not learned that? I thought you were supposed to be a smarty pants?"

The tease is silly, but it works, making the moment lighter. "I *am* a smarty pants, but more importantly, I'm a smart ass. So there's reason one why not. It's fun to jab with you, but that won't last. You're going to get tired of my always pushing your buttons. Everyone does. And I'm not sure I'm ready for your level of *casual* fun. It's a bit of a bigger deal to me. I think your way sounds . . . dangerous."

He rubs at his chin like he's contemplating my arguments, but I can see the light in his eyes. "Agree to disagree. I find your button pushing endearing in an odd way. Can't say I can explain it, but it's true. And you say dangerous like it's a bad thing, but what I'm hearing is that you might enjoy a little danger. Fuck knows, I would. And you seem rather risky to me too, Brat." His voice is full of promise, the hazards seeming fewer than the possibilities when he says it like that.

I smile at the idea that of the two of us, I could be the dangerous one. Ridiculous. "Okay. Agree to disagree. But what I think we can both agree on is that you have a paper to write tonight and we should get to work."

He grumbles, muttering something about 'this conversation not being over', but he pulls out his laptop and book. "Okay, now what?"

I sigh. "Now, you write. Here's the outline we worked on last night. Use it to do the opening paragraph and then we'll reread it to clean it up."

His nod is reluctant, but he gets to work, his fingers deftly flying cross the keys as he writes. A mere fifteen minutes later, he sits back in his chair. "Done."

He turns his laptop toward me and I begin to read his introductory paragraph. It's good, better than I would've expected if I'm honest, though my harshly judgmental thoughts embarrass me a bit. "Good job. Next paragraph is based on this quote . . ." I point to the one in his notes.

But he doesn't get to work. Instead, he smirks at me knowingly. "You thought it'd suck, didn't you? That a dumb jock like me wouldn't be able to write for shit. But I'll let you in on a little secret. I aced English in high school and can actually string together a sentence, using commas and everything. This professor and me just don't click, and I particularly hate *Paradise Lost*."

I blush, the truth a bit of a jagged dig, but probably no more so than my expectation of him. "Honestly, yeah. Sorry for the preconceived idea. Stereotypes aren't always true. Hell, they're *usually* not true."

"Apology not accepted this time, Brat. Gonna take more than that," he says, reaching forward to wrap a tendril of my hair around his finger. It feels intimate with the rest of my hair piled on top of my head, like his finger is *this close* to brushing against the silky skin of my neck.

"Zach, what are you doing? What are you talking about? We agreed—" I say, but my voice is quiet.

"*You* decided. I didn't agree to shit. I just blasted one of your judgments about me. Tell me something that'll change one of mine about you."

I think he's trying to stall on his work, but he seems genuinely interested. I quickly rack my brain for something, then offer, "People think I'm spoiled sometimes, like I get everything handed to me because of my dad. But that's not true. He's more of the 'work hard and earn it' camp than the 'want my kids to have it better than I did' group. He does pay for some things, my tuition and my apartment, and I know that's a *huge* benefit lots of people don't get. But it comes with strings, and we butt heads sometimes when he expects me to give in to what he wants. He raised me to be a leader, a fighter, but then he wants me to fall in line like one of his underlings at work." It's a big share for me, and a rarely-voiced criticism of my dad. He's a good man and a good father, but no one is perfect.

Needing to get back on more solid ground, I flip the switch and let my armor pop back into place. "So, that's me . . . poor little rich girl." Zach eyes me thoughtfully, like he can see right through my shield, so I try to distract him. "So if it's not *Paradise Lost*, what is your favorite book?"

He leans close, whispering in my ear, "Right now, I'm thinking my favorite book is the *Kama Sutra* because whatever is on page sixty-nine, I'm game for it." He sits back, smirking. I know I walked right into that, but it almost feels like he's directing us back to lighter, looser, sexier conversation because he knew I was uncomfortable with what I shared. Like his dirty joke was actually to be nice to me.

So I respond as expected, playing along, "Ugh, disgusting. Is that all you think about? Your brain is going to need a transfusion if the blood stays in your *other* head all the time."

He chuckles and grabs at his crotch like he's checking for blood flow, then knocks on the side of his temple. "Nope, I think we've got an appropriate division of blood supply. A little going north, a little going south."

We both laugh, and then I tap on his outline, signaling that we should get back to work.

And that's how each segment of his paper goes. He works, I

read over it, and we pause for conversations. Somehow, through the evening, I feel like I get to know him a bit better.

He's not quite the cocky bastard jock I thought, though there's a heavy dose of that on the surface. But beneath, he's actually a nice guy, albeit one with a wicked tongue that he uses to lash at me deliciously, both literally and figuratively.

His barbed banter is exciting, making me anticipate what zinger he's going to lob my way next. He sometimes goes for the lowest common denominator joke, usually sexual, but then he'll turn right around and surprise me with something a bit more high-brow. I swear there was even a comment about *The Great Gatsby* but I'm going to need to check my quote source to be sure. Of course, I didn't let him know that.

But he's also used that sinful tongue to drive me crazy in a much more literal way. Around paragraph eight, he slipped his hand around the back of my neck, pulling me toward him as I read, to lay little licking kisses along my skin. The only skin I left exposed, I think, recognizing the irony in that.

By paragraph twenty, he whispered dirty promises in my ear as he slipped my skirt up my thighs to get at my hot pussy. I'd protested for a second, more out of some feeling that I should than because I actually wanted to. I'd been desperately close to coming again, but he'd recognized that I'd finished reading the paragraph and stopped, going back to work on the next section. I'd growled and told him not to start games he couldn't finish. But he'd just grinned evilly and said that he planned on finishing . . . the paper *and* me.

It's almost eleven when he finally finishes his essay, clicking *Submit Online* to turn the completed assignment in. I look around and realize the library has cleared out, though our secluded corner has been pretty quiet all night. I find that I don't want the night to end. The tutoring has been fun, almost like a team effort to get his paper done by the deadline. But more importantly, it has been fun to spend time with Zach, and he's got me on edge from all his touches and dirty whispers. Hell, I never knew having to be quiet in the library could be so damn sexy.

But I'm not sure what he's thinking. Has this just been fun and games to pass the time while he got his work done? Hell, for all I know, he's off to some party full of sorority girls and cheerleaders, and I'm going to go home to get myself off to thoughts of him. Again. Even though I know I shouldn't.

"So, now what?" I ask, adding a bit of sass to my tone and lifting one eyebrow, hoping he hears the challenge and takes me up on it but knowing that if he doesn't, I'll have my answer right there.

He smirks. "I told you, Brat. I was gonna finish my paper and then finish . . . you."

I should say no. I know that I should not do this. It's epically stupid in so many ways. But Zach checks all the boxes on my checklist, both good and bad. Football player, cocky jock, bastard asshole, kind, funny, quick-witted, sharp-tongued . . . Zach.

And I know I'm going to give in. But I won't do it easily. That's not who I am.

"You think you can? Hmm, I don't know. Guys sometimes have a hard time closing the deal. I could probably tutor you there if you want," I say, letting false doubt fill my voice. I have no qualms that Zach could probably get me off in minutes, especially considering the way he's been building me up all night.

He leans in and kisses me full on the lips. It's fierce and hard, communicating in no uncertain terms that he's ready to meet this challenge. My inner bitch jumps for joy, clapping with excitement.

He pulls back, both of us panting, and then he gives me that arrogant smirk. "I don't need a damn bit of tutoring for this, Brat."

He gets up, and I'm confused for a second at where he's going. But with a quick look around, he drops to his knees and crawls under the table. He grasps my knees and forces them wide, sitting on the floor between them. And then he flips my skirt up to my lap. Damn maxi skirt that was supposed to protect me from this, but right now, I'm thanking God that it's making my pussy easy-access for whatever Zach is about to do.

He grabs my inner thighs, kneading them in his rough grip as he inhales me. "Fuck, Norma, dressing like a good girl but wearing sexy Victoria's Secret panties like a bad girl," his voice rumbles, so close to where I want him, the heat of his breath good, but I tilt toward him, looking for more.

"This is such a bad idea. We're going to get caught . . ." I murmur, but my brain is already shutting down all the solid arguments for why I should definitely not be doing this. Not here, but most of all, not with Zach. This has danger written all over it, for my body, my heart, and my career. Almost like he can hear me but interprets the same situation differently, Zach smiles ferally against my thigh.

"We won't get caught if you're quiet, Norma. Think you can be quiet while I eat your sweet little pussy? Or maybe you like that someone might catch us, might watch me fuck your cunt with my tongue? That little bit of danger get you off?" He emphasizes each question with a stroke of his thumb against my clit, but it's through the silk of my panties . . . good but not enough.

I whimper, biting my lip to try to stay quiet.

"Say yes or I'll stop. I want to hear you give in, knowing that you're choosing this." Zach's voice is a hushed growl.

Needing to fight him and not wanting to give in, I reach down and slip my panties to the side myself, exposing my pussy to him. I hear his breath hitch and then he groans. "Say it, Norma." He's begging me to give in, and I feel like though I'm saying yes, he's the one who gave in first.

"Lick my pussy, Zach. Make me come . . . right here in the library where anyone could come upstairs and see you on your knees under the table. Is that what you want? That hint of danger?" Somehow, whispering the filthy words makes it easier to say them.

"Fuck, yes," he snarls, and then he dives into my pussy. He shoves my hands out of the way, pulling my panties to the side and spreading me wide open with his hands.

His tongue laps at me, tickling and teasing along my lips and then around my clit. I gasp at the onslaught, the sensations so good, but mixed with the risk of getting caught, it's so much more. I never knew that would be such a turn-on, but it is.

He moves his attention to my clit and sucks hard. I have to cover my mouth to stifle the moan bubbling up in my throat, threatening to loudly let loose. Zach chuckles against me, the vibrations adding a new feeling to his ministrations. "That's it, Brat. Let yourself go. You know you're loving every second of this just as much as I am. I want to see that soft Norma coming undone for me."

I grab at his hair, trying to get him back where I want him without answering the challenge of just how much I'm loving this. Because I am, I so am.

He licks a long line from my entrance to my clit and then sucks my clit into my mouth, using his tongue to flick against it fast and hard in the vacuum he's created around my tender bud. The world pulls tight for a moment, centered on my core, and then it explodes in a flash of white light.

My hips shake and my thighs quiver as I come for the first time from a man's touch. From Zach's touch. My body clenches and then sags as the orgasm washes over me in waves. I think I'm quiet, though right now, I don't really care.

Zach lays one last kiss to my clit, and I shudder, pulling away. "Too sensitive. Fuck."

He moves my panties back in place and lays a gentle pat to my mound, eyes looking up at me from under the table. "Never met a girl as sassy as you are, Brat. Never had one as tasty either. You're like fucking honey."

His eyes are glazed over, and I wonder if I look as shell-shocked as he does. I don't know what just happened or what it means. Maybe it doesn't mean anything, but it was amazing.

He climbs out from under the table and bends down to kiss me. I can taste myself on his lips. He smirks. "See? You're fucking delicious."

He stands up, and I can see him, thick and hard inside his jeans. I reach out to touch him, cupping his length through the denim, wanting to pleasure him the way he just did me.

He seems to read my desire on my face because he takes my hand, pulling me to my feet and guiding me over to the endcap of one of the rows of books.

Zach licks my ear, making me whimper. "I thought so. You dressed up so sweet and innocent, giving me attitude . . . but you've got a dirty side, don't you?"

I tremble, my hips grinding on their own against his cock, and I bite my lip before admitting, "Maybe."

"Get on your knees, Norma." His tone is hard, something different from before but still with that undercurrent of a light dare.

I obey but can't help but sass him. "No jokes about me sucking you off or making me beg for the privilege?"

He cups my jaw in his rough palm. "Fuck that. If you want to suck my cock, I'm not gonna risk your ire and screw up this chance. I'll shut my fucking trap, bite back any words I might have, and thank God for the opportunity to be in your hot, sassy mouth."

I can't help but smile at the odd twist of compliment he just bestowed on me. Most people, guys especially, don't even consider shutting down their mouthiness. No, they just want me to stop mine. But Zach's different. He seems to like my mouth. Well, if that's the case, I'm going to make him fucking love it.

I undo his jeans, letting them fall wide open and pulling his boxer briefs down to let his cock free. He's . . . huge and gorgeous. I should've known. Football god like him would have an amazing cock to go along with it. Some people get all the blessings. Right now, I'm sure fucking glad though.

His thickness is a bit intimidating, so I lick around the head, teasing him and tasting him. I let my tongue slide along the length of his shaft, from root to tip, and then I take the plunge, filling my mouth with as much as I can take. My lips stretch wide, and I have to pull back, letting my saliva coat him inch by inch as I take him deeper, exploring the limits of my mouth and then my throat.

I find a rhythm, three shallow thrusts and then a slow, deep one that makes him groan in pleasure. The fourth time I do that, his hands tangle into my hair and my silk scarf headwrap falls off.

Zach grins mischievously. "Wait. Wait." I pop off his cock, surprised to hear him say that. But then he bends down and grabs the silk scarf.

"What are you gonna do with that?" I ask, not sure I like where this is headed.

But his smile is soft. "Give me your hands." I obey slowly, and he grabs my wrists in his massive hand before slipping the scarf around one wrist and then the other, loosely looping them together behind my back. It's not tight, and I could get out if I wanted to, but I find that the thought of being restrained is rather erotic. Like the thought of getting caught. I don't think I would want to be full-on, tied down at his mercy, just like I don't actually want someone to catch us and watch. But the fantasy of it, so close but not quite real, is somehow extremely sexy.

"You good?" Zach asks, a light in his eyes.

In answer, I suck him back into my mouth, moaning against his heated flesh. Looking up through my lashes, I can see that he's gripping the bookcase behind me so hard his knuckles are going white. He's trying to let me lead here, let me take him. But suddenly, the thought of his being in charge is rather enticing. Another thing I thought I wouldn't be into. I feel like I'm learning more about myself tonight than ever before.

I lick a lazy circle around his head, knowing he's on the edge and liking that I'm doing that to him. "Zach?" I whisper.

He grunts. "Yeah, Brat?" and his cock jumps, bumping against my upper lip.

"Fuck my mouth," I tell him, a little louder so that I'm sure he hears me. I'm ballsy as fuck, but I don't know if I can say that twice.

His smirk is full of delight, and he feeds me his cock in one smooth stroke, deep into my mouth. His hands don't leave the bookcase. Instead, he uses the leverage to loom over me, forcing me to look up, which lets him into my throat even easier.

"Fuck, Norma. Swallow my cock, take me deep," he says, getting a bit loud. I whimper against his skin, the sound a warning to be quiet.

He grimaces, forcing back his moans, and picks up the pace. His cock pumps into my mouth, sloppy with the combination of my saliva and his pre-cum, and I try to swallow it all down in preparation for what I know is coming. I can feel a drop running down my chin, but with my hands tied, I can't wipe it away. The trickle ends and I realize it's dripped onto my shirt.

But Zach doesn't stop, closer and closer with every stroke. And then he slips further into my throat and I feel the pulses as he comes, his hot cum filling my mouth as I fight to gulp it down. He cups the back of my head with one hand, holding me deep as his cock jerks over and over.

He throws his head back in release, his mouth open in a silent roar before a shudder runs through his whole body. It's a powerful sight to see him unfettered, and I wonder if this is why he was looking at me so glazed earlier. I wonder if he got this kind of joy from watching me come. The thought makes me smile.

Slowly, his head falls forward and his eyes meet mine. "Fuck, Brat. That was . . . fuck."

I like that he's speechless, that maybe I'm not some orally super-skilled football groupie, but I did that to him, and judging by the look in his eyes, he fucking loved it.

I smirk at him. "Might have to expand your vocabulary a bit for the next paper," I tease.

He laughs. "You fucking brat. I think you sucked all of my vocabulary words out of my cock. Get up here." He pulls back, slipping his softening cock into his jeans before pulling me to stand in front of him.

I'm expecting him to untie me, but he kisses me first, apparently having no qualms about tasting himself on my tongue. I don't have any squeamishness about it either, and I actually rather like the dirty thought that he tastes like me, I taste like him, and our flavors are co-mingled within our kiss. But after a moment, he pulls back and spins me in place.

He makes quick work of the loopy knot in the silk scarf and then spins me back around.

"We should go. I don't know about you, but I have an eight AM class tomorrow," he says, though his tone says he wants to stay right here. Just that little hint resolves the whisper of doubt, of question in my mind and heart.

I smile. "Get some sleep. Eight tomorrow night again?" I hold my breath for a split second until he agrees.

"Definitely. See you tomorrow, Norma." His grin is wide as he struts out of the library.

It's not until he's gone and I'm alone that I think, *What the fuck did I just do?*

ZACH

She freaked out. I knew she would. But in the four days since that first bit of oral exchange, of the sexual variety, not our usual banter, I've managed to calm Norma down. I knew she'd have second thoughts, could tell she was inexperienced, but fuck if that didn't make me love it even more, that such a sassy spitfire could be so innocent but somehow push just the right buttons and let me push her too. Buttons I didn't even know I had.

I've had sex, though not nearly to the manwhore scale Norma thinks. But none of it compared to what Norma and I did in that library.

In public. Where anyone could've come up to see.

With her hands tied, at my mercy as I fucked her mouth.

No, that was on a whole different level.

So the next night, when she'd come in, ready to argue that we go back to a more professional level of tutor-tutoree, I'd been expecting it. Her doubts, her fears, all masked in vinegar and snark.

The battle had been fierce and many bites had been given, but in the end, I'd won. Mostly.

"Are you sure about this?" Norma asks, looking at me like I've lost my ever-loving mind. "I mean, no one knows shit and we could just keep on meeting in the library. No need to throw a parade or anything."

We're standing outside the school food court, where we're about to go in and grab a slice of pizza for lunch.

This shouldn't be a big deal.

But it's such a big fucking deal. And we both know it.

It's part of my reassurance to her that I'm not just looking for some convenient pussy for the semester, some acknowledge-ment of the fact that I can't date anyone else when I'm suppos-edly dating Norma, cover story and all. I hate that it took me damn near flunking English to meet her, hate that there's this question lingering over our heads. But I wouldn't change a thing.

The fact is, I *am* dating Norma. And she's probably the least convenient pussy around me at any given time. Which might be why I want it so damn much.

"You don't get a choice here, unless it's cheese or sausage, because we're getting lunch," I say, making sure that she hears the lack of options here. She needs this, both the public acknowledgement and for me to force the issue and push her buttons a little because I know that even when we study and spend every night at the library touching and exploring, my fingers deep inside her or her lips wrapped around me again, she's questioning whether it's real. All because the setup was fake.

She grins, and I can see the devil in her eyes. "What if I say sausage and we head on over to my place so I can get my taste?" She glances down at my cock, knowing it doesn't take much to get me rock-fucking-hard for her.

I adjust myself, squeezing a bit hard to let the pinch of pain deflate my cock. "God damn it, Brat. Lunch. Let's go."

I open the door for her, and she steps inside, back held straight and shoulders squared. She looks like the tiniest warrior fairy ever, ready for battle. She stops just inside the door, and I stop beside her to take her hand. I look down at our clasped hands, and she looks up at me. She baits me. "Welcome to the funeral of your social standing, Football God."

The fire in her eyes belies the fact that she's nervous. She's not worried about my social standing. She's worried that this is going to lead to some 'who's that girl' situation and that she'll be on the losing end of the spectrum against the cheerleader types. Maybe for some guys, that'd be the case, but not me. Definitely not now.

Now, my type is a sassy, snarky little redhead who makes me work for every damn inch of her submission and then falls apart in a gorgeous shattering of sparks when I earn it. It's fucking addicting and I want it all the damn time.

I lead her across the cavernous room. If this were a Hollywood movie, a hush would fall over the crowd of people, chairs would screech as people turned to stare, and jaws would drop.

None of that happens because it's just a college food court, and for the most part, people are buried in their own work and food.

We grab our pizzas and cokes, and she does get sausage, though I think it's mostly so she can take big, mean-looking chomps of it as a pseudo-threat to my manhood. Which she does as soon as we sit down at a table for two.

"You that hungry for sausage, Brat?" I tease, letting her know that she's not fooling me and that I'm on to her transparent symbolism.

"Ravenous. Wish I could eat the whole damn thing in one gulp right now," she says with a wink. Then she grabs her drink, letting her tongue slip out to catch the straw and then taking a cheek-hollowing suck.

It's an almost comical caricature of flirting, but damned if it doesn't set me off anyway because I know she's doing it intentionally to irritate me. "Keep it up and you'll get to," I promise her.

She tosses her napkin to her plate, grabbing the edges of her tray like she's ready to bolt out of here, but I lay a staying hand on hers. "After lunch."

She sighs and sits back in her chair. "Okay, bullshit aside, Zach. Why are we doing this? There's no need, really. The whole" —she lowers her voice to barely a whisper— "cover story was a just-in-case scenario." She looks around the room. "You know, if someone saw us and questioned why we're hanging out. But we don't have to invite people to the fucking wedding by showing up in the middle of the day to the most populous place on campus."

As if to prove her words, a guy bumps along the edge of the table as he passes by.

LAUREN LANDISH

I weave my fingers through hers, holding her hand on the tabletop. "I know. And as much as I appreciate your help and your agreeing to that stupid fucking idea, I don't want to be the asshole who keeps you like some dirty little secret. You're better than that. And I figured you'd be the first person to stand up and demand to be treated like a damn queen. So why the hesitation? Unless you don't want to be public with me?"

Admittedly, the thought hurts and is something I hadn't considered. I mean, technically, dating a 'football god' is a good thing for most girls, but I'm well aware that Norma isn't most girls and can likely see problems coming a mile away that no one else would. Hell, she could probably drum some up if need be with her sharp mouth.

She bites and then purses her lips, cheekily challenging me. "What if I like being your dirty little secret?"

I growl, leaning forward, my voice thick. "Do you want to date me for real, Norma?"

She must hear the serious tone in my voice because all humor leaves her eyes as she nods. "Yes. I'm just scared."

I nod back. "I get that, but I'm here. I want to date you, for real. We're doing this together." She seems reassured. Serious talk done, I let the light back into my eyes. "Now, about that 'dirty little secret.' You won't *be* one, but we can sure as fuck *have* some dirty little secrets. That work?"

She leans forward. "Actually, there's something I've been meaning to tell you, but I wasn't sure how to."

My cock thickens in my pants at her words, and my brain starts shooting off in every imaginable direction, thinking she's about to tell me some dirty fantasy she wants to enact. Whatever it is, I'm on fucking board. "Tell me anything."

She tries to pull her hand away, but I clench it tighter, wanting the connection when she says whatever this is, holding her in place, close to me, though the table separates us.

"Zach, what we've been doing in the library . . . has been great. Better than great. But —"

Oh, shit. There's a 'but.' I hadn't considered this sentence was gonna have a 'but' in it.

"But I feel like I should tell you . . . I'm a virgin." She lets out a whoosh of air with the whispered word, and it takes my brain a minute to process what she just said.

"A virgin?" I parrot back quietly, disbelieving. She looks down at the pizza, like she can't meet my eyes. I use my free hand to tilt her chin up, locking her in place with my gaze. "All this sass, all this sexiness, all this mouthy brattiness . . . and you've never had a man inside you?" I ask, running my thumb along her full bottom lip. Her tongue peeks out to wet her lips and she catches the tip of my thumb too.

"Do you want me to be your first?" I ask, though my tone is more begging for the privilege.

"Fuck, yes," Norma moans, the words breathy.

"Let's go . . ." I say, standing up and taking her hand. Normally, I'd be the nice guy who clears our table, throwing the trash away and returning the tray. But today, I've got places to be. Namely, inside my Brat. Right the fuck now.

I drag her outside and around the corner of the building, a small concession to not fucking her up against the glass of the building's front. Instead, I press her up against the brick, caging her in my arms and taking her mouth in a kiss.

Her hands grab my T-shirt, her nails digging slightly into my chest for a split second before she fists the fabric, holding me in place. "Fuck, Norma. I'm gonna fuck you right here in the quad if we don't get out of here."

LAUREN LANDISH

She sputters as I press off the building, pulling her by the hand. "We can go to my apartment. It's just off campus. We can even walk there."

I shake my head. "Oh no, Norma. I'm fucking you at *our* place . . . the library."

She argues the whole way there, and I let her rage and rile, knowing that once I get her there, she'll want it just like that.

I go not to our usual corner but to a quiet study zone room on the third floor instead. She huffs as I press her to the closed door, her head turned so she can see me even with her cheek against the wood.

I'm running on instinct here, letting what I honestly feel is the right choice pour from my lips to her ear. "I'm fucking you here, Brat. In our place. Not some cheap hotel room or a frat party bedroom, and not your sweet, innocent bedroom at home. Not this time. You deserve your first time to be great, and I can give that to you, right here where we met, where we belong."

"Someone's gonna see us," she pleads, even as she arches her back, rubbing her ass along the length of my cock. Her body is telling me exactly what she wants. It's like she's in a war between what she knows is the 'right' thing to do and what she really wants. What she wants every time we do something naughty here.

I grind against her, growling in her ear. "Listen to me. Just be quiet or cover your mouth if you have to, and no one will have a reason to come check the room."

"Fuck . . . that feels good," she whimpers as my hand cups her pussy.

"I can make your first time so good, Norma. Fill you up and rub your little clit until you come all around me." I spin her around, yanking her shirt and bra off and pressing her bare back against the door. "So fucking pretty, Brat." I dip down, taking her nipple into my mouth as I cup her tit, holding it up to my mouth.

The need is burning me up from the inside. We've been building up to this, day by day, conversation by conversation, touch by touch. And I can't wait anymore.

I pull her over to the big library table, yanking her shorts and panties down in one swoop as she kicks her shoes off. "Up you go . . ." I tell her as I help her lie down. I pull my T-shirt over my head and reach for the button of my jeans. Norma makes a mewling sexy kitten sound and I look up.

She's watching me, just as hungry as I am. I realize with a start that this is the first time I've seen her fully nude. I've pulled her shirt up and sucked her tits, I've spread her wide on a chair and eaten her out, and I've fingered her against more bookshelves than I can count.

But this is different. This is Norma, my Brat, spread wide and naked, every vulnerability exposed without armor, ready to take me for the first time. I take a mental snapshot of her writhing on the tabletop for me. It's a fucking honor and I can't wait. But she doesn't want my sweet words right now. That's not who she is, not who we are, at least not right now.

"You ready? You want to get fucked for the first time in the library, Norma? Behind a door that doesn't lock. Anyone could just waltz right in here." She bites her lip and tilts her head back, looking at the door upside down. I grab her ankles and pull her to the edge of the table, not sure it'll hold us both. Her legs spread wide around my hips, and I finish unbuttoning my jeans, shoving them down, and then my boxer briefs follow.

I take my cock in hand, pumping the shaft a few times as she watches. "Say it," I order her.

She grins, and I already can't wait to hear what she's gonna say. "Yes, Zach. I want you to fuck me, right here where anyone could walk by that tiny window in the door and see you balls-deep in my virgin pussy. You think you can handle that?" All sass and brattiness and challenge. I fucking love it.

I groan as pre-cum leaks from my tip at her words, and I use it to smooth my hand's way up and down my rock-hard length. I tease my head along her clit, not entering her yet but wanting to feel some part of her pussy against my cock. "Just think . . . it's dangerous, but it's a rush, isn't it?" She probably thinks I'm talking about the door. I'm really talking about her. She's fucking dangerous as hell, a sweet little innocent wrapped up in a prickly, ball-busting brat who drives me insane.

I aim lower, letting her feel me right against her entrance, and freeze. I lock eyes with her, wanting to watch to make sure she's okay with every bit of this. Her blue eyes shine back at me brightly, so I slide in ever so slowly. She's so tight. It's like nothing I've felt before, and I want to live buried in her pussy forever.

Just the head of my cock is in, but I pause, letting her get used to the feeling. Sex is like football. Sometimes, you need to no-huddle hurry up, but usually, it's better to take that extra heartbeat to make sure things are just right before you throw the ball downfield. "It's okay . . . do it. I'm so fucking ready, Zach," she encourages me. Touchdown.

I pull back and thrust further, breaking her cherry and causing her to cry out, the pain muffled by her forearm as she tries her best to stay quiet. I hold still, letting her adjust until the pain washes away and I start thrusting again slowly.

It's not only because she's a virgin that I'm taking my time. It's something else too. It's the look in her eyes as she starts to fuck me back a little, the challenge and the vulnerability all tied up in one as my cock turns the pain into the pleasure that rolls through her as she realizes she's taken a step that she can never retreat from. She gets more into it, thrusting with me, and her mouth drops open as my hips smack against hers and her pussy clenches around me.

"Oh, fuck, Zach," she whispers. "You feel so good inside me."

I look her in the eyes. "Norma, you feel good inside me too." She gasps as she realizes the depth of my words, her hands clasping as she holds them to her chest. It almost looks like she's praying, but the muffled sounds coming from her are more devilish than angelic.

I give her a hard stroke, holding deep inside her and grinding there for a second, then reach down to the floor to grab her panties. No scarf right now, though I know there's probably one in her bag, but I'm not leaving the glory of her pussy to get it. This will have to do. I take the silky scrap and wrap it around her wrists, feeding her hands through the leg holes. It's not a perfect restraint, but it never is. It's more the illusion of it that gets us both off.

Her fingers tangle and clasp again, the dark green of the panties bright against her fair and freckled skin, and she squeezes around me. It didn't mean anything when I tied up her wrists that first time. It was just something I felt, but now it's become one of our things, and it's so fucking sexy when she gives herself over to it and to me.

Her sweet tightness is doing me in, and somehow, she finds the strength to keep pushing into me, encouraging me to fuck her harder and give her more.

I slip my thumb to her clit, swirling it in tight circles, and she bucks beneath me. I lay a hand on the table next to her head,

LAUREN LANDISH

leaning over to get an up-close view of the first time she comes on my cock. This is something that will only happen the first time once, and I'm not going to miss a bit of it. She moans, louder than usual, but I'm sure not going to tell her to be quiet. Instead, I tell her, "Say it, Brat. Tell me what you want."

Her breath hitches, but her eyes are clear enough to meet mine. "Rub my clit, Zach. Fuck me hard until I come. I need to come before someone sees me."

"I see you, Norma." The words hang in the air a split second, and then she detonates all around me.

"Yes!" she rasps as her body convulses in waves. Her eyes roll back and her mouth opens in a silent scream. It's the prettiest thing I've ever seen.

My cock swells, and her tight pussy clenches around me one last time, pushing me over. "Fuck, Brat!" I fill her up, crashing with waves of white light as she milks me for every drop of cum before we both sag. I place a palm on either side of her head and bend down to sip at her lips softly. "You good?"

I feel her lips spread into a wide grin. "No, I'm fucking fantastic." And then she giggles, that little girl sound I can pull from her every once in a while.

I agree with her. "Yeah, you are, Brat."

NORMA

Dear Diary,

I'm pretty sure I've met my match. I wore that virgin badge so proudly, certain that any guy able to match my bites wouldn't stick around long enough to earn my cherry. Until Zach. Oh, yeah, I'd say I gave it to him, but it's more like he took it from me. Although I was damn sure willing . . . willing to do it in a public place, willing to let him loop my panties around my wrists, willing to let him say filthy things to me and

314

say some of my own back, willing to let him fill me with his cock and cum. All that . . . so fucking willing.

He seems pretty set on us actually dating too, not just the secret cover story. I'll admit that I don't fully trust that. His words seem heartfelt, but I just can't believe that a guy like him wants someone like me.

But I'm playing along either way, dating or 'dating', and really tutoring him. He got the B he needed on his Idolatry in Paradise Lost *paper, a B-plus, in fact. I think it was worthy of an A, but the professor probably wasn't expecting A-quality work from him. Harsh but true.*

He's even been texting me pictures of him, full of sweaty workout hair and goofy grins with captions like 'You wanna kiss now?' I didn't tell him that I'd happily kiss him when he's all gross. I sent him back a picture of me holding my crinkled nose with a caption of 'No thanks, stinky boy.' But the teasing banter continues between us, sometimes juvenile, sometimes sexy, and sometimes sharp. I love every bit of it.

I've met my match.

THE LAST NOTES OF SUNSET ARE JUST DISAPPEARING INTO the horizon as I unlock my apartment door and head inside. Yeah, it's Sunday, and yes, most people have a history of taking Sundays off.

Zach and I, though . . . well, it's only been two Sundays, ten days since he took my virginity, but Sunday is already my favorite day of the week. Ten days . . . and he's fucked me nearly every day possible.

The only days we've missed were this past Friday and Saturday, since he had an away game. But I watched the game, only the third football game I've ever watched that wasn't a newspaper assignment, tuned in the whole time as Zach ripped apart the other team for five touchdowns. Sure, the other guys on the team helped, but I can tell he's the glue that holds them together. A responsibility he's told me he takes very seriously.

Today, after getting his text, we met up again . . . this time at the stadium, shortly after the team left from their post-game wrap-up. We reviewed class notes and how to structure an argumentative essay in the home team locker room before Zach pushed me up against the lockers and finger-fucked me while pinching and kneading my nipples.

We've yet to have sex in a 'regular' place. Besides the stadium, we've tried out many of the musty old parts of the library, and once in a closet while people walked by, oblivious to him thrusting his cock into me with his hand covering my mouth.

I keep thinking we're going to get busted, that we should either stop this entirely or at least be a little more discreet. Maybe use my empty bedroom instead of hiding in the shadows of the library.

But every time he touches me, every moment we're together, I'm unable to think about anything else. I'm willing to take any risk to be with him. Hell, the risk of being with him in those wild places is half the fun. Okay, maybe not half. It's mostly fun because of Zach, but the chance of getting caught definitely adds to it.

He seems to be telling the truth about wanting us to really be a thing, though that's still so hard for me to believe. I mean, the nerd and the jock? How fucking cliché is that? People would be more likely to believe it was some tutoring cover story than that we actually like each other and have things in common to talk about.

But the way his eyes light up when he sees me, the way he shares with me and the little things he does—like actually fucking study—tell me that this is real, that he sees me as more than just a fun fuck.

The thought warms my heart, and then I hear the ding of a reminder on my phone. Sunday evening . . . phone call time. I dig my phone out of my bag, plopping on the couch to call my big brother, Liam.

It rings a few times, then I hear the call connect before Liam's voice rings out. "Norma Jean Blackstone, is that you? I thought something had happened to you since you haven't called to bust my balls in so damn long."

I grin. "Oh, my apologies, brother. You need me to insult you a bit? I'd be happy to oblige," I tease, intending to start listing his faults in a humorous manner, but the words don't come. And then I realize how soft of a lob he's throwing me, and I laugh as I tell him, "Besides, isn't it Arianna's job to bust your balls now?"

Liam laughs a hearty chuckle. "That it is, little sis. And she does a fine job of keeping me in line, no worries there."

"How is she? I haven't seen her around, though I usually don't since we don't have any classes together," I ask. Arianna is Liam's secretary-slash-girlfriend and she attends classes at the university with me. But that's where the similarities end. Arianna is stunning and made of steel, laser-sharp focused on business, and she somehow managed to actually fall in love with my arrogant brother.

"She's doing well, settled into her fall class schedule and set up her work schedule accordingly. I think she wants to have dinner soon, just the three of us. Unless there's a fourth you'd like to bring . . ." He lets the prying inquiry trail off.

"No . . . yes . . . well, kind of, I guess," I say with a laugh. "I'm not sure. I am seeing someone, but I don't know if we're at a dinner with the family stage yet."

I hear a crackle of leather and I can visualize Liam sitting down on the couch, probably shocked at my words. I'm not

317

exactly a frequent dater so my admission is tantamount to telling him I'm nominated for a Pulitzer.

"My baby sister is growing up. I'm so proud of you, Norma Jean." His voice is pure sarcasm, much like mine usually is, but the sentiment is real, just like mine usually is too.

"Thanks, Liam. Your CEO-intern love story was rather inspirational and made me open to finding my true love. Just think how many relationships the Hallmark movie of your and Arianna's taboo affair will inspire." I'm totally full of shit about the movie, but they really did have a hard time at the office when their relationship came out. That seems to have settled down now, though, and I'm glad for them.

"Ha-ha, but if you tell Arianna that, she'd probably love it. She's a hopeless romantic. So, speaking of romance, what's the unlucky bastard's name?" His tone is casual, the insult smooth as silk, but I'm not a newbie to his games.

"Nice try, but I'm not telling you his name so you can run a background check on him. He's fine, I swear." I roll my eyes at his overprotectiveness, but I secretly love that Liam wants to protect me. I'd never let him know that though. "Besides, if he wasn't fine, I'd cut him off at the dick long before you'd get your chance."

Liam hisses through the phone. "Please, for the love of fuck, Norma . . . I do not want to hear you use the word *dick*. You're my baby sister and I remember when you were a cute little thing on the couch, watching cartoons. I can't handle you and . . . dicks."

It's a reasonable request, so I blatantly ignore it. "Why, Liam, if you don't like me saying 'dick', how about 'cock' or 'pussy' or—gasp—what about 'cunt'? He starts singing in my ear, *la la la la la la*, and I laugh. "Okay, okay, I'm done. Promise." I enjoy when we can have these little moments of childishness again because it reminds me of how close Liam and I have always been.

There was a rough patch for a while when Liam was finishing college and our dad made the mistake of telling Liam that he wasn't going to bring him up in the family business. Well, I'm not sure of the exact wording because I was still in elementary school, but basically, their relationship, which had already been tenuous, imploded. They rarely talk anymore, though I know Dad is proud of Liam's success. But even then, when Liam was refusing Dad's calls, he'd hang out with me, his whiny kid half-sister. He even chose to deal with my mom, his stepmother, to pick me up instead of coordinating it through Dad. Whatever their drama, we've always made it a priority to not let it affect our relationship, and that's something I'm thankful for.

Liam laughs once more and then sobers. "Seriously, though, does he treat you right? Make you happy?"

I smile, even though Liam can't see me. "Yes and yes. He's a good guy. I think you'd like him, but give me some time."

He sighs but agrees. "You got it, Sis. But if you really do have to chop his dick off, don't say a word and use your one phone call for me. I'll get you a lawyer."

I bark out a laugh, the thought absolutely preposterous, which makes Liam's entertaining it even funnier. I always press his buttons and give him shit, but it's a rare treat when he's on fire and shoots back just as much as I do. "Got it. Hey, I gotta go hit the books. Talk to you later?"

"Sure thing, Norma Jean. Bye." He hangs up and I disconnect on my end too.

It was fun to spar with Liam, but the thought of sitting around his table with Zach at my side for dinner is throwing me for a loop right now. There's a pit in my stomach that says don't ask for too much, but there's another part of me that says it sounds like a good outing.

That night, I dream about introducing Zach Knight, Football God, to my business-dry brother and dad. I wake up in the middle of the night with my heart racing, not sure if it's because the dream was going so well or so badly.

———

"So, HOW'S THE TUTORING COMING?"

I look up from my story, a quick little no-brainer about an upcoming show the art department is doing, to see Erica sitting down next to me, keeping her voice low. "What do you mean?" I ask.

"I mean, can he tell the difference between a comma and an apostrophe?" Erica sarcastically hisses, rolling her eyes. "Milton, dammit! How's he doing on Milton?"

"Just fine. His grades have been better," I reply, inwardly cringing. Tutoring Zach on *Paradise Lost* has me reading it myself, of course, and the parallels between Milton's long-winded narrative on temptation and innocence lost and what I'm currently going through certainly haven't escaped me. "He doesn't like it, but I can't fault him there."

I grin for maximum effect, because I know almost nobody likes Milton. Still, it's a staple. Hopefully, Erica buys it, but as she keeps studying me, I grow frightened. Here's where she's going to bust me, I just know it.

Still, I'm not lying. Zach's grades have improved on the two papers he's recently written. And no, I didn't do the work for him. He's more than capable, with plenty of brains to go with his sublime body. He's just been trying to bullshit his way through a class without even taking the time to read the Cliff Notes.

Erica purses her lips, then nods. "Okay. Listen, keep up the good work. I know Zach's hard, but you seem to be on top of him."

More like underneath, in front of, and on my knees with . . . but I've been on top too, I think, trying not to choke on my own horrified laughter. Did I almost say that?

"Are you using the cover story or has no one caught on? I mean, surely, someone has noticed the two of you in the library every night, right?" Erica asks.

Before I can stop the words, they shoot out. "God, I hope not." I think back to our study sessions and how careful we always are. We've never spotted anyone near us at all, but that doesn't stop us from enjoying the 'might get caught' taboo factor.

Erica is taken aback by my answer for a split second and then her eyes narrow as she analyzes me. I'm reminded of why she's the boss of the school paper. She's shrewd, with great instincts, and great at reading people. A flush steals up from my chest to my face, but I keep my mouth shut.

"You're fucking him, aren't you?" Erica asks, clucking her tongue. "Damn, I thought you'd be immune, but I guess no one really is."

I still don't deny or confirm her suspicions.

"Look, just be careful here, Norma. I really didn't mean for you to get tangled up with Zach like that. Figured the cover story was a last-ditch effort if someone caught up to you. Honestly, I figured you were a bit stronger than his flirtations too."

I shrug. "He's nice, and we've been spending a lot of time

together." Even though I still haven't said yes, that we're seeing each other, she gets the drift.

"Do what you want, girl. But that guy is a manwhore, and I can't imagine that you're into that. Don't let him play you with slick words and sweet nothings. You need to come out the other side of this unscathed."

Nodding, I tell her, "I hear you. I swear, I'm good. Promise."

She purses her lips like she doesn't believe me, but she holds her tongue. But her words continue to ring in my mind just like she intended.

Erica leaves, and I quickly finish my article before rushing to the library. I'm early and do my own studying until Zach shows up. I'm immersed in my math assignment when I feel arms wrap around me from behind. My instinct is to elbow back, maybe bite at the hands trying to cover my mouth, but then I realize it's Zach and settle, a giggle escaping my mouth.

"What are you doing? This is a library, you know!" I chastise him, though he knows I love it.

He grins, taking my hand and leading me up to the fourth floor where we drop our bags on our usual table.

Over the next few hours, we study, we flirt, and I come all over Zach's fingers, bucking for every stroke. But Liam's and Erica's words echo in my ear like opposing drums. *One . . . be happy. Two . . . he's playing you.*

And as we go over the argument between angel and fallen angel in book six, I wonder if I, too, will end up discarded when my usefulness is over.

ZACH

"Come on, put some leg into it!" Coach Buckley says as I scramble through the cones, stopping and heaving a long bomb downfield. It's a missile, sixty-five yards, that flies in a beautiful arc to drop into Lenny's arms.

"That's how you do it! Be ready to do it again, just like that, for this weekend's game." Coach yells, excited. "Jake, you're up!"

I watch as Jake takes the snap, dropping back, dodging the orange cone, and chucking it downfield to Lenny.

"Fuckin' A!" Jake says, pumping his fist as his ball hits Lenny in stride. "That's a starter's arm there!"

I say nothing as Jake continues his celebration. I really don't care about his bragging as long as Coach isn't considering that Jake might be right. But Coach Jefferson isn't even watching Jake's passes. Sixty-five yards on a two-step stop is great, but there's more to the game than being able to throw it downfield. Practice continues, and afterward, Jake's still riding high as we get changed in the locker room.

"So, Knight, you feeling the heat about losing your spot yet?" Jake asks as I come out of the shower. He's got a big shit-eating grin on his face like his takeover is imminent. "Because it won't be long before you feel me coming up on your ass."

A few of the guys instantly stop to see if this gets out of hand, knowing there's already animosity between us. "Snake, I'm naked and fresh out of the shower. Do you really want to talk about coming up on my ass? I already told you, if you want the starting job, show what you can do. Until then, keep holding that clipboard on the sidelines."

Maybe that last part was a bit too harsh, but I don't need him in my face, talking shit. It'd be different if he were just fucking around. But when he says it, it's out of sheer jealousy and animosity. He really does think he's the better player, the better leader for our team, and that he deserves the QB gig just because he's played longer, as if it's something you earn with seniority, not skill.

And while I may be a cocky asshole, I earned my spot as the QB with hard work, something my dad instilled in me from day one. I still remember his telling a Peewee football-sized me that 'hard work beats talent when talent doesn't work hard.' It'd been a few years later, after putting forth the effort to really learn the game that I loved, that we realized I might have some real talent. But he never let me rest on my laurels, insisting that I had a responsibility to keep working hard to make the best of the gift given to me.

And I've worked my ass off, on and off the field, running myself to the ground to be physically better than I was yesterday and striving to gain the coaches' and players' respect. Something tantrum-throwing Jake will never have.

Jake's face turns a deep brick red as he stomps out of the locker room. I look around and realize damn near the whole team was watching the exchange. "Show's over, guys. Same damn rule stands today as it did yesterday and the day before that. We're all here to do our fucking best and earn our way. There are no handouts and we could all lose our spots if we fuck off."

There are murmurs of agreement, and Lenny gives me high-five, bro-ing out with a "Fucking A, man. That's the truth." Everyone is still pulling their shit together, the long practice wearing everyone down. But I'm ready to get out of here and get to Norma. I quickly toss on sweats and a T-shirt and run my fingers through my hair. It's nothing fancy, but we've gotten more comfortable around each other and practicality dictates that my baggy grey sweats are way easier for her to slip her hand inside for a bit of hand action. In contrast, she's taken to wearing little cotton skirts that twirl out when she spins, and more importantly, they flip up easily for me to get at her pussy.

I'm distracted by my dirty thoughts as I walk across the parking lot, taking a direct path toward the library instead of following the winding sidewalk path. But I'm broken out of my mindlessness by a revving engine.

At the last minute, I look to my right and see Jake gunning for me in some twisted version of chicken. I don't think he's actually going to hit me, but he seems intent on scaring the shit out of me. I jump out of the way, and as he flies by, I can see the evil grin on his face so I yell out at him. I doubt he heard me, though, because he doesn't even slow as he peels out of the lot. In his fucking Mercedes. The one I'm sure his dad bought for him. I don't begrudge him nice things, but it's just another symbol of his being handed everything on a silver platter and not knowing how to handle it when he doesn't get what he wants.

I'm tempted to chase after him, yank him out of that fancy-ass car, and set him straight on the proper way to behave with teammates. Knowing that's probably the worst thing I could do right now in the mood I'm in, I hoof it straight to the library, hoping that seeing Norma will be the distraction I need.

But even as the fall evening air blows against my overheated skin, I can't let the anger go. Seeing the way Jake looked at me as he gunned his engine has me more and more pissed with every step. I'm going to have to deal with him eventually, not just let Coach handle it. I'm going to have to challenge him face to face the way he keeps doing me. I'm definitely fucking willing to do that, but I have to be smart about it. A QB who flies off the handle on a teammate isn't attractive to coaches or scouts, whether it's him or me.

When I get to the library, Norma is waiting for me in the lobby of the library. She looks cute and sexy, wearing a frayed-hem denim skirt and a white blouse. Her hair is pulled back at the nape of her neck and she has a folded red scarf wrapped around her head. And if I were more focused right now, my cock would already be at full staff from seeing her lips, which are satiny-smooth with bright red lipstick, an obvious sign that she plans on blowing me tonight. She turns to show off her shoes, a pair of polka-dot heels that might bring her up to five-seven when she stands tall, and I know she wore them just for me. She's got a whole naughty modern 50s pinup vibe going on. To top it off, I know that underneath her skirt are some sexy silk panties. She's worn them almost every *study* session we've had since she discovered how much I like them on her.

She's saying so much with her clothes, and I get the message loud and clear and appreciate the effort she put into dressing up for me. If only I were in the mood . . . but after the locker room shit and then nearly getting run over by an asshole who's trying to take my job, sex is actually, for once, the last thing on my mind.

We head upstairs to our spot on the fourth floor. "Whoa," she says as I try and fail to avoid slamming my books onto the table. I drop into my seat, and the wood actually creaks dangerously under the strain. "You okay?"

"Yeah, just . . . a fucking asshole tried to run me over in the parking lot," I growl, reaching for my dog-eared copy of Milton. "Don't sweat it. It's fine. I'll get it figured out."

Norma looks at me for a minute, then shakes her head. I'm not sure if she realizes I'm being literal about the near-miss with the car. She reaches over and puts her hand on mine. I've got big hands, the better to grip a football with, and hers looks almost like a kitten's paw on top of mine. "I'm sure you can figure it out, but talk to me. What happened?"

I look into her eyes, and before I can let any self-doubt stop me, I nod. "I'd rather not do it here. Maybe we could go for a walk?"

Her lips lift in a small smile. "I've got one better. C'mon." She grabs her stuff and I follow suit. Holding hands, I let her lead me out of the library and out to the parking lot.

She digs keys out of her bag and unlocks a new black Volkswagen Jetta that sparkles in the parking lot lights. I whistle. "Wow."

"Gift from my dad," she says, and I remember that her family is rich enough that my potential pro-ball money might not even qualify as pocket change to them. I'm struck by the fact that, in contrast to whiny, entitled Jake, Norma doesn't seem effected by her family's wealth. Sure, she's had opportunities afforded by their funds, but she's got good core values and is a good person underneath the privilege.

I get in as she starts up the engine and we pull out. I don't ask where we're going. I don't really care. I just want to get away. But as she drives, I get the sense she's taking us away from campus. "So, talk to me," she says as we get on the highway. "What's got you worked up today?"

"Jake Robertson," I reply, sighing as I lean back. "Sorry. I shouldn't have been so pissed off about it all."

"No, it's okay," Norma reassures me. "Who is he?"

"My backup on the team," I admit, looking out the window as the lights go by, lulling me into a trance. It's nice in her car, quiet except for the motor, and the soft scent of her perfume somehow calms me. "He's got issues with me."

"Why's that?" Norma asks. When I shift around, she glances over, her voice serious. "Zach, this isn't for the paper. This is just for you."

327

I nod, even though that wasn't even on my mind. "Jake's a redshirt senior. You know what that means?"

"I've heard the term, so kind of. He's actually been at school five years? Why'd he redshirt a year?"

"When he got here, the team had two guys ahead of him, good players. One went pro in Canada, and the other got some chatter from the League but ended up coaching high school ball instead. He's at some uber-competitive 6A school in Texas. So Jake redshirted that first year to study, fill out, and get a solid year of college under him. He backed up the younger of the two guys for a year and actually started his sophomore year."

"How'd he do?" Norma asks, and I shake my head, snorting derisively.

"Let's just say when I showed up for freshman ball the next year, it was a serious fight between me and him for the starting job. That burned him hard, especially since I was just a freshman who, in his eyes, hadn't paid his dues. But then when the team went out and lost the first five games, Coach Jefferson took a chance and put me in. I lit it up, and I've had the job since."

"So, what made the difference?" Norma asks. "I mean, I'm pretty ignorant of football besides that you're one hell of a player." She smiles with the compliment, and I give her a half-hearted lift of my lips to show I appreciate it.

I shrug. "He's not bad, and it wasn't all on him. The team just didn't have all the right pieces then, and it's a team for a reason. But there's got to be a leader on the field, and he gets rattled and off his game easily," I tell her. "Then he starts making mistakes and can't take the heat when it falls on his shoulders. He blames everyone else when it's a shared final score, win or lose. He just made everyone play worse overall.

Anyway, this is his last shot, so he's getting frustrated and desperate. I'm not worried about his taking my spot—that's not fucking happening—but if he keeps pushing my buttons, he's gonna get decked. Shit, that might even be part of his plan, but I'm trying to keep my cool."

I huff, shaking my head. "I can't believe he actually tried to buzz me with his fucking car." Norma gasps, and I think she realizes I wasn't exaggerating. She looks me up and down, like she's checking me for injuries, and I reassure her. "I'm fine. Really. Just pissed me off because that was fucking dangerous, and he was grinning like it was some big joke."

"Shit," she breathes. "Why does it matter to him that much? Does he actually think he has a shot at the pros?"

"No, it's too late for that for him. Besides, Jake's family is pretty well off, and from what I've heard in the locker room, he's going to be working at his father's company. I think he just wants to have that thing to hang his hat on that *he* did, something that's his own and not his father's."

"Is that why you play? To have something of your own? What's your family think about all this?" she asks.

I smile a big smile at that, years of my parents' cheering in the stands coming back in an instant. "They love football too. Probably why they put me in it when I was barely bigger than a football. They've been supportive all along, but this year, especially, with all the interest from the pro scouts, they've been telling me to get my degree first and play pro later." I mimic my dad's voice because I can totally hear him saying that, so vivid it's like he's here, but it's only because he's said it dozens of times. "I'm the first in my family to go to college. I used the golden ticket football afforded me, and I plan to use it to get to the next phase too."

"Then what? What's the plan after the pros?" She asks it

naturally, but it takes me by surprise. No one ever asks me that. Playing in the League is the goal, the final step, the be-all-end-all. You play until you're too injured or they won't offer you a contract, and then you fade off into obscurity. There is no plan for after, or at least not one that most folks give a shit about.

"Put my degree to work, I guess. I've got this year, plus one more, on my Sports Management degree. Figured that'd help me with my own contracts and negotiations in the pros, and then when I can't play, I can help other guys get fair deals. But it's all football, always football. It's all I've ever known, and I love it just the same today as I did when I was five. Maybe more."

"I'm just guessing here, but I think that's why you're better than Jake Robertson," she says.

I interrupt her, teasing and feeling better after getting everything off my chest and talking about my parents. "You don't even know if I'm better. You're just taking my word for it."

She laughs a bit. "Should I take it that you're full of shit then? That this Robertson guy is better than you?"

I growl. "No. I'm better than he is."

She nods. "Duh. Then as I was saying, I think you're better than him because you have such a passion for the game. It's not about making your own mark on the world to stand out of your dad's shadow. It's just about your love for football and leading the team to victory. You want what's best for all the guys, not just yourself."

I nod but then smirk. "Well, all the guys except for Robertson. He can drive that fancy fucking Mercedes off the road somewhere and never show up to practice again. I wouldn't be sad, wouldn't shed a tear. And we'd win games all the same without him." They're harsh words but tempered with the snobby humor in my voice. I don't actually wish harm to Jake. I just want him to get his shit in line.

She purses her lips, weighing my seriousness. "Oh, he's back, the cocky bastard who can do no wrong. Too much serious talk for you, caveman?" She makes a silly grunting noise to drive her point home, but it's too cute to be insulting.

I glance to the road, noting that there are no headlights for miles, and lean across the console, breathing in her ear. "But you fucking love it when I go all 'caveman' on your bratty ass, don't you?"

She sticks her tongue out at me but admits, "Maybe."

"Stick that tongue out again, Brat, and I'm gonna put it to work," I warn her, but she doesn't back down. I knew she wouldn't. I hoped she wouldn't.

"Work?" She gulps, but I can see her eyes flick down to my groin.

"On dinner. Let's get something to eat. I'm starving," I say, delighted at the way she deflates that I didn't say something sexy. But I really do want to grab a bite. "And then after that, maybe you can stick that tongue out again for my cock, leave a nice ring of that pretty red lipstick on me like you're marking your fucking territory."

Norma signals, getting off the highway and pulling into a parking lot. "While door number two sounds delightful, I think I'll take door number one . . . a dinner date."

NORMA

I know it's not a typical first date, where the well-dressed guy picks the nervous girl up and drives her to a restaurant for polite conversation. But this is us, and through some twist of fate, grabbing a bite to eat after a long drive is our actual first date. Not just meeting in the library or grabbing lunch in the food court. Not secret sexcapades or conversations about centuries-old poetry. Our first date is real conversation, connecting as Zach works out some sketchy shit with his team, and a steak dinner. Okay, and probably some racy action later, I think with a small smile.

But a secret thrill goes through my body when Zach holds the door open for me like a total gentleman and then takes my hand as we approach the hostess stand. He keeps the link until we reach the table and then he gestures for me to sit before sliding into the booth next to me. His muscular thigh is pressed against mine under the table, and when he places his palm along the bare stretch of skin below the hem of my skirt, I fully expect him to start working his way higher.

But he doesn't. He just rests it there, casually and comfortably, like it's the most natural thing in the world. And instead of sparks of arousal at his touch, I feel a warmth settle in my heart.

"What are you thinking?" Zach asks, his eyes scanning the menu.

I look over my own plastic-coated list of choices, glad that I'm not one of those girls that only eats organically paleo vegan or whatever. I think everything on this menu, including the menu itself, probably consists of beef. "I'm going for the Angus burger," I finally say. "Oh, and a strawberry milkshake."

He smiles, and I can't help but say the same thing I do every time I order a shake, though I keep it quiet so the next table over doesn't hear me. *"My milkshake brings all the boys to the yard . . ."* I can't sing for shit, but I add a little shoulder move to spice it up a bit.

Zach barks out a laugh, then leans in close, his growl in my ear. "You'd better not bring any boys to the yard, Brat. Just me. I'm the only one in your yard, and don't you forget it." He leans back, his eyes hard and hot as they glance over my face, now flushed from his words.

"What are you going to get?" I ask, disappointed that I don't have a snappy comeback, but when he looks at me like that, I swear my brain shuts down in favor of other body parts getting priority functioning.

He smirks, knowing he got me. "Sirloin and veggies, with iced tea. Maybe a bit of your milkshake." I'm ninety-nine percent sure he's not talking about the frozen drink the waitress is going to bring.

Luckily, my brain is starting to be useful again and I fire back, "You think I'm gonna share my shake? Ooh, that's a big ask, Zach Knight. We'll have to see if you play your cards right to see if you can get a . . . *taste*."

Our shared smile is one of silly humor, but more importantly, it's one of finding someone to play with and have fun.

After ordering, we sit back and conversation flows easily. I don't want to get Zach riled up about Jake again, so I stick with checking in on his English progress. "So, how are your grades in English now? I know you've had several papers that were B or higher, but have you checked your overall? Your eligibility shouldn't be in jeopardy now, right?"

Zach grabs his phone from the table top and clicks for a second and then flashes the screen at me. He's logged into the university's app and the screen shows his current overall grade . . .75! "Oh, my gosh, Zach! That's great! Congratulations! By the time midterms roll around, you might even have a B if you keep up the hard work."

Zach looks at the screen like he can't believe it. "Not bad for a dumbass jock, huh?"

I smack his bicep. "Don't talk like that. You're not a dumbass and you know it. You said you did well in high school English and all your other college courses are going well. You're smart. You just checked out on *Paradise Lost* and that's totally understandable."

He smiles. "I know you're right. I've just always done better with a football in my hand than a book. I can get by, but I won't claim to be *smart*."

"I think you've got plenty of brains," I reply, slipping my hand around his bicep and holding him loosely, not forcing his hand to stay on my thigh but certainly not dissuading it either. "You're juggling college with football, and that's a lot. How big is your playbook?"

Zach thinks before answering. "Over a hundred plays easily, plus formation variations."

"And every week, you have to adjust that to the other team, right?" I continue. "Then you have to execute on the field, and you're making decisions in what, thirty seconds at a time?"

Zach nods. "Something like that, though we have an offensive coordinator who sends in plays."

"That takes brains, Zach. And before you tell me that there's a system, a formula to your plays and all, guess what? I've got a formula too when I write. My brother has a formula he uses when he looks at business deals. Sometimes, we even have to break the formula when our guts say to do so."

"Is that what you did with me? Break your formula?" He's teasing, but I can see the hint of realness to his question.

"I think we both broke our formulas here. But so far, I'm thinking this play has gone pretty well." I raise one eyebrow, daring him to disagree.

His eyes trace down to my red lips, and he whispers, "Yeah, I'm pretty sure this audible is gonna lead to a touchdown."

I grin and whisper back, "Does football talk as seduction usually work for you?"

"Oh, yeah. Watch this . . ." He leans in close, his lips brushing my ear. Then he says, "Rally . . . six-nine . . . connect and smash."

A breathy sigh escapes my lips and then what he said filters through the fog of my arousal and I grin. "That's not even a thing, is it?"

He smirks like the cocky bastard he can be. "Not even close, but I'm not calling plays on the field. I'm calling plays on your body, and smashing into your sweet pussy sounds like the game-winning move."

I laugh at his arrogant outrageousness, our smiles mirrored on each other's faces. The waitress stops by, dropping off our food, and a pleasant tension fills each bite as we look forward to what's going to happen after dinner. It's another new change to our dynamic. Normally, when we meet up for studying, it seems the sex comes out of nowhere with no leadup. Oh, there's plenty of foreplay, but not like this.

I take a big bite of my burger and Zach grins. "I feel like we've been talking about football all night. Tell me . . . why journalism?"

He waits while I chew and swallow, using the moment to gather my thoughts. "I've always been inquisitive by nature, I guess. I like finding out about people, what makes them tick, what makes them do the things they do. And watching my dad, while he's a good guy, there's just so much behind-the-scenes shit that goes on. I think that in some cases, the public deserves to know what's happening with their friendly global corporate monopoly."

He nods. "You ever think about going into the family business? You said your brother started his own company too. But what about you?"

I shake my head. "Hell no. I like the nuances of business, but I like reporting on them, not directing the success or failure of the whole thing. My brother and dad are like two peas in a pod, though they'd kill me if they heard me say that. Both are super-driven and competitive, willing to work themselves to the bone, but with just enough charm that they're benign leaders of their companies, not cartoonish evil empire villains. Although it was touch-and-go there for a while with Liam, until he met Arianna. But she got him whipped into shape. I think you'd like him . . . now."

He looks at me in surprise. "Are you asking me to meet your family, Brat?"

The look of horror on his face has me stuttering. I didn't mean my comment like that, but he doesn't have to be so put off by the mere thought of meeting my brother. "No . . . no, I just meant, you two would get along, I think. But not like there's a family dinner I'm asking you to or anything . . ." I trail off, heat flushing my face and burning the backs of my eyes.

Zach realizes it and cups my cheek. "Shit. I'm sorry, Norma. I was just kidding . . . seriously. I would love to meet your infamous brother, and your mom and dad too, if you want. Let's have a whole fucking pony parade and I can meet them all if it'll make you not cry."

"No, it's fine. I'm sorry. You were just pushing my buttons like we always do. I'm not sure why that one just felt like a sting instead of a tease." I huff out a breath, letting my unexpected reaction go as I realize that it was only in my head. Just a momentary uprising of doubt. About myself or about Zach, I'm not sure which. Or maybe just about us. In the back of my mind, there's a whisper . . . *the jock and the nerd* . . .

so cliché. But I force it away, knowing that Zach has done nothing to make me think he's not just as into this thing between us as I am.

ZACH

The drive is quiet as we head back to campus, and finally, I can't take it. "Pull over somewhere."

She looks at me questioningly but does as I say, finding a dark side road that's deserted and stopping the car. "Now what?" she asks, and I can hear the hesitation in her voice.

I get out and walk around the driver's side of the car, opening her door and leading her out. I lift her up and set her on the hood of the car. Her skirt rides up as I step between her knees, forcing her to spread to give me room. With my hands on her hips, I hold her in place.

"On the side of the road? Going for something extra-kinky now, are we?" She's teasing me, and I know that if I laid her back, she'd let me fuck her tight little pussy right here, right now. But I can hear the hurt in her voice, her usual spark lacking.

"Brat, that's not what I'm doing. Or at least not yet. First, we need to talk. And not snarky fun this time. Serious and real. You in?" I ask, but I'm not going to let her say no. This conversation is happening.

"Ooh, cocky bastard is back, is he?" she tries once more, her eyes begging me not to do this. But I think she doesn't quite know where I'm going with this conversation and that's why she doesn't want to give in to having it.

"Stop. I'm not fucking around, Norma." Her eyes flash fire at me, and if looks could kill, I'd probably be dead where I stand. I reach up, pulling the scarf from its near-constant place

337

around her head, and move to use it in the other place it usually resides. "Put your hands together."

She sighs but gives me her wrists, and I loosely tie them together. She could get out, same as always, but the symbolism of her letting me be in control is more powerful in this moment than ever before. I know she's kicking and screaming against this conversation on the inside, but it's what we need, a dose of seriousness in the midst of all our usual play.

She rests her bound hands in her lap, but I lift them, placing them behind my neck and crowding into her, face to face. The bumper of her car presses against my knees, but I need to be close to her for this. "Listen to me. I detested the idea of needing a tutor in the first place. Thought the whole secret girlfriend shit was stupid as fuck. And then I walked in that library and you busted my balls like no one ever has, completely unimpressed with me and my shit." Her eyes drift down, but they snap back up at my next words.

"I *liked* it. Liked your sass and your backbone and the way you can use words like knives but only do it in a fun way. When you sparred with me verbally, it made me feel like I was a worthy opponent. And fucking you, here, there, and everywhere, has been hotter than I could've ever imagined. Being the first man to be inside you is an honor I will always cherish."

I can see the tears glistening in her eyes, but strong-willed woman that she is, she holds them back along with any verbal indication of what she's thinking. My girl who usually won't shut up isn't saying a word.

"I wasn't looking for any of this, but I found it. I found you, and I will shout from any damn mountaintop you want me to that we're together. I'll meet your brother and your parents. We can walk hand-in-fucking-hand along the field at half-time if you want. Tattoo your name on my ass in that fancy scripty font girls like . . ." I'm running out of grand gestures to list so I thank God when she laughs.

She sniffs a bit, her nose runny from the unshed tears, but the smile is back on her face and her laughter is like a balm. "No tattoos, hero. But the rest sounds pretty stellar." She sobers, though this time, it feels like she's with me, no walls and unfiltered. "I'm sorry, Zach. Truly. I wasn't looking for this either, and I don't exactly have the best track record with guys hanging around. Sure, I'm fun to be *friends* with and have literally been told that I'm great in small doses, so I just keep waiting for the other shoe to drop, for you to figure out that I'm not worth the effort to hang around. I'm not easy and I know that, and you're . . . you. You could have any girl on campus you want, so why would you be with me?"

The admission seems like it hurts her to say, and I realize that for all her strength, my Brat is a softie underneath, scared to get hurt just like the rest of us. It's a surprising revelation, though I guess it shouldn't be. She's human and victim to the same insecurities we all are. She just hides hers a bit better than most, deeper in the shadows of her heart, not one to show her weak spots.

Wanting to soften it for her, I let just a hint of tease into my voice and let her see the sparkle in my eye as I say, "Let's be clear. I'm a fucking football god. I could have virtually any woman I want, period. Not just on campus." She rolls her eyes, and I continue as I grasp her chin, forcing her to see the truth in my words. "And I chose you. I choose you every damn day, Brat. You keep me on my toes, keep things interesting. Choose me back."

She chuckles a bit. "Fine. I choose you too." The words are full of humor, like she's giving in to something silly, but I can hear the honesty in them, feel the weight of them, and I know they mean just as much to her as they do to me.

She looks around us, the dark night pressing in like a blanket, stars above us twinkling like fairy lights, and down below, the occasional headlight or taillight passing on the main road. "So . . . you said you like to keep things interesting, right?"

I can hear the dare in her voice, the challenge to fuck her right here on the side of the road where anyone might drive by or even someone on the main road might notice if they looked up at just the right time.

I yank her from the hood of the car, her hands scrambling to grab at me, but they're uselessly tossed over my head still and she can't get purchase. I grab her head in my hand, tilting it the way I want and taking her mouth in a hot, passionate kiss. She moans into me, and I swallow every sound, wanting to keep not just her sass but her submission as my own.

I step back, lifting her hands over my head and spinning her in place. A press to her back has her bending over the hood, ass presented perfectly for me and her hands reaching toward the windshield. Our conversation . . . the truth and the heaviness ride me, and I need to claim her, make sure she fucking knows that we're in this together. That she's mine.

She is mine. See those hands? They aren't letting go of that knot. And she has just as tight a grip on my fucking heart. She's mine, and I'm fucking hers.

I rip her skirt up, exposing her ass to the night air. Her panties are soaked, the silky white covering of her pussy almost sheer with her arousal. My already rock-hard cock throbs in my pants, and I'm tempted to take her right here. But this is about showing her more, showing her something new, and I lick the fabric, her breath catching as I tease her clit through her panties. "Zach . . . oh, God."

I reach up, hooking my thumbs in her panties and rolling them down her thighs. Folding them in half, I tuck them in my pocket, for a half-second wondering if Norma knows I've kept four other pairs from special encounters. Regardless, the scent of her arousal hits me in the face, my mouth watering as I start licking and sucking on her sweet folds and silky soft lips.

"Spread wide for me." She steps her heeled feet wider without the restriction of the skirt, and I growl, grabbing a handful of her ass in each hand.

She cries out, pressing into my palms. "Please, Zach. Just fuck me. I need you."

I lay one long lick to her pussy, starting with a flick of my tongue against her clit and then through her folds, up to the puckered rosebud of her asshole, where I swirl my tongue. She bucks, and I know it's her first time being touched there. The thought makes me want to take her virgin ass too. But not tonight.

I pull my sweatpants down, letting my cock spring free to tease along her slit, getting myself coated in her juices. "Goddamn, you're fucking soaked. So sexy. Tell me, Norma. Use those damn words of yours and tell me what you want."

She squirms, trying to impale herself on my cock, and I press her hips to the hood, not letting her take it without saying it. She lets out a cute kitten growl of frustration and finally gives in. "Fuck me. Slide that awesome fucking cock of yours into my pussy and make me come."

At her order, I do it, slamming balls-deep in one stroke and going full-power from the get-go with no time for her to adjust. My hips slap against her ass, and she bucks, trying to fuck me back. I grab her hips, helping her move. It's hard, rough, and passionately violent. It's exactly what we need after all the truth of the night.

But I know there's more.

"That's not all though, is it, Brat? You don't just want me to fuck you. You want me to fuck you in the shadows of the library, in the dark of night on the side of the road. Where someone might see you being my fucking dirty girl, getting plowed so hard and raw you have to fight back the screams. You want me to fuck you with your hands tied up in the silk scarves I know you only wear as a way of wordlessly asking me to do this to you. This is what you want, to be my tied up, submissive fucktoy, and you like that someone might see you getting filled by your arrogant bastard jock boyfriend." Every word of my filthy talk is true, and I pound home each one with another powerful stroke inside her.

She's trembling beneath me, her pussy a mess of her cream and my pre-cum as she gasps out with every thrust. "Ohh . . . Zach . . . I'm gonna come." Her voice is getting higher-pitched and louder. In the shadow of night, it carries, and I love that down the street, someone might be letting their dog out for the night for a bedtime piss and instead, they hear us.

"Not until you say it, Brat. Tell me I'm right," I grunt, "look over there at those headlights, any one of which could be someone who sees us." I tangle my fingers in her hair, holding her head to the side so that her eyes can lock on the vehicles driving by, not exactly close, but close enough to feel taboo. I grind deep inside her, giving her time to see a few headlights pass.

She cries out at the change in sensation, and faster than I'd meant for her to, she falls off the edge. Shudders rack her body and her pussy squeezes me like a vice, but mixed in with her shouts of pleasure, she gives me what I demanded. "Yes . . . it's all true. Fuck me anywhere, even if we might get caught. I just want you, Zach!"

Her admission and naughty words are my undoing, and I

follow her over, coming hard and groaning loudly as rope after rope of my cum fill her tight pussy.

Panting as we both come back to earth, I help her stand up. Turning her head toward me, I kiss her, the smack of our lips replacing the smack of my hips against her. "Fuck, Brat. That was amazing."

I let my cock leave her body, instantly feeling the loss, and she whimpers a bit too. I spin her, untying her scarf and handing it back to her. "Now what? You ready to head home? It's pretty late." I look up to the pitch-black sky and then at all the shadows surrounding us.

Norma smirks and then sasses, "You promised me door number one and door number two earlier."

I have no idea what she's talking about, my brain pretty much fried after sex and our conversation. I lift my brows in question.

"Earlier, you said door number two was dinner. But door number one was something else." She sticks her tongue out, licking her red lips, and like a flash, I remember. I told her she could suck me off and leave that red lipstick all over me. The lipstick is still there, must be some of that fancy kiss-proof shit girls wear, but I'm all for trying to get it to smudge.

"You gonna clean me off, Brat? Suck me off right here?" I ask, letting my thumb trace the edge of her lip.

She bites her lip, narrowly missing the pad of my finger, and smiles naughtily. "Nope. Get in the car, asshole."

"Asshole? Is that what you call guys when they make you come like a damn freight train against the hood of your very practical and reliable fancy car?" I tease, liking that we're back to this space between us.

"Apparently, but you'd be the only one who'd know." She

smirks, and I hear the compliment in the words. That I'm the one she chose to give her virginity to, and as much as she may give me a hard time, we both know that was a big deal. That *we* are a big deal.

Norma drives for a few minutes, looping down toward the main road but then pulling off at an exit and parking again, just off the highway on the shoulder. And then she looks at me with a devilish grin.

"Here?" I ask, surprised. "We're literally on the side of the road."

"Yep," she says, letting the word pop her lips. "I watched the cars like you told me to. There's only a few going by, no traffic or anything."

I turn and look behind us. "What if a cop stops?"

She widens her eyes, looking innocent as hell, but I know it's a front because my Brat is anything but innocent. "Guess you'll have to keep your eyes open and keep watch."

I grin back, knowing we're doing this. I gesture to my cock. "All yours, Brat. Show me what you've got."

She looks in the rearview mirror one time and then lies over the console. I help her slip my dick free of my pants and then she breathes on me. I'm impatient, ready for this in a way I don't know that I've ever been. Sure, she's sucked me in dim corners at the library, but this seems riskier somehow. I fucking love it.

She laps at my tip, swirling her tongue around it before taking me into her mouth. "Fuck, Norma, I love it when you do that."

She hums against me and goes deeper. I spread my legs to give her room to work, letting one of my hands drift into her hair and the other down to hold myself straight up for her, giving her a better angle. She dives in, covering my whole cock with the wet warmth of her mouth, and she begins to suck me, each stroke up and down better than the one before as she takes me higher and higher as she goes deeper and deeper.

I groan, trying but failing to keep my hips still. I buck into her mouth, already about to come. I glance in the mirror and see headlights coming up behind us.

"Don't stop, don't stop," I beg. Norma thinks I'm talking to her, and maybe I am, but I'm also praying that car doesn't stop and get a view of my girl's mouth full of my cock. Because if someone tapped on the glass right now, I don't know that I could let her pull off me. I need this, so close . . .

The car whooshes by in a whir of speed, and I come, filling her mouth as I cry out, my hand gripping the headrest behind me as I lift my hips so that my Brat can take every bit of me. "Fuck . . . yeah!"

When she sits back up, there's no red on my cock and her lips look just as pristine as they did when I picked her up. But we're both undone from the night.

We might not have studied for shit, but I feel like I got a great big lesson in all things Norma Jean Blackstone.

ZACH

I don't think I've ever enjoyed college this much. On the football field, the Ravens are undefeated. Now the pursuit is for the conference championship, and if we can do that, the sky's the limit.

But it's not just football. The weeks that I've been studying with Norma have been . . . something. My little Brat makes studying at least tolerable, and while Milton isn't going to be on my Kindle for away games anytime soon, I'm doing well.

How well? Well, enough that my weekly essays are coming

back with Bs and even an A on one of them. I've got a B in English already, and if I stick with it, I might even pull out a B-plus. Hell, might set my sights on an A with her help.

Part of it, of course, is her sassy mouth. I can't make a single statement in our discussions without having to justify it. Norma knows just how to press my buttons too, and while the acid that used to coat her tongue isn't there any longer, she still gives as good as takes, verbally speaking. And she doesn't let me just skirt by easily. When we're in study mode, I can't even seduce her . . . most of the time.

Not that we don't seduce each other. She's even taken the lead sometimes, and the more she does it, the more it thrills me. I'll never forget the time she gave me a surreptitious hand job in the middle of the library for getting an 'A' on that essay, her face impassive as she talked about temptation and Satan's role as an anti-hero. Meanwhile, underneath the table, her hand was milking my cock, and I had to untuck my shirt to make it back to the dorm without giving myself away after our 'tutoring.'

Simply put, sex with her is awesome. Every time is more fun than the last, and we're constantly one-upping the other with how intense and fun we can make it.

And that's what makes Norma different. She's . . . special. It can work.

The thought is undeniable as I jog out onto the field for Home-coming. The Ravens have homecoming relatively late, and this year, it's an important game. If we win this, we're nearly locked for the conference championship in three weeks. The only games we've got left are against teams we should beat. All we have to do is play our game the way I know we can.

"How're you feeling, Son?" Coach Jefferson asks as we wait on the sidelines for the senior captains to do the coin toss. "We're on TV today. You know some scouts are going to be watching, maybe here but definitely later." He scans the crowd, like he could spot a scout at this distance.

"Don't sweat it, Coach. There will be plenty of highlights to choose from for my reel," I promise him. "You just get ready for the Gatorade bath."

I glance up in the stands, but I can't see Norma in the mass of tens of thousands of fans here to see the Ravens take on the Bulldogs. But I know she's here, wearing a team shirt to support me and ready to cheer like crazy.

I put it out of my mind as we take the field, needing my brain to focus because it's time to work. We run the first three plays just as Coach scripted, burning the Bulldogs for two good passes before we get stuffed on the third play.

Looking over at the sidelines, I watch as Jake gets the play from Coach, sending in the signals. "What the fuck?" I mutter.

Settling into the huddle, I call the play. "Trips left Camelot, Rodeo 82 Ninja on three."

"Are you out of your fucking mind, man?" Will Franklin, my left tackle and our senior captain, asks. "They're stacking the box."

"Coach called it. Now run it," I say, putting that tone in my voice that says cut the bullshit. Will shuts his mouth, and the huddle breaks, but as soon as I settle into the shotgun, I know Will is right. This makes no sense.

They're coming at me hard. They have to, so why this play? I'm only going to have five guys protecting me. Everyone else is going deep. This is a play we normally only run in long ball, no-pressure situations. Now, I'm not afraid to stand in the pocket. Every quarterback's expected to take a shot from time to time, but this is suicide. Tugging on my facemask, I make a decision to overrule coach and audible it.

It's a risk. The crowd's going nuts and I'm not sure anyone can hear me, but I have to trust that my teammates can. The ball snaps, and I roll right, avoiding the manic Bulldog rush as I look for an opening.

Nothing. I've got half a second to make a decision to either run or pass when I see it. Not even breaking stride, I laser the ball downfield to our tight end, who takes it the rest of the way in for a touchdown.

Jogging off the field, Coach Buckley gives me a pat on the shoulder. "Great call, Son! Can't argue with a touchdown."

"No problem, but why did you send in that play?"

Before he can answer, Coach Jefferson calls him over and I can't get an answer. For the rest of the first half, though, I keep getting strange signals from the sidelines, and more than once, I'm changing plays at the line. When we go in for halftime, we're up, but it's not by what we wanted.

"What the hell's going on out there, Zach?" Coach Buckley asks as the locker room door closes. "You keep changing the play at the line out there."

"Coach, I'd call them like you send them in, but the signals aren't making any sense with what's happening on the field!" I growl, trying to keep my voice low. Coach is a good guy, and I learned to never disrespect a Coach where others can hear you. "I swear, every time we're in a position to run for the first down or work the short routes and sidelines, you're wanting me to stand back there and throw bombs!"

Buckley stops, tilting his head. "What the hell do you mean? I know they're trying to pressure you."

"Then why do you keep sending in plays for me to sit in the pocket? That's what Jake's signaling."

Coach stops and looks at Jake, who's trying to look innocent and failing. "Jake? What the fuck are you doing out there?"

And though my attention laser-focuses on Jake, I'm aware that there is a whole room full of guys watching and listening to the exchange now.

Jake seems to realize the same thing, looking around at the team with his hands held wide. He hems and haws. "I don't know what you mean, Coach. I just send in what you tell me to. But if Zach can't handle it, that's on him. You know I'll step in for the team if he's pussing out."

Coach's eyes narrow, looking between the two of us. "I don't have time to deal with this shit. Second half, I'll send in the signals myself. Jake, sideline. Zach, win the damn game."

He walks off, and I turn to Jake, shaking my head. "You really are a snake, aren't you? You trying to get me fucking injured out there?"

Jake looks at me, his jaw clenching as he stares at me. "The team would be better with me out there. I should be the one getting the headlines, goddammit."

"Don't fucking stab your own teammate in the back. That just shows why you *shouldn't* be out there," I growl.

I should say a lot more. Hell, I'm *this close* to beating the shit out of him. But I have no proof he's done it on purpose. It's obvious now that he did, but he'll weasel his fucking way out of it with Coach and I'll be the one talking shit like a crybaby. But with the whole team watching, this isn't about the coaches. Every man in this room knows in his gut that Jake just tried to have me sacked on the line so that he could get some grass time.

And that shit doesn't fly. Not with any team, but especially not with the Ravens. The circle of guys gathers closer and I think Jake can see the sea of fury encroaching.

He pushes past one of the smaller guys and makes a break for the locker room door. "Whatever. Glory hound," Jake says, turning away.

I look around at the guys, who are waiting for my signal on how we want to handle Jake's breech of the football code. "Fuck that asshole. We have a game to win." Will takes over the pep talk from there, and we run back out, ready to rock.

The second half is a total turnaround. With Coach Buckley running the signals directly to me, our offense clicks on all cylinders, and we unleash hell on the Bulldogs. We're so far ahead, the Bulldogs don't have a chance at recovering, so Coach pulls me out and lets Jake get some field time . . . and to ensure I don't end up with some stupid injury that didn't have to happen.

I'm pretty satisfied when the whole defensive line seems to instantly falter and a lineman gets through to Jake, sacking him to the grass. The same thing happens on the next play. Jake's time on the field is basically useless as he keeps eating the turf. We keep the Bulldogs from making any headway, but the team sacrifices gaining any ourselves.

It's still a shootout, though, and as the guys pile off the field, they all give me high-fives. Will stops, pressing his helmet to my forehead and talking low. "Ravens don't put up with that shit. But you need to let it go now. We fought your battle for you so that you wouldn't fuck up your future. You got me?"

I nod back, the significance of what he's saying sinking in. "Thanks, man. You didn't have to do that. But thanks."

He grins and gives me a big wink before letting out a big whooping yell. "We were gonna win, no matter what! Ravens forever! Let's hear it for my man, Zach!"

And like the bottle's been uncorked, the excitement bubbles over. Everyone's congratulating me, and Coach Jefferson doesn't even wait until we're back in the locker room to toss me the game ball in front of the stands. "You earned it, Son. Damn fine job today!"

I smile and nod, telling him thanks. The team lines up near the student section for the Alma Mater, but before we're even started, I see Jake turn and storm off the field. Whatever. I bet Coach will chew his ass for it, and in the future, I'm going to insist he doesn't relay the calls. He's got a knife, and it's pointed right at my back. Luckily, the rest of the guys have me and I have them.

The music plays on, and it's a great feeling to stand here with my team, knowing we're playing our best season ever. But regardless of how much everyone might be pounding my shoulders and congratulating me, I should be enjoying this whole thing with my girl.

Yes, *my* girl.

I look out into the crowd, and at that moment, I see her in the stands. I wave to her, feeling slightly stupid, but when she waves back, it feels good to know I've been playing a great game in front of her.

Suddenly, the guys all crowd around and in one big mosh pit of craziness, I'm shuffled to the locker room amid the celebration. I manage to poke my head up above the mass and yell, "Norma, meet me by the locker room!" I think I see her nod before I'm carried away.

NORMA

The game is amazing! I'm kind of ashamed to admit it, but I've never been to one of our college games. Not until Zach. Sure, I've seen them on television, and I went to a few of the important games in high school, but it's nothing like the rush of a college Homecoming game. The stands are a sea of black and gold for the Ravens and red and white for the Bulldogs. There's an undulating energy to the crowd, everyone cheering and booing in unison as the teams battle it out on the field. And watching Zach play the game that he loves, I'm suddenly struck with understanding why he loves it so much.

Somewhere after half-time, I hear my name being shouted from the stands below me. I scan the crowd and see Erica waving at me. I smile and wave back and she starts to work her way up to me. Luckily, the couple sitting next to me seem to be on a bathroom break and Erica sneaks into one of their seats for a minute.

"Hey, girl! Never thought I'd see you at a game! What do you think?" she asks excitedly. I grin, enjoying seeing my usually serious and hard-pressing boss a bit crazy. Her hair is pulled up in a big cheerleader bow that's almost as big as my palm and she has logoed eye black on her cheeks, her right proclaiming *Ravens* and her left *#1*. She's also wearing a team shirt and has a pompom on a stick. She's a fangirl, which surprises me somehow.

"I love it! Look at you . . . you're totally a football groupie!" I say with a laugh.

She laughs and shakes her head. "No, more like a super fan. I'm not a dick-hopping groupie when I've got a good one of my own." She leans close and points back down where she was sitting, where as if he sensed she was talking about him, a good-looking guy turns around and smiles at Erica. She gives him a little finger waggle and he laughs before going back to watching the game. "So, you here for Zach?"

I nod. "Yeah, I'm meeting him after the game for some HoCo team party. Supposed to be fun, but I'm nervous." The admission is truer than I'd like to admit. What we have together is awesome, but introducing me to his team feels like it's on par with me introducing him to Liam. Major.

"Ooh, have fun! That's probably a big deal to take someone as your girl, not your flavor of the week. Seems like maybe I was wrong about Zach and you. Maybe you do have a magic pussy that can tame the wildest of manwhores? You'll have to tell me all your secrets." She says it jokingly, and I realize she's probably mildly drunk and not filtering, but it's still a bit of a sting.

"Oh, yeah, pussy whipped him right into shape," I joke, playing off the pseudo-compliment.

But she doesn't stop, "Girl, I would've bet money that you would've barely been able to tutor him successfully, much less turn his eye. Not because you're not gorgeous, because I mean, have you seen you?" She grins loopily. "But he's just . . . Zach Knight, Quarterback Extraordinaire. He could have pussy twenty-four, seven if he wanted."

She's not wrong. Hell, I basically said as much to Zach. But he reassured me that he wants only me and I believed him. I do believe him. But it's hard to remember that when Erica is verbalizing the same insecurities that I already have.

"Yeah, good thing he's got mine then, I suppose," I say with a bit of a bite. Luckily, the couple returns from the bathroom right then and saves me from any more of Erica's drunken disbelief at my relationship with Zach.

She waves and heads back to her guy, magically not stumbling on a single step. So maybe not that drunk. Just enough to insult me, apparently. I give a moment's thought that maybe she's more sour-grapes-jealous than surprised. Her whole outfit and enthusiasm could be school spirit, but right now, if someone told me she was a bit more toward the groupie end of the spectrum, I wouldn't be surprised.

I try to let that temper the effect of her words, to let them go and enjoy the game.

And as the third quarter turns to the fourth, I'm pretty ensnared in the game again, even when Zach gets pulled to the sidelines for a bit. From listening to the fans around me, I figure out that the Coach is letting Jake get some time, but once Zach is off the field, I quit watching the game and instead watch him on the sideline.

And when we win, pandemonium breaks out and the hugely wide grin on Zach's face is beautiful. When he looks up to find me in the stands and we wave back and forth, it feels like he invited me in to this special moment, shared his joy with me across the distance separating us. I see his head pop up as the crowd pushes toward the end zone and see him pointing and mouthing, "Meet me outside the locker room." I nod back, but he's gone in the mob.

I wait for the stands to clear a bit before working my way down and out, following the throng of people before turning off to head toward the locker room hallway. Down here, the mass clears a bit, giving me a clear sightline to Zach leaning up against the wall. I smile at the sight of him, freshly-showered damp hair mussed, a black T-shirt stretched tight across the muscles of his chest, and what are quickly becoming my favorite grey sweatpants. I'm so busy checking him out that it takes me a minute to realize that he's smiling while talking to someone.

I follow his gaze to see a blonde Barbie-looking girl standing in front of him. She's looking up at him with a flirty smile, twirling a lock of hair around a manicured finger as she chats back. I don't need to hear the words to know that she's basically propositioning him because her every intention is being broadcast absolutely one hundred percent loud and clear.

A stab of jealousy, hot and bitter, punches me in the gut. I'm torn. There's the one side of me that wants to haul ass over there and basically mark my damn territory, push Blonde Barbie the fuck away from what's mine. But I'm pissed at myself to admit there's a tiny wiggle deep in my brain that says I should've known. Like Erica said, Zach has always been a bit of a manwhore, and while he's been nothing but gentlemanly with me, at the least, maybe he'd prefer someone easier, less prickly and snarky?

And just like always, when I get a bit out of sorts, I react by going full-throttle. I basically stomp my way over to Zach, but about halfway there, he turns and sees my incoming fury. His smile just pisses me off more.

My voice is stone-cold as I get to his side. "Zach."

He puts an arm around my shoulder, pulling me to his side. "Hey, Brat! Been looking for you."

My eyes shoot daggers and his grin grows. I swear he even chuckles a bit. "Norma, this is Beth. Beth, this is Norma. Beth is 'like my biggest fan ever!'" he says, obviously mimicking Beth's voice. "Norma is my girlfriend."

I watch Beth's eyes widen and then narrow as she very obviously looks me up and down, judging my worthiness. My inner bitch is yelling *you can fuck right off, Beth.* And though every instinct is telling me to verbally slice and dice her, I know that's not the best move here and would only make me seem bitchy and insecure. And while that's probably true, at least to some degree, I force myself to calm down and take the high road.

I channel the cool demeanor I've seen my dad give to opposing business forces, the one my mom has given to waitresses the world over when they flirt with my dad in front of her, and give Beth the smile that says I consider her less than a worthy opponent. That I consider her inconsequential, less than a footnote to the highlights of my day. "Nice to meet you, Beth."

She smiles back, just as fake as the boobs pressed up damn near to her chin, but she doesn't address me, instead keeping her lasers locked on Zach. "Oh, your *girlfriend*. Right. Well, I guess I'd better be going for now then. See you *later*, Zach." Every word is designed to sound like she's covering some big secret between the two of them. She blows a smacking kiss at the air, aimed right for his mouth, then pivots and sashays away, her hips exaggeratedly swinging right and left.

To his credit, Zach doesn't even watch her go. Instead, he steps in front of me, caging me in his arms and pressing me back against the wall. "You surprise the hell out of me, Brat."

I look away, refusing to meet his eyes, but he tilts my chin, forcing me to.

"You are so fucking jealous. You were strutting over here like some sexy Valkyrie about to demolish that girl. I'll admit, I was a little excited to see you trash talk her, reduce her to a crying puddle on the ground, because I know that sharp tongue of yours could do it in a heartbeat. But instead, you went all responsible and mature on me, like you knew that I was yours and wasn't going anywhere, not when I have something as special as you in the palm of my hand."

To emphasize his words, he lets one hand cup my ass, squeezing hard enough to make me gasp. "I had a moment where I almost made some vulgar joke about her fake tits or bottle blonde, but when they make it that easy, it's almost a pity to use it. Lowest common denominator shit," I admit. "And it hit me that I was jealous because of the possibility, not that you were actually doing anything or even considering it. And that opportunity is always out there. I don't want to be *that* girl. You don't deserve for me to be that way because you've given me no reason to mistrust you. It's just my own fears and doubts."

"So don't be scared. Don't doubt me, and sure as fuck don't doubt us. Because it's me and you, Brat." His words are serious, solemn like a promise. "You need to do some territory marking to get it out of your system? Because I could be down for that." He grins, like it's a joke, but leans close to whisper in my left ear, "You need to leave a mark on my neck before we go to this party?" He tilts his head, almost like he's deferring to me, and the expanse of his neck is right there, so warm. I can see his heartbeat racing, so I lean forward to lick it and then lay a soft kiss, letting the beat pulse against my lips.

I move to his ear, whispering back. "I don't need to mark your neck like I've got something to prove to everyone else. They can fuck off. All I care is that you're marked here . . ." I lay my palm against his heart, and my other against my own. "And so am I."

His breath hitches. I'm holding mine. The moment stretches, and I can almost taste the three little words in the pregnant pause between us, neither of us willing to say them yet but both acknowledging that they're true. That this is real. So fucking real.

"Goddammit, Brat. That's the sexiest thing anyone's ever said to me. Come on." He grabs my hand, dragging me down the hallway and around under the bleachers until we find a deserted corner in Section 67.

He pulls me close and crushes my lips in a fierce kiss. I melt against him as we descend deeper into the shadows, out of view, though I can still hear people moving through the stadium a little bit away.

He nibbles on my ear, making my thoughts and our previous

357

conversation scatter like the wind. "You were a god out there today."

He cups my breast, teasing the stiff nipple and pinching me lightly. "Did you like watching me play?"

I slip my hand inside his sweatpants, grasping his thick cock and stroking it to rock hardness while he tugs at the button of my jeans, undoing them and rubbing at my drenched panties. "What do you think? I wanted to—"

"Hey, Louie, you gettin' the brooms?"

We freeze as a voice calls out, seemingly just outside the alcove we're hiding in. It's one of the stadium workers, probably getting everything together for cleanup.

"Don't move," Zach whispers, but he spins me, shoving my jeans and panties down. Suddenly, his cock is right at my entrance, and without notice, he thrusts inside me. He clamps his hand over my mouth to stifle the moan he knows is coming when he fills me.

The stadium worker is oblivious as Zach starts stroking in and out of my pussy, my body clenching, already on the edge from the feel of him inside me and the thrill of what we're doing. It's impossible to be totally quiet, the soft wet sounds of my pussy taking his every plunge seeming to echo around us, but no one peeks around the corner to catch us.

I turn my head, my eyes swimming with lust . . . and something more, needing to see it reflected in Zach's eyes. His blue eyes lock onto mine and he nods. There wasn't a question, but I know he's telling me that he feels this too. My body ramps up, tighter and higher, my lips pressed together behind his palm.

We hear the stadium worker talking, his voice getting quieter and quieter as he walks away from our hiding spot. Zach growls in my ear, "That was so hot, wasn't it, Brat? You wanted to come all over my cock knowing someone else might hear you, might see you getting fucked under the bleachers by your football god."

I nod as he hammers into me, whimpering as I try to hold back my cries.

But he's not done. He rumbles, "You might be evolved . . . not need to mark me up, but I'm just a cocky bastard caveman. I know I have you here," he says, taking the risk of removing his hand from my mouth to place it against my chest. His thumb flicks at my nipple, but I know he means my heart. "But I need to mark you inside and out because you're fucking mine, Brat."

His other hand grips my hip tightly, dimpling in the skin, and I know it'll leave bruises. I welcome them, want his mark if that's what he wants. Hell, I'm rethinking my previous stance on leaving a hickie on his neck because being in his rough grasp is heaven.

I hear footsteps, but it's too late. There's no stopping us now.

Zach pounds into me, hips slapping my ass with every thrust like he's given up on being quiet. I tighten my pussy around him, and it's enough to send us both over. I clench my teeth, and a glance over my shoulder shows Zach's jaw clamped tight too, both of us trying to contain our cries as our orgasms rock our bodies. I feel him fill my pussy with his cum, and I milk him, wanting every last drop.

We sag as Zach pulls out, breaths panting and happy smiles on both of our faces. We got away with it. Again.

"God, you make me so fucking crazy. That was hot," I whisper, tugging my panties up. "I couldn't believe you kept going."

Zach steps closer, stopping me from pulling my jeans up though his sweatpants are already back in place. He cups my pussy through my wet panties. "I couldn't stop. Didn't care if we got caught as long as I got this sweet pussy. And now you're marked . . . inside." He touches my chest like he did before and then grinds his palm against my lips. He smirks. "And out." He smacks my ass over the sensitive area he'd been gripping, the sound echoing around us as it bounces off the metal bleachers.

I grin back, liking the way he thinks. "So caveman, Zach," I tease.

But he knows. "Just the way you like me, Brat. Now let's get to the after-party. The guys are all dying to meet you. Fair warning, I might've talked about you . . . a lot."

I blush. "Oh, God, what did you tell them?"

I swear Zach blushes a bit, but surely, that's just a trick of the lights. "Just that you're bratty and prickly and can cut just about anyone down in under ten words. You probably need to get your game face on because they're ready for you to wow them."

"Shit, no pressure or anything though, right? And you tell me this now? After fucking my brains out, where I have no hope of forming coherent sentences."

He winks at me. "Well, I had to give them a fair shot. It's like a head start for them, because they'll need it against you. I might've also told them that you're my girlfriend, and now they want to meet the 'witch who cursed me', though I think that's supposed to be a dig on me more than any commentary on your spellcasting abilities."

I sigh, looking heavenward as though I need strength. "Well, let's do this then," I say, sounding like I'm dreading every bit of this. I'm actually excited to hear that Zach's been talking about me with his team. And nervous to meet them because these are Zach's people. And meeting someone's people is a big deal.

Zach looks down at me like he knows every thought that just ran through my mind. Hell, he probably actually does. "You'll do fine, Norma. They're gonna love you and you're gonna love them."

I swear I thought he was about to say his team would love me like he does, but the words didn't come. I'm not disappointed though. I feel like we're there, just hovering on that edge of admission, and it's a sweet moment of anticipation, knowing that it's coming. For him and for me.

NORMA

Dear Diary,

The past weeks have been amazing! I feel like Zach and I have reached a place of excited-comfort. Yeah, I know those two words are pretty much the antithesis of each other, but it's the best way I know to describe where we are.

I guess I never realized that my lack of positive romantic relationships had done a bit of a number on me. That maybe my jump to sarcasm was preemptively defensive. But with Zach, there's no need to be constantly on alert. And we've had some rather insightful, deep conversations, acknowledging feelings that I usually hide behind snark, and even building some bridges over my insecurities. My trust that he's going to hang through the challenge of being with me hasn't dulled my sharp tongue, though. But it's . . . evolved? I guess that's the right word. We zing each other but then bust up laughing, high-fiving as we say 'good one' or lobbing a verbal softball to let the other slam-dunk it. It's easy, fun, and . . . comfortable.

But it's not all prose and slam poetry, which though they are thrilling, are nothing compared to our sex life. I almost can't believe that I can actually say that . . . my sex life! From virgin to fuck-me-anywhere-and-anytime in a whiplash of 'Oh, God. Yeah!' Definitely exciting.

Somehow all mixed together, though, Zach and I have reached a place I wasn't sure I'd ever get to. Excited comfort. Him, my cocky jock who puts up with my prickliness and calls me on my sass. Me, his mouthy brat who challenges him to use his brain and supports his dreams on and off the football field.

I'VE GOT BIG PLANS TODAY.

Big, responsible plans that include such titillating endeavors as writing a three-hundred-word article on the new smoothie cart in the quad, studying vocabulary words for biology, and reading the last section of *Paradise Lost* for my *study* session with Zach tonight. But all of that has to wait until I finish my cup of coffee and take a shower because I need the wake-me-up to get rolling on my list that doesn't sound bad but will definitely keep me busy while Zach hits the weight room with the team this afternoon.

I'm mid-caffeine fix when my phone rings. Recognizing Madonna's "Papa Don't Preach" and hoping that my dad will listen to the prayer, I answer.

"Hey, Daddy!" Somehow, my voice usually reverts to a younger version of myself when I talk to him.

"Norma Jean. There's my little ladybug. How're you doing, baby?" He regresses to the childhood nicknames he's always called me too. Secretly, I love it, though I sometimes tease him that I'm not quite as small as a 'red-headed ladybug' anymore. He always winks and tells me that to him, I'll always be his ladybug.

"Doing great, working hard at the paper and keeping my grades up in all my classes. The usual. How're you doing? What are you and Mom up to?" I ask, knowing that these are just pleasant niceties until we get to the meat of the conversation. I love my dad, and he loves me, but he's a dedicated businessman through and through, not one for small talk, though I know he keeps up with what's going on in my life through Mom.

"Good to hear. Keep working, Norma Jean, and you're going to be running *The Chronicle* by your senior year." I smile at his certainty, knowing that's my hope too. "Your mother is industrious, as always. I believe her current charity du jour is something about rescue dogs? Oh, greyhounds . . . that's it, rehoming race dogs. She actually mentioned bringing one home, if you can imagine, but when I reminded her that dogs tend to make her sneeze, she doubled down on finding twice as many their forever homes. I think that's a win-win, for me and the dogs."

I laugh. Though I've already heard the story from Mom, it's interesting to hear my dad's take on the conversation. My mom's version featured him grumping that she 'wasn't bringing an animal that had never known grass to live in a penthouse apartment because it'd be torture for the poor critter even if it was luxury to them.' That's my dad . . . steel exterior that he shows to the world, and the softest teddy bear center he shows to my mom, and sometimes to me.

"Well, good for them . . . and for you, then." I wait, knowing he'll get around to his real reason for the call if I give him the opening.

"I wanted to see if you're available for lunch today. It's a business thing and my associate is bringing his son, so I need my daughter there to represent the family name." His tone has switched to a more clipped professional cadence and I can vaguely hear papers flipping in the background.

"Dad, I've got to study today. Maybe some other time?" I say, hoping for the out. I'd love to have lunch with him, but a dry business lunch sounds ridiculously boring and irresponsible with my limited time.

"Norma. I'd like to have lunch with my only daughter today. It'll help me out, and my associate will be grateful to have someone age-appropriate to engage with his son while we talk business. Please." He's not asking, he's telling me that I'm doing this.

"Fine, Dad. What time and where?" I say, making sure the eyeroll is audible in the sigh I add to the words.

After a quick breakdown of lunch expectations, we hang up.

So much for a useful day of productivity.

"LADYBUG, SO GOOD OF YOU TO COME ON SUCH SHORT notice," Dad says as he opens the door. It's his version of acknowledging that this is a big ask and saying thank you.

I nod. "Of course." As I come in, I see that Mom has had the foyer painted again . . . or at least I think it was blue last time I was here. Truth be told, I don't come to this property often. It's right downtown, near Blackstone Industries and close to campus, but Dad's rarely here. He spends most of his time in luxury hotel rooms on his innumerable business trips. And Mom prefers to stay in the 'country house' just outside the city limits. Yes, that's actually what they call it. Admittedly, I live in a strange world, straddling the ridiculous wealth I grew up in and my own rather middle-class current situation, but even that is funded by my parents. But one day, I'll be self-sufficient. I can't wait to have a little studio apartment of my very own with my name on the lease. Maybe an odd dream for a 'spoiled little rich girl' but it's the truth. I want to make it on my own. Just like my dad. Just like my brother.

"Come, let me introduce you." I follow my dad into the living room where two men stand up as I enter. They're obviously father and son, looking like a time-progression photo of the same person. "Norma, this is my friend, Joe, and his son, Jake. Joe, Jake, this is my daughter, Norma."

Joe offers his hand, which I shake politely. He's probably my dad's age, late forties or maybe a well-preserved fifty, but a bit broader with a slight paunch beneath his dress shirt. "The photos Lewis has shown me don't do you justice, my dear," he says complimentarily.

"Thank you." And then I turn to shake Jake's hand and freeze. Why does he look familiar? I can't place him, but something about him tickles along the periphery of my mind. He shakes my offered palm, not giving me anything to work with about how we might know each other.

We sit down to dinner, the dry chatter between Dad and Joe boring me to tears, especially as Joe waxes on about Jake joining him in the family business. But it gives me time to try to tease out the mystery of Jake.

And then like a bomb, Joe offers the answer. "Norma, I hear you're a journalism major now? Jake's in college too. Plays quarterback for the Ravens, actually." He says it with pride, patting Jake on the shoulder.

My eyes jump to Jake, who's smiling mischievously. "Yeah, I think I've seen you around campus. Seems I've heard you're *dating* one of the guys on the team, right?"

Dad chokes on his water. "You are? I didn't know that, Norma. When do I get to meet this young man?"

This cannot be happening. One, the slimeball sitting across from me is Jake Robertson, the guy who pissed Zach off so badly and almost ran him over with a fucking car in a dangerous flare of temper. Two, he just outed my relationship with Zach to my dad. No, I'm not hiding Zach in any way, and I'm actually damn proud to be with him, but there's a step-by-step to these things, and jumping from seriously-

LAUREN LANDISH

dating to meet-the-parents skips a few rather important steps.

Jake smirks, obviously pleased with himself for stirring up drama. I narrow my eyes at him, trying to figure out his game because he's got to have one. But I realize my dad is saying my name and turn to look. "When I'm ready, Dad. And not a moment before." I let the hard tone I learned from him coat the words, and he must hear the warning because he doesn't press, though the look in his eyes says this conversation is far from over.

"Yeah, I hear you've been helping Zach study quite a bit, even got his English grade up from failing to an A. A girlfriend better than any tutor. Say, you're working with him on *Paradise Lost*, right? Maybe you could read over my final essay for class too? Give me a few pointers, you know, since you're already helping him?" Every word is said with the sweetest of smiles plastered to his face, like my helping him would be the ultimate kindness. If I didn't know better, I'd even believe him. That's how well he has this good guy act down.

"Oh, I don't know about that. I'm just so busy these days. And I'm not tutoring Zach. We have study dates. I guess the extra time hitting the books is paying off for him." I let saccharin sarcasm drip from every word as I say, "I guess I'm just a good influence like that."

Jake laughs. "God knows, I need a good influence. How about we let the father figures talk business, and you meet me over at the school library? You could look at my paper really fast, and I know it'd help me so much."

Before I can say no, Dad interjects. "I'm sure Norma would love to help you, Jake."

I hiss, "Dad," and then school my features into the placid steel

366

of my mother. "May I talk to you in the kitchen for a moment, please?" It's not a question.

He nods deferentially to Joe and follows me into the kitchen, but before I can say a word, he whispers, "Norma, I don't know what's going on out there, though I realize there's more than what's on the surface. But I also know that Joe is an old friend and a business associate I'd like to maintain a positive relationship with. So, read his paper, give him a few suggestions, and be done with it."

"Dad, I'm not some pawn to be used in your business deals, and that guy out there is basically Zach's nemesis. He's using his dad and you, and probably me. I just don't know what his end game is yet."

"Then go with him and see if you can figure it out. That's one of your special talents, isn't it? Investigate what his nefarious plan is." Though he says it like it's a silly idea, it's actually not a bad one. His voice softens, the dad I know and love and who loves me. "It's not a big deal, ladybug, unless you say no and make it one."

"Fine," I agree, though it's the last fucking thing I want to do. But Dad's right. Maybe I can use the time to figure out what Jake's up to, because he's sure as fuck up to something.

Back in the dining room, Jake is already looking smug. It doesn't help when I say, "Sure, Jake, I can go to the library now, if you want to go get your paper."

He's up out of his chair faster than a blink, gesturing for me to go first. "After you."

I give my goodbyes to Mr. Robertson and Dad, making sure to give Dad a bit of a stink eye.

LAUREN LANDISH

At the library, I sit down at a table right up front, surrounded by people entering and exiting, grabbing snacks from the vending machine, and surrounding us at all times. I want the safety net of a crowd. I wish I could've gotten ahold of Zach on the way over, but the phone reception in the concrete-built basement weight room is non-existent.

"Okay, so . . . let me see your paper," I say brusquely as Jake comes in a minute or two after me and sits down.

Jake grins and pulls it out of his backpack. "Thank you for doing this." Something about the way he says it seems off, though he's smiling calmly.

I take it from him, careful not to touch his hand, and begin to read it over. It's fine, not great literary critique, but nothing that warrants a tutor, for damn sure. I hear my dad on one shoulder, telling me to give a few tips and suss out any ill intentions. But there's the prickly, mouthy brat Norma on my other shoulder, begging to just put it all out there and see what happens.

The devil wins.

"Your paper's fine, Jake, though I'm sure you knew that," I say, narrowing my eyes, and he has the grace to look chagrined. "So, what's this all about? Why the smokescreen? Especially when you know it's only going to cause problems with Zach and with the team."

He sits back in his chair, looking casually calm as if he hasn't a care in the world, and rubs a thumb along his bottom lip. "Look, I'm not a nice guy, or at least not always a nice guy," he says with a shrug, like it's beyond his control. "But I just don't like the way Zach's treating you and I didn't know how to talk to you without the ruse. That's why I got my dad to arrange lunch with Lewis and you today. If I just came up to you randomly, I figured you'd blow me off, but I just don't think

368

it's right and you deserve to know." He shakes his head, puppy dog eyes looking at me sadly.

I sigh, not believing his schtick for a minute but figuring that maybe this'll get me the information I'm looking for. "Fine, I'll bite. What's he saying?"

I'm expecting him to say Zach's engaging in some colorful locker room chatter. Goodness knows, he's got enough ammunition for some racy stories, though I don't think he'd blab like that. What I'm not expecting are Jake's next words.

"He keeps talking about how he needed a tutor and Coach set him up with some fake girlfriend thing to cover it up, but that he's such a fucking god that he turned it into a pussy-on-demand situation for the semester. Basically, he says he just uses you as a place to stick his dick, if you'll pardon the vulgarity." His tone is sincere and disgusted, like he can't believe someone would say that.

There's so much information in what he just said that I can't even process it all at once, and instead, I have to take it in bits and chunks. My mind whirls.

Okay, there is no way, I mean literally no way, Zach is talking about me like I'm a cum receptacle with no emotions, not after everything we've shared. And the mere fact that I don't even consider that a possibility speaks volumes about just how far we've come. No doubt, no second thoughts, no insecurity. I know without question that Jake is lying about that and using the obscene insult to poke at my emotions, expecting my horror.

But I'm not horrified. I'm furious but force the explosion of words bubbling in my throat down as I consider the rest of what Jake said.

Tutor. Fake girlfriend. That was our original cover story. But no one is supposed to know that. Just me and Zach. Coach and Erica. And it's certainly not true now. I don't think it ever really was.

I wonder if Jake overhead Coach talking about it to Zach or maybe to someone else? He is around the locker room with the rest of the guys, so it's definitely possible, I suppose.

And then an image pops in my head. Of Erica in full Ravens gear. Like a super fan. Like a . . . groupie.

And though I have no reason to think Jake and Erica know each other, every instinct I have says that's who told him the whole secret setup.

Jake looks at me expectantly, waiting with a sad face for my breakdown, but I can see the eager glee in his eyes. I take the fastest second to compose my thoughts and then strike.

"Tell me, is Erica part of your whole evil plot to destroy Zach? Or did she just share some pillow talk after what I'm sure was a disappointing fuck?" My face is stoic, nothing more than mere curiosity.

Jake's jaw drops. "What? Erica didn't say shit, and she's a better fuck than you are. I know because Zach's been mouthing."

I smirk. "Oh, so you *do* know Erica? The editor of *The Chronicle*, who it seems is rather unable to keep her mouth shut. Kind of an important skill for a reporter, wouldn't you say?" Anger lights up in his eyes, and though I know it's a dangerous button to push, I can't stop my mouth. "And I wasn't talking about her being a shitty fuck. I was talking about you, *Snake.*" I say it like it's beyond obvious that it's the most ironic nick-name in the world, like the guys in the locker room who called him that were joking about his size, or the lack thereof.

"You fucking bitch! I was this-fucking-close to finally getting my shot. Zach was almost failing, mostly on his own right, but a little cash here or there never hurt, and it was going to be mine. I should be the star quarterback of the Ravens, the one the team looks up to, the one the scouts come to watch, the one headed for the pros. And if it wasn't for that fucking contract-blocker, it would be me. Me!"

His anger is getting out of control, his voice louder, and we're drawing an audience in the quiet of the library. I'm pretty sure I even see a few cell phones recording Jake's apparent break-down, and he follows my glance around, seeing the attention centered on him. But though he seems to want it on the field, deserved or not, right now, he wants out of the limelight.

He grabs his paper and backpack, slinging it over one shoulder as he points at me, saying loudly enough for everyone to hear, "Fucking whore . . . sold your pussy to the quarterback. And for what? An interview with Coach? You're worse than a whore. You're a cheap slut."

There's a collective gasp, and then Jake stomps out of the library. All eyes turn to me, questions and judgments and concern in every one of them. I dig for a shield, throwing up some sass, and say with a tiny laugh, "Sold my pussy to the quarterback? He means my *boyfriend*. And trust me, I gave it freely because . . . have you seen him? Whoo!" I let a saucy smile take my face, and my weird response seems to have put most folks off. I guess they were waiting for my breakdown too. Fucking vultures.

I grab my bag, knowing that Zach's in the weight room and that I need to talk to him now. And Coach. And Erica.

But Zach first.

ZACH

"All right, man. Throw that weight up and give me three. I got you covered," Tim Perkins, one of the wide receivers, tells me.

I spread my hands wide on the cool metal bar, pressing it up before lowering the weight to my chest. I do the three reps and set it back on the rack.

Standing up, I stretch a bit. "Okay, your turn," I say as we switch places and he lies down on the bench.

All around us are guys working out. It's not the whole team because it's not an official practice or mandatory weight session, but it's understood that unless you have class or class-related shit, you'd better have your ass in here pumping some iron.

Music is blaring, the guys are bro-ing out as we smack talk about the upcoming game, and it's like I'm home. These guys are my family and I'll be sad to see them go when the season's over. Not everyone is leaving, of course, and there is plenty of off-season work to do, but some of the guys are graduating, and others get side-tracked with different priorities when there's not a game every week.

The warm, fuzzy moment comes to a screeching halt when the door swings open and Norma walks in. No, that's not right. She doesn't walk in. She blows in like a fucking hurricane, fire in her eyes, and I swear her red hair is blowing in some sort of invisible wind because she's crackling with fury.

I can't help it. My first instinct is to think . . . *what did I do?* But then I see beneath the whirling storm to my Norma. And she's scared shitless.

"Brat! What's wrong?" I yell. Someone chooses that moment to turn the music off and my voice echoes in the sudden silence.

"We need to talk. Now." Every man knows that those are words you don't want to hear, and the guys around me cringe. Norma must see their reactions because she restates, "Not like that. But we need to talk. Where's Coach Jefferson?"

I'm thoroughly confused now. Why does Norma want to talk to Coach? "Uhm, his office, probably. But . . . why?"

She doesn't answer, just gives me one of those looks that silently communicates a thousand words. And I realize that this is about us and the tutoring. That's the only reason she'd need to see Coach. "C'mon."

I grab her hand and drag her down the hall, knocking hard twice but opening the door at the same time. "Coach . . . sorry to interrupt, but—"

Norma doesn't give me a chance to play nice. "Coach Jefferson, I'm Norma Blackstone, Zach's girlfriend and *tutor*." Her emphasis on the word is intentional, giving it a deeper meaning that Coach instantly catches.

"Yeah, yeah. Come in, I guess? What can I do for you?" Coach asks.

Norma sits down in the chair in front of the desk uninvited but stays perched on the edge, leaning forward. Coach sits down too, hands crossed in front of him.

"Sir, this is a lot. Please, let me see if I can get this all out." She takes a big breath, as if she's about to spill the longest story ever and needs oxygen to do so. "I work for Erica Waters at *The Chronicle*. I'm the one she asked to do that favor for you and tutor Zach with the whole fake girlfriend thing."

Coach gets up, holding a staying hand out, and Norma pauses as he shuts the door. When he sits back down, she continues. "Today, Jake Robertson schemed to get me alone at the library—"

"What the fuck?" I yell.

Norma grabs my hand, holding it tightly. "My dad asked me to do it as a favor. He didn't know," she tells me before she looks back to Coach. "I didn't know just how unhinged Jake has become." She lets that sink in for a moment. "He said he needed help with a paper, but it was a ploy. He tried to tell me that Zach was saying uhm, *unflattering things* about me, about us."

I interrupt again. I can't help it. "What did that asshole say now?"

Norma blushes but she says it without a tremble. "He said that you were using me for sex, basically that we're still fake but that I'm the only one who doesn't realize that."

"Mother fucker, I'm gonna kill him." I turn to the door but stop when Coach growls.

"Son, you'd best sit your ass down in that chair and shut your mouth. Let the woman speak, for fuck's sake." He gives me a hard look, but even years of training to listen to my coach's instructions without question aren't enough to hold me back from tracking Jake down right this fucking minute. But what is? Norma looks at me, eyes pleading for me to do as Coach says, so begrudgingly, I do. But only until she's done, then I'm Snake hunting.

Norma looks at me. "Obviously, I didn't believe him." Her words shoot to my heart. I hadn't considered for a moment that she would believe something so ridiculous, but then I remember how unsure my Brat used to be. But when someone basically told her that her worst nightmare was true, she didn't doubt. Didn't doubt me, or herself, or us. It's a beautiful ray of sunshine in the midst of this shit.

"But more importantly, I realized that he said Zach was mouthing about his *tutor* and his *fake girlfriend*." She emphasizes the words but doesn't give me time to process what that means before continuing, "No one knew, at least no one was supposed to. I did a bit of quick deduction and realized that football groupie Erica told him. And though he didn't exactly mean to, Jake confirmed it. He got really angry then, stood up and started yelling about how Zach was almost failing on his own but that 'a little cash never hurt', implying that he bribed Zach's English teacher, I'm guessing to grade him poorly and cost him his eligibility, so that Jake could play. He went on a bit of a rant, and the theme was basically me, me, me."

Coach huffs. "Shit. That's . . . a lot." He shakes his head a bit and then seems to pull it together, but there's a knock at the door. "Not now, go the fuck away."

But the door opens anyway and Will pops his head through the crack. "Sorry to interrupt, but sir, you need to see this." He holds up his phone and Coach holds his hand out to take it. He clicks the *Play* button in the middle of the screen and Jake's voice fills the room. It seems one of those people who were filming his tirade posted it online.

Coach watches it through twice and then hands the phone back to Will, who's looking at me with unspoken promises in his eyes. "Send me that, please. If you'll excuse me, I have some business to take care of."

Norma and I stand, hearing the dismissal. "Of course, sir. Me too."

"Stop right there, Zach." I turn to look at him, and he steps right up to me, invading my space. He's a big man, but several inches shorter than me. Even still, I have no doubt he could make me cry uncle. "Let me be clear. I want you to stay here while I get this shit sorted out. You are not, in any circumstances, to approach, speak to, or lay a hand on Jake Robertson. The last thing I need is his daddy getting you arrested for being a dumbass. Do I make myself clear?"

"Sir—" I try to argue.

But he cuts me off, turning to Will. "Senior Captain, I think I need you to take the defensive line, and anyone else who wants to go, out for some drills on the field tonight. Really make sure everyone's working together as a team. But I need every one of you, all of my star players, ready for the game this weekend. Understood?" Will nods his head and then looks at me.

Coach just gave them the go-ahead to go after Jake. Without me. I hate that they're fighting my battle for me once again, especially when this one is so damn personal, but I know I'd do the same thing for them. And as mad as I am, I don't know that I'd stop at beating the shit out of Jake. And Coach is right. I can't be stupid about this or Jake wins and I lose anyway.

Coach walks us back down the hall, already on his phone. "Yes, Dean, I need to have an emergency meeting with us, Erica Waters, Jake Robertson, and Professor Ledbetter. Yes, right now."

Back in the weight room, the guys are all looking at their phones, so I know they've seen the video of Jake. Will gathers everyone up and says, "Drill time." Usually, there'd be a few moans of whining about having to hit the field, but tonight, everyone knows it's something different and there's a chorus of 'Fucking right, it's drill time.' and 'Hell, yeah.' As the guys file out, they each give me a high-five or touch their forehead to mine, assuring me that the team has my back and that we protect our own, even when it's from an internal threat.

Lenny is the last to walk out, and after fist-bumping me, he stops in front of Norma. "Don't you worry. We all know you aren't a whore. You're a goddamn magician who got my boy here locked down. And Norma, you've got some big clanging brass balls on you. Badass bitch." Norma beams at the praise.

And then we're alone.

I'm so on edge I think I'm going to crawl out of my damn skin. I'm pacing, hot anger pumping through my veins, encouraging me to scour the campus and find Jake. Or at a minimum, to follow Coach and demand some answers. But Norma stops me with a soft touch.

"Hey, calm down. It's going to be okay, Zach. Coach is handling Erica and Professor Ledbetter, though is it wrong of me to hope Jake misses that meeting because he's running drills with the team?" She does little air quotes so I know she caught on to what's happening tonight. I have a split second of question on whether she's down for back-alley justice, but then she spits out, "I hope they find that fucker before I do because he'll get off easier with them than with me."

I smirk at her trash-talking. "You are so sexy when you're being all bitchy and bratty. Like fire personified, inside and out. My little fire fairy brat."

My answer seems to surprise her, shocking her out of her flash of anger too. "Oh, that wasn't bratty. That was a reality check." A tiny smile tilts her lips. "Okay, maybe a bit bratty."

Needing to touch her, I pull her to me, crushing her in my arms. "Fuck, Norma. This is so messed up. I never thought he'd—"

She cuts me off with a kiss, and I realize that we don't need words right now. We need each other.

Though he didn't stand a chance at driving a wedge between the two of us, Jake's threat is dangerous in a different way. The thought reminds me of how pleased I am that Norma didn't question us for a second, that not only have we come so far, but she has come so far. Still my mouthy Brat who takes no shit but dishes out prickly barbs with laser accuracy, but also my girl who knows that she's mine and I'm hers, unequivocally.

Our kisses become more frantic. "Norma, I need you."

"I need you too. Take me," she says, panting for air.

I reach up, encircling her neck with my hands for a moment, and she freezes, mouth open and eyes wide, saying yes without words. I untie the silk scarf there and then pick her up, carrying her across the room.

"What is this thing?" she asks, looking at the big metal rack above her.

"You'll love this. It's a power rack," I say, chuckling. I pull her shirt and bra off unceremoniously but lay a quick kiss to her sternum as she shudders. She offers her hands, and I tie the scarf around one wrist. "Hands up, Brat, and look in the mirror."

The air, or maybe it's the anticipation, raises goosebumps along her arms as I loop the scarf over the pullup bar and tie her other wrist. Like usual, it's not tight, but it's become our thing and she so willingly and beautifully gives herself to me each and every time this way, wanting it as much as I do.

The automatic lights have cycled off, leaving portions of the room in shadow and little pockets of light from the spotlights in the ceiling. Right above Norma, a beam shines down, high-lighting her body in sharp relief, shadows and light dancing along her skin. "You look fucking glorious, Norma." In response to my words, her nipples harden, tempting me to lick, suck, and bite.

I pull her skirt down, tossing it aside after she steps out of it, and grab her ass, massaging her cheeks in my big hands. She whimpers, pressing back for more, so I wrap my arms around her and grind my cock against her ass. Even through my workout shorts, my cock tries to penetrate her.

But I need to taste her first. I drop to my knees, kissing along her spine and then biting her sweet ass. She steps wide without my telling her, and I use my hands to guide her to arch her

378

back, letting me see all of her. I lean in, and she moans needily, so I spread her cheeks and tease at her puckered hole.

She lets out a keening cry. "Oh, God, Zach." I do it again, and then go lower, tasting her honey and circling her clit. Her hips sway, and I focus on her clit, letting a finger slip inside her tight pussy. She covers me in cream, and I spread it up to her ass, tapping on her rosebud as I lick her clit. Her cries become incoherent, just high-pitched sounds, begging, and then she shatters.

Her body shudders and I lap at her juices, wanting to swallow every drop. Needing to be inside her, I stand up, shoving my workout shorts down at the same time.

The head of my cock slips inside her, and we both groan. "Everything's going to be okay, Brat. You're all mine," I whisper as I fill her up.

"I am," she confirms. I'm still for a moment, letting her adjust, and I think I hear something. A thud, maybe? But it sounds far away.

I meet her eyes in the silvery mirror where she's watching like I told her to. "You'll have to be quiet so we don't get caught fucking in the weight room. Pretty sure that's against the team's rules." Her pussy clenches around me, and I know she likes the thought of being naughty.

I start stroking in and out of her, and I know she wants to push back against me, but the scarf is holding her, forcing her to stand tall. I like her at my mercy, but I can't tease her right now, both of us needing to connect on a physical level and deeper.

I speed up until we're both trembling, gasping. "Is this what you want, Brat?"

"Fuck . . . yes!" Suddenly, I hear a sound again and freeze, not pulling out but keeping her full of cock. I barely move, just grind my cock back and forth slowly against that rough spot deep inside her, careful not to push her over so we don't make a sound.

When I don't hear anything for a few seconds, I give her one powerful thrust. Her air rushes out. "Zach!"

"That's it, Norma. I'm gonna fuck you and fill you with all I've got, reward you for knowing that you belong to me. And I sure as fuck belong to you." My words are whispered, growls that vibrate against the silky skin of her back.

My hips slap against her ass as I fuck her deeply, our breath coming in short gasps as we both get closer and closer. Her pussy squeezes around my thick cock like a vice, and I clamp my teeth down to hold back the roar as I explode, my cock coming deep inside her.

She's watching in the mirror as I come, and it triggers her orgasm too. She whimpers, biting her lip, but she's still louder than she probably should be. It makes me feel like a beast that I can make her forget herself that way.

When we catch our breaths, I reach up and untie her wrists, massaging her fingers. "Why do you do it?" I ask as I kiss each fingertip. "You don't have to let me tie you up. It doesn't really matter to me. I've never done that with anyone but you."

"I know I don't have to," she says softly, laying a sweet kiss to the corner of my mouth. "But, Zach, sometimes, I feel like there's all this pressure on my shoulders to do amazing things and be this hard-hitting powerhouse. But you help me understand that by surrendering to you, by letting you be in charge, you make me stronger. I feel like can breathe and just . . . *be*."

I smile and kiss her squarely on the lips. "With you by my side, I'm stronger too. And better, like I have a purpose beyond the field."

We pull our clothes back on as we talk quietly, making sure the room is reset so no one is the wiser, and heading down the dim hallway. I don't know where we're going, but I can't stay here any longer. If nothing else, we'll go to Norma's place until I get word from Coach or Will that things are handled.

"I don't know anyone stronger," she says with a smirk. "You're going to make one hell of a pro quarterback."

I nod, her confidence in me a boost but nothing compared to the thought deep in my heart. "And if everything goes the way I dream, I'll be playing in big games and signing big contracts."

She thinks that's all I had to say and smiles before adding, "Big records too."

"Fifty," I say with a smile. "I think that's a good start."

She looks at me, confusion in her eyes. "Fifty?" As we step out of the building, the late November chill surrounds us. I pause to pull my jacket off and lay it around Norma's shoulders. She slips her arms into the sleeves, but she's basically drowning in it, the cuffs hanging well past her hands.

"Fifty years. Of marriage. That's the main record I want, just like my parents. They're not there yet, but they will be. That's what I want. More than football, though I seriously want that too. But I want someone to share it all with, to be in the stands cheering me on, to make a life with during football and after football."

She looks up at me. "That sounds . . . nice. Are you thinking about anyone in particular?" She's grinning, but there's more hope than tease in her voice.

I chuckle, pulling her close. "Brat, I think you and I are thinking the same damn thing."

She lifts to her tiptoes, and I bend down to catch her lips in a kiss, but just before I make contact, a loud voice calls out, "Payback, bitch!"

I try to push Norma behind me, not sure of the threat but wanting to protect her regardless, but she twists in my arms and then cries out in pain as there's a loud crash.

She's panting as a dark figure pushes past me. Before I can think, I lower her to the floor, and though she's crying from the pain, she's chanting, "I'm okay, I'm okay." I take her at her word, and with a quick kiss to her forehead, I take off after the shadowy attacker.

ZACH

"9-1-1, what's your emergency?"

I yell as I run, making fast headway at catching up with the ghost who's zigging and zagging as he runs. "Ravens football complex, a guy just jumped me and my girlfriend. She's been hit in the leg."

I have a good idea who's in front of me, and red rage seeps into my vision as I pour on the speed to chase him down. Talking with the phone in my hand is slowing me down, though. "Sir?"

"My girlfriend was attacked," I repeat, forcing my voice to be as calm as possible. "Parking lot, the Ravens football practice complex. Send campus cops and a fucking ambulance. I'm chasing the motherfucker who did this."

"Sir, that's not a good idea—"

I hang up my phone, dropping it to the pavement as I sprint harder. I use both arms and force my breathing into a rhythm as I close the gap quickly, tackling him from behind.

"You motherfucker," I growl as we roll on the ground. He gets a punch in to my face, but I quickly pin him down, ripping off his mask. I'm not surprised. "I fucking knew it."

"I–I didn't mean to hit her," Jake stammers, holding his hands up. "I was going after you!"

"You mistook a five-foot-four girl for me because of what? A team jacket?" I ask, my voice dripping with fury as I yank his shoulders up with a fistful of his shirt. Before Jake can respond, I punch him in the nose, enjoying the satisfying crunch of his bone under my blow.

Jake tries to fight back, but my rage has inoculated me to pain. Instead, I hammer him again and again, smashing his face with all my might.

"I'm sorry!" Jake howls, his eyes already getting puffy from the blows.

"Not as sorry as you're going to be," I rasp, every instance of him undermining me on the field, trying to get me hurt with wrong signals, almost running me over with his car, and most of all, hurting Norma, riding me hard and giving me an ugly desire to destroy him.

I'm staring down at him in disgust when suddenly I hear a scream. "Zach!"

It's Norma, and her obvious cry of pain pierces through the hot fire of my anger. I scramble from the ground, needing to get to her, but I yell back, "Don't you fucking move. The cops are the way."

He tries to crawl, belly dragging the dirty ground, but I know he won't get far.

I crouch next to Norma, brushing the hair back from her forehead. Her eyes meet mine, utter agony and incomprehension mixing in equal measure. "Fuck, Zach. It hurts so bad. Why?"

"It was Jake," I tell her, putting a hand on her shoulder to keep her still. She keeps trying to sit up, but I can tell by the way her leg is lying, she shouldn't be moving. "He meant to hit me."

"Why?" Norma repeats, her own pain making her not understand. Instead of trying to explain any more, I hold her, letting her pour her agony against my chest.

"I'm so sorry, Norma. The ambulance should be here soon," I tell her as the sound of the siren gets louder.

Norma sobs, her tears soaking my shirt before the ambulance and cops arrive. Unsure what the hell's going on, they let me ride with her to the hospital, although I do notice that a cop car follows us as well.

The whole time, I apologize to Norma, who's crying and whimpering with every bump in the road. She whispers through her pain. "How bad is it?"

I glance over at the paramedic, who seems unsure. "I don't think it's that bad, but we don't know for sure. I think it's a clean break, but they'll get X-rays and everything at the hospital."

"Even if it's broken, don't worry," I tell her, putting on my best face. "We'll rehab together, Brat, and you'll be kicking ass in powder puff before next season."

That at least gets Norma to sniffle and smile a little, though it's more of a grimace. "There is no powder puff football at our school."

I give her hand a little squeeze, trying to force a smile at her. "Then I'll start a league, and you can be the star player."

When we get to the hospital, Norma has to roll into an exam room to get checked out and the nurses stop me at the door, saying that they need room to work and will come get me soon.

That's when the cops start by getting me into a conference room. I try to answer their questions as honestly as I can, but my brain's running a hundred miles an hour while at the same time, it seems to be going in slow motion.

"So you hit the girl, then —" the one cop, a detective with a permanent 'fuck you' scowl on his face, starts.

I shake my head, trying by sheer will alone to not jump out of the chair and yell at him. "No. Jake hit Norma, and I chased him down. Norma's my girlfriend. Why would I hurt her?"

"Well, why would this Jake fellow hit her?" he asks. "Is this some love triangle gone wrong?"

Before I can argue, there's a big commotion and a man in a custom-tailored suit comes in. Behind him is a cute girl I've seen Norma with in pictures. So if this is Arianna, then he must be . . . "I'm Liam Blackstone. Zach Knight?"

I nod, and the cop looks like he's about to pop a gasket. "Mr. Blackstone, I'm sorry, but —"

"Zach is done talking," Liam says, handing the cop a card. "Here's my attorney's card. Mr. Knight has nothing to say until he gets here."

The cop grumbles, then nods. "Fine. Mr. Knight, you're not under arrest, but don't leave the hospital just yet."

He leaves, and in the muted hospital silence, Liam and I study each other.

He tilts his head, appraising me, and I'm not sure if he's going to find me lacking, especially considering tonight's happenings. He must find me acceptable somehow, though, because he continues, "Who hurt my sister?"

"Jake Robertson. He's my backup quarterback on the team

and has been gunning for me all season. He tried to involve Norma today, but we didn't dream he'd do something like . . . this." My voice breaks, and I plop back to the chair, my head buried in my hands.

"Robertson . . . I know that name," Liam growls after a moment, his fists bunching. Liam might be about fifty pounds lighter than me, but he looks like he could handle himself well. He's certainly built well enough. "Where is he?"

"Probably getting treatment too. I nearly curbstomped him after I chased him down and caught him," I admit. "Might have charges coming my way because of it, actually."

Liam shakes his head, pulling out his phone. "Not when my lawyers are done. Arianna, could you go out to the lobby and get with the doctors and see if you can get an update? I'll talk with the campus cops. I want every security camera in the vicinity of the football complex pulled and one of our lawyers with the cops when they go over it. Tonight. Oh . . . and Zach should probably call Coach Jefferson. I figure he'll want to know as well."

Arianna nods before stepping out. Liam dials a number, and his conversation is brief. "Dad? It's Liam. Norma was attacked at school by Jake Robertson. Yes, *that* Robertson. Figured you should know. I'm at the hospital. I'll give you an update as soon as I hear something, but get here when you can. 'Bye."

Liam hangs up and then looks at me. "So . . . rumor has it you've been seeing my sister."

I stand up, offering him a hand since this is crazily our first time to meet, though I feel like I know him from Norma's stories about her big brother who always made time for her. "I'm more than seeing her, but yes."

He shakes my hand, squeezing harder than need be, and I

squeeze back. We have a bit of a staring contest and then he asks, "How much more?"

I let go of his hand and give him a nod. "I think I'll discuss that with her first. But she's the most important thing in my life."

"Even more important than football? You're supposed to have a pretty bright future on the field," he says doubtfully.

I nod, clearing my throat. "Even more than football, and I don't say that lightly."

He smiles. "All right then. Let's see what my brat of a sister is up to." I flinch and he notices. "What?"

I know my face must be turning pink because I can feel the heat. "Uhm, that's what I call her. Brat." His eyes narrow, and I rush to explain, "But it's a . . . term of endearment."

He pales, then chuckles. "And I will never call her that again. All you, man."

It's awkward as fuck but also feels like some spark of male connection was just forged between us. I don't think we're ever going to play Never Have I Ever or some shit, but I think we could probably grab a beer sometime. After this mess is done.

About fifteen minutes later, the doctors come and get the two of us. Norma's still in an exam room, her left leg in a Velcro splint, but she's smiling as the curtain opens. "Hey . . . Arianna told me you two talked. That must've been *awkward*." Her voice lilts at the end.

"Hey, Little Sis," Liam says, taking her left hand. "They have you on the good stuff?"

"I'm flying high," Norma agrees. She squeezes Liam's hand, then looks at me. "Zach . . . ohmygawd, I'm so sorry."

I shake my head, tears threatening at the corners of my eyes. "You've got nothing to be sorry for. I should be apologizing to you, Norma. This whole fucking thing is my fault. Jake was after me."

Norma forces her tossing head to still, eyes meeting mine, and for a second, I think she's lucid. But then she singsongs, "Fuck, you're so pretty. I love you so much. Did you know that? I love you, Zach."

I can't help the grin that splits my face, and Liam shrugs. I chuckle, bending down to tell her, "I love you too, Brat."

"Ooh, yeah . . . I'm your Brat. Hey, do you think when they let me outta here, you could tie my hands behind my back again? Or—oh—maybe over the hood of the car again? Yeah, that!"

Liam clears his throat, his cheeks blushing now. "I, uh, think I'll step out for a minute. Check on Arianna's progress on her to-do list."

I lift one shoulder, some version of an attempt at 'sorry, man' for his having to hear that. Something tells me that while Norma won't remember this conversation at all, Liam and I are never going to forget it. Though he's probably going to remember being mortified at his little sister's sex life, I'm going to remember it as the first time we said *I love you*.

NORMA

A few days later, after a quick surgery to reset the bones in my leg, I'm finally home, albeit with a clunky cast that reaches from my toes to just below my knee.

"You're actually tough as steel now, Sis," Liam tells me teasingly.

"The metal they used is actually . . . ti-tan-iuumm," I sing loudly and badly. Liam busts out laughing and I grin back.

"When's your next appointment? Do you need me to take you?" He already has his calendar app open on his phone like he's going to add my appointment to his to-do list. But I know he's already got the appointment listed there because he's Liam.

"No, Zach said he'd take me. Doc said I'd need a check this week to make sure nothing's changed since I was discharged from the hospital and then another follow-up in four weeks, and then hopefully, the last one two to four weeks after that when I get my cast off. Then, the fun of physical therapy starts." I shudder a bit at the memory of my orthopedic surgeon telling me that the real work of healing started on my first day of PT and that it was going to be hard and painful, but absolutely necessary. "Zach already said he'll work with me on that too. I think he's got some vision of us being workout buddies. Like he's going to cheer me on for every rep of toe point and flex, and then I'm gonna fall into his arms, grateful for his time and patience. I'm expecting it's going to end up with me whiny and bitchy about how hard it is and him smacking me and telling me to 'suck it up, buttercup' in some growly amalgamation of every football coach he's ever had."

Liam opens his mouth and then promptly clacks it shut, his eyebrows going high.

"What?" I ask, curious of what just ran through his mind.

He shakes his head. "I was going to make a joke about you liking it when he smacks you, but then I remembered your drug-induced tell-all and decided I didn't really want to know any more details than you've already over-shared."

I blush, mortified at the things I apparently was spouting off, loudly and vehemently, when I was medicated. Liam hasn't teased me too badly, but Zach has given me so much shit for it that I threatened to never let him tie me up again. But when he'd mimicked my high voice, 'I looove it when you tie me up, Zach . . . can you do it again?' I'd eventually laughed and given in because I was telling the truth and I do love it. No need to punish myself for my mouthiness, not when Zach can do that for me.

"Yeah, maybe it's best that we skip those jokes. I'm friends with Arianna now, too, you know? I might know a little more about my brother than I'd like to."

We meet eyes, silently agreeing to never speak of this again. "So, the game starting?"

"Yes, the game. Let's watch the game," I say. Liam hits the kitchen for a few drinks, a bottle of beer for him and a Coke for me since I can't mix anything stronger with my medications.

Sitting on the couch, just the two of us, reminds me of our younger days when a teenage Liam would voluntarily give up his Saturday mornings to watch cartoons with a younger me. It's not the usual cartoons and movie marathons we once had, but watching my man play the game he loves with Liam by my side is a nice progression.

When the Ravens win the conference championship, we're both yelling so loudly that my neighbor downstairs bangs on the ceiling. We try to quiet down our celebration, especially since I know the poor lady is going to have to deal with me stomping around clad in a cast for the next two months. No need to start off on the wrong foot now. I grin to myself at the stupid joke . . . the wrong foot.

Hours later, I almost have to pinch myself at the vision in front of me. Actually, that's not a bad idea considering these pain meds pack a wallop of a punch. Maybe I am hallucinating. "Ouch!" I say. "Nope, not a dream, I guess."

Zach reaches for my hand, stopping me from pinching myself

again just to be sure. "Why the hell are you pinching yourself, Brat?" Liam clears his throat, and Zach rephrases, "You okay, *Norma*?" He gives Liam a mildly apologetic look, but I can tell he's not the least bit sorry. It's just what he calls me and I like being his brat. God knows, everyone at this table knows what a pill I can be.

I look around the table at the people surrounding me, the ones who put up with my shit willingly and lovingly. Zach's question means every eye is on me, and I meet each one with a smile. Zach, Liam, Adrianna, Dad, and Mom. "Just so glad you're all here. It means a lot," I say, choking up. Tears threaten at the corners of my eyes.

Liam groans. "Fuck, you broke her, dude. She never used to cry before you. She'd just smack talk us all about not having anything better to do on a Saturday night than crowding around her tiny ass table."

His outburst makes everyone laugh a bit, breaking the spell and giving me a moment to compose myself. I grin through the drying tears. "I'd like to think maybe he fixed me more than broke me, but if you'd rather me go back to busting your balls, that can be arranged. In fact, Arianna was just telling me the other day —"

"No," he interrupts, and Arianna laughs, shaking her head and clearly mouthing, 'I told her nothing.'

Dad's voice is a bit louder than need be, but it does the trick, getting everyone to quiet down about things that would probably make Mom's socialite crowd faint. "So, Zach, tell me about the game, the team. It seems the drama didn't interfere with the win."

Zach straightens, unconsciously sitting taller. He's relatively comfortable with my dad after they both spent the last few days sitting by my hospital bedside, but I think there's always that little spark of fear when a guy talks to his girl's dad. "The team was a bit shook up, understandably, but we pulled together and did our best. Coach Buckley had my back on offense, and Coach Jefferson kept the whole team solid. We're proud, not just of the win today, but of the way we played as a whole."

Dad grins. "Damn fine interview answer. Guess my daughter's been coaching you on what to say to reporters too?" He looks to me proudly.

But Zach corrects him. "No sir, Norma's a damn smart girl and has definitely helped me out with school and so much more, but I've been talking to the press for years. I know what to say, and if I didn't, Coach Jefferson would've held me back from ever seeing a microphone."

My dad smiles at the bold answer.

"Hey, speaking of school . . . what did Coach say about his meeting with the dean? Everything got a bit crazy and I never heard, or if someone told me, the conversation washed away with the pain meds," I ask Zach.

Zach grimaces. "It was bad, honestly. Professor Ledbetter lost her job since she wasn't tenured, and taking bribes to change a student's grades is a pretty serious offense. She admitted she did that early in the semester but got cold feet, and my later work was more correctly scored, but she did change all of my papers and quizzes to their appropriate grade. At least she still had copies to do that with. I easily have a B-plus, might even that A I've been wanting if I ace the final essay."

"I'll help with that! Not like I'm doing much else, sitting here for the next few days. Oh, and thanks for getting my paper-work from my professors, Arianna. Most of it can all be done online. My math professor even offered to let my study group leader film the lecture so I could watch it at home. But there's always those few things that need to be handed in or returned old-school-style on paper. I should be able to stay pretty caught up, though, and not affect my grades too much."

Arianna smiles. "Happy to help. Don't you have an article to write too, though? That's going to be a big chunk of work, so don't overdo it." Her motherly words are sweet, and judging by the look on my mom's face, she approved of this message of over-restraint. She probably asked Arianna to say it since I'd begged her to chill after the fiftieth time she'd tried to force me back on the couch. A mother's love. Can't live without it . . . can't live with it, sometimes, I think faux-sourly. Truth is, my mom has been a pillar of support, and there were some moments before surgery that I really just wanted my mommy and she was right there by my bedside, soothing my fears away like moms do.

"I do need to work on the write-up. Trey, he's the newly-promoted editor, stopped by while I was in the hospital to see if I wanted to write it or have someone else do it. I demanded the assignment, of course," I say, throwing my hands out to the side as if there'd been any chance I would turn that opportunity down.

Trey seems like a nice guy, but when he'd come by to introduce himself as my new boss, I'd been surprised. Apparently, Erica resigned as editor, though legally, she didn't do anything wrong. She wasn't involved in Jake's plans, but her sex-induced loose lips were a catalyst, and she'd burned some bridges with the administration, our paper staff, the whole football team, and Coach Jefferson. I think she mostly wants to just finish out her senior year with as little attention as possible, but she did send me a text that simply said, *I'm so sorry.*

Trey told me that my position with the paper was secure, but not to think that my in with the football team would get me any more bylines than any other lowly reporter learning the ropes. I'd smiled and told him I didn't want any special favors and most definitely don't want to be the sports column reporter, but that I'd be happy to write a few football team-centric pieces from interviews with the guys and coach about the incident, sprinkling in my own injury at the end.

He'd agreed and told me to 'be careful with those crazy football guys.' He'd had a teasing smirk, and I could appreciate the humor with Zach at my side and in light of Jake's actions, though I refused to shrink away like some broken victim.

"Make sure you include the final penalties for Jake Robertson too. It should be more, so much more, but I did the best I could for you, ladybug. I'm so sorry I ever pushed you to help him." His words are broken, his guilt at having had any hand in this obvious.

"Dad, you didn't do anything wrong. I was pissed at the time, and no, I don't want to be involved in your business dealings." I quickly correct myself, "Unless you're setting me up for an interview, of course. But none of us had any idea that Jake was going to go off the rails like that. I'm not sure he even knew the pressure was getting to him and it was that dire of a situation."

In the end, Jake's injuries had been significantly worse than mine. He'd had a broken nose and cheekbone from Zach's punches, and when he fell, he'd hit the pavement wrong and had some internal bleeding. He'd been placed under arrest while still in his hospital bed, handcuffed to the railing as the police read him his rights and stationed a guard outside his door.

His dad, Joe, had raged about his son being treated like a common criminal and had hired some big-shot lawyer to launch his defense.

That was when Dad had taken over and the whole thing had turned into a twisted version of a business negotiation. I forget sometimes what a cold, calculating monster my Dad can be when the situation calls for it, and hurting his only daughter had triggered some pretty serious viciousness for him. But through it all, he was the dad I've always known, powerful and strong but soft and sweet to me.

I think dealing with all of that might've even brought Dad and Liam together a bit, allies against a shared foe. They're never going to be tight, but at least they're both here together, something that was previously a rare occurrence.

In the end, Jake plead guilty to assault for his attack on me, and attempted manslaughter for almost running Zach over, because you can be sure that Liam got the parking lot video for that too. We each got a permanent restraining order against him too. Jake won't do time, but he's on a parole for a long time and has to do anger management classes and seek help for some daddy issues that were worse than we'd ever thought. He was expelled from school too, so no more football.

I won't say I feel sorry for him, because I don't, but I can imagine that having your whole life implode, especially when it's through your own doing, is hard. I just hope he gets better and stays the fuck away from Zach and me.

After dinner, everyone is slow to leave. Mom, especially, offers to tuck me in or set up a work station in the living room, but I reassure her that I'm fine and that Zach will be here to help. That seems to make her smile, and I guess she approves of Zach wholeheartedly, because she leaves without my Dad having to drag her out like he has the last few times.

I lie back on the couch, my head on the arm and my foot propped up high on the couch back. "Ahh, alone at last," I say, a smile on my face though my eyes are already closing.

"You tired, Brat?" Zach asks, and though it's a sweet question, like he's ready to tuck me in if I say yes, I can hear something more in the undercurrent.

I crack one eye. "Maybe. Why?"

He smirks. "Oh, if you're tired, I'll let you rest. I just thought with me winning the championship today, you might want to celebrate a bit."

My other eye opens, all thoughts of sleep evaporating at his cocky look. The one that's pointedly looking me over, head to toe. Sexy as fuck . . . well, until he hits my cast. "Actually, maybe I should let you rest. You've had a long day."

"Scared of a cast, Zach? I promise not to bang you over the head with it if you bang me." It's a stupid joke, not even funny, but it makes Zach laugh and reconsider.

"You sure you're okay, Brat?" he asks, and I know if I said no, he'd patiently take care of me all night.

"I'm okay, except that I need you inside me. It's been days, Zach. And after everything, I just . . . I need you." My voice is soft, no filter and no façade, just raw truth.

Zach lies down on top of me, his thickening cock pressed right up against my pussy as he holds himself up. He watches my face to make sure he's not hurting me, but my leg is supported and out of the way. Once he's certain I'm not hiding any twinges of pain, he brushes a lock of my hair out of my face, his face serious. "Norma, I know we said this before, when you were a little out of it, but I want you to know I mean it with all my heart. I love you, Norma Jean Blackstone."

My breath hitches. I knew I'd said all kinds of weird shit at the hospital, but I remembered telling Zach I love him because it was the truth. The one I'd been too reserved to say. But now, I have no doubts, no worries, which sounds odd, considering my current predicament, but a broken leg doesn't affect my heart in the least. "I love you too, Zachary Thomas Knight."

The moment sparks, and we both smile, the love and light filling us, leaving no room for any shadow of a doubt.

And then Zach bends down and takes my mouth in a kiss and the beautiful light explodes into fiery passion.

Our kiss becomes messy, hungry as we fight for more. "Fuck, Norma," Zach says as he grinds against me, and I moan at the hard ridge of him against my hot pussy. But suddenly, his weight is gone. He stands, ripping his shirt over his head and helping me get my shirt and bra off.

He crouches down, his shoulders between my thighs, one of my knees hooked on the back of the couch and the other bent to let my foot touch the floor. He shoves my skirt up, too inpatient to take it off me since it'd mean rearranging my legs again. Instead, he leaves it puddled around my waist and grips my panties. "You attached to these?"

I shake my head. "Not at all." And with a fierce tug, he rips them from my body, tossing them over his shoulder carelessly because now he has what he really wants. My pussy, spread wide in front of him, juicy with desire for him.

He licks me, devours me, giving no mercy. There's no tease or buildup. It's full-throttle from the first touch, driving me wild. But he holds my hips firmly in place, not letting me move against him. On some level, I know he's doing it so I don't hurt myself, but on the surface, I like him holding me down, making me take his tongue-lashing. "Oh, God, Zach," I cry out, already on the edge in just minutes.

"Come for me, Brat. Come all over my face with your sweet cream so I can get inside you. Fuck, I need inside you." The desperation in his voice commands me to obey, and I fly off into the dark abyss, letting the blackness behind my lids consume me as lightning shoots through my body, making me shake in ecstasy.

Zach stands, and dropping his jeans and boxer briefs at the same time, he kicks his shoes off, nude in an instant. And then he's hovering over me, cock poised at my entrance.

"I love you, Brat."

"I love you too, Zach."

And then he fills me in one stroke, and though my hands aren't tied this time, I have never felt more bound. Connected to this man, to what we have together, silk strands between us and surrounding us, creating something better together than we are alone. Not Norma, not Zach. But *us*.

And as his cock pushes into me, jackhammer hard and fast, he roars as his orgasm rips through him. And the knots in the metaphorical silk binds cinch tighter, just like my pussy as I come again with him.

ZACH

The Sapphire Bowl isn't the biggest bowl game around, but it is on New Year's Eve, which makes it extra-special. Beyond the obvious football incentives, I've got some bonus motivation sitting at the fifty-yard line. Norma is sitting in her seat, watching my every move, her small body more or less draped in one of my old jerseys. Liam and Arianna sit on her right. My parents sit on her left.

Unsurprisingly, my parents *love* Norma. Norma was nearly gutted when my mom heard us giving each other hell, sure that they'd think we were seriously bickering and an obvious match made in hell. But I knew better, and when my mom had come in the room, she'd addressed Norma first before even giving me a hello kiss, telling her, 'You get him, dear. Keeping a

Knight man in line is dang-near a full-time job.' But Norma's been overly sweet ever since, to the point my Dad quietly asked me if the Brat nickname was supposed to be ironic. I assured him that Norma was being extra-sweet because she wanted to make a good impression but was a strong-willed, sassy, prickly brat who kept me on my toes and in my place. And I liked her that way. He'd grinned and told me 'Good job, Son.' I think that was the best compliment he's ever given me, even better than all the football praise he's heaped on my shoulders over the years of playing.

But of course, Norma is sitting instead of standing because of the cast still clunking along on her lower leg. She's almost to Freedom Day, as she calls it, but also known as cast removal day, and she's ready, counting down the days on her calendar. But she's managing pretty well. I, Arianna, and Liam pitch in when she needs something, and her parents helped too until they left a couple of days after Christmas.

I give them all a wave and catch the kiss Norma blows me for luck before turning back to the field. "You feeling it, Zach?" Coach Buckley asks me. "This could be your last game." I can tell he's pumping me for info without asking outright.

I shake my head. "Nope, I haven't told Coach Jefferson yet, but I did a lot of thinking over winter break. I'm coming back next year. I want to be a Raven one more year, finish my degree, and then see about the pros."

Coach Buckley grins. "You haven't told Coach Jefferson yet?"

I chuckle. "Just haven't had a chance with the holidays and practices to be ready for today. Besides, I'm sure you've noticed how nice he's been to me? He thinks I might declare early for the draft and is trying to make me forget about the five AM practices and the two-a-day drills. But I remember, and I'm still staying."

Coach Buckley claps his hands, the sound loud even on the riot of the sideline. "Well, all right, then. Let's play some damn football then!"

To say it's a good game is a ridiculous understatement. We're playing the Jaguars, and while they're a great team, we strike hard and fast. By the end of the first quarter, we've already scored twenty-one points.

"You planning on slowing down?" Coach Buckley asks me as I come off after the third touchdown. "Or are you just trying to shatter the TD record?"

"Not stopping until the game clock hits zero," I reply, grabbing a Gatorade and giving Norma a thumbs-up. She waves a pompom on a stick madly, making me laugh because she's suddenly my favorite fucking groupie ever. Her little cheer gives me new energy, which helps because our defense is struggling and the Jags hit us for two straight long touchdowns.

It becomes a shootout, and as we enter the final two of the fourth quarter, I know the guys are exhausted. Sweat drips off every facemask and every player's chest is heaving. "Okay, let's keep it going. Almost there, guys."

"Zach," one of my linemen says, his white jersey nearly gray with sweat. "There ain't much left in the tank, man."

I want to slap him in the head, tell him to man the fuck up . . . but looking around at the other guys, he's right and just saying what they're all thinking. I'm being fueled by something super-human, something that they don't have. I have Norma. Chuckling, I nod. "Okay . . . then let's run a Bratty Norma Special."

It's a new play, something we've run once or twice in practice as a 'fuck it, let's have some fun' type shit. The guys grin, and it's my ass if this goes badly.

400

At the snap, everyone goes directly at and nails the closest Jaguar, looking like something out of a bar fight rather than football. It's chaos, it's anarchy . . . it's just like my girl, fighting on every damn front. And just like in real life, I run through it all, slick and smooth through every obstacle and diversion and battle, like I'm playing Frogger on the Interstate. In seconds, I only have one guy left to beat, Prince Ellsmore, an All-American strong safety who's been gunning for me all game.

"Sorry, Prince, but I'm the fucking King," I growl as I lower my shoulder, hitting him right under the chin. It sends him flying, and I go the rest of the way untouched for a fifty-three-yard touchdown run.

It proves to be the knife in the Jaguars' heart, winning the barn burner with a score of 56-45.

The trophy presentation is a huge event. The Ravens haven't won a bowl game in almost a decade, and Coach Jefferson looks like he's about to cry as he holds it aloft.

"And now the MVP of the Sapphire Bowl," the cable TV host says, bringing out another trophy. "Zach Knight, get up here!"

The crowd's going nuts, but when they stick the mic in my face, I look down at the trophy, the reality more surreal than every dream I've ever had of this moment.

I try to find my mind, remembering to thank my team and my coaches. I hear the TV host ask about a repeat performance next year, and I smile as I see Norma making her way slowly and carefully through the crowd. The guys notice her too and help her get a front-row seat for my moment because that's what family does, and these guys and Norma are my family, my chosen tribe. "I'd love a repeat of this next year. I'll be here to help make it happen as the starting senior quarterback for the Ravens."

I let my eyes flick to Coach for his reaction, and his jaw is dropped open, and the tears that threatened flow freely now. He closes his mouth and gives me a thumbs-up, a look of pride in his eyes.

And with my interview done, I can finally do what I've been wanting to do since the timer buzzed. I rush to Norma, picking her up and spinning her around in joy. Her tiny hands fist my jersey, and she pulls me into a deep kiss, our lips still smiling even as we try to pucker. The crowd's cheers get even louder.

We part just a bit, and she whisper-yells, "You think you can put up with all this plus me for another year?" A sassy smirk is on her face as she challenges me with those words.

I give her a cocky grin back. "Brat, I'm fucking sure I'm gonna be putting up with you for at least fifty years."

Thank you for reading the Virgin Diaries series! I hope you enjoyed the books. If so, please take a moment and leave a review. Make sure you join **mailing list** so you never miss a new book or giveaway.

PREVIEW DIRTY TALK

BY LAUREN LANDISH

Chapter 1
Katrina

"CHECKMATE, BITCH," I EXCLAIM AS I DO A VICTORY DANCE that's comprised of fist pumps and ass wiggles in my chair while my best friend Elise laughs at me. I turn in my seat and start doing a little half-stepping Rockettes dance. "Can-can, I just kicked some can-can, I so am the wo-man, and I rule this place!"

Elise does a little finger dance herself, cheering along with me. "You go, girl. Winner, winner, chicken dinner. Now let's eat!"

I laugh with her, joyful in celebrating my new promotion at work, regardless of the dirty looks the snooty ladies at the next table are shooting our way. I get their looks. I mean, we are in the best restaurant in the city. While East Robinsville isn't New York or Miami, we're more of a Northeastern suburb of . . . well, everything in between. This just isn't the sort of restaurant where five-foot-two-inch women in work clothes go

403

shaking their ass while chanting something akin to a high school cheer.

But right now, I give exactly zero fucks. "Damn right, we can eat! I'm the youngest person in the company to ever be promoted to Senior Developer and the first woman at that level. Glass ceiling? Boom, busting through! Boys' club? Infiltrated." I mime like I'm sneaking in, shoulders hunched and hands pressed tightly in front of me before splaying my arms wide with a huge grin. "Before they know it, I'm gonna have that boys' club watching chick flicks and the whole damn office is going to be painted pink!"

Elise snorts, shaking her head again. "I still don't have a fucking clue what you actually do, but even I understand the words *promotion* and *raise*. So huge congrats, honey."

She's right, no one really understands when I talk about my job. My brain has a tendency to talk in streams of binary zeroes and ones that make perfect sense to me, but not so much to the average person. When I was in high school, I even dreamed in Java.

And even I don't really understand what my promotion means. Senior Developer? Other than the fact that I get updated business cards with my fancy new title next week, I'm not sure what's changed. I'm still doing my own coding and my own work, just with a slightly higher pay grade. And when I say slightly, I mean barely a bump after taxes. Just enough for a bonus cocktail at a swanky club on Friday maybe. *Maybe* more at year end, they'd said. Ah, well, I'm excited anyway. It's a first step and an acknowledgement of my work.

The part people do get is when my company turns my strings of code into apps that go viral. After my last app went number one, they were forced to give me a promotion or risk losing my skills to another development company. They might not understand the zeroes and ones, but everyone can grasp dollars and cents, and that's what my apps bring in.

I might be young at only twenty-six, and female, as evidenced by my long honey-blonde hair and curvy figure, but as much as I don't fit the stereotypical profile of a computer nerd, they had to respect that my brain creates things that no one else does. I think it's my female point of view that really helps. While a chunk of the other people in the programming field fit the stereotype of being slightly repressed geeks who are more comfortable watching animated 'girlfriends' than talking to an actual woman, I'm different. I understand that merely slapping a pink font on things or adding sparkly shit and giving more pre-loaded shopping options doesn't make technology more 'female-friendly.'

It's insulting, honestly. But it gives me an edge in that I know how to actually create apps that women like and want to use. Not just women, either, based on sales. I'm getting a lot of men downloading my apps too, especially men who aren't into tech-geeking out every damn thing they own.

And so I celebrate with Elise, holding up our glasses of wine and clinking them together in a toast. Elise sips her wine and nods in appreciation, making me glad we went with the waiter's recommendation. "So you're killing it on the job front. What else is going on? How are things with you and Kevin?"

Elise has been my best friend since we met at a college recruiting event. She's all knockout looks and sass, and I'm short, nervous, and shy in professional situations, but we clicked. She knows I've been through the wringer with some previous boyfriends, and even though Kevin is fine—well-mannered, ambitious, and treats me right—she just doesn't care for him for some reason. So my joyful buzz is instantly dulled, knowing that she doesn't like Kevin.

"He's fine," I reply, knowing it's not a great answer, but I also know she's going to roast me anyway. "He's been working a lot of hours so I haven't even seen him in a few days, but he texts me every morning and night. We're supposed to go out for dinner this weekend to celebrate."

Elise sighs, giving me that look that makes her normally very cute face look sort of like a sarcastic basset hound. "I'm glad, I guess. Not to beat a dead horse," —*too late*— "but you really can do better. Kevin is just so . . . meh. There's no spark, no fire between you two. It's like you're friends who fuck."

I duck my chin, not wanting her to read on my face the woeful lack of fucking that has been happening, but I'm too transparent.

"Wait . . . you two *do* fuck, right?" Elise asks, flabbergasted. "I figured that was why you were staying with him. I was sure he must be great in the sack or you'd have dumped his boring ass a long time ago."

I bite my lip, not wanting to get into this with her . . . again. But one of Elise's greatest strengths is also one of her most annoying traits as well. She's like a dog with a bone and isn't going to let this go.

"Look, he's fine," I finally reply, trying to figure out how much I need to feed Elise before she gives me a measure of peace. "He's handsome, treats me well, and when we have sex, it's good . . . I guess. I don't believe in some Prince Charming who is going to sweep me off my feet to a castle where we'll have romantic candlelit dinners, brilliant conversation, and bed-breaking sexcapades. I just want someone to share the good and bad times with, some companionship."

Elise holds back as long as she can before she explodes, her snort and guffaw of derision getting even more looks in our direction. "Then get a fucking Golden Retriever and a rabbit. The buzzing kind that uses rechargeable batteries."

One of the ladies at the next table huffs, seemingly aghast at Elise's outburst, and they stand to move toward the bar on the other side of the restaurant, far away from us. "Well, if this is the sort of trash that passes for dinner conversation," the older one says as she sticks her nose far enough into the air I wonder if it's going to be clipped by the ceiling fans, "no wonder the country's going to hell under these Millennials!"

She storms off before Elise or I can respond, but the second lady pauses slightly and talks out of the side of her mouth. "Sweetie, you do deserve more than *fine*."

With a wink, she scurries off after her friend, leaving behind a grinning Elise. "See? Even snooty old biddies know that you deserve more than *meh*."

"I know. We've had this conversation on more than one occasion, so can we drop it?" I plead between clenched teeth before calming slightly. "I want to celebrate and catch up, not argue about my love life."

Always needing the last word, Elise drops her voice, muttering under her breath. "What love life?"

"That's low."

Elise holds her hands up, and I know I've at least gotten a temporary reprieve. "Okay then, if we're sticking to work, I got a new scoop that I'm running with. I'm writing a piece about a certain famous someone who got caught sending dick pics to a social media princess. Don't ask me who because I can't divulge that yet. But it'll be all there in black and white by next week's column."

Elise is an investigative journalist, a rather fantastic one whose talents are largely being wasted on celebrity news gossip for the tabloid paper she writes for. I can't even call it a paper, really. With the downfall of actual print news, most of her stuff ends up in cyberspace, where it's digested, Tweeted, hashtagged, and churned out for the two-minute attention span types to gloat over for a moment before they move on to . . . well, whatever the next sound bite happens to be.

Every once in awhile, she'll get to do something much more newsworthy, but mostly it's fact-checking and ass-covering before the paper publishes stories celebrities would rather see disappear. I know what burns her ass even more is when she has to cover the stories where some downward-trending celebrity manufactures a scandal just to get some social media buzz going before their latest attempt at rejuvenating a career that peaked about five years ago.

This one at least sounds halfway interesting, and frankly, better than my love life, so I laugh. "Why would he send a dick pic to someone on social media? Wouldn't he assume she'd post it? What a dumbass!"

"No, it's usually close-ups and they're posted anonymously," Elise says with a snort. "Of course, she knows because she sees the user name on their direct message, but she cuts it out so that it's posted to her page as an anonymous flash of flesh. Look."

She pulls out her phone, clicking around to open an app, one I didn't design but damn sure wish I had. It's got one hell of a sweet interface, and Elise is using it to organize her web pages better than anything the normal apps have. It takes Elise only a moment to find the page she wants.

"See?" she says, showing me her phone. "People send her messages with dick pics, tit pics, whatever. If she deems them sexy enough, she posts them with little blurbs and people can comment. She also does Q-and-As with followers, shows face-less pics of herself, and gives little shows sometimes. Kinda like porn but more 'real people' instead of silicone-stuffed, pump-sucked, fake moan scenes."

She scrolls through, showing me one image after another of body part close-ups. Some of them . . . well damn, I gotta say that while they might not be professionals or anything, it's a hell of a lot hotter than anything I'm getting right now. "Wow. That's uhh . . . quite something. I don't get it, but I guess lots of folks are into it. Wait."

She stops scrolling at my near-shout, smirking. "What? See something you like?"

My mouth feels dry and my voice papery. "Go back up a couple."

She scrolls back up and I read the blurb above a collage of pics. *Little titty fuck with my new boy toy today. Look at my hungry tits and his thick cock. After this, things got a little deeper, if you know what I mean. Sorry, no pics of that, but I'll just say that he was insatiable and I definitely had a very good morning. ;)*

The pictures show a close-up of her full cleavage, a guy's dick from above, and then a few pictures of him stroking in and out of her pressed-together breasts. I'm not afraid to say the girl's got a nice rack that would probably have most of my co-workers drooling and the blood rushing from their brains to their dicks, but that's not what's causing my stomach to drop through the floor.

I know that dick.

It's the same, thick with a little curve to the right, and I can even see a sort of donut-shaped mole high on the man's thigh, right above the shaved area above the base of his cock.

Yes, that mole seals it.

That's Kevin.

His cock with another woman, fucking her for social media, thinking I'd probably never even know. He has barely touched me lately, but he's willing to do it almost publicly with some social media slut?

I realize Elise is staring at me, her previous good-natured look long gone to be replaced by an expression of concern. "Kat, are you okay? You look pale."

I point at her phone, trying my best to keep my voice level. "That post? The one right there?"

"Oh, Titty Fuck Girl?" Elise asks. "She's on here at least once a month with a new set of pics. Apparently, she loves her rack. I still think they're fake. Why?"

"She's talking about Kevin. That's him."

She gasps, turning the phone to look closer. "Holy shit, honey. Are you sure?"

I nod, tears already pooling in my eyes. "I'm sure."

She puts her phone down on the table and comes around the table to hug me. "Shit. Shit. Shit. I am so sorry. I told you that douchebag doesn't deserve someone like you. You're too fucking good for him."

I sniffle, nodding, but deep inside, I know that this is always how it goes. Every single boyfriend I've ever had ended up cheating on me. I've tried playing hard to get. I've tried being the good little go-along girlfriend. I've even tried being myself, which seems to be somewhere in between, once I figured out who I actually was.

It's even worse in bed, where I've tried being vanilla, being aggressive, and being submissive. And again, being myself, somewhere in the middle, when I figured out what I enjoyed from the experimentation.

But honestly, I've never been satisfied. No matter what, I just can't seem to find that 'sweet spot' that makes me happy

and fulfilled in a relationship. And while I've tried everything, depending on the guy, it never works out. The
boyfriends I've had, while few in number considering I can
count them on one hand, all eventually cheated, saying that
they just wanted something different. Something that's
not me.

Apparently, Kevin's no different. My mood shifts wildly from
self-pity to anger to finally, a numb acceptance. "What a
fucking jerk. I hope he likes being a boy toy for a social media
slut, because he's damn sure not my boyfriend anymore."

"That's the spirit," Elise says, refilling my wine glass. "Now,
how about you and I finish off this bottle, get another, and by
the time you're done, you'll have forgotten all about that loser
while we take a cab back to your place?"

"Maybe I will just get a dog, and I sure as hell already have a
buzzing rabbit. Several of them, in fact," I mutter. "You know
what? They're better than he ever was by a damn country
mile."

"Rabbits . . . they just keep going and going and going," Elise
jokes, trying to keep me in good spirits. She twirls her hands in
the air like the famous commercial bunny and signals for
another bottle of wine.

She's right. Fuck Kevin.

DERRICK

My black leather office chair creaks, an annoying little trend
it's developed over the past six months that's the primary
reason I don't use it in the studio. Admittedly, that's probably
for the better because if I had a chair this comfortable in the
studio, I'd be too relaxed to really be on point for my shows.
Still, it's helpful to have something nice like this office since it's
a hell of a big step up from the days when my office was also

the station's break room. "All right, hit me. What's on the agenda for today's show?"

My co-star, Susannah, checks her papers, making little check-marks as she goes through each item. She's an incessant check-marker, and I have no idea how the fuck she can read her sheets by the end of the day. "The overall theme for today is cheaters, and I've got several emails pulled for that so we can stay on track. We'll field calls, of course, and some will be on topic and some off, like always. I'll try and screen them as best I can, and we should be all set."

I nod, trying to mentally prep myself for another three-hour stint behind the mic, offering music, advice, hope, and some-times a swift kick in the pants to our listeners. Two years ago, I never would've believed that I'd be known as the 'Love Whis-perer' on a radio talk segment called the same thing. Part Howard Stern, part Dr. Phil, part DJ Love Below, I've found a niche that's just . . . unique.

I started out many years ago as a jock, playing football on my high school team with dreams of college ball. A seemingly short derailment after an injury led me to do sports reporting for my high school's news and I fell in love.

After that, my scholarships to play football never came, but it didn't bother me as much as I thought it would. I decided to chase after a sports broadcast degree instead, marrying my passion for football and my love of reporting.

I spent four years after graduation doing daily sports talks from three to six as the afternoon drive-home DJ. It wasn't a big station, just one of the half-dozen stations that existed as an alternative for people who didn't want to listen to corporate pop, hip-hop, or country. It was there I received that fateful call.

Looking back, it's kind of crazy, but a guy had called in

bitching and moaning about his wife not understanding his need to follow all these wild superstitions to help his team win.

"I'm telling you D, I went to church and asked God himself. I said, if you can bless the Bandits with a win, I'll show myself true and wear those ugly ass socks my pastor gave me for Christmas the year before and never wash them again. You know what happened?"

Of course, everyone could figure out what happened. Still, I respectfully told him that I didn't think his unwashed socks were doing a damn thing for his beloved team on the basketball court, but if he didn't put those fuckers in the washing machine, they were sure going to land him in divorce court.

He sighed and eventually gave in when I told him to wash the socks, thank his wife for putting up with his shit, and full-out romance her to bed and do his damndest to make up for his selfish ways.

And that was that. A new show and a new me were born. After a few marketing tweaks, I've been the so-called 'Love Whisperer' for almost a year now, helping people who ask for advice to get the happily ever after they want.

Ironically, I'm single. Funny how that works out, but all the good advice I try to give stems from my parents who were happily married for over forty years before my mom passed. I won't settle for less than the real thing, and I try to advise my listeners to do the same.

And then there's the sex aspect of my job.

Talking about relationships obviously involves discussing sex with people, as that's one of the major areas that cause problems for folks. At first, talking about all the crazy shit people want to do even made me blush a little, but eventually, it's just gotten to be second nature.

Want to talk about how to get your wife to massage your

prostate? Can do. Want to talk about how your girlfriend wants you to wear Underoos and call her Mommy? Can do. Want to talk about your husband never washing the dishes, and how you can get him to help? I can do that too.

All-in-one, real relationships at your service. Live from six to nine, five days a week, or available for download on various podcast sites and clip shows on the weekends. Hell of a lot for a guy who figured *making it* would involve becoming the voice of some college football team.

So I want to do a good job. And that means working well with Susannah, who is the control-freak yin to my laissez-faire yang. "Thanks. I know this week's topics from our show planning meeting, but I spaced on tonight's focus."

Susannah nods, unflappable. "No problem. Do you want to scan the emails or just do your thing?"

I smile at her. She already knows the answer. "Same as always, spontaneous. You know that even though I was a Boy Scout, being prepared for this doesn't do us any favors. I sound robotic when I read ahead. First read, real reactions work better and give the listeners knee-jerk common sense."

She shrugs, scribbling on her papers. "I know, just checking."

It's probably one of the reasons we work so well together, our totally different approaches to the show. Joining me from day one, she's the one who keeps our show running behind the scenes and keeps me on track on-air, serving as both producer and co-host. Luckily, her almost anal-retentive penchant for prep totally doesn't come across on the air, where she's the playful, comedic counter to my gruff, tell-it-like-it-is style.

"Then let's rock," I tell her. "Got your drinks ready?"

Susannah nods as we head toward the studio. Settling into my broadcast chair, a much less comfortable but totally silent one,

I survey my normal spread of one water, one coffee, and one green tea, one for every hour we're gonna be on the air. With the top of the hour news breaks and spaced out music jams, I've gotten used to using the exactly four minute and thirty second breaks to run next door and drain my bladder if I need to.

Everything ready, we smile and settle in for another show. "Gooooood evening! It's your favorite 'Love Whisperer,' Derrick King here with my lovely assistant, Miss Susannah Jameson. We're ready for an evening of love, sex, betrayal, and lust, if you're willing to share. Our focus tonight is on cheaters and cheating. Are you being cheated on? Maybe *you* are the cheater? Call in and we'll talk."

The red glow from the holding calls is instant, but I traditionally go to an email first so that I can roll right in. "While Susannah is grabbing our first caller, I'll start with an email. Here's one from P. 'Dear Love Whisperer,' it says, 'my husband travels extensively for work, leaving me home and so lonely. I don't know if he's cheating while he's gone, but I always wonder. I've started to develop feelings for my personal trainer, and I think I'm falling in love with him. What should I do?' "

I *tsk-tsk* into the microphone, making my displeasure clear. "Well, P, first things first. Your marriage is your priority because you made a vow. For better or worse, remember? It's simple. Talk to your husband. Maybe he's cheating, maybe he isn't. Maybe he's working his ass off so his bored wife can even *have* a trainer and you're looking for excuses to justify your own bad behavior. But talking to him is your first step. You need to explain your feelings and that you need him more than perhaps you need the money. Second, you need to get a life beyond your husband and trainer. I get the sense you need some attention and your trainer is giving it to you, so you think you're in love with him. Newsflash—he's being paid to give you attention. By your husband, it sounds like. That's not a healthy foundation for a relationship even if he is your soulmate, which I doubt."

I sigh and lower my voice a little. I don't want to cut this woman's guts out. I want to help her. "P, let's be honest. A good trainer is going to be personable. They're in a sales profession. They're not going to make it in the industry without either being the best in the world at what they do or having a good personality. And a lot of them have good bodies. Their bodies are their business cards. So it's natural to feel some attraction to your trainer. But that doesn't mean he's going to stick by you. Here's a challenge—tell your trainer you can't pay him for the next three months and see how available he is to just give you his time."

Susannah snickers and hits her mic button. "That's why I do group yoga classes. Only thing that happens there is sweaty tantric orgies. Ohmm . . . my . . ." Her initial yoga-esque ohm dissolves into a pleasure-induced moan that she fakes exceedingly well.

I roll my eyes, knowing that she does nothing of the sort. "To the point, though, fire your trainer because of your weakness and tell him why. He's a pro. He needs to know that his services were not the reason you're leaving. Next, get a hobby that fulfills you beyond a man and talk to your husband."

I click a button and a sound effect of a cheering audience plays through my headset. It goes on like this for a while, call after call, email after email of helping people.

Well, I hope I'm helping them. They seem to think I am, and I'm certainly giving it my best shot. In between, I mix in music and a hodgepodge of stuff that fits the daily themes. Tonight I've got some Taylor Swift, a little Carrie Underwood, some old-school TLC. I even, as a joke, worked in Bobby Brown at Susannah's insistence.

Coming back from that last one, I see Susannah gesture from her mini-booth and give the airspace over to her, letting her introduce the next caller. "Okay, Susannah's giving me the big foam finger, so what've we got?"

"You wish I had a big finger for you," Susannah teases like she always does on air—it's part of our act. "The next caller would like to discuss some rather incriminating photos she's come across. Apparently, Mr. Right was Mr. Everybody?"

I click the button, taking the call live on-air. "This is the 'Love Whisperer', who am I speaking with?"

The caller stutters, obviously nervous, and in my mind I know I have to treat this one gently. Some of the callers just want to laugh, maybe have their fifteen seconds of fame or get their pound of proverbial flesh by exposing their partner's misdeeds. But there are also callers like this, who I suspect really needs help. "This is Katrina . . . Kat."

Whoa, a first name. And from the sound of it, a real one. She's not making a thing up. I need to lighten the mood a little, or else she's gonna clam up and freak out on me. "Hello, Kitty Kat. What seems to be the problem today?"

I hear her sigh, and it touches me for some reason. "Well . . . I can't believe I actually got through, first of all. I worked up the nerve to dial the numbers but didn't expect an answer. I'm just . . . I don't even know what I am. I'm just a little lost and in need of some advice, I guess." She huffs out a humorless laugh.

I can hear the pain in her voice, mixed with nerves. "Advice? That I can do. That's what I'm here for, in fact. What's going on, Kat?"

"It's my boyfriend, or my soon-to-be ex-boyfriend, I guess. I found out today that he slept with someone else." She sounds

417

like she's found a bit of steel as she speaks this time, and it makes her previous vulnerability all the more touching.

"Ouch," I say, truly wincing at the fresh wound. A day of cheat call? I'm sure the advertisers are rubbing their hands in glee, but I'm feeling for this girl. "I'm so sorry. I know that hurts and it's wrong no matter what. I heard something about compromising pics. Please tell me he didn't send you pics of him screwing someone else?"

She laughs but it's not in humor. "No, I guess that would've been worse, but he had sex with someone kind of Internet famous and she posted faceless pics of them together. But I recognized his . . . uhm . . . his . . ."

Let's just get the schlong out in the open, why don't we? "You recognized his penis? Is that the word you're looking for?"

"Yeah, I guess so," Kat says, her voice cutting through the gap created by the phone line. "He has a mole, so I know it's him."

There's something about her voice, all sweet and breathy that stirs me inside like I rarely have happen. It's not just her tone, either. She's in pain, but she's mad as fuck too, and I want to help her, protect her. She seems innocent, and something deep inside me wants to make her a little bit dirty.

"Okay, first, repeat after me. Penis, dick, cock." I wait, unsure if she'll do it but holding my breath in the hopes that she will.

"Uh, what?"

I feel a small smile come to my lips, and it's my turn to be a little playful. "Penis, dick, cock. Trust me, this is important for you. You can do it, Kitty Kat."

I hear her intake of breath, but she does what I demanded, more clearly than the shyness I expected. "Penis, dick, cock."

"Good girl," I growl into the mic, and through the window

connecting our booths, I can see Susannah giving me a raised eyebrow. "Now say . . . I recognized his cock fucking her."

I say a silent prayer of thanks that my radio show is on satellite. I can say whatever I want and the FCC doesn't care.

I can tell Kat is with me now, and her voice is stronger, still sexy as fuck but without the lost kitten loneliness to it. "I recognized his cock fucking her tits."

My own cock twitches a little, and I lean in, smirking. "Ah, so the plot thickens. So Kat, how does it feel to say that?"

She sighs, pulling me back a little. "The words don't bother me. I'm just not used to being on the radio. But saying that about my boyfriend pisses me off. I can't believe he'd do that."

"So, what do you think you should do about it?" I ask, leaning back in my chair and pulling my mic toward me. "Is this a 'talk it through and our relationship will be stronger on the other side of this' type situation, or is this a 'hit the road, motherfucker, and take Miss Slippy-Grippy Tits with you?' Do you want my opinion or do you already know?"

"You're right," Kat says, chuckling and sounding stronger again. "I already know I'm done. He's been a wham-bam-doesn't even say thank you, ma'am guy all along, and I've been hanging on because I didn't think I deserved better. But I don't deserve this. I'm better off alone."

Whoa, now, only half right there, Kat with the sexy voice. "You don't deserve this. You should have someone who treats you so well you never question their love, their commitment to you. Everyone deserves that. Hey, Kitty Kat? One more thing. Can you say 'cock' for me one more time? Just for . . . entertainment."

I'm pushing the line here, both for her and for the show, but I ask her to do it anyway because I want, no need, to hear her say it.

She laughs, her voice lighter even as I know the serious conversation had to hurt. "Of course, Love Whisperer. Anything for you. You ready? Cock." She draws the word out, the k a bit harsher, and I can hear the sass, almost an invitation, as she speaks.

"Ooh, thanks so much, Kitty Kat. Hold on the line just a second." My cock is now fully hard in my pants, and I'm not sure if my upcoming bathroom break is going to be to piss or to take care of that.

I click some buttons, sending the show to a song, Shaggy's *It Wasn't Me* coming over the airwaves to keep the cheating theme rolling. "Susannah?"

"Yeah?"

"Handle the next call or so after the commercial break," I tell her. "Pick something . . . funny after that one."

"Gotcha," Susannah says, and I'm glad she's able to handle things like that. It's part of our system too that when I get a call that needs more than on-air can handle, she fills the gap. Usually with less serious questions or listener stories that always make for great laughs.

Checking my board, I click the line back, glad that Susannah can't hear me now. "Kat? You still there?"

"Yes?" she says, and I feel another little thrill go down my cock just at her word. God, this woman's got a sexy voice, soft and sweet with a little undercurrent of sassiness . . . or maybe I really, really need to get laid.

"Hey, it's Derrick. I just wanted to say thanks for being such a good sport with all of that."

"No problem," she says as I make a picture in my head of her. I can't fill in the details, but I definitely want to. "Thanks for helping me realize I need to walk away. I already knew it, but some inspiration never hurts."

"I really would like to hear the rest of the story if you don't mind calling me back. I want to hear how he grovels when he finds out what he's lost. Would you call me?"

I don't know what I'm doing. This is so not like me. I never talk to the callers after they're on air unless I think they're going to hurt themselves or others, and I certainly never invite them to call back. But something about her voice calls to me like a siren. I just hope she's not pulling me into the rocky shore to crash.

"You mean the show?" Kat asks, uncertain and confused. "Like . . . I dunno, like a guest or something?"

"Well, probably not, to be honest," I reply, crossing my fingers even as my cock says I need to take this risk. "We'll be done with the cheating theme tonight and it probably won't come back up for a couple of weeks. I meant . . . call me. I want to make sure you're okay afterward and standing strong."

"Okay."

Before she can take it back, I rattle off my personal cell number to her, half of my brain telling me this is brilliant and the other half saying it's the stupidest thing I've ever done. I might not have the FCC looking over my shoulder, but the satellite network is and my advertisers for damn sure are. Still . . . "Got it?"

"I've got it," Kat says. "I'll get back to you after I break up with Kevin. It's been a weird night and I guess it's going to get even weirder. Guess I gotta go tell Kevin his dick busted him on the internet and he can get fucked elsewhere . . . permanently. I can do this."

LAUREN LANDISH

"Damn right, you can," I tell her. "You can do this, Kitty Kat. Remember, you deserve better. I'll be waiting for your report."

Kat laughs and we hang up. I don't know what just happened but my body feels light, bubbly inside as I take a big breath to get ready for the next segment of tonight's show.

Get the Full Book Here!

ABOUT THE AUTHOR

Join my mailing list and receive 2 FREE ebooks!

Other Books By Lauren

*Irresistible Bachelor*s (Interconnecting standalones):
Anaconda ‖ Mr. Fiance ‖ Heartstopper
Stud Muffin ‖ Mr. Fixit ‖ Matchmaker
Motorhead ‖ Baby Daddy ‖ Untamed

Get Dirty (Interconnecting standalones):
Dirty Talk ‖ Dirty Laundry ‖ Dirty Deeds

Bennett Boys Ranch:
Buck Wild

Connect with Lauren Landish.
www.laurenlandish.com
admin@laurenlandish.com

facebook.com/lauren.landish

twitter.com/laurenlandish

instagram.com/lauren_landish